W9-ATW-948

# GABRIEL
## a novel

# GABRIEL
## a novel

### HARRY
### POLLOCK

**McGraw-Hill Ryerson Limited**

Toronto  Montreal  New York  London  Sydney

GABRIEL

1 2 3 4 5 6 7 8 9 10   BP   4 3 2 1 0 9 8 7 6 5

ISBN 0-07-082242-5

**Printed and bound in Canada**

For Vera

*In tuo ingente amplexu tota est mihi vita.*

Catullus,
*Poems to Lesbia*

# 1

Gabriel was three years old. He was lying in a wooden crib. His baby brother was asleep in a smaller cot with wooden sides to keep him from falling out. The parents were visiting with the old ones who lived in the basement of the building. The grandparents had the most comfortable bed in the world with an immense feather comforter. Set in the chalky wall was a big oven. There was a long table and two unpainted benches. Grandfather was a cobbler. He sat hunched by the window tapping nails into the community's shoes, in the Polish town of Opatow.

It was a mild summer evening. Gabriel had been awakened by a great clamor, the ringing of gongs and shouts in the street below. He tottered to the window. On toe tips, eyes wide open, he saw the orange glow of the fire intermittently obscured by the billowing smoke.

Suddenly he was pulled back into the room. Whack. His bottom smarted. Whack.

—Come quickly, his mother shouted. We'll all be burned alive.

They stumbled down the creaking staircase. Gabriel in the tight clutch of Sara's hand. Noah slung over her right breast, her palm secure upon his back. Down past excited voices and screaming children and barking dogs out into the cindery street.

—Hooray for the volunteers! Long live the firefighters! A feeble spray issued from the single hose. Jerzy, the town idiot, at the well was pumping spastically. The water sloshed into the pails and onto his person. He was grinning, pumping, shivering.

—*Psiakrew Cholera. Yoptvoyamotch.* Screaming obscenities the volunteers ran toward the blaze, buckets of water splashing indiscriminately in wide arcs at the flames, onto the ground and about the throng.

The fire left charred ruins. The dispossessed were granted asylum in the homes of their neighbors. Sara and Aaron

returned with their children to the flat on the fourth floor.
—Praise God our building was spared, she whispered as
she hovered over her sleeping sons. Aaron recited a prayer
of thanksgiving.

By the time he was almost four Gabriel was familiar with
every aspect of the town. The stream that ran under the
bridge where he peed when he couldn't hold back any
longer. The orchard with the juicy apples and the tall grass
for playing in. The market square. The broad street. The
Opatow Gate. The hospital. The roads leading to Staszow
and Kielce and Radom and Lagow. The brewery. The
Cathedral.

One day the police came in a black van. The engine
coughed and white farts sputtered from the exhaust.
Gabriel's grandfather was taken away.

—Only a few *zlotys* he owed, the grandmother wailed.
What will we do without him? Who will sit in his place at
the Sabbath meal? Who will bless the wine and the bread?
Who will sing: Beloved come the Bride to meet. The
Princess Sabbath let us greet?

On Sundays the Jews of Opatow brought parcels to the
prison to their incarcerated relatives and neighbors.
Gabriel's family trooped to the prison compound with a
packet of eatables: Home baked chala, chicken, gefilte
fish, egg kichel. For the prisoner, Judah the Lion
Gottesman.

Gabriel's father lifted him up to the grating in the
metal-ribbed door. He searched out his grandfather and
spied him in a corner of the communal cell, reading his
prayer book.

—*Zayde*, Gabriel shouted. *Sholem Aleichem.* We're here.
Shouts of encouragement from the other visitors. A volley
of Yiddish.

—Don't despair. It won't be long. We'll pray for your
return.

Gabriel went to the synagogue every Sabbath and on the
Festivals. In the modest *beth hamidrash* the men sat on
benches, separated from the women by a partition. They
prayed lustily, their voices rising in a testament of faith.

—Who is like unto our God, they chanted, pendulums of

piety. Who is like unto Thee in Holiness, performing wonders.

In the fullness of time Judah was released from his debtor's confinement. Once again Gabriel accompanied The Lion to the bath. It was a ritual they observed every Friday. At the edge of the pool of warm, softly-lapping water they paused to splash themselves before immersion, then descended the stone steps, concaved by time and erosion, deeper and deeper until he was totally submerged. Then the grandfather pulled him back to a safe level.

Sometimes Gabriel urinated in the water. It was his secret. He watched the yellow stream slowly fade into the wider blue. Usually he did it like the others behind the house or in the field, or under the bridge where his uncles emptied their bowels.

—Reb Shmuel says the boy dreams too much at Cheder. He doesn't pay attention, Sara complained to Aaron. The *melamed* says he'll have to use the *kantchek* on him, to discipline him.

In the dingy chamber with the sawdust-covered earth floor eleven youngsters bent over their prayer books. Eight hours each day they sing-songed the Hebrew phrases in time to the whistling beat of the birch rod wielded by the gaunt, dyspeptic Reb Shmuel. From the courtyard the odor of manure seeped in through the open window. Sometimes Gabriel could hear the soft plop-plop of the cowflops and a relieved mooh. Gabriel laughed.

—Attention to the book. Eat not of the bread of idleness. Raise your voices in praise of the Everlasting One, Reb Shmuel ordered.

—V'ohavtoh es Adonai alohechu b'chol l'vovchoh. Motty the hunchback had the loudest voice. Gabriel stopped to listen. His shoulders felt the sting of the birch. He resumed the chanting. All day the high trebles poured forth the litany that led to Grace while the *melamed's* horse-faced wife cooked and baked and the *melamed's* shy daughter sat in a corner and sewed buttons on shirts.

On the Sabbath there were special studies in the Synagogue. Gabriel sat amidst the learned men and listened to their wisdom. When asked he recited and earned the pleasure of the elders with his interpretation of selected passages from the Gomorrah. His other grandfather, the farmer, who lived a little way outside the town, prophesied:

—In the New World he'll forget everything. The Jews in America are becoming like the goyim. Atheists.

First it was Gabriel's Uncle Eli who emigrated. After a year he sent for his older brother, Aaron.

Gabriel remembered his father's departure. One day — it was after the Passover and the sun was bright in the deep blue sky — many people assembled in the flat. Everybody was talkative and unusually gay. But the outward happiness was tinged with the sorrow of imminent loss. The guests — relatives, friends, neighbors, the whole Jewish community, it seemed to Gabriel — had turned out to bid Aaron farewell. He was to depart the next day even before morning prayers. By train from Ostrowiec to Warsaw. Then on to the Baltic coast, then a boat to London for a stopover, then directly across the great Atlantic Ocean to Canada. Gabriel's father showed him on a map.

—See. Here is Halifax. Here is Montreal. And there is Toronto where Uncle Eli has a room all ready for me. And a job. He patted Gabriel tenderly on the head. Come, Gabriel, let's go in to our guests.

The room smelled sweetly savory. Honey cake. Almond cookies. Lokshen kugel stuffed with raisins. Sara, perspiring, bustled about, covered in her white apron from neck to knees. She set out the pastries and the homemade wine. A bottle of vodka. She urged everybody to eat and drink.

—*Mazel Tov*, Aaron. Good fortune and long life. May it not be long until you are reunited with your family.

—*L'chayim.* I drink your health.

—*Chayim Tovim Sholem*, Aaron responded. Sara mopped the tears from her face with a corner of the apron.

—You'll see, Sara, it won't be so long. Before another Passover you and the children will be with Aaron.

—Amen, Sara said. Amen. Out of your mouth into God's ears. The thin woman with the apple-red cheeks of a farm girl, the devoted wife and sacrificing mother, forced a smile as she dabbed at her eyes. She would worry about

4

her husband. He was going so far away. There would be nobody to care for him. Can a brother take the place of a wife? Oh the days until they would be together again.

Sara worried all the time. She was concerned about everything and everybody. All the years of her life she worried. About her children and their illnesses. Small children, small problems. Big children, big problems. May the Lord spare them and afflict me instead. After all, that's what a mother is for.

She lamented Aaron's odyssey.

Gabriel wandered away from the buzz of sound into the bedroom. His father's articles were arranged neatly on the bed. His Sabbath suit, double-breasted, navy with white pin stripes. A white shirt with stiff collar. A black tie. Black felt fedora. Black shoes. An ensemble fit for a sport. Aaron was particular about his clothes. He spent a lot of time brushing away the lint. He looked like a dandy, handsome with his closely-trimmed beard and mustache.

Gabriel would miss his father. He moved his fingers about the things on the bed. The murmurs in the other room swelled into a greeting or a response. His father's voice. Would Gabriel ever see him again? He dropped onto the bed and the tears came. It was all so confusing. Almost unbearable, the pangs of separation. He lay there for a long time. Then he joined the guests. His mother gave him a glass of warm milk and a piece of cake.

When Gabriel awoke the next morning Aaron had gone. Somehow it didn't seem to matter so much. His mother assured him:

—We'll all be together, God willing. Away from here in a new land. A good land. Canada.

—Where the streets are paved with gold, Gabriel said. Papa says it's the *goldene medina*.

It took Aaron twenty-six months to save enough to send for his family. Awake at five in the blackness of wintry mornings. Wrapped in his prayer shawl and phylacteries, enunciating the first prayers of the day. A slice of black bread and a cup of tea. Then the long walks to the shoe factory, arriving at seven. Susskind's Sport Shoes for Men. Handmade. Cutting the leather. Shaping it. Cementing.

Tacking. Finishing. Polishing. Half hour for lunch. A sandwich and tea. Work again until seven. The evening walk home along Adelaide Street and up Spadina to Dundas where he turned left until he came to Augusta and the lonely third floor room. Evening prayers. Soup and bread for supper. Sometimes a bit of meat. A sweet biscuit and a cup of tea. Writing a letter to Sara: I miss you and the children. I hope to have you with me soon. I am getting along fine.

Off to sleep in the brass bed. Up the next day, back to the shop. Every day except Saturday. Aaron would not desecrate the Sabbath. Forty-one years on the job and he kept the Sabbath day holy. He worked Sundays to make up for his day of rest.

The envelope was postmarked: Toronto Feb. 7, 1926. In her excitement Sara almost tore the remittance it contained.

—It's come, she shrieked. Praised be the Lord who hath sustained us and brought us to this day. We're finally going.

The letter in Aaron's neat, Hebraic hand contained the details. Departure day and time. Final arrival in Toronto beginning of June.

But first there were documents to be obtained. Passport. Exit visas. Health certificates. Sara was anxious about Gabriel. His eyes were bothering him. He sometimes awoke unable to open his eyes. The lids were cemented by a nocturnal discharge. He was having trouble seeing the words in his prayer book. A specialist's advice would be sought. Sara took him to Warsaw, a day's journey. They traveled third class all night. The next day the old eye doctor examined Gabriel's eyes through an assortment of instruments. He grunted and made notes as he peered.

—Trachoma, he announced. No longer active. Nothing to worry about for the present. As for the other problem. Iritis. Mild.

The medicine man wrote out a magic formula. Eye drops. Any chemist would supply it.

Mother and son returned to Opatow. Sara had her own remedy. Soft bread, soaked in warm milk, applied to his lids, secured by a handkerchief. In the morning the soggy mess was eased away from Gabriel's eyes. The lids opened miraculously.

—Praised be God, all our papers are in order, Sara announced. We leave in three days.

A farewell of tears and strained jollity. Bright assurances of reunion. Then Sara, fretting Sara, indomitable Sara, clutching a multitude of bags and suitcases, issuing injunctions to Gabriel and Noah to stay close to her, waved and shouted her goodbyes to the assembled well-wishers.

They traveled steerage from Danzig across interminable miles of ocean, in the hull of the S.S. Lituania, pride of Poland. Old men with scraggy beards, walking aided by sticks, struggled against the roll of the ship. Women with babushkas, heavy dresses and sweaters and shawls, coarse stockings held from falling down around their beefy ankles by elastic bands twisted into knots.

Thin, nervous young men in their best suits, shoes polished, attempted an attitude of sophistication. Mothers shepherded noisy children, giving the teat to screaming infants. Seasick passengers moaned and vomited, wan faces looking to heaven for deliverance.

Every evening after supper there was a movie. Gabriel like the one about the immigrant best of all. Good old Charlie. With his big shoes and cane and dirty bowler hat. There he is running around, in one door, out the other, pursued by the uniformed officers. Isn't it funny what he does with his stick? And look. That poor girl. She is all alone. Charlie comforts her. He shares his bread with her. He tips his hat and smiles. She shyly smiles back at him. The boat tilts. There goes Charlie sliding away over to the other side. What's this? A young man has spotted the girl. He sits down beside her. She smiles. She snuggles up to him. They're in love. But where is Charlie? He has landed in the middle of a card game and has scattered the cards all over the place. Now the gamblers pursue him in anger. The piano player who has been accompanying the movie pounds out the final chords as the chase on the screen reaches its climax and the film ends with Charlie leaping

7

into the boat's ventilator shaft.

Gabriel remembered the beat of ship's engines. Thud. Thud. Thud. Thud. Like a giant heart straining. Sometimes he was allowed to go to the galley. One of the staff, in grease-stained white, lifted him off the floor up to a high table where the shining machine was guillotining slices of fresh, white bread. As he reached for his piece he could look through the porthole at the churning, white-flecked waves. He felt dizzy and asked to be put down.

—Halifaxu! Halifaxu! The S.S. Lituania slipped smoothly into the Canadian port.

The passengers were herded into galvanized steel sheds. Gabriel and Noah huddled with their mother in the women's enclosure. Sara unclothed and told the boys to do likewise. She had to help them.

Gabriel marvelled at the accumulation of nakedness. Heavy breasts with nipples that were stiff in the raw morning air. Sagging bellies. Bushes of tangled hair — auburn, blonde, black — where the legs joined. Heavy bottoms. Rancid smells assailed his nostrils.

A woman in a long, white coat moved slowly down the shivering queue, poking, palpating, asking questions through an interpreter. She scanned papers and stamped approval.

## 2

Leonard Avenue was an abrasion in the backside of the Toronto Western Hospital. Faded, red-brick, three-storey houses huddled intimately for support. Prouder in its poverty than Cabbagetown in the east end, superior to nearby Kensington with its stinking, open-air market where the smell of chicken shit mingled with rotting vegetables and fat, spiced herring, lacked the gentility of the more affluent neighborhoods north of College and west of Bathurst Street.

Leonard was a cauldron in which the differing races simmered without yielding up their individual biases. A challenge to the social services of St. Christopher House stuck in the middle of the area like a prim dowager.

After the excitement of reunion at the station, Aaron took his family to No. 43. He ushered them into a two-room, second-floor flat with shared toilet.

The first night in his new world, Gabriel was awakened by screams from the hospital. Gabriel wondered was he born amidst such anguish?

They were confined to just these two rooms. The house was dominated by the Jacobsons. With four boys and two girls the Jacobsons occupied all the other rooms in No. 43. Selma Jacobson, a blubbery, asthmatic woman was always coughing or belching or farting. One afternoon Gabriel sat obediently beside his mother in the downstairs parlor and watched intently as Mrs. J. sucked up a mouthful of tea from her glass, choked over it and went into a coughing spasm that dredged up the liquid from her stomach and erupted in a red-brown mass of vomit. It oozed all over the teapot and cups and saucers and cake and the white linen table cloth which the landlady reserved for her social occasions.

When the spasms finally ended, the wheezing began. A thin, forlorn sound. A broken-down accordion. Hmnnnnn-hraugh—hmnnnn-hraurrgh. The tiny eyes watered. The belly quivered like the lumps in the curdled milk that was Gabriel's Saturday supper. Hmnnn—hruaghh. I'll huff and I'll puff and blow the house down.

When she had coughed herself out, her husband quietly assured Sara that everything was once again as it should be. All's well that ends well.

Solly Jacobson was a thin willow. Taciturn, introverted. Selma's flatulence moved him — upwind. He returned to his *Morgen Journal.* He was glad that Sara was visiting. She would help clear the mess. The Jacobsons granted their tenants minor privileges.

—Do come downstairs Mrs. Gottesman. A little chat. Relax a bit.

Other times: Don't let those damn kids run around the flat. They're making a helluva noise above my head.

Gabriel and Noah entered the house, two Buddhists, shoes removed and left outside the front door. Tiptoe upstairs. Walk softly. Do not run. Shhh. Old Jacobson will get you if you don't watch out.

On Leonard Avenue the language was polyglottal basic. Gabriel heard and remembered:

—You goddam ball? (Where's the ball I gave you? Polish-English.)

—*Salma Dupa.* (Kiss my ass. Straight Polish.)

The first English words Gabriel heard in his expanding universe: Fuck. Fuck you. Fuck off. Sonofabitch. Bastard. Shit. Piss. Cock. Prick. Cunt. The daily expletives of the street. Strange to the ears of the young Talmudic scholar. He learned to use them in self-defense. He practiced their sounds with Noah — a badinage of vulgarities.

—Fuck off, Noah.

—I won't, you sonofabitch.

—You fuckin bastard. Suck my cock.

The epithets added spice to the Yiddish jargon of the family. Until Sara, puzzled by the foreign words creeping into the boys' vocabularies, discovered their meanings and threatened corporal reprisals if the words were not abandoned immediately.

—Nice Jewish boys don't use such nasty expressions. In the house we use Yiddish. At prayer, the Holy Tongue.

Gabriel was already fluent in both: the coarse patois of the eastern European *shtetl* and the Hebrew: although the grandeur was flattened in the race between the Rabbi and the congregation, to see who could finish first.

\* \* \*

—I'll knock your fuckin heads off if you don't stop fuckin around my house. Sheeny kikes.

That was Big Irish talking. O'Hara and his boozing parents occupied the sagging storey-and-a-half frame structure at No. 48A. Big Irish. His voice the most strident in the neighborhood. Just turned twelve, he was big (almost six feet) and fat (210 pounds). He roared his demands. Acquiescence was expected and immediate. Big Irish had a secret weapon. Standing in the midst of a group of the kids, pretending to be interested solely in what was going on, he would cunningly unleash from the depths of his bowels a mute fart of staggering power. The smell fanned out over the area sending the young vagabonds running, fingers clutching at noses.

Big Irish breathed deeply, appreciatively and sliding his right hand into his pants, farted again, withdrew the palm, smelled it with relish and clapped the offensive mitt over Gabriel's face.

—Smell that, Jew boy, he commanded.

Gabriel held his breath under the pressure of the Irishman's grip. Useless. Succumbing, he inhaled the noxious odor. Big Irish, guffawing, released him and sauntered away, obsessed by the growing bulge in his trousers.

—Christ, what a hard-on! Just like the old man. Maybe catch them at it again. At confession tell the priest only about the jacking-off. Bet he does it himself.

—Beware the sin of Onan, my son.

Are you coming, Onan? Anon. Anon. And on.

Big Irish came in two ways. He masturbated himself. Or got one of the younger kids to pull him off.

—Here, Bert. Suck this and I'll give you a penny.

Little Bert, encouraged by the ring of trolls encircling him and his mentor, knelt and lollipopped the uncircum-

11

sized head. In time, Big Irish began to quiver and yell. Gouts of sperm shot into little Bert's mouth.

—Swallow it. Swallow it!

Bert gagged, then brought up all over Irish. Bert ran crying home. Irish nonchalantly wiped himself with Bert's sweater.

The O'Haras moved away in the middle of one night. When the gang gathered the next day there was no sign of any of them. Bits of furniture still sat abjectly in the shanty. Two men arrived in a van and took away an old, sagging sofa, one scratched end table and a bridge lamp. They left the old boxes in the kitchen. They padlocked the front door.

All that summer Gabriel absorbed the language and the folkways. Sara washed and waxed and sewed and cooked. She helped Mrs. Jacobson, in return for a reduction in rent. Aaron worked on at the factory. Every Friday he received six dollars.

Beginning in September, Gabriel had to be registered. He was led to school by a spindly eight-year-old with long, black pigtails. Zipporah. She had arrived in Canada a year before. She spoke English haltingly but well enough.

The morning after Labor Day, a morning that was sultry and humid, down Leonard Avenue Gabriel and Zipporah ambled. Through wooden gates across the school yard teeming with shouting, running children, they passed into the aging, yellow-brick building named in honor of the great Canadian educator Egerton Ryerson. Their sneakered feet trod the stone steps that let into the first floor hall. Hollow sounds resounded from wooden floors, wooden walls, splintery, wooden desks; everything creaked.

They ascended, respectfully, the broad wooden staircase. On the first landing they approached the Principal's Office: David A. Davidson. His secretary Florence Wheeler greeted them in the anteroom.

—Yes?

That was all. Just—Yes. There was so much to do that first day of school, Miss Florence Wheeler felt bothered. She couldn't waste time, on civilities. Especially on immigrant kids. The city was full of them. Too many Yids,

Eyetalians and Polacks for her liking. What was the country coming to? All that flotsam. Or was it jetsam? The huddled masses. Go print it on the Statue of Liberty. This isn't America.

—Yes? She managed a tentative smile.

—Please, Miss Wheeler, Zipporah tried once more. Please. I have a boy here who would like to go to school.

Miss Wheeler scrutinized, from behind her pince nez, the little waif posing as would-be scholar. Get it over with. Jot down the particulars. Assign him to Mrs. Pendergast.

—Well then. Miss Wheeler sighed sadly and reached for an admission form. She dipped her long, tapered pen with the broad nib into one of the double, glass ink wells — blue ink for registration. What is his name?

—Yechiel, said Zipporah brightly.

It was his Biblical name. All the kids on Leonard Avenue called him Yechiel (when they weren't calling him fuck-face or other epithets).

Miss Wheeler looked confused. So Zipporah blinked her brown eyes with the long black lashes, smiled and repeated:

—His name is Yechiel.

—What kind of a name is that? How do you say it?

—Yechiel, repeated Zipporah.

—Yechiel, reiterated Gabriel.

Miss Wheeler attempted to pronounce the name. In vain. The phonics eluded her. Ah, Florence Wheeler, repeat after me. I come from Loch Lomond. I've been to Loch Neagh. My hope is in Holy Loch. My redeemer is Yechiel.

—Heel? She tried again. No success. Oh well, that's no name for a Canadian. Let's call him, let's see, something you can pronounce, a name that suits him.

She turned to her page of prior registrants, noticed that the last entry was one for a Frederick. She pondered for an instant and decided, beadle-wise:

—Gabriel. Henceforth young man you'll be called Gabriel. How does that sound to you? A fine name. Gabriel — the angel of the Lord. Yes indeed, Miss Wheeler was pleased.

—What did she say, he inquired of Zipporah in Yiddish.

13

—She said that from now on your name is Gabriel.
—Not Yechiel?
—No. Not Yechiel. *Gabriel.*
—Sonofabitch! Yechiel voiced his amazement. *Gabriel?*
He grinned at Miss Florence Wheeler. O.K. Gabriel.

\* \* \*

As his familiarity with the new language flourished, Gabriel delved into the limitless world of the written word. One after the other, like beads strung together, he sounded syllables to make words to make sentences to discover meanings. Fascinated by type faces. Upper and lower. Italics. Roman faces marching along the page of the primer. Gothic on broadsides.

Gabriel read omnivorously. The way of the world discovered, in the pages of old newspapers that served as wrappers for beef. Squares of newsprint used in lieu of toilet paper had messages of import, the most exciting part beginning usually at the torn bottom of the square, and no amount of rummaging through other sheets stacked on the bathroom floor could provide the sequel. There were newspapers on the kitchen table and on the floors. To be perused while sitting or kneeling or prone.

Gabriel read tales about school boys in English magazines: *TRIUMPH. WIZARD. CHAMPION.* High jinks in the dorms. Raggings. Out-witting the dons. Mistakenly accused. A world of the British Public School and how it turned out impeccable leaders from among the scions of the aristocracy. And the odd poor, scholarship boy.

Best of all, though, Gabriel liked fairy tales. Seated in a straight-backed chair at the kitchen window, feet propped up on the fender of the stove, munching on buttered rye bread, he read. Immersed in the adventures of The Snow Queen and The Red Shoes and others from the imaginative store of Hans Christian Andersen and The Brothers Grimm.

There were story hours at the library next to St. Christopher House. In the enchanted circle of childhood

Gabriel listened while Jean Ordway read, clothing the words with animation and color. Blonde Miss Ordway was beautiful and soft-spoken. She was Anglo-Saxon. She exuded a fragrance of apple blossoms. She developed literary and art projects during the summer months for her special group. Gabriel adored Jean Ordway. He sat close to her to breathe in her perfume. He gave her all his attention. He was quick to volunteer for her. He trembled when she touched him in approval of a correct answer.

—I think you are absolutely right, Gabriel. It *was* Hans Brinker and the Silver Skates. She smiled at him and murmured, the honeyed suspiration issuing from her dainty mouth. Y-e-s-ss-ss, Gabriel. It was Hans Brinker.

In a fantasy Gabriel saw himself grown up and utterly changed. He was Sylvester Thornton-Smith. He and Jean Ordway were more than friends. They were together always. He was tall and Anglo-Saxon. English came trippingly on his tongue. He was a member of the Granite Club. Black tie or white tie, he was equally comfortable. He and Jean Ordway lived happily in high society. The world of Masseys, Drews and Macleans. He read fairy tales to polite, scrubbed, upper-middle-class Christian children.

Gabriel's ethereal affair with Miss Ordway was interrupted. He and Noah were being sent away to stay with relatives in another part of the city. Sara was going into hospital to have the lump in her breast removed.

The Rajanskys lived in a grand house on Palmerston Boulevard. Eleven rooms, all elegantly furnished. Uncle Rajansky owned a business on Spadina Avenue. He was one of three partners in the Zenith Cloak Company. He was the designer. A bit of a simpleton in matters outside the purview of his cutting table with the patterns and thick lays of cloth.

His wife was a friendly, open-faced woman. A meticulous housekeeper and a gracious hostess. She pressed tea and cake on all visitors.

There were only two offspring. Howard was in medical school. He had a real skeleton in his study and treated it like a companion, joking with it, asking advice of it, embracing the bony hands in greeting, flicking cigarette ashes into its skull. He called it Yorick.

—Alas poor Yorick, you look discomfited today. Has that rascal Polonius been around bothering you? You'd prefer Ophelia, you randy devil.

Then, looking at Yorick's groin, Howard would emit a low moan:

—Ah, quite chapfallen. No balls at all. You are no genitalman.

His twin sister Sophia proclaimed her elevated station with an arrogance that was just barely hidden beneath the veneer of good manners. Sophia coached her mother in the graces. Table cloths instead of newspapers. Highly-polished hardwood floors with expensive hall runners and Indian rugs instead of linoleum. The decor was professional and subdued and tasteful. Sophia Rajansky floated about the house in a delicately-flowered peignoir. She read the best selling novels, listened to The Boston Pops. She was *au courant* with the affairs of the world and had formed definite opinions on how to resolve all the world's problems. Unlike her brother who was a bluff, unaffected young man, Sophia was pained by the uncouth nature of her father's relatives. Uncle Horsetail, flat and florid, who belched in company, was one of her constant regrets.

Howard was completely involved in his studies. He emerged from his smoke-filled room only to relieve himself.

Gabriel and Noah accompanied by Aaron were welcomed by the Aunt one Sunday afternoon in mid-November. It was a chill, drizzly day. They wore bulky, brown, mouton coats, in Sara's anticipation of a sudden winter frost. Gabriel carried a pillowcase stuffed with a change of underclothing.

After the tea ritual Aaron thanked the Rajanskys. He kissed his sons and quietly departed.

The two boys were shown the bedroom and the toilet and warned against disturbing Howard. Nor were they to venture into Sophia's room. Sophia made that clear herself. They could read, they could listen to the radio, a highboy with standard and short wave reception and police

16

calls. And they could play with Princess, the thoroughbred white collie.

—Yes, let's play with Princess, the two agreed.

Princess was a superb bitch, with a placid disposition. She was well-trained and knew many tricks. Lie down and play dead. Shake a paw. Walk on your hind legs, Princess. Heel, Princess. Fetch the slippers, Princess. She was the friendliest dog in the neighborhood and in consequence was always in peril of getting knocked up.

Not that she was allowed to roam at will. She was walked on a leash. After her stroll, in the company of Uncle Rajansky, she was kept on the verandah for awhile and the uncle would shoo away the other dogs with a broom.

—Garonne away from here you rotten dog. Leave Princess alone.

The collie was to be bred with a prize stud. However, before the contracted act could be consummated, a scruffy, black mongrel got into her. The uncle was dozing over a newspaper and the mongrel, grown wily after bouts with the broom, waited until he saw no further movement from the Uncle. Sensing the all-clear, the predator sneaked up to Princess whose wagging tail wafted the odor of receptiveness to his eager nose. Uncle Rajansky slept on, unaware of the impending ravishment.

The male mounted the not unwilling Princess and plunged with fast, short strokes. The uncle started awake at the squealing of the two conjoined dogs. Princess was being pulled backwards down the veranda steps by the mongrel in his desperate attempt at retreat.

—Here, Princess. Come here, Uncle Rajansky commanded.

She strained to reach him, advanced, but with each tentative pull forward Princess was dragged farther away by her lover. The uncle commanded again.

—Come here, Princess. Bad dog. Come here. Then at the mongrel: You bastard dog. I'll kill you. Let go of Princess.

The altercation brought the family and the neighbors out to investigate. Gabriel and Noah left the antics of Amos and Andy on the radio and rushed out to marvel at the sight of two dogs joined back to back.

The uncle pulled at the white dog's collar. Still stuck. He gave the mongrel a kick in the ribs. The dog slithered away dragging Princess with him.

Advice from the neighbors.

—Clap your hands.

—Get a big stick and beat the black dog.

—Light off firecrackers.

—You pull one dog and I'll pull the other.

—And get your fingers bitten off?

Gathering of kids, converging from blocks and blocks. Come and see. Two stuck dogs. Have you ever seen such a thing in your life as two dogs stuck?

More advice.

—Hot water. Pour it on them. That's the answer. Hot water. Works every time.

Uncle Rajansky allowed himself to be persuaded. A pail of hot water. He approached the two fornicators now standing abjectly. Carefully he aimed and slowly he upended the full pail, splash! all over the mongrel. The dog yelped, then ran howling, pulling Princess with him, then stopped. The Uncled, pail refilled, readied himself for the second deluge. An error of judgment. The steaming liquid descended over Princess who writhed and whined. Pulled. Remained stuck.

—Come Princess. Uncle Rajansky beckoned. Good dog. Come. Home, Princess. He patted the collie, then tugged again, then swore and sweated. He left for more water, vowing to kill that goddam mongrel.

The Aunt stood on the verandah, praying for the deliverance of the collie. Sophia was long gone indoors, refusing to be part of this shameful scene. In her twenty-two years she had never been with a man. Never would she place herself in such a predicament. Howard had shown her pictures and diagrams of the male genitals in his medical books. They looked huge. Jokingly, he had cautioned her about being nailed by a superabundant nigger.

Gabriel ventured near Princess. He patted her. Nice doggie. Good doggie. Noah, unafraid, patted the mongrel. Good doggie. Nice doggie.

It was at this time that natural laws produced the resolution. The mongrel's corona assumed its normal state. The collie's sphincter loosened and the unwelcome guest was released.

A great o-o-o-o-h went up from the multitude.

When the Uncle emerged with his pail Princess was on the verandah amidst solicitous wellwishers. The mongrel, a short distance away, was licking his sore shaft. The Uncle stroked Princess. Then he glared at the mongrel, raised his arm, aimed and hurled the pail at the mutt, hitting it on the head. There was a thud like a tire blow out. The black dog stood immobile for an instant, then shook himself and bolted away up towards Bloor Street.

A great shout rang out. HOORAY. HOORAY.

* * *

After the escapade of the conjugal canines, Gabriel became more interested in his own organ. It would grow erect, stay that way for a bit then become limp. He thought about trying to do what the mongrel had but he was afraid of getting stuck. Besides, it was very messy. Princess was leaving blood on the floors and the carpets. Miraculously, the dripping ceased after the encounter with the mongrel.

Anyway, Gabriel was more interested in Judy. Shy, nine year old Judy, a cousin who lived on Markham Street and came visiting. Gabriel and Judy played games together. In the Rajansky house or at her place. She had only a mother, a sickly woman who was always alone in her room, taking medicine or sleeping or crying quietly.

To Judy's place on a sleepy Saturday afternoon Gabriel came calling.

—Judy. Judy. Where are you? To which she responded with a low whistle.

—Judy. Judy. I love you. She whistled again, two notes, ascending.

He found her on her bed, curled up with the furry teddy bear whose buttoned belly concealed the pajamas inside.

—All alone, Judy? She opened one eye and closed it

again.

—Uh, huh, she said. All alone. Helen's at the playground. Mom's asleep.

—I'm here to take care of you, he said, and the game began. He embraced fumblingly her little girl's body. The legs thin, the hips not yet rounded, the tiny nipples on her non-breasts.

Judy felt him, small and bony. Only his bottom was soft. For awhile they were silent, listening to the heart beats.

—Let's play house Judy. Do you want to? I'll be the father.

—All right, she said. I'll be the mother. I'll make tea. Tea was quickly disposed of.

—What shall we do now? Is it time to go to sleep? Yes, it's late now and you've had a busy day. Let's go to sleep.

Together they lay, boy child against girl child. Whispering. Giggling.

—Let's take our clothes off. Do you want to?

—Oh yes, said Judy.

A flurry of shirt, trousers, dress, slip, panties, undershirt, stockings. Quite naked. Innocent in Eden.

—What shall we do now Judy?

—I don't know.

—Let's touch each other. All over. Look. My nipples are bigger than yours, Judy.

—Let's wrestle, said Judy.

Arms and legs entwined, Gabriel wrestled Judy off the bed onto the floor. Tired. Panting, Judy pins him down.

—That was fun, she said. What shall we do now. Oh, I know. Let's kiss.

Gabriel kisses her on the cheek. On the neck. On the arms. In the navel.

—Look, Judy. You have a hole right here. He touches the hairless lips. Kiss Judy? She nods assent. Gabriel brushes his lips against the flesh.

—Now it's your turn Judy. Here. Gabriel shows her the juncture of his legs. The small pouch with twin balls. The toy penis rising to her touch.

—Kiss Gabriel?

—Yes, Judy. Kiss. She encompasses the head.

—There. What else, she asks. More exploration each of the other's body. He thinks they should play at having babies but he doesn't understand how to get inside her. Both of them too small, too unknowing.

The pre-puberty territories, having been assayed, are abandoned for more rewarding activities.

—Let's get dressed and go out for ice cream.

## 3

Oh see dat watermelon
A smiling on de vine.
How I wish dat watermelon
It was mine.
Oh de white folks must be foolish
Dey need a heap of sense
Or deyd never leave it dere upon the vine.
Oh, de hambone am sweet,
And de bacon am good,
And de 'possum fat an berry, berry fine,
But gib me, yes gib me,
Oh how I wish you would—
Dat watermelon dere upon de vine.

They sang the song at St. Christopher House. The Nigger Song. All the kids knew it. On a hot August afternoon gathered in a circle in the playroom Mr. McKenzie shouted:

—See dat watermelon.

Gleefully, aware of the rewards for an enthusiastic rendition, the kids sang, shouted, grimaced. Gabriel too. Watermelon and fat nigger lips.

—Man, whatcha got there, hidin behind yo back? Is dat watermelon? I sho would like some of dat mouth-waterin fruit. I sho would.

In the movie house crafty Felix the Cat steals the hunk of watermelon from the darky in the cotton field. He lollops away on speedy feline feet and finds a secluded spot behind a bush.

—See dat watermelon.

With greedy gulps Felix swallows the pinky-red pulp and throws away the rind. The darky picks it up mournfully and shuffles off picking at it with white nigger teeth.

—How I wish dat watermelon it was mine.

Eyes sparkling, voices high and loud in tribute to the gourd, the boys and girls at St. Christopher frolicked in sing-song confraternity.

After the last raucous cadence died away the watermelon

was brought in. Mr. McKenzie performed the ritual with a long, glinting carving knife. The sphere was halved and the halves were halved and in turn sliced into smaller slivers until there was a segment for everybody. Multiplication by division.

Mr. McKenzie was the only male social worker. He provided counselling for the boys, physical education instruction, woodwork technique and enforcement of the law. Miss Ricketts looked after the girls. Between them they offered a plethora of activities for the juveniles of the area. Every problem had a solution. If a situation became unmanageable, the police were called. Usually just the threat was enough to defuse a brawl.

St. Christopher was a hop, skip and jump from No. 43 Leonard Avenue. It was a wide gabled structure on Bellevue Place built in the Elizabethan style, containing an office, gymnasium, carpentry shop, billiard room, and an auditorium with a little platform stage. On the second floor there were clubrooms, a parlor and two bedrooms. A lawn of close-cropped grass lay in front overshadowed by three immense chestnut trees. The front door of great glass rectangles was always locked. You rang. Eventually the rheumy caretaker opened it, two-fingers wide, and inquired about your business.

—It's four o'clock, Mr. Brady. Jolly Chums Meeting time.

Mr. Brady nodded, opened wider and you rushed inside.

During the summer the fellows played baseball all day. The girls played charades. They learned to sew. They discussed such things as dating and how to grow up to be proper young ladies. And experimented with the excitement of life in dark corners in the evenings beyond the range of supervision. Kissed. Pawed. Probed.

Horny Fox leered: No virgin ever walked under the clock at St. Christopher. Not for long. If she were intact it was the duty of McTavish to introduce her to the joys of coupling. McTavish was the leader of the rites.

He was also the particular bright star of the Spring Concert at St. Christopher. He could imitate Harry Lauder. When he made his appearance on stage dressed in Scottish kilt and carrying a knobby cane and said:

—*It's a braw, bricht moonlight nicht tonicht*, there was a burst of applause. He danced about the stage as he sang *Roamin in the Gloamin* and *I Belong To Glasgow*. He brought forth tears with his rendition of *Annie Laurie*. The homesick Scottish ladies in the audience, the Yiddishe mamas too, caught up in the special poignance of the moment, listened and were touched by the plaintive quality that McTavish brought to the song.

McTavish wooed avidly. Big smile on his roguish face. Moving in for the conquest. One hand reaching up to scratch his head, the other winding around the buttocks. A friendly caress. Then quickly, a kiss on the mouth. Then up with his kilt and the revelation of the hairy pubis and dangling genitals.

—Look. Genuine heather, he announced. *In hoc signo.*

Slap. Across his face. Girlish giggle. Turn and run away. Invitation. Come again? Upstairs to the lounge.

—Oops. Sorry Miss Ricketts. Didn't see you.

Across the hall, down the rear stairs. Out of the building. Behind the bushes.

—Caught you.

—Don't, please.

—Aw, come on, you'll like it. McTavish is your darling.

He felt for her breasts, then under her dress and into the sweat-stained panties. Fast feel. McTavish the pride of St. Christopher. Cocksure in his conquests. In his prime of sixteen years, he screwed the daughters then the mothers. Or reversed the vice.

His mating song, learned at the Bowmanville Reformatory:

> I love a lassy.
> She's dirty but she's classy.
> She's as tight as the paper on the wall.
> She has an awful habit.
> She fucks just like a rabbit.
> Mary—my Scotch blue balls.

Gabriel kept away from McTavish.

—Hey jew-boy, what does your tribe do with their foreskins, McTavish taunted.

Gabriel dared to reply.

—We plant them and they grow up to be pricks like you.

24

McTavish mauled Gabriel for that retort. Gabriel thence-forth kept his silence and his distance. He preferred the company of Bob Reed. Big, black, affable Bob. Everybody called him Snowball.

—Hey Snowball, throw the fuckin ball. Hey Snowball, had your watermelon today?

Bob matched them with a smile, a wink, sometimes a fast flick of the fingers against the backside.

—Up your ass, man, he shouted.

Bob lived with his mother, a white-haired, dun-colored widow. She scrubbed floors at the hospital. Bonded by circumstance and loneliness the two shared a second storey flat up the street near Nassau. He was her epitaph: mild mannered, soft spoken, courteous —traits assimilated with his mother's milk. She washed his clothes, mended them, ironed them and presented Robert daily to the world with pride and affection.

Gabriel and Bob were street buddies. The friendship was always interrupted at the door of the Reed apartment.

—White and black don't mix, Mrs. Reed reminded her son.

Carver mixed with everybody. Carver Washington came to St. Christopher House all the way from Grange Street. He was the eldest of seven brothers. He was a mathematical genius. He could add, subtract, multiply, divide, all in his head. Like his namesake he was going to be a great scientist.

Carver wasn't bothered by color.

—Shit man, that don't mean nothin to me. Just don't call me nigger. And don't lay out in the sun too long. Your white skin gonna get awful burned before it gonna look like mine.

Carver visited Gabriel frequently. He was warmly received at the Gottesmann home. He conversed in fluent Yiddish.

—*Vos machst du, Mama*, he greeted Sara with a kiss. *Vos is tzu essen?*

He delighted Aaron with stories from Sholem Aleichem.

—Where did you learn these tales Carver, Aaron wondered.

25

*—Fun meine shvartze mama*, Carver sometimes replied. At other times he laughed: *Fun der Rebbe.*

During the Jewish festivals Carver strolled to the Kiever Synagogue with Gabriel and Noah. In the little *shul* with its twin minarets of burnished gold, Carver stood, prayer book in hand and swayed with the other worshippers, alert to the comments that his presence provoked.

*—A shvartzer in shul?*

*—Ya. Er is der shvartzer Yid.*

*—A yid? Nein! Ummeglich.*

*—Ya. Ya. A Yid. Carver der Yid.*

*—Sholem Aleichem*, Carver bowed in greeting. And returned to his Siddur in a concentration of piety.

Salvatore Puzzo introduced Gabriel to spaghetti and lasagna and minestrone soup. He showed Gabriel how to say *Fuck You* without uttering a sound. You just bent your right arm up to a vertical position and put your left hand under the elbow and made an upward gesture.

—Try it next time somebody gets to you, Salvatore urged.

It happened for Gabriel during Yom Kippur in the synagogue. While the shawled figures were rocking away at prayer, Gabriel leaned from his position at the end of the pew and opened a window. The place was fetid with the accumulation of stale breaths. But it was forbidden to open windows. The *shammes* spotted the misdemeanor and whacked Gabriel across the back of the head.

—Close it up. Shut it.

Gabriel turned to his oppressor and with full deliberation gave him the sign. For emphasis he mouthed the words silently: Fuck You. Then he closed the window.

\* \* \*

At St. Christopher House Gabriel met Pegeen O'Sullivan. Beautiful, fresh-faced, eternally-smiling Pegeen O'Sullivan. Dark, moody Gabriel. She was twelve. He was eleven. He swooned over her.

The two appearing in the St. Christopher musical extravaganza *FLYING HIGH.* All about a group of kids taking a

26

trip. They were going up in an airplane. Gabriel, a member of the chorus, was singing:

—Flying higher, higher, higher.

To his left, in the wings, he could see Pegeen, the star of the show, peering out onto the stage. At him. At him!

—In our airplane way up high. We'll fly to London Town.

Gabriel finished and held out a bottle. Smelling salts for air sickness. Then the curtain closed for the end of Act One.

During the interval while the stage crew — Horny, Sal and Carver — changed the scenery and the mothers peeked under the drapery for a sight of their child actors, Pegeen drifted over to Gabriel.

—Why, you have a smudge on your nose, she breathed at him an exhalation of roses. Mustn't appear that way on stage. You probably brushed your face against the set. Here. I'll fix it.

From inside her bodice she withdrew a pink handkerchief and with a delicate dab removed the speck of dirt from the tip of Gabriel's nose.

Oh that I were a glove upon that hand. Oh to be a handkerchief between those breasts. Oh to be with Pegeen forever and ever and ever. Amen.

Sick with love for Pegeen O'Sullivan, Gabriel chronicled her every gesture in his direction as a token of affection. He would love her all the years of his life. And if his mother would only let him he would marry her. Gabriel's Irish Pegeen. He would change his faith for her. Because never again would he fall so passionately in love. Pegeen, with a voice like soft spring rain.

Pegeen was pleased to be his friend. Just that. She could never reciprocate his love. Her mother wouldn't allow him inside the Catholic Irish home on Lippincott Street. The lilt of Pegeen's laughter went out of his life.

The St. Christopher Shakespearean Players were born of the Great Depression. The order of the day was *Do It Yourself*. Theatricals were the very thing. St. Christopher set high standards.

—I know there is so much talent in this group, the social

worker beamed at the circle of delinquency gathered about her on the floor of the great hall. What would you like to do?

A contemplative silence. Mick fingered his cock through the hole in his trouser pocket.

—Gabriel, do you have any suggestions?

—Let me think, Miss Ricketts.

Think about her freshly starched white cotton blouse with the open vee and the swell of her breasts. Think about Miss Ricketts sitting demurely, legs curled up beneath her. Miss Ricketts shifting animatedly in her enthusiasm, her legs covered in beige-colored silk stockings that ended above the knees where the pink flesh flashed and the satin panties covered you-know-what. Virginal Miss Ricketts, caring for an aged, phthisic mother in a third-floor flat near Alexandra Park. M.R. Social Worker.

Dear Miss Ricketts. You had such a niche of pleasure for these pubescent street urchins. You might have yielded up your sacred treasure.

Look, Gabriel. How soft my thighs. Wouldn't you like to touch them? Mick, look. See what I offer. An exploration around the mound of Venus. Place your finger there. Oh, so tender. Oh, so moist. Gently, gently. So. Now deeper. There's ecstasy! What are all the social sciences compared to such an experience? I offer myself to you completely. Like St. Christopher, I bear your burden. A jubilation. An exultation amidst the blight of your lives. For you who share your loins with me today shall be my lovers.

—Why don't we do a play by Shakespeare, Miss Ricketts legs unfurled. I know just the one. *A Midsummer Night's Dream*. There are lots of characters in it. Dukes and Duchesses and Fairies.

—Fairies? Bob goosed Mick who hooted in delight and made obscene sounds. The girls clapped their hands excitedly.

—Oh, Fairies, Miss Ricketts. How wonderful.

—And a Queen of the Fairies too, Miss Ricketts said. That would be a splendid role for you Jane. You see, Titania falls in love with Bottom...

28

—Kiss my bottom, said Mick.

—Then Oberon, the King of the Fairies, gets jealous. Whom shall we get to play Oberon?

—Get Fox. Horny Fox, the shout went up.

Melville (Horny) Fox leered at the prospect of a free feel in the service of Thespis.

—Oh, then we must have people to play the common laborers who put on a play for the Duke.

—Get my father, Louella Smyth suggested sourly.

—No. No, shouted Salvatore. My old man is more common than anybody. Just give him a couple of beers and a fat ass to tickle and he'll give you the greatest performance you've ever seen.

—Can that jazz, man. We don't want old farts in the Dream, said Snowball.

Horny Fox said, I'll play any part you want me to, Miss Ricketts. I'll play them all. Just so long as I don't have to be no fuckin fairy.

—Your language Melville, Miss Ricketts admonished him. Your language. Try to leave out the F words.

—I'll play the Duke, Mick said.

—That's the spirit, Miss Ricketts shouted gaily as she stirred from the sitting position.

—Let me help you, Miss Ricketts, Mick's palm under her rising posterior.

—Oh, don't do that, you naughty boy. Miss Ricketts rouged. Upright, she adjusted her skirt. She straightened her blouse and smiled benignly. We'll meet here next week. I'll have the scripts.

When she was younger, her first years as a social worker, she called at their homes. But the kids were often downtown or running around the neighborhood in search of unprogrammed diversions. The mothers were out shopping or working. The fathers lay in wait for her.

At first Mary Ricketts tried to find explanations for such anti-social behavior. Cultural. Economical. Political. The simple facts eluded her. She was younger, hence more desirable than the enervated European mamas. She was always newly-coiffed, laundered and dressed. She had an eager, inquisitive air. When she knocked on the door and shouted, Yoo-hooo — Is there anybody there? Gregor Polonsky, father of four, fantasizing on the couch was sure his prayers for a new piece of ass had been answered.

—Please to come in, Miss Mary Ricketts, he bowed extravagantly and ushered the Social Worker into the kitchen. Please to have a glass of tea with lemon.

—Well, thank you, Mr. Polonsky, but I really came to talk about Ivan.

Gregory clumsily pulled Miss Ricketts onto his lap. No talk now, he whispered. Talk later. Now we go for horsy ride.

—Oh, Mr. Polonsky, don't do that. I'm surprised, Mr. Polonsky. Really!

M. R. stopped visiting. She issued invitations and held court in her office where, seated behind the formidable oak desk, she could safely confront her clients. A bleeding Jesus on the cross hung in an ornate frame on the wall behind her.

*A Midsummer Night's Dream*, duly (and dully) cast, went into rehearsal. Gabriel made his debut in the role of Thisbe. His understanding of the part: Little. His enthusiasm: Nil. His shame: Much. Why? Because of Wall. Why Wall? Because that part was played by a black girl and Gabriel had to put his mouth up to the hole in the wall (artfully contrived by thumb and index finger of each hand of the girl) and kiss.

—You see, Thisbe kisses Pyramus through the hole in the wall, Miss Ricketts explained.

When Gabriel delivered himself of the lines: *I kiss the wall's hole and not your lips at all*, there were jeers, catcalls, myriad sucking sounds from the other actors.

—Kiss my hole.

—Nigger hole.

—Black hole of Calcutta.

Gabriel was unhappy about this outpouring of affection in public, but Miss Ricketts told him it was a good role and it would make a fine actor out of him.

—You'll see. You'll enjoy it. Don't let the others bother you, she counselled.

The fascination for Theater ignited in Gabriel, and he

continued to rehearse and to learn the Shakespearian lines with their involved rhythms.

The *Dream* was presented on an August night, hot as a Jewish baker's oven. Everyone related to the actors pushed into St. Christopher for the special event.

Jane, in gauze tutu, was a radiant Titania. She admonished Stanley Wolchuk's tall, skinny Oberon. Horny Fox watched from the wings, waiting in horned impatience to get on stage, to lie beside her as Bottom, bedecked with fairy ribbons and caressed by Jane's hot hands.

Who waited for Gabriel's appearance? Sara and Aaron Gottesman, and brother Noah. They sat and waited while other actors appeared and were recognized and applauded. Their likenesses treading the boards to the rhythm of the Bard. Seeing in their youngsters the opportunities that had passed them by. Evoking memories of the bleak spring morning of a midland town or the bittersweet remembrance of their lives in a Polish village.

THESEUS: How shall we beguile.
The lazy time, if not with some delight?

PHILO: There is a brief how many sports are ripe;
Make Choice of which your Highness
will see first.

THESEUS: A tedious brief scene of young Pyramus
and his love Thisbe; very tragical mirth.

PYRAMUS: Yonder she comes.

Gabriel entered and advanced with mincing step over to Rosemary Bush and applied his mouth to her hole in the wall.

THISBE: O wall! full often hast thou heard my moans,
For parting my fair Pyramus and me:
My cherry lips have often kissed thy stones,
Thy stones with lime and hair knit up in thee.

—That's Gabriel, Noah shrieked in glee.

—Dressed like a girl? Aaron was perplexed.

—It's Shakespeare, Sara explained.

—Why is he kissing the black girl's fingers, Aaron wanted to know. What is he saying?

Gabriel, the first born, the sage of the Gottesman family continued to recite unfamiliar words in the strange saga of Pyramus and Thisbe.

*Enter* LION *who roars and seizes* THISBE'S *mantle. Exit* THISBE *pursued by* LION. *Enter* PYRAMUS.*He stops. Sees the rent garment. Woeful lament. Out sword. Into* PYRAMUS' *body.* PYRAMUS *dies. Gradual collapse onto stage floor.* THISBE *enters, sees, reacts, builds to big climax.*

THISBE:    Asleep, my love?

What, dead my dove,

O Pyramus, arise!

Speak, speak! Quite dumb?

Dead, dead. A tomb

Must cover thy sweet eyes.

These lily lips,

This cherry nose,

These yellow cowslip cheeks,

Are gone, are gone!

Lovers, make moan!

His eyes were green as leeks.

O, Sisters Three,

Come, come to me,

With hands as pale as milk;

Lay them in gore

Since you have shore

With shears his thread of silk.

Tongue, not a word!

Come, trusty sword:

Come, blade, my breast imbrue!

*(Stabs herself)*

And farewell, friends:

Thus, Thisbe ends!

Adieu, adieu, adieu.

Gabriel slumps to the floor in attitude of slow death. General applause. Hurrah. Wonderful. What a performance. Fine actor. Did you see how well he (she) killed himself (herself)?

—Killed himself!

Noah rushes to the stage, shouts at Gabriel: Are you hurt? Get up. Where are you bleeding from? Noah tugs at Gabriel. Lifts his tunic in search of the gore. Gabriel opens one eye, whispers *sotto voce:* Beat it. It's only pretend. Gabriel dies again.

Everybody rushes to get a good look at the dying actor. Director decides to end play. Fast curtain.

* * *

There were other theatrical diversions at St. Christopher. *Twelfth Night* with Gabriel belching Sir Toby upstage and down pursued by a limping Horny Fox as Aguecheek. These two in turn chased Jane as Maria. The script indicated it, the director encouraged it. Jane was stroked, patted, slapped and mauled.

—Har, har, Horny bellowed, this is a really good play. He came to every rehearsal.

Jane's body was as tantalizing to aspect as to touch. Her appearance in Act One Scene V was a voyeur's delight. The word went out to the baseball field: Jane is on. The heavy hitters threw away their bats and gloves and mitts and masks. They plodded into the auditorium, sat and waited.

Jane played Maria like Zasu Pitts suffering from a Theda Bara hangover. The director — nineteen-year-old John O'Keefe, a psychology student, knew the value of catharsis. Because of his own yearnings for Jane he evolved a touch-tear-tantrum approach to the play. The romantic was greatly overblown. The bawdy was magnificently eroticized. He told Salvatore Puzzo, who was acting the Clown:

—Don't worry about the lines, about their meaning. Just look at Jane and when she talks to you, let your eyes run all over her body. She's being coy. She's only pretending. She really wants you to feel her up. So let her have it, O.K.?

To Jane he said privately: When you play the scene tease

him. Work him up. Make it stand up for him.

To the whole cast O'Keefe explained the double entendres. The kids enjoyed them. In their street brawls and shagging activities they spoke a similar vernacular, hot and forceful. Shakespeare sure could make up good words. He was one of them. He belonged.

Now Jane was onstage. Right leg extended, pelvis thrust forward in the Kotex Position favored by fashion models. She took a long breath, expanded her chest and with wildly nictitating eyelashes upbraided Clown:

MARIA:     Nay, either tell me where thou hast been
               or I will not open my lips so wide as a
               bristle may enter in way of thy excuse.

Having established the symbolism, the balance of the scene proceeded at an accelerated pace. Part Shakespeare. Part John O'Keefe. Part Jane (More. More). Tragical. Comical. Pastoral. Genital.

Rehearsal over. Chocolate milk and peanut butter sandwiches.

—Hey Jane. Whatcha doing tonight? Nothing? How about meeting us? Where? Your place. O.K.?

—Nope.

—Why not?

—Mom's home.

—How about the empty house near the dairy? What time? Nine.

—Well...awright.

The word went out. Jane was the word. Made flesh.

## 4

In the courtyard behind Garbriel's house, accessible via a driveway between No. 51 and Zimmerman's Grocery, two crumbling dwellings leaned mournfully against each other. Their sagging timbers wheezed in the winter winds and rotted away with the summer rains. The Reingold family inhabited one of these, the Slomczynskis cohabited in the other. The hastily thrown together slats looks like a Hollywood set designer's sketch for *Tobacco Road*.

Mrs. Reingold was a twittering canary. She saluted the morning with song. She warbled her vespers. All day, every day, her thin, reedy soprano sneaked through the cracks of the house and floated away into oblivion. Mr. Reingold was a carpenter, emaciated and balding. He rose at six and left at seven, his tool case scraping against his one good leg, his wife's fervent farewells pinging against his ear drums. The Reingolds had four children: three young girls and a boy, Felix, who was Gabriel's age.

Felix was the only kid with roller skates. One day Gabriel and Salvatore Puzzo ambushed Felix as he grunted past on silver wheels. Bam. A punch in the back. Zok. A kick in the ass and Felix was down in the road. The skates were seized and divided between the assassins. Felix shouting for succor. Up and down Leonard Avenue and around the block, balancing on one foot, they flashed dodging horses and trucks and bicycles, outdistancing the crying, pursuing Felix and his distraught mother. After a promise by Felix to share his worldly possessions the skates were returned, forgiveness sought and obtained. Amity prevailed.

The Slomczynskis in the other shack came from Staszow. They spoke and cursed in the mother tongue, aided by select English expressions brought into the house by their children. Mrs. Reingold was always shooing the Polish kids off her property. They were snotty and scrofulous. They urinated in the dust of the courtyard. They showed off their private parts. As they grew older their exploits became more specific and consequently more shocking to those neighbors who observed with great circumspection and greater satisfaction the randy revelations.

Roman Slomczynski, the head of the family, was on relief. The handouts from the city sustained them and gave them a night of boozy revelry every Friday. The festivities led to mayhem. With the dawn came the summation. Bleeding noses, blackened eyes, torn brassieres, crashed crockery.

In the beginning the police used to answer the riot call placed by Mrs. Reingold from Zimmerman's place. Then they refused to get involved. Just a family affair. A Polack celebration. Everybody sobers up. Everybody friendly again. Besides, the Slomczynskis in the clutch of alcohol were inseparable in the face of interference by outsiders. They would not be torn apart by neighbors' pleadings or police order.

The Slomczynskis had one major problem. Their daughter Mary. By the age of 18 she was only forty-six-and-one-half inches high, a chunk of flesh with a wrinkled dwarf's face. Mary sat around most of the time. She was slow-witted. The Slomczynski son, Staszek, a year older, a plodding ox, amused himself by playing with Mary's heavy pendulous bubs. Once he took out his organ and showed it to her. She fondled it, stiffened it and cooed over it. He toppled Mary onto the bare splintery floor and pulled down her woollen knickers. He shoved desperately. She began to cry with the pain. He soothed her with a five cent piece. In return she agreed to suck him off. Her piggy bank filled up with nickels.

Three grocery stores competed for the relief vouchers: Wineapple's (the sign in big, white, ceramic letters on his window) across from St. Christopher; Zimmerman's in the middle of Leonard; and Hershberg's at Nassau. Mrs. Hershberg was a widow, spare and nervous. When her husband Isaiah died leaving her with three sons and a mother-in-law, she embraced the business and perpetual celibacy. Her eldest son Ephraim helped serve the customers. He was sixteen and known by all, because of the depth of his knowledge, as Einstein. He read everything and remembered most of what his spectacled vision perceived. The residents came to him for advice about welfare forms, police summonses, and local and universal problems. Einstein had opinions and answers. He knew why there was a depression and how long it would last. He was aware of the latest treatment for cancer developed at the Western Hospital. He read up on medicine and knew how to relieve headaches, piles, chilblains, asthma. He knew how women became pregnant. (He had illustrations of male and female organs.)

Gabriel came to Einstein with stories about St. Christopher House. Einstein dispensed anecdotes about the things that were going on in the neighborhood. About the widow Prokosh.

—I wonder about her, Einstein mused. You know the milkman was in the house with her yesterday for over an hour. And the other delivery people. She must be very popular.

Gabriel tried to assess the charms of Mrs. Prokosh, a plump, full-lipped, preening pouter pigeon. He would ask Jane about her mother.

Jane was always straightforward. Ma went out last night. She didn't get in till morning. Three o'clock.

—Say, Einstein, confided Gabriel, we're going over to the empty house on Nassau tonight. With Jane. Want to come along?

—Can't, said Einstein. Gotta help my Ma in the store. Besides I just received the new copy of *Science Fiction*. All about space travel. Trip to the moon and the other planets.

—Well, Gabriel promised, I'll tell you all about it tomorrow.

—Gabriel, the scientist's voice fell to a whisper. Be careful. You can get an awful disease. Clap. You know, V.D. You're better off jerking off. Although you can get bald if you do it too much.

Gabriel had felt the slight tug at his genitals. The constriction of the testicles. The awakening and the surging erection. Soaring sexual activities imagined from the first moment of his discovered potential. It happed six months ago. He had finished with his toilet and was idly observing the whirlpool within the bowl carrying away his excretory

37

melange. He was buttoning up his white flannel combinations when he heard girlish laughter in the courtyard beyond the bathroom window.

Mona laughed like that. Gabriel had been thinking about Mona and her deep contralto chuckle and the movements of her body as she ran and dodged and slid into her seat in the classroom. Mona had white thighs. Gabriel saw them one afternoon at school. He was coming down the hall and made a right turn for the exit. There was Mona, her blue serge skirt pulled up. She was adjusting the legs of her cotton bloomers, pulling at them, smoothing them. Gabriel felt the heat in his face. He stood there, staring, fixing for all time the blessed vision, then mumbled:

—Oh, sorry, and dashed out.

Mona's thighs and bulging bottom stayed with him from that time. He knew from pictures that Mick showed the gang that Mona too had a cleft up where the thighs came together. That's where you were supposed to put your penis.

Thoughts about Mona excited him. His horn demanded attention. He started stroking. It felt good. Slowly first, along the tingling shaft. Up tempo amid increasing tightening. The climax arrived with a gush of seed spurting everywhere, splattering the linoleum floor, the unpainted plaster wall. When the working of his left hand finally ceased he was breathing more quietly. He regarded his gradually subsiding instrument. He thanked Mona for the inspiration of the event. Life was for jerking off. All the days ahead of him. Four times a day and more. He could will from his imagination as his fucking partner any girl he wanted. The horny response came at the thought of Mona's ass or Jane's tits bouncing as she skipped rope. Or from reading *I Am A Young Stenographer* or from looking at the sexual antics of Tillie The Toiler, Mutt and Jeff, Blondie or Popeye in the secretly circulated comic books. When the one-eyed sailor took out his battering ram and shoved it into his lady friend's hole, Gabriel's own whizz-bang was an eager partner. Olive Oyl fucked them both.

He willed himself again deep inside Mona, her legs wrapped about him, feeling the tightness, the moist, warm softness. His member distended in anticipation. Would it be better actually doing it with a girl? Everybody talked about it.

Wait. Tonight. Maybe. God, he wished it could be tonight. With Jane. Big, round, blue eyes, fair face haloed by gently-falling, sunny hair. Long-legged as she loped around the corridors of St. Christopher. The print cotton skirt secured at the waist by two mother-of-pearl buttons, curved over her rounded hips down to just above the dimpled knees. Jane wore sky-blue ribbed cotton sockees. Tan Saddle shoes. Three blue metallic bangles at each wrist. A shiny silver crucifix hung around her neck on a filigree chain. When Jane was in trouble or wanted something very badly she grasped the ornament in both hands and with eyes tightly-closed prayed.

—Oh, God, dear God, please don't let my geography mark pull me below passing grade. In the name of the Father and the Son and the Holy Ghost. Amen.

In their way, Mick and the others prayed as fervently but in vain for a chance at Jane. She tormented them with glimpses of her thigh-length pink satin underpants. Jane was content to merely frolic, gamboling innocently and outrunning her pursuers, evading capture. She indulged in hand holding, tolerated surreptitious breast fondling and giggly, tight-lipped kissing. With Robert McKenzie and John O'Keefe at St. Christopher, with the interns at Western Hospital she was a friendly tease. To the adult males of the neighborhood she proffered a cheery hello and a fast pass by. No webs of entrapment for this little fly.

The setting sun was sending thin stripes of blood into the August sky. The humidity washed in from the lake, bathed the asphalt and concrete, hung suspended in the early evening air and dampened the wallpaper in the Gottesman kitchen.

Sara was clearing the supper dishes from the newspaper-covered table. Mick's father (he sold sandwiches on the Montreal-Toronto train run) dozed on the porch, a half empty bottle of ale lodged between his bony legs. Mrs. Fox, gaunt and grey, mother of Horny, was reading one of her evangelical tracts. Washed in the blood of the Lamb. Roman Slomczynski was engaged in the evening ritual:

—You goddam supper for me? Why you no goddam supper ready when I come home for work at factory? Why?

Slap. Crash. Crunch.

Jane's mother was instructing cuddly, Baby Doll Jane.

—Mom's going out Janey, honey. Is my make-up on O.K.?

Lipstick, powder, rouge, comb, handkerchief, swiftly stuffed into her big, beige, canvas bag.

—Bye dear. Be a good girl, huh? And lock up when you go to bed. Not too late, huh? School tomorrow.

A peck on Jane's cheek. Open-lipped. Mother cares about her baby.

—Mom, you look beautiful. You always look *scrumptious.* I love you.

Mom grins. She confirms her appearance in the dresser mirror and strides toward the door humming.

—There's a small hotel, by a wishing well.....

Mrs. Prokosh at thirty-plus still desirable. Available to select males who like a good time and have money to guarantee same.

\* \* \*

Jane's house on Nassau is a three-story, semi-detached red brick with wood trim painted layer upon layer in creams and greens. Five battleship-grey wooden steps leading to a wooden verandah with wooden columns supporting an upper porch. Six foot partition between houses for privacy. Mr. Moshe Greenspan, lean, quarrelsome, sixtyish, bachelor, peddler of pots and pans, in two rooms on the third floor. Below him are the O'Reillys. The Irishman digs ditches for the city works department. His wife stays home with infant triplets and keeps house for Mrs. Prokosh.

James and Mary O'Reilly are from Belfast. Ulster by birth. Ulster by inheritance. Ulster in their attitudes toward work, toward merrymaking, toward sex. Sober. Industrious. Mrs. Prokosh lusted for O'Reilly. Protesting at first — think of Mary, it wouldn't be right — he, Irish Protestant, succumbed to the happy task of ploughing the Magyar landlady's furrow. O'Reilly purchased ice cream in cones for everybody from the Surrey Ice Cream Company next door owned by Lou Alexiou, a Greek from Mycenae. Lou sells wholesale to Hershberg's Grocery Store and to Zimmerman and Wineapple. To drug stores, variety shops, restaurants. In the hot summer evenings Lou sells retail. Queue up by the open window and reaching it shout your order.

—Single. Double.

—Pistachio. Vanilla. Chocolate.

—Nickel for a double. Nickel for two singles.

Cold, refreshing, Surrey Ice Cream in cones. To bite into. To lick. To feel the cold of it going down, down, in three delicious flavors.

To the west, approaching Lippincott Street, Nassau pauses at a lane. The corner house empty. The Rosenbergs once lived there. Master tailor Meyer Rosenberg from Pinsk and his crafty, parsimonious wife and two snivelling *hoydens*, Adele and Ada. The sound and fury of domestic family strife gone. Moved to a bigger house in the better neighborhood of Montrose and College.

The silent Rosenberg house waiting for such a summer evening. Waiting for Horny Fox and Mick and Felix and Adam (whose right cheek is puffy-pink from the skin graft that never heals). Waiting for Four-eyes Bleiberg with the rancid armpits. Waiting for Jane.

Jane. Naked in the cluttered bedroom she shares with her mother. Jane looks at Jane's mirror image. See Jane's lips. Carmined. Pouting. Full. Salve-smooth with the application of Mom's lip rouge. Jane opens lips into oval of desire. Tongue issues seductively serpentine, sweeps about periphery. Pretend with eyes shut tight. Pretend with Mick who waits to receive Jane's snake tongue. A cunning linguist. Jane commands and Mick's mickey stands. Hard pressed for entry between Jane's thighs. Everybody's mickey stands for Jane.

See Jane's breasts. Round hillocks. Soft. Supple. Sensitive. Think Mick again. Jane imagines nibble on nipple. Jane fingers deep in imagination. Jane feels sensation shooting down, detour around her dunny funny belly button. It darts downward to the virgin shrubbery. Legs-widespread, quivering on orangy bedspread covered bed, see Jane fingerfuck within the golden mist of maidenhair. Into the tropical moistness between the twinlipped portal. Massage. Start slowly. Eyes closed. Increasing rhythm. Circular strokes. Here we go round the mulberry bush. Jane's mulberry bush, raspberry lips, strawberry nipples. Mick's mickey. Polish sausage. Bottle of Coke. English cucumber. In and out. Round and about. Faster. Faster. Ooooo. Oooohhhh! Coming. Coming. Aaaaahhh. Aaaahhhhh. Subside. Wet in the bed. Essence of Jane. Eyes unlash, staring at the twenty-five watt electric bulb hanging from the flyspecked ceiling.

Mom on this bed. With Dad on this bed. With others who came to visit when he was away buying chickens in Cooksville. After Dad was killed in the truck accident Mom asked Jane to sleep with her. It was lonely without him. She needed the company. In bed in the freezing winter nights Mom was warm and savory. Before retiring Mom anointed the lobes of her ears, the cleft of her bosom, behind her knees. The smell wafted deliciously towards Jane. In dreams Mom tossed and moaned, whispered and sighed. Jane caressed awake by the agile digit and the oral embrace. With Mom through Paradise. Mom and Jane in amorous plenitude. The first sweet, dizzying, almost-fall from innocence. Jane still *virgo intacta.*

Tonight. Epithalamium for Mick and Jane. The burden or proof or reproof is on her. St. Christopher carried ONE. ONE was almost too much. Tonight, Jane, unknowing must carry all. All who creep to the vacant Rosenberg house. Celebration of the mass.

The celebrants enter. Wan candles flicker. The side door hangs diagonally open on one hinge. The front door newly decorated with a death's head in aluminum paint against the peeling black. Kick sharply. The latch gives. Push. Creak open. Enter. Creak shut.

—Jane not here yet?

—She'll come. She's gotta come.

—Then everybody will come.

Whispers. Jokes. Run to the window to look. Where is Jane?

* * *

Gabriel puts away *The Operas of Gilbert and Sullivan.* He is, for the nonce, finished with Sir Joseph Porter, KCB. His preparation for *H.M.S. Pinafore* must wait. Thoughts of Jane have marred his concentration. His loins are knotted. Can't wait. Run up the time worn stairs. One. Three. Five. Seven. Nine. Eleven. Thirteen. Fifteen. Dash in before somebody beats you to it. Shut the door. Hook and eye closure. Safe enough. Unbutton bursting fly. Pants down. Longjohns. Unbutton. Sara insisted that he wear them.

—Don't talk back. Do as I tell you. You're never too old to listen to your mother.

Defiantly, grudgingly, Gabriel acquiesced. Child. Boy. Man. In bondage to mother. Wore his combinations. Through all seasons.

Released, Gabriel's penis bounded out and up. Gabriel cupped his left hand, embraced the shaft. Thoughts of his mother interfered.

—Fuck off, he muttered. Gabriel's mother fucked off.

Jane came into focus. Gabriel stroked lightly. Jane loomed larger then disappeared. Vision fugitive. Gabriel stroked with determination. He was on a bucking stallion carried away to Olympus. Jane on Olympus reached out and touched Gabriel. He drew her to him and kissed her on the lips, on the neck. He lingered on her breasts. Lyre music. Jane banished her grecian robe with a magic wave of her blonde hair. She touched Gabriel with a feather from the lyre bird and Gabriel stood undressed before her.

Now they were in the chamber of Aphrodite. Jane beckoned him to the couch. As he advanced it dissolved into a multitude of soft white feathers. Gabriel beside

Jane, amidst a snowstorm of feathers, his arrow of flesh gradually sucked into Jane's golden orifice. Plumes swirled about them in slow motion with each Gabriel thrust, with each Jane heave. They reached their climax simultaneously, precisely as prescribed in the pamphlet: *Family Life.* Available at City Hall. Ten cents.

The semen showered down into the tub where the fish were kept alive until Friday, slowly sinking great gobs of milky sperm, into the gaping mouths of the scavenger carp.

His mother confronted him at the front door.

—Going out again? Why don't you stay home and do your school work or read? Always running around with the *shkotzim.*

Nay mother. Tonight I seek the Princess Rosamond. I, Prince Gabriel, shall try my valor in the resurrection of the maiden of my dreams. When in the end the Prince arrives at the tower and ascends the winding stair he tries the door of the small chamber wherein the Princess Rosamond lies. She looks so lovely in her deep slumber that he is transfixed by her beauty. Finally he bends down and softly places a kiss upon her rosy lips. Behold, she awakens. Her eyes open and she regards him with kindness and affection. She arises and hand in hand they go forth. Her royal parents, the King and Queen awake also, as does the entire court. They gaze on each other in startled wonderment. Then the horses in the yard get up and shake their sleepy flanks. The dogs jump up and bark and wag their tails. The doves on the roof pull their heads from beneath their wings, look about them and fly away into the field. The flies on the wall stir and creep on apace. The fire in the great kitchen comes to life with a roaring blaze, the meat begins to roast, the cook gives the scullion a great box on the ear that he cries with pain and the maid carries on plucking the bird. The wedding of Prince Gabriel and Princess Rosamond is held in great splendor. And they live happily together ever after.

—What's the matter with your leg? Got a cramp? I'll phone the doctor, Gabriel's mother insisted.

Gabriel's wet penis adhering to his combinations. He tugged inside one pocket shifting his leg carefully. That does it.

—No Maw, it's nothing. My leg's stiff from all that exercise. Playing baseball at St. Christopher.

Christ, did I flush the toilet. Recurrent doubts about pulling the chain. Somebody, his father or Noah or his all-wise mother would walk in and see his shame in the cracked toilet bowl. Or glistening against the wallboard. Once he was so frenzied in his spasms that he shot all over the mirror. The Jaffa Orange wrappers, zealously collected by his grandmother from Hershberg's grocery in lieu of toilet paper, made ideal wipers.

—Where you going, the inquisition continued.

—Over to St. Christopher.

Tonight we shall examine the anatomy of the Fairy Tale. Our sampling will be selected from the Brothers Grimm. The Frog Prince. Faithful John. Hansel and Gretel. Rapunzel. The Fisherman and his Wife. The Valiant Little Tailor. Cinderella. The Musicians of Bremen. Clever Alice. Little Snow White. Rumpelstiltskin. The Golden Goose. The Wolf and the Fox. The Goose Girl.

—What's at St. Christopher, she pursued.

—Gilbert and Sullivan. *We sail the ocean blue and our saucy ship's a beauty. We're sober men and true and attentive to our duty.* Look maw, wait till you see me all dressed up like an admiral of the Fleet, in blue and white and gold, veddy, veddy English, you know. Dancing and singing and kissing all the *shikses* in the chorus. *A maiden fair to see, the pearl of minstrelsy, a bud of blushing beauty.*

—I don't believe you, she said, feet rooted, arms akimbo. Her prescience was unerring. He couldn't keep a secret from her. If he wouldn't tell she would ask Noah.

—Where's Gabriel off to? Did he tell you? Think. Try to remember. He's going to get into trouble unless you tell me. *Vey is tsu mir. Gottenyu.* What will the neighbors say?

A good name is better to be desired than riches. Sara was poor. But she had pride.

—I told you I'm going to rehearsal. If you don't believe me come along and watch.

He pushed past her, beyond the door and down the three

porch steps into the street. Sara following observed him sauntering towards Bellevue Place. Gabriel entered the settlement house by the front door, nodded to Elsie the office girl who was chatting on the telephone, looked in at the basketball game in the gym and went out into the empty playground.

He left by the rear gate. He walked whistling down Casimir Street. *He is an Englishman. For he himself has said it. And it's greatly to his credit.* Along Dundas with the mean little cottages on the north side and Alexandra Park across the street car tracks he ambled until he reached the Variety Shop at Denison. Up past the square with its fountain and benches, beyond the Kiever Synagogue until he came to Nassau. He purposed a left turning here but rejected the plan in the event that Sara would be waiting for him outside Hershberg's.

Sara ruled the household and everyone within it. Gabriel could not escape. Unlike the Jews of ancient days who fled Pharaoh's wrath under the aegis of the Paschal Lamb and recounted their flight from bondage every year at the Passover Seder, Gabriel was the prisoner of Sara's consuming motherhood. She hovered over her boys. Scrubbed their backs in the bathtub. Mended their clothes. Bought their suits. Selected shirts and ties. Gabriel rebelled when he could. He was open to all new perceptions, new experiences. The cantor's son introduced him to toasted bacon sandwiches at the Rainbow Tea room on College Street.

He questioned the validity of the encrusted Orthodoxy of his religion; then of all religions. He yearned to escape beyond the pale.

When at a concert he heard the treacly outpouring of the fat tenor rendering *My Yiddishe Mama*, Gabriel smirked, frowned, groaned, fidgeted, and agonized. All about him the Jewish boys and girls were unable to hold back the tears.

My Yiddishe Mama. I need her more than ever now.

My Yiddishe Mama. I'd love to kiss that wrinkled brow.

Gabriel would have sold his Jewish soul to any non-Kosher Mephistopheles to get his Yiddishe Mama off his

46

Yiddish back for just a little while.

Like that pleasant afternoon. Tuesday it was. Two o'clock. Sara was shopping at the Kensington Market. Aaron humped over his last at the shoe factory. Noah at the playground. Gabriel all alone. Midsummer stillness. Seated on the porch bench Gabriel sought diversion. What to do until supper?

The window facing him showed the backside of old lady Gwozdz. Fat hemispheres of flab churning within the housedress as she stooped to dust and polish the things in the bedroom. The Gwozdz and the Gottesmans weren't talking to each other. The altercation began with the raising of dust from the carpet beating in the Gwozdz backyard. It drifted next door and through the open windows into Sara's kitchen. Name calling ensued—in Polish—with Mrs. Gwozdz baring her rump and turning it to Sara with the injunction:

—*Salma Dupa.*

Whereupon Sara bared hers and invited Mrs. Gwozdz to kiss *her* ass. Better to stay away from the old Polack and the possibility of a broom handle up the rear end. Gabriel wandered by and eyed the next dwelling. On the second floor the window was raised and a woman put out her head. A newcomer just moved in but already the recipient of numerous male visitors. A heavily-powdered and painted good-natured straw blond of thirty-eight. She was called Lily. His mother told him to stay away from that woman. There were reasons. Too shameful to talk about. Her appreciative callers left pieces of silver. Some brought food. Or cases of beer.

Lily leaned out of the window. Gabriel could see her tits slop-slopping inside her scoop-necked sweater.

—Hi, she shouted gaily to Gabriel. Whatcha doing?

—Nothing, Gabriel said. Nothing.

—Wanna come up? Need your help. Door's open.

Gabriel considered.

—Come on, she urged. Won't eat you up. Scaredy cat?

—O.K. I'm coming, and he dodged inside and ran up the steps. Fifteen of them, two at a time.

—In here. Gabriel approached and gave her his hand. She

grasped it, shook it, then gave him the secret password, forefinger scratching his palm. She grinned as he blushed.

—Hey, help me with this. She gave him a cylinder of tomato juice and an opener. Can't get this thing to work. See. I cut myself already.

—Oh, that's easy, Gabriel said. The contraption fitted around the rim of the can. It had a lever that you turned to put the opener in a cutting orbit. But first you had to pierce the tin with the sharp edge of the opener. He exerted pressure.

—Here, we'll do it together, Lily said. She bent beside him and put one hand over his. Her other fell on his lap. He felt her breasts and smelled her rose water. His pants grew tight.

—Aw, shit, Lily said, when their joint efforts failed. Forget about the juice. Let's have some beer instead. Going to the ice box she brushed against his thigh and felt his stirring member.

—Hey. That's some hardon ya got. Didn't think you were old enough. Embarrassed he turned his head away.

—Come on let's see. Over here to the window. She laughed in her boisterous way and knelt down. She was unbuttoning him when it happened.

Crack. Bone thudded on his head. Whack. Another blow to his back. His right arm was pulled behind him.

—You come away from here. Right away. You hear? Gabriel's mother pulled at her son. And you — she gasped at Lily, you...hoo-er. Leave my boy alone.

Sara dragged Gabriel and his erection down the stairs, berating him for bringing shame to the family.

—What will the neighbors say, she moaned. *Lieber Gott.* That I should have a son who doesn't care how much pain he brings to his mother. Who always brought him up so carefully. Taught him to be a decent, upstanding human being. It's a *shande* and a *charpe.* At supper she told the story to Aaron. Noah listened in wonderment. Gabriel was doing something bad? Aaron simply said:

—Not nice, Gabriel. Not nice.

The incident remained current in the Gottesman annals for months. Gabriel openly recanted and promised he would never even look at Lily again. He vowed inwardly that he would fuck and fuck until his cock wore off but he would never again be discovered and humiliated.

He continued north from Nassau Street to Oxford and turned left at the Bell Telephone exchange until he reached the lane and came to the back of the empty house.

* * *

Jane made sure her front door was locked. She hopped down the steps and skipped along the sidewalk (dodging the cracks). The street lamps were burning dimly. It was not quite dark. Mick greeted her at the deserted house.

—Hi Jane. Eagerly.

—Hi Mick. Demurely.

—How come you're so late. Been waiting for you a long time. Boy is it spooky in there. Been running all through the place. Fell down the stairs. Boy did I hurt myself. Wanna see?

Seated on the verandah, Mick pulls up his jersey.

—Feel.

Jane traces the rough, torn abrasion above Mick's waist. He guides her land lower. Jane, giggling, withdraws.

—C'mon inside. Mick pulls Jane upright.

—Oh, I don't know. It's so nice out here.

—Aw come on, Jane.

—Well, maybe just for a little bit. She unrumples her skirt, smooths her blouse, bounces on soft, rubber soles into the haunted house.

Flickering candles held by Jolly Chums reveal past ravages. Flowered wallpaper with peeling petals. Splintered floorboards. Crumbling mantlepiece above blackened fireplace. Metal chandelier crazy-hanging with empty light sockets. Eyes behind candlelight peering out at Mick and Jane. Night light filters through dusty windows.

—Holy smoke, Jane pouts. You got the whole Coxie Army here.

—Three cheers for Jane! Good old Jane. The shouts go up. Jane mellows. What are we gonna do now?

—We're gonna play Hide the Body, Mick says. Mick is in charge. He makes the rules.

—Me and Jane first. We hide. The guy who finds us gets his turn with Jane. O.K. Give us five minutes.

Grumbles of discontent. Who chose Mick to be first? Nobody dares to contradict him. Everybody agrees, hoping his turn will come. Gabriel too.

—Up you go Jane. Mick propels her ahead of him up the broken stairs. His hand on her back slips down to her buttocks in a sweeping caress, then under her skirt. Along the curving backside, down the sloping loins, around to the rear again.

Jane with difficulty, with sweet awareness stumbles upward. Mick hobbles close behind. On the first landing they pause. Shaft of moonlight points the way.

—Don't Mick. No more. Jane draws away.

—Come on Jane. Up to the top. Into the attic. Secret hiding place. He pulls Jane after him. On the third floor there is a small dirty room. Standing on rickety chair Mick reaches up and dislodges a section of ceiling.

—There it is. Mick panting now with the exertion. I'll hoist you up and get in after you. Then we'll replace this piece. They'll never find us.

—Don't want to get dirty. Jane holds back.

—You'll be O.K. Come on. Up. Jane. That's it. The two together in total blackout.

—Gee, it's dark up here, Mick.

—Lie down Jane. Jane stretches out. Mick alongside. He fondles Jane's breasts. She objects.

—No Mick. Don't.

—What do you mean don't? Haven't I felt you up before?

—I don't want to right now. I can't see. It's getting awfully hot and stuffy. Mick. No. I told you, I don't want to.

Mick isn't easily put off. Didn't he set up the whole affair tonight? He promised the guys it would be a gang lay. He knew all about women. He had been layed once before. A fast fuck with the sister of big Irish.

He reached between Jane's thighs, tore at her underpants. Jane squirmed. He pried at her legs with elbows, knees, fingers. Her panties came away in a thin, ripping sound.

—Mick. Don't. You're hurting me.

Mick lunged at Jane. His penis thudding against her. Again. Ill-aimed. Too high.

—Goddamit.

—*I don't want to.* I don't *want* to.

A plunge again. Well placed. Powerful enough to enter into Jane's virgin cunt. A momentary obstacle of membrane, then gradually deeper. Jane's screams mounting.

—I'm hurt. Mick, you bastard. You've done something bad. Let me go. Jane slashes Mick's bare back. Mick won't release her. Jane jerks away. Dislodged, Mick comes all over Jane's blouse. Jane sobbing.

—I'm bleeding. I can feel it.

—Jesus, Mick cries, I'm all wet.

Downstairs the hounds are seeking their quarry. Hey Mick. Hey Jane. Where are you?

Scared now, Mick lowers himself from the hiding place. Jane in pain scrambles after him. No longer Baby Doll Jane. Dishevelled. Dirty, tear-stained face. Lipstick smudged. She discovers the deep red oozing down her limbs. Jane sobbing: I'm hurt.

Felix suddenly appears. Behind him the others.

—Got you Jane. Got you Mick. Felix jumps on Jane. They fall to the floor. He fingers her.

—Christ, she's bleeding! Felix springs away. The others back off and look to Mick for direction. He says nothing. Felix leads the pack down the stairs.

—Let's get the hell out of here.

A cacophony of sound as feet run, trip, hurdle obstacles, out into the night, out of the house where ravaged Jane, bleeding Jane wails a threnody to her lost maidenhood.

## 5

Sara was the daughter of a farmer. A Jewish farmer from a hamlet near Ostrowiec. She was down to earth and stubborn. She was deeply religious. She invoked metaphysical assistance for all kinds of conditions. For warts she tied a handkerchief into thirteen knots and buried it in the soft earth of the basement. When the fabric disintegrated, the warts would disappear. She was superstitious. Always wear shoes in the house: stockinged feet are a portent of death. D'ont praise a child for fear of The Evil Eye. Leave a light in an infant's bedroom to ward off Lilith. Beware of the Angel of Death.

She was ingenuous and kind. Easily moved by a sad story, she doled out a measure of financial assistance, then regretted her generosity. She vowed never again, and no sooner tested than she would acquiesce.

The hegira from No. 43 to No. 47 Leonard Avenue, recently vacated by the Frankels, was made necessary by the anticipated arrival of the newcomers. There was much to do before the in-laws arrived. Sara's own family would occupy the first floor. The living room became the bedchamber — twin beds and a wardrobe — for Sara and Aaron. The dining room, used only on important occasions, was also the parlor for entertaining guests on weekends. Every day after school Gabriel switched on the green porcelain lamp that sat in the middle of the massive, round, oak Duncan Phyfe table and spread out his homework. An oversized bureau against the wall housed linens, dishes and cutlery. A narrow lounge with thin lumpy mattress and tired springs pulled out into a double bed for Gabriel and Noah. The kitchen was furnished with a deal table and four chairs. There was a kitchen cabinet of light maple. A black metal coal-burning stove with nickel trim hulked hugely against one wall. The stove pipe, assembled in crimped sections, stretched diagonally across the room into the chimney outlet in the opposite corner. It was secured to the ceiling by loops of wires.

Every morning when Sara lit the stove for cooking and

for heating the water tank, the smoke billowed out between the joins of the pipes and from under the heavy circular stove lids. Sara and the kids catapulted out of doors during all seasons, eyes watering, throats raspy, heads swimming. Once, the fire department had arrived and analysed the situation. The inspector made some unsuccessful recommendations on how to increase the draught then departed amidst sirens and bells. The stove smoked and the family choked. The cockroaches under the sink thrived.

The gloomy hall was illuminated by a single weak bulb that dangled abjectly from the ceiling. A black box-telephone was strapped to the wall just where the stairs led up to the second floor. At the head of the stairs was the bathroom. You shit in the bowl, washed your hands in the tub and wiped them on your pants. There was no ventilation except a miniature window at the end of the low-ceilinged chamber. The stink clung with fecal ferocity. It obeyed the natural law of gases. It rose to the ceiling and, finding no escape, hung there. Despair of hope all ye who enter. The sounds from the toilet—urinary, defecatory, masturbatory—echoed into the kitchen on the other side of the cardboard wall. A square cell and a room with a verandah looking out onto the street completed the second floor. Eleven winding stairs ended in two attic rooms on the third level. The back room looked out onto a row of garages and the shacks of the Reingolds and the Slomczynskis. The front room had sloping walls. An old, luxurious chestnut tree brushed its leaves against the window and provided shade during the stifling summer days.

\* \* \*

Five o'clock on a Sunday morning at the beginning of June. Then if ever come perfect days.

—Up. Up. They're coming today. Quick get dressed. We're all going down to the station to meet them.

Aaron already awake. Phylacteries donned, prayer shawl

over his shoulders, *siddur* in hand, nodding as he prayed softly in one corner of his bedroom. Morning devotions. An extra prayer for safe arrival.

Gabriel and Noah identically dressed for summer in shorts and shirts and socks and running shoes.

Gabriel runs to the kitchen, slaps water over his hands and face, quickly dries with rough all-purpose towel. Noah next. Hasty prayers. Noah reciting quickly to catch up to his older brother. Seated at the kitchen table. Breakfast dishes and utensils on the unvarnished wood. Corn flakes with Jersey milk, rye toast with butter and hot chocolate. Sara putters about, nibbles on her bread, gulps the coffee. Aaron has two soft-boiled eggs broken into a bowl and fortified with a pat of non-salted butter, toasted chala baked Friday by Sara before the onset of the Sabbath. Washed down by a glass of milk.

The clock in the tower of the red-brick fire hall was hollow-sounding six when Aaron turned the heavy key in the slot of the front door. He tried the handle. Secure. The *mezzuzah* on the doorpost kissed by all in turn, a last careful look around the house, then the group stepped down the street for the morning's long-awaited adventure.

Cotton candy clouds drifted overhead in the sky. All quiet. The houses breathed in slumber. At this hour no doors banged shut. No windows screeched open. No kids running up and down the stoops. No yelping mutts. No housewives sloshing greasy water out of pans into the gutter. No cowboy serenades from the Slomczynski gramophone. No shouts. No curses. No wails. The curtain was still to rise on the street theatre for the day. The instant before creation.

Along Bellevue Place. More mute dwellings. The metal cleats in Aaron's shiny Oxfords proclaimed pting...pting... pting...pting...pting. Sara's summer sandals, a more sedate ka-lop, ka-lop, ka-lop, ka-lop. The youngsters' sneakers, sa-wish, sa-wish, sa-wish, sa-wish.

They turned right at Denison. Dundas Street ahead.

P-ting, ka-lop, sa-wish, sa-wish. P-ting, sa-wish, sa-wish, ka-lop. P-ting, p-ting, ka-lop, sa-wish, sa-wish, sa-wish, sa-wish. Gabriel ran ahead, Noah close behind to the street

54

car stop. Sara shouted:

—Careful. Not so fast.

Aaron did not shout to his sons. He did not hear Sara. He was thinking of the imminence of reunion. He was a good son. Quiet. Respectful. Caring. He kept his emotions submerged. He lacked articulation to give them voice. Joy illumined briefly his features then retreated.

Between the silent, sailing clouds the sun shone forth. It was a morning for rejoicing. Life was good. Despite the absence of the promised treasure in the streets of the new world. Aaron had found no gold anywhere in the six years since his arrival. Beaded in perspiration, he hammered countless nails for each copper he earned at the shoe factory.

But there was freedom here. A man wasn't afraid to voice his opinions. He himself wouldn't criticize of course but he enjoyed listening to his neighbors. Politics. City Hall didn't know the problems of the people. They should be thrown out at the next election. The Province was controlled by the Tories. But the most venom was reserved for Richard Bedford Bennet up in Ottawa. What did Bennett know about the working man?

Aaron marvelled at the audacity of his landsmen. In Opatow a Jew could get a cracked skull and a term in prison for a minor disagreement with authority.

—Here comes the street car. Noah spied it first. It lurched toward them from Bathurst Street. The T.T.C. red and cream car with vertical wood slats. During the sleety winter months the ticket man tossed lumps of coal into the stove beside his perch. Sometimes two cars were joined together.

The tram sparked to a stop. The doors clanged open. Sara pushed the kids before her. She urged Aaron to hurry. Hurry. Hurry. Sara's perpetual heavy-handed guidance. Everybody needed her help. Aaron couldn't be trusted to succeed by himself. She wouldn't wait for him to fail. He had to be shown the way in all things. Blessed are the meek for they shall inherit the earth. Whatever the strong leave of it.

Cash or tickets in the fare box. Four for a quarter for

adults. Children under fifty-three inches tall, twelve for twenty-five cents.

The street car started up spasmodically. Aaron fumbled in his worn black, leather change purse. Pennies and nickels carefully scrutinized and placed in Sara's outstretched palm. When she had assembled the correct amount she shouted to Aaron:

—Enough.

She thrust the coins at the conductor. He pointed to the fare box. When the silver and copper discs had rattled to the bottom of the glass cage he counted out four paper transfers and handed them to Sara.

Gabriel and Noah sat in the very back. Aaron and Sara in front of them, watching the mean little shops and houses unroll and fade past.

At Spadina an old laborer in denim overalls got on followed by two charwomen. A new model, all-metal TTC tram made a left turn at the intersection. The morning light bathed the cobbled streets, the Roman Catholic Church, the Dominion Bank, Shapiro's Drug Store and the Standard Theatre, home of Yiddish drama. Very few stirring yet in this new dawn of revelation.

The motorman advanced the rotary accelerator and the vehicle jerked forward until it reached its maximum speed, maintained if for half a minute then gradually braked and eased to a full stop at Beverley Street.

On the left a solid, eight-foot brick wall enclosed the Casa d'Italia. The consulate was impregnable.

—McCaul Street, next stop. McCaul.

The iron fence of the Art Gallery of Ontario blurred by. No travellers boarded at McCaul. None alighted. The morning city was immobile in the grip of Sunday paralysis.

At University Avenue a constable in blue serge with maroon trouser stripes, silver buttons winking, his pointed English style bobby's hat secured by chin strap, stepped briskly inside. He saluted the driver, then propelled his convincing bulk along the swaying aisle. He grunted down beside the two boys.

—Behave yourself, Sara whispered anxiously to them. Then she assured the policeman. They're good boys. They don't make any trouble.

At Elizabeth Street, Chinatown. Exotic names in English letters. Lum Fun. Wong Pow. Kuomintang. Yew Shew. And the New York Café.

*Chink. Chink. Chinaman.*
*Wash my pants.*
*Put them in the toilet*

—And make them dance........the refrain pranced across Gabriel's memory. A ditty learned during recess at Ryerson Public School. Chinkee. Chinkee. Chinaman. His cousin, Ruth, a beautiful girl with high cheek bones and slit eyes was called Chinkee. But Chinks were evil like Fu Manchu. The Chinese laundryman was a good Chink. He brought the Gottesman family a package of Lichee Nuts and a Chinese calendar every Christmas.

The Ford Hotel appeared ahead of them. Two red columns. They transferred to the Bay street car heading south. Shea's Vaudeville Theatre featuring Ben Blue, Borah Minnevitch and his Harmonica Rascals, Henry Armetta, Ethel Shutta and the Shea's Dancing Girls. Gabriel would be an actor one day. Happiness in an amber spotlight. Make mine make-believe. The tinsel. The glitter. The romance. The beautiful women who kiss with open lips.

The clock in the tower of City Hall tolled the hour. The stonefaced Victorian structure sat impassively like a grand dame, attended by Eaton's and Simpson's department stores and Bowles Lunch.

They passed between the lofty edifices of the financial center — the Stock Exchange, The Bank of Commerce, The Evening Telegram, the Globe, the National Club.

—Front Street. Union Station, the motorman bawled.

There it was. The long, buff building, handsome with Greek columns and porticos. Inside, a huge hall with a high, curved ceiling. A clock in the center. Numerous ticket wickets flanking one side. A shop that sold candies, cigarettes and newspapers and magazines and souvenirs. Checked luggage. And a horde of bustling people. Two constables promenading, ready for any emergency.

It was ten minutes after seven.

—The train from Montreal. Where is the train from

Montreal?

Sara questioned a porter, found the answer, ushered the family down a flight of cold, white stone stairs to the waiting room. A welcoming committee had preceded them. A babble of voices. Yiddish. Italian. German. Polish. Uncle Eli spotted Aaron and motioned for him to squeeze into the place next to the roped off area. Push. Sorry. Push. Beg your pardon. Push. Squeeze. Ah.

Seven thirty-seven. A rumble of steel thunder. Then the metallic harshness of the brakes. Then silence.

—Here they come, somebody shouted in Yiddish.

A shriek of welcome as a group of sideburned Chassidim in long black coats and fur hats came into the concourse.

—*Baruch Haba.* Blessed be ye who come in the name of the Lord.

A young, dark woman emerged and was embraced by an older man. Saucer-eyed children hanging onto mothers hanging onto husbands. The seed of Israel.

Aaron was the first to see them, lugging cloth packs of belongings. Joshua, the youngest brother in knicker-bockers. Samson peering out of watery, myopic eyes. Sadie, finger in nose. Sniffling Freda, sinus plagued. His mother in black, a lace shawl covering her wigged head. And the father. Judah the Lion. A little man with sable-colored van dyke beard; on his head a black, peak cap. On his body a black suit; on his feet, black shoes. All of them searching about in an agony of uncertainty.

—*Mamanyu! Tatanyu! A danken Gott!*

The immigrants from Opatow heard, then saw, then stumbled in the direction of the waiting brethren. They embraced, re-embraced, kissed, wept.

—*Sholem Aleichem. Aleichem Sholem.*

Aaron offered up a prayer.

—Blessed art Thou, O Lord our God, ruler of the universe who hast granted us life, sustained us and permitted us to celebrate this joyous occasion.

Peg Leg Pete, twelve-year-old consumptive buccaneer, baptized Alfred Bruce Smith, brought a new distraction to the neighborhood. He arrived at No. 41 Leonard on a summer evening with two younger snotnosed sisters, a haggard apathetic mother and a thin dissolved-in-drink Pa.

Alf hobbled down the ramp of the truck. Yo ho ho and a bottle. His tapered rubber-tipped prosthetic bump-bump-bumped down the incline to the sidewalk. The door of the frame cottage unlocked, the unloading began. Faded furniture. Cracked crockery. Chipped bric-a-brac. The accumulation of the years. And one thing special: a tattered Union Jack to be unfurled on Victoria Day. *Dulce est pro patria moriri.* Finally a case of O'Keefe Ale (two dozen dark-green bottles) transferred reverentially by Pa Smith himself.

The two girls ran into the weedy back yard. The mother stood on the little porch. She leaned against one of the thin uprights. Horatio Smith uncorked his first drink.

The Peg Leg waved the huge flag, stomping and singing — Rule Britannia, Britannia rule the waves. He wrapped the red, white and blue linen about him and scanned the widening circle of foreign faces.

—Get the flag off you, Fiona Smith bleated. And find your sisters.

Horatio, second bottle in hand, appeared at the door.

—Wat's this about the flag now? She pointed to her son posturing *cap à pé* in the symbol of British ascendancy. Shocked at the desecration, Horatio hurled the half empty bottle at the boy. It struck him on the head spilling its suds over the flag.

—Let's have the bleeding flag. Come on, into the bleeding house with you. A couple of kicks in the backside and Alf proceeded jerkily, hollering with pain, past the assemblage of the curious, indoors.

Alf's leg was a recent acquisition, the reward for racing against a freight train, and losing. The other three had jumped from the trestle into the water below; A.B. Smith was not fast enough. The engine wheels sheared off his left limb just above the knee and he fell, a crippled bird trailing blood into the Don River. He was pulled from the shallow stream and ambulanced, sirens oscillating to the Hospital for Sick Children on Elizabeth Street.

For a while Alf was a somebody. Pictures in the *Star* and *Telegram* and the *Globe.* All kinds of photographs. Alf, alone in his hospital bed, propped up by two pillows, attempting to smile. Alfred and his two sisters eating ice cream cones. A photograph of Horatio and Fiona Smith hugging their hero offspring. A shot of the mighty locomotive with the engineer leaning grimly from his cab. There were radio reports of the mishap every hour for the first day. The Movietone News people chronicled the event for movie goers. The saga of Alfred, at the first run theaters downtown.

When asked by one reporter what Mr. Smith thought of his son's escapade, Pa reflected briefly and finally conceded:

—He made it by jiminy. He made it. Got lots of spunk that lad has. Should have run a little faster though. Fuckin train was speeding. Should have slowed down. Railroad company says they'll take care of our Alf. Not to worry about the expenses. Welfare promised to look after us. And the boys at the Canadian Legion Post took up a collection. Y'see....I'm a vet. Went over in 1915 with the Princess Pats. Jesus, those were good times. Yup, fuckin good times. Lots of action. Lots of beer. Fought for my country. Lance Corporal Horatio Wellington Smith. Demobbed in 1919. Got a pension on account of shrapnel wounds. And mustard gas. Can't work you see. God bless the king. He's been looking after me all right. All right.

Eventually up and about, clomping everywhere on his peg leg, Alf enjoyed the notoriety. The story of his ordeal embellished by repetition ending always with the question:

—Wanna see the stump?

Whether he did or not, the listener was shown the way the curved flesh of the aborted thigh fitted snugly against the leather cradle with its criss-cross of laced tapes and the smooth-finished, varnished wooden peg.

60

Alf ran races. Erratic movements of flesh and wood competing against each other, the peg leg a rigid piston pulling the other to catch up.

Alf broad jumped, landing in the raked earth with the peg leg pointing heavenward. Ludicrous. A source of merriment. There goes Peg Leg Pete. Ass over elbow.

He imitated Cap'n Kidd, a patch over the eye, an empty wine bottle gripped fiercely in one hand, doing the hornpipe. As a finale he hurled the bottle at whatever unfortunate creature hove into view. An alley cat, a sparrow, a pregnant mutt. Or high up into the air to fall again to the road in a shower of sharp splinters.

He was a little ruffian. His was the power and the glory. He insisted on halfers of all the plunder. Chunks of ice from the ice wagon. Lumps of coal pilfered from the sacks. Loaves and cakes from the bakery wagon. If refused he flopped to the ground, removed the portable leg, levered himself to a standing situation again with its help, then hopped on his good leg towards his quarry, the wooden shaft swinging viciously before him. Ultimately he let go and sent the weapon hurtling at the victim. Thrown off balance by the force of his thrust, he fell to the pavement and began to whine about the mistreatment of a cripple with only one leg.

Tired of the forays against them, the gang trapped young Smith in the lane. A thin wire was cunningly stretched across his unsuspecting path. Stomp. Stomp. Contact. Raise wire. Pull sharply. One buccaneer laid out flat. They whacked his ass with a two-by-four, dragged him by the good leg along the street and deposited him outside his door. Then they peed on him and ran to St. Christopher House.

After this debacle Alfred stayed on his porch and glared at everyone who passed by. The bruises healed and he began to feel more confident about facing his peers again. He made vocal sallies at the girls playing double dutch and hop scotch. In vain. Until one day Mona came by.

—Jesus, will you look at that, he whistled his approval of the rolling ass and the bouncing bubs.

Mona allowed herself to glance in his direction, saw him

seated on the stoop, the peg raised at a sixty degree angle. Alfred Bruce Smith's disability held a phallic fascination for Mona.

—Wanna see it? he invited her.

—What, she retorted, have you got that I haven't seen before, bigger and better?

—You've never seen anything like this I bet. C'mon over here. I'll show you.

—Mona allowed herself to be shown. Seated in the tall grass in the field behind the house she watched the ceremonial removal of the peg leg. Straps unlaced with great deliberation. The concave receptacle eased away from the flesh. Alf shifted closer to Mona. With a deft, sideways twist he presented his stump into her lap.

—Look. Wanna feel it?

The gristle and flesh had been surgically shaped into a smooth, rounded terminus of gleaming skin. Mona edged her fingers lightly around the sensitive perimeter. Alf, aroused, urged her on.

—Do it some more. Some more. Wriggling in sexual response.

Mona saw the bulge rising inside Alf's short pants. He released it, pulsing, a thin, rigid member. He wedged the stump between her legs and scraped against her wide-opened thighs as she jerked him off. He achieved his climax just about the time Lucy Northwright, messenger of the Lord, was delivering the tidings of salvation.

> Beautiful lamb,
> Wonderful lamb,
> Wonderful lamb of Jesus.
> Wonderful lamb,
> Beautiful lamb,
> Beautiful lamb of God.

The thin specter in garb penumbrous strode by No. 47 Leonard Avenue on her way to Nathaniel House. The dark lady announced her coming in a piping tremolo, vocalizing her favorite hymn with evangelical fervor. The Jewish mothers pulled the children out of her path and spat three times on the sidewalk to ward off the *ayin hora* of Lucy

62

Northwright.

Miss Lucy was the slightly-mad incubus of an alien God. Her mission — to spirit away and convert the *cheder* boys.

It had happened before. Forced conversion. In 1858 the seven year old Edgardo Mortara, beloved son of the well-known Jewish family of Bologna, was kidnapped and given to Roman Catholics for upbringing, on the pretext that he had been baptized six years earlier by his Catholic nurse. There were world-wide protests especially from representatives of the Jewish Community. Pius IX appealed to, refused to return Edgardo to his parents. The Pope was busy with the Vatican Council of 1869 and the proclamation of the Dogma of Papal Infallibity. *Ad Majorem Dei Gloriam.*

It wasn't going to happen in 1929 in the vicinity of the Kiever Synagogue. Hear, O Israel, the Lord our God is One.

Between stanzas of her *Agnus Dei* Miss Lucy showered blessings:

—Praise the Lord. Oh yes, Praise the Lord.

The Jewish kids responded.

—Crazy Devil. Crazy Devil.

Gabriel's mother joined from the verandah.

—Not Crazy Lord. Crazy Devil. Crazy Devil.

Infuriated, Miss Lucy shouted in a growing crescendo:

—Praise the Lord. Praise the Lord, and heard, mistakenly, the sacrilegious reply:

—Praise the Devil. Praise the Devil.

She riposted: Hallelujah. Hallelujah.

—I'm a Bum, tendered the street urchins.

—Hallelujah. Praise to God. Gabriel recited the Hallel, the Psalms of David. In that context the word Hallelujah had majesty. In ghetto English it tumbled in tatters from the glory of heaven.

—Hallelujah I'm a Bum.

—Hallelujah Bum Again.

Abraham Silberfogel, the *meshumid*, supervised the activities of the Nathaniel House with the zeal of the convert. White-maned, with a little beak of a nose and protruding chin, he hovered about like a great bird of prey, seeking juvenile apostates.

He had been reborn to the way of the cross and accepted Jesus as his Savior. He became a Jewish-Christian, the label devised for belated converts to the-once-and-future Messiah.

Honest Abe was assisted by a small congregation of the faithful — three females of tepid temperament and indeterminate age. Genteel readers of the Gospelers — Ma-ma-lu-jo. Bringing light unto the Jews.

Their efforts were profitless. The ghetto bonds could not be so easily sundered by the blandishments of earnest amateurs who had only a superficial awareness of the Old Testament and a colored-by-faith familiarity with the New.

Their earnest activity became more animated as Christmas drew nigh. They offered in addition to salvation, parties and presents. The invitation urged:

> Come to the Nathaniel House and welcome Jesus
> into your hearts. For Jesus said: *I come to fulfill*
> *the prophecy.* Bring your friends. Refreshments.

Gabriel, accompanied by some of the finest young scholars in the Jewish community, knocked on the premises of the large colonial mansion at 225 Bellevue. They would suffer themselves to be shown the true path to salvation.

—Praise the Lord, intoned the Silberfogel.

—Crazy Devil, mumbled Gabriel, in Miss Northwright's direction.

She was echoing — Praise the Lord. Oh yes, Praise the Lord.

The Sunday morning Bible class, led for this special occasion by Silberfogel, began with a reading from St. Matthew, the familiar tale retold in the Director's Yiddish-accented English:

> Now the birth of Jesus Christ was on this wise;
> When as his mother Mary was espoused to Joseph,
> before they came together, she was found with child
> of the Holy Ghost. Then Joseph her husband, being a
> just man, and not willing to make her a publick ex-
> ample, was minded to put her away privily. But while
> he thought on these things, behold the angel of the

64

Lord appeared unto him in a dream, saying: Joseph, thou son of David, fear not to take unto thee Mary thy wife; for that which is conceived in her is of the Holy Ghost. And she shall bring forth a son, and thou shalt call his name Jesus: for he shall save his people from their sins.

The flight to Nazareth (Mary went all the way on her ass).

No room at the inn (for Joseph it was no in at the womb).

The birth in a stable (Away in the manger. No crib for His bed. The Little Lord Jesus, laid down His sweet head).

The star that shone that night (Star of wonder, star of light).

The wise men (We three kings of Orient are).

Pictures of the Christ child were distributed. Cows peering, cud-chewing, down at Him, a chubby little cherub, blonde, tilted nose. Like Pegeen O'Sullivan's baby brother. Gabriel wouldn't have given him much of a chance of growing up to become God. Not the God of Moses. Of Abraham, Isaac and Jacob. Of David. Not the Lord of Judah the Lion. But Gabriel cooed over the pictures and later colored in with greasy crayon, the empty spaces. *The Christian Child's Coloring Book of the Nativity.*

Every Sunday during November and into December, they were wooed with stories and sundry diversions. Songs and recitations Christological. Chocolate milk and salmon sandwiches. Gold and silver stars awarded for excellence, pasted on a chart with all their names. I am the way, saith the Lord.

Two weeks before Christmas Miss Lucy announced there would be an examination. A quick review in preparation. She was satisfied. Honest Abe himself appeared.

—I am so pleased with the progress you have all made. My, but you know so much. Jewish children are so clever. I know you have enjoyed learning about our Savior. And His disciples. Peter and Paul and the bread and fishes. And

Mark and Luke and John and Matthew. But oh my, I mustn't give away all the answers. You see there are questions on this sheet for you to answer. When you are finished Miss Northwright will collect and mark them. Those with fifty per cent correct answers (or more) will get a very pleasant surprise. A Christmas surprise. Now then. Here you are. And good luck.

Mr. Silberfogel distributed the papers. Where was Jesus born? Why did Saul change his name to Paul? State the Golden Rule. Why is Jesus the Messiah? Who betrayed Jesus? How? Why did Thomas doubt Jesus? Why did the Jews want to crucify Jesus?

The queries received replies facetious and factual, simple and involuted. The crucifixion response was varied. The Romans nailed him to the cross. The Jews were too busy on the eve of the Passover. What kind of a BULLSHIT question is this?

Gabriel drew a picture of Jesus with gossamer wings affixed to a torn, bloody robe, flying up between a space in the clouds above which he marked the word: HEAVEN. Felix sketched a big penis which he labelled the father of Jesus. Goudie Garfinkel drew a figure covered entirely by a white sheet with the words across the chest: The Holy Ghost. The apocryphal tales about the genesis and ultimate fate of Jesus that Gabriel heard within the family did not find utterance: The foetal Jesus, prematurely aborted, being flushed down the toilet. Jesus, the bastard, no father (even in heaven) to admit parentage. Jesus, of ornithological origin, via the wayward dove that dropped his seed into Mary's ear. A silberfogel.

Despite the graffiti, the students passed the examination. And were suitably rewarded. A Christmas stocking packed with an apple, an orange, candies, little wooden toys, puzzles. As a bonus each neo-Christian received a pocket-sized, black, leather-bound New Testament inscribed: To our devout brothers in Christ Jesus, with the sincere hope for a full life spent in His footsteps. Signed discreetly: Abraham Silberfogel, Director, Nathaniel House.

Afterwards, the Christmas party. Soda pop. Sandwiches.

Cakes. A great deal of singing. The Director beamed at the congregation and visitors from the other missions. Miss Lucy at the piano leading the singing:

—Good King Wenceslas looked out, on the feast of Stephen...

Everybody sang, *serioso-giocoso.*

—The stars in the bright sky looked down where He lay. Omnium gathered around the creche — a *papier mâché* family, the infant, Mary, Joseph, livestock.

>We three Kings of Orient are
>Tried to smoke a rubber cigar
>It was loaded and exploded
>Now we are on a star.

Music traditional. Lyrics unknown.

>Star of wonder, star of light.
>Lead us to the dynamite.

The doggerel obscured by Miss Lucy's authorized version.

Miss Lucy soloed into:

>Loving Jesus meek and mild.
>Look upon a little child.
>Make me gentle as thou art.
>Come and live within my heart.

Then she dissolved with a soft flourish of arpeggios into:

>Jesus loves me this I know
>For the Bible tells me so.
>Little ones to Him belong
>They are weak but He is strong.

—Now, everybody: Yes Jesus loves me.

>Yes Jesus loves me
>Yes Jesus loves me
>The Bible tells me so.

In a sudden expression of devotion similar to the high-spirited ending of the *Ayn Kelohaynu* in *shul,* Garfinkel added a coda (immediately caught up by the other pranksters):

—I am Jesus little lamb

>Yes, by Jesus Christ, I am.

* * *

Sara's third little lamb was delivered on the third day of Hannukah — Christmas Day — at the Mount Sinai, the Jewish Community's general hospital on Yorkville Street. Confined to two adjoining houses, converted into an institution of healing, the Mount Sinai was a congested organism. In-patients and out-patients. Emergency cases. Obstetric. Chronic illness. Emotional problems. The afflicted were deposited in the halls and left amidst catheters and intravenous apparatus and other pro-tem paraphernalia, pending the discharge of prior patients.

Sounds of clinical activity reverberated throughout. Visitors, invalids, and staff mingled freely, raucously. The Mount Sinai was staffed by Jewish doctors who were prevented by a gentiles-only policy from obtaining residencies in the big, well-equipped, non-sectarian institutions.

Dr. Irving Rosen, avuncular and predisposed to small talk even during moments of crisis, was in attendance when Sara was admitted. Her brief period of labor was spent shrieking in a screened section of the first floor hall. As soon as one of the two small operating rooms became vacant she was wheeled into the presence of her doctor.

—I'll have you out of here in a jiffy, Sara, he hollered to her from the wash basin.

It was a routine delivery. Outside the Christian children were singing carols. In the hospital chapel the visiting rabbi was lighting the candles on the menorah. O Lord, our God who hast commanded us to kindle the Hannukah lights.

Sara abided eight days. She was visited by Aaron every evening. On Sunday Gabriel and Noah were sneaked in and at the approach of a nurse were concealed under Sara's high bed.

For Sara it was a holiday. Attentive nurses. Lots of rest. Kosher meals prepared by others and served to her. Body massages. Alcohol rubs. Friendly people everywhere. Sara allowed herself a few guilty moments when she thought of Aaron and the children trying to manage without her.

From her bed she could see onto the quiet snow-covered street with its solid homes. In the adjacent house, Catherine Kingston resided in splendid anonymity. Mabel Chambers, two doors distant, a lady of means, walked her black toy poodles on their diurnal round. But private residences were beginning to give way to commercial and professional enterprises. The Mayfair Club at the corner. Across from it the Presbyterian Home for Girls. A Chinese laundry. Despite these incursions, the Loyal True, Blue Protestant Sons and Daughters of Albion formed a city-wide phalanx against foreigners.

> For inspite of all temptations
> To belong to other nations
> He remains an Englishman....

In an attempt at economic and social assimilation, Mr. Grotowski changed his name to Grove. Shmuelevitch to Sanders. Petrofsky to Peters. Cohen to Conn. Garibaldi to Gary. Doxiades to Dixon. The Wangs, Wongs, Lims, Lams, Lums, Chins, Chans and Chens, trapped by pigmentation and physiognomy remained undeniably Wangs, Wongs, Lims, Lams, Lums, Chins, Chans and Chens.

Aaron helped Sara out of the big, black Dodge Taxi. She cradled in her arms the fruit of her womb, the first of her children born in Canada. Aaron paid the driver. He escorted his wife into their bedroom where an upholstered wicker basket was ready to receive the new guest.

—*Baruch Haba.* Welcome, Aaron said. He watched as Sara unwrapped the baby and placed it into the cradle.

The other inhabitants of No. 47 appeared. They provided unrequested opinions.

—So small. Probably sickly. Won't amount to much.

Aunt Sadie stood, stared, withdrew her right index finger from her nostril and pulled with it a gob of mucous. She regarded its color, contemplated its texture. She wiped the jelly on her blouse, returned the finger to her gaping mouth and sucked in imitation of the infant.

Uncle Joshua, green and fifteen, forced a smile and said kitchy-koo and wandered away.

Uncle Samson peered benignly through barely-open, puffed lids. His children, he vowed, would be strong, handsome, healthy, heroes, mighty doers. He mumbled un-heartfelt congratulations and sidled into the backyard where his rusting CCM bicycle was leaning against the clapboard fence. It was guarded by his German Shepherd dog

Rex. He leashed the dog to the rear frame and pedalled heavily out into the courtyard, waved at Roman Slomczynski and chugged through the lane into Leonard Avenue, up to Nassau along to Bathurst, down past the Sanitary Steam Baths and the Greek Orthodox Church, down to Queen Street and the full four miles to Sunnyside. Rex bounding, slavering behind him.

Aunt Freda, sniffling hay-feverishly, suddenly sneezed. Aaron hollered for her to get out, wouldn't want to give the baby a cold.

The infant began to whimper then cry then shriek. Sara in her convalescent bed reached for him to nurse him. Gabriel and Noah were shooed out. The others, Sadie and Freda and the grandparents, left with Aaron. Sara sighed a sigh of great sacrifice. She pulled out her breast full of milk and presented the ripe nipple to the babe.

Suckled. Satisfied. Both slept.

## 7

Behind the long, wooden counter Einstein stood, cutting flimsy sheets of Kraft cheese from a great block. As the slices fell into position on the waxed paper he brushed to one side the crumbs (he would nibble at these later) and looked up at Sara, waiting for her to call out.

—Enough, she finally said. Enough.

Einstein weighed the result and translated it into cost.

—Anything else? he asked.

—And a head of lettuce, two pounds of potatoes. Sara offered up the vegetables pre-selected for the best choice.

And a half pound of unsalted butter.

—Cash or charge? Einstein asked as he pushed the purchases to her.

—Charge. Sara hoped it would be all right to charge just this little bit more. I'll pay as soon as Aaron goes back to work. Most likely next week. Yes, next week, I should be able to pay back for everything.

Einstein opened the thick ledger with the dog-eared pages and flipped them expertly to the page marked Gottesman. To the accrued debit of $7.59 he added the current purchase: 63¢.

—That's O.K., Mrs. Gottesman, he assured her. I know you'll pay it off. Anyway, I hear the City will be helping out soon. Relief. Relief for everybody. Don't worry about the bill.

He echoed his mother's belief in the morality of her customers. Mrs. Hershberg insisted with saintly assertion that the cash would come in. The Depression couldn't last.

Two years already. Mrs. Hershberg's mother-in-law, heavy-set, loose-jowelled, spat on the floor in disagreement and dragged her weary weight and arthritic bones into the kitchen at the back. She set about to prepare another batch of cheese blintzes. She did all the cooking and baking and serving and cleaning up. The agreeable smells attracted kids and adults for samples of the old woman's cuisine.

Sara's family ate regularly and enough. Great gobs of starchy concoctions. Thick, soured milk — a homemade yogurt — with bread hunks bobbing about in the crests and depths. Noodles and potatoes drowned in hot milk. Noodles and cottage cheese sprinkled with sugar. Beet borscht. Cherry borscht. Spinach borscht. Mounds of mashed, boiled or browned potatoes topped with fried onions. Thick slices of bread. Rye. Black. Onion buns and kaiser rolls. Bagels on Sunday. Chala on the Sabbath. Beef freshly-ground at the butcher's under Sara's hovering eyes. Scrambled eggs with chopped onions. Meat dishes. Dairy dishes. Never both at one meal. Sara performed culinary legerdemain with plebian ingredients.

She bargained and bartered and begged for credit. Charity, dispensed by the Jewish Family and Child Service, took the form of cast-off clothing. Other agencies provided exotic forms of succor. The handwriting on the postcard left by the mailman bore the announcement:

—Food parcels will be given out on Thursday evening. Present this card at the Food Depot, 17 Nassau Street, between the hours of 7 and 9.

Aaron set out with Gabriel. The Depot was located in a former school near Spadina. They arrived at half past six. Better to be early, Sara advised. About eighty recipients of the food message were already there in a wavering queue. Father and son took their places. Gabriel shouted greetings to young acquaintances. Aaron averted his head, eyes lowered. Shame shrivelling him.

At twelve minutes after the hour a door opened. The procession started to shuffle forward. Twenty minutes later Aaron presented himself and the card to a person at a desk who confirmed: Name? Gottesman. Status: Married. Address: 47 Leonard Avenue. Unemployed? Yes, but hope to get back to the job soon. Aaron, clutching Gabriel, was passed on to a spectacled hunchback who handed him a loaf of Weston's bread wrapped in white paper. From another shelf a quart bottle of milk from City Dairy. A small, round, white, unlabelled carton was handed to Gabriel. The hunchback warned him not to eat it all himself. It was for the whole family.

—Peanut Butter. Good for you. You'll like it.

Sara was waiting for them at the door.

—What did they give you?

—Milk. Good. Bread...Hmm. She felt the softness.

—Makes great toast, Ma, from Gabriel.

—What's that you have, she asked her son. He handed her the carton. Sarah removed the cover and inspected the contents. Looks like paint, her nostrils flared as she smelled the oily substance floating at the top. Pooh, as she pushed it away.

Gabriel inserted a knife and plumbed for depth. The metal struck a crusty substance. Gabriel excavated some of it to the surface.

—Looks like shit, Noah, newly-arrived said. Like the shit in the baby's diapers.

—Doesn't smell like shit, Gabriel sniffed the knife. Stale peanuts, that's it.

—Such food the *goyim* can eat, Sara declared. I won't have it in the house. Throw it out. Pea-nut But-ter. Hah!

Gabriel stirred the unhomogenized mess to make a blend. He sang in time to the circular motion of the knife.

—Here we go round the mulberry bush, the mulberry bush, the mulberry bush. I bet Gerty Bush likes peanut butter. Mmmm, good.

He stirred. Easier now. Solids absorbed into the oil. He sang *sotto voce*: here we go into old Gerty's Bush, that smells like peanut butter.

Gabriel the adventurer spread the lumpy mass onto a piece of Weston's bread. Close your eyes and open your mouth and see what the good lord will bring you. He champed down on the cotton batting and bit off a mouthful. He tasted and chewed, grimaced and chewed, and swallowed the peanut butter-flavored pulp.

—Tastes not so good, Gabriel said.

—Tastes like shit, huh? Noah bet it tasted like shit.

Gabriel, agreeing that it was an inferior morsel nevertheless finished the piece. He spread some on a second slice. Bit off bigger hunks. Managed to radiate enjoyment. Not so bad.

Gabriel ate everything. Ate while reading. Doc Savage.

The Shadow. School texts. The details of the cloacal system of the frog and the urino-genital tract of the rabbit did not diminish his appetite. Deep in his reading he dipped his spoon into the mashed potatoes, scooped and delivered into his mouth, opening and closing reflexively. Masticating. Swallowing. While the other diners argued, Gabriel ate and read. Everybody's unwanted food was Gabriel's fare, furtively placed on Gabriel's plate.

Gabriel looked up to discover with amazement that his portion was undiminished.

—Eat. Eat, his mother said. It's good for you.

The arguments began when Sara hollered through the house: Supper's ready. Noah asked, What have you got? Sara said, Chicken burgers. Noah said, I won't eat. David said, Me no eat neither.

—Leave the room, Sara rejoined.

Reluctantly the two younger boys sat down. Gabriel and Aaron already eating. Noah takes a forkful of meat. Holds it, staring before him.

—Eat, Sara commands. Noah has no appetite. Sara curses her luck.

David tastes and spits out. Sara cuffs him. Eat David. Eat Noah. It comes out: David, eat, Noah. Noah, eat, David. Everybody laughs except Sara. She catches Noah depositing potatoes on Gabriel's plate. Sara shouts, Stop this nonsense. Eat.

Argument about school. Principal's office phoned. Noah came late three times this month. The Principal is a goddam liar, shouts Noah. Sara believes Mr. Davidson. Noah starts to cry, runs away from table. Sara shouts, Come back, you hear me? Noah reluctantly returns. Gabriel has to relieve himself. Where are you going? Sara cries after him. Upstairs. Noah eats. Aaron eats. Sara hasn't tasted anything yet.

Noah has to pee too. He runs up the stairs to join Gabriel. They criss-cross their streams, missing the bowl. Onto the fading linoleum floor.

—A fine way to bring up children, Sara glowers at Aaron. She curses. Runs to the foot of the stairs and hollers: Gabriel! Noah! What's the matter, haven't you finished yet? No answer.

—If you don't come down right away there'll be no supper for you. I'll throw it out. See if I don't. This time I'm not fooling.

The toilet is flushed. The brothers slide down the bannister, hit the end post with a smack, dismount and run into the kitchen. A few mouthfuls and Noah runs away again.

Sara is crying, God has cursed me. Gabriel has finished and is reading by the window. Aaron sits staring forlornly at his wife. She wipes her eyes, scrapes the leftover food onto her plate and spoons it into herself. Without joy. Finished, she clears the table, washes the dishes and scours the pots with steel wool and kosher soap. She pours generous heaps of cockroach powder all around the kitchen sink. The roaches scurry madly out of the way.

* * *

Nothing perturbed Rivka Blumenthal, the social worker at the Jewish Federation on Beverley Street. She had a full case load and handled the problems of her clients with cool precision. An antiseptic woman of forty, she displayed the symbols of her sensibility in her dress (plain) hair style (arranged in a bun at the back) and demeanor (clinical).

Sara presented the note from the school nurse to Miss Blumenthal, who read: Preliminary examination of the eyes of Gabriel Gottesman indicates the desirability of spectacles. She pursed her full, pale lips in reading; finished, folded the paper and placed it on her desk. She looked at anxious Sara and the sullen youngster at her side.

—Are your eyes bothering you, young man? It would be impossible to lie to Rivka Blumenthal.

—Oh yes, Sara answered for him. He needs glasses. His eyes are strained from too much reading. I tell him he shouldn't read so much but he won't listen to me. After all, I'm only his mother. He reads all the time.

—Is that correct, young man, the social worker shot the

75

question at Gabriel.

—Yeah, I guess so.

—He has awful headaches, Sara said.

—Is that so, Miss Blumenthal seemed genuinely interested. Is that right, young man.

—Yeah, sometimes.

—Oh, he really needs eyeglasses, Sara continued, trying to convince. But we can't afford them. My husband is out of work. We're on the pogy. Sara admitted the last fact slowly, with embarrassment.

—Well, let's see what we can do, Rivka brought out a form and began to write on it with her fat, black, Shaeffer's fountain pen. Big, backhand letters. Name?

—Gabriel Gottesman, Sara answered for him.

—Gabriel, is it? she turned to him for confirmation. He nodded.

—Speak up, young man, she encouraged.

—Yeah, Gabriel muttered.

—You mustn't say Yeah. It's not nice. Say yes. Yes. You mustn't speak like an ignorant *shaygetz*. Remember, you should always say YES. And PLEASE. And I BEG YOUR PARDON. And of course THANK YOU.

—I tell him all the time to say PLEASE and THANK YOU, Sara interjected. All the time. Sara shook her head in a please-believe-me affirmative motion.

Miss Blumenthal made some more notations and affixed her name with an authoritative flourish. She handed a card to Sara.

—Take this to Dr. Gold.

Sara thanked her effusively. Gabriel, anxious to leave, was admonished by Rivka Blumenthal of the Federation of Jewish Philanthropies to be sure and behave himself and set an example in all things, especially in his school marks.

—Say thank you for everything, Sara scolded him.

—Thank you, he said, suppressing a grimace. Gabriel's *Ode To Rivka* took shape:

Rivka Blumenthal, social worker,
Rivka Blumenthal is no shirker.
What, dear God, will be her fate?
Does Rivka Blumenthal menstruate?

76

She steers clear of dirt and muck—
Does Rivka Blumenthal ever fuck?

\* \* \*

The steel-rimmed eyeglasses were ready prior to the Sabbath. The myopia corrected, the astigmatism reduced. Gabriel wore them, tightly pressed at the nasal bridge, to morning services, the Sabbath of the new month, at the double-domed Kiever Shul. The print in his *siddur* was sharper. The Hebrew letters marched nobly across the page from right to left. Looking up he could make out the design woven in gold threads on the maroon velvet curtain before the Holy Ark: two lions rampant, holding between them the Scroll of the Torah. The bubble of the ceiling appeared azure blue, fading towards the apex into whiteness. On the three panels surrounding the balcony where the women sat, a primitive painter had etched the twelve Zodiacal signs. Aries. Taurus. Capricorn. Saggitarius. Gemini.... The animals pranced about in abandon. Virgo, in Garden of Eden innocence but loosely robed. Figured in deep blue against buff. Plaster peeling in spots.

Afterwards, peering from behind the lenses on the leisurely stroll homeward, Gabriel, four-eyed, anticipated the jibes at the movie matinee. But first, the heavy dinner of chopped chicken liver, fat chicken soup, baked potatoes, roast chicken, apple sauce and cherry soda-pop. Aaron contemplating the *menuchah*, the peace of the seventh day. The Sabbath afternoon siesta.

For Sara too. Disposing of the utensils, the luxury of indolence in bed until dusk. Lots of time until the Saturday night laundry. Water boiled in the copper container. Transferred to the round steel tub with Aaron's help. The addition of soap suds and Javel Water. In with the soiled clothes: stained underwear, sweat-stiffened stockings, food-pocked shirts, sheets, pillow cases, a slip, girdle, brassiere, bloomers. Allowed to soak while the family went shopping. Then scrubbed with a bar of Sunlight soap on the glass ridged washboard, rinsed, wrung out and taken downstairs into the musty basement to dry.

She gave the boys a nickel each for admission to the Liberty and another nickel for a treat. She cautioned them to mind their manners and to watch out for the cars.

—What's playing? Noah wanted to know as they ran towards Dundas Street.

—Tom Mix, I think. Or Jack Hoxie. No. I think this week is Rin Tin Tin.

—I like Rin Tin Tin, Noah said. The bravest dog in the whole world.

—Hurry up, Gabriel shouted as Noah stopped to tie a shoe lace. He didn't want to be late. The cowboy serials were the best. The Masked Rider was his favorite. And he was in one hell of a predicament. At last week's showing the Masked Rider was tied up and buried alive by the bad guys, just as the episode ended. The doomsday voice boomed out into the dark theater as the screen went blank:

—What will happen to the Masked Rider? Will he escape from the grave? Or is this the end? Be sure to see the next thrilling chapter of *Alone In the Saddle* with the Masked Rider at this theater.

Gabriel was sure his hero would escape this ordeal as he had those of the previous eight episodes. But how? Like the resurrection of Abraham Silberfogel's Jewish-Christian Lord, the Masked Rider's defiance of death would be a major miracle.

Noah stumbled and fell, bloodying his nose on the cobblestones. Unable to stanch the flow Gabriel dragged him, crying, back home. They missed the show. The following week the Masked Rider appearing in the final chapter, showed no effects from his previous ordeal. He had triumphed. The cowboy galloped off into the sunset waving his hand.

Intermission. Everybody scurried to the lobby. Ice cream. Popcorn. Chocolate bars. The brothers trotted to the toilet. Noah peed on his trousers. Gabriel sponged the stain, hollered to Noah to watch out next time.

They stayed for the second showing. In the middle of the Bugs Bunny cartoon the projector sputtered out and all was dark. The hand clapping started. Then foot thumping. The manager ran up and down the aisles stabbing points of light at the culprits, threatening expulsion if they didn't stop the racket. The carbons replaced, the mayhem on the screen resumed to the accompaniment of whistles, and shouts.

Sometimes, alone, Gabriel sneaked into the Garden Theater on College Street. That was where he saw her: the top-hatted singer in revealing dress and silk stockings. She sang in a deep voice and enticed the bearded professor who made strange noises. She sang:

*Ich bin von Kopf bis Fuss an Liebe angestellt,*
*Weil dass ist meine Welt und sonst gar nicht.*

He kissed her feet and ran away with her and became old and stooped. She stayed beautiful. Gabriel dreamed himself into her boudoir and ravished her.

Frankenstein was playing at the Orpheum. Noah was scared to see it. Gabriel went alone with a bag of cookies and apples. The Orpheum was old and dark. It was scary just to sit in the auditorium with the mice running between your feet. The toilet was in the basement. You had to go down a long flight of steps through a dark corridor and push open a squeaking door. The one marked Gentlemen had a dirty toilet bowl and a urinal. A sixty watt bulb dangled from the ceiling. Spiders ran across the walls. Cockroaches scurried over the floor. Two flies chased each other around the sink.

Gabriel stood on his toes to get his penis over the edge of the urinal. He was the only one there. He turned around suddenly to confront the Monster. Nobody. Reassured, he began to pee. He was just a little scared. Maybe the Monster wasn't really dead.

Suppose Boris Karloff was standing behind him ready to grab him. Gabriel whirled about. Nobody. The Monster was hiding behind the door. If only Dr. Frankenstein were here, he would know how to handle him. Gabriel did up his trousers and prepared to leave. Nobody in the corridor. He walked, feigning confidence, then panicked and ran to the stairs. He could feel the breathing behind him, the hands clutching at him. Another sprint, beyond the door.

Safe.

When he left the Orpheum it was dusk. Gabriel hurried home, the Monster at his heels all the way.

\* \* \*

SCENE: *Kensington Market on a Saturday night. With a cast of hundreds including* SARA *and the three boys.*

*On Nassau Street just short of Augusta they pass the* Shochet, *ritual slaughterer, gazing out of his messy window. They will come back here later to the white-bearded, skull-capped sage. With their squawking poultry-geist.*

MR. RABINOWITZ *settles down to wait. To muse. Remembrances of days of devotion, of the* shtetl *in Poland, a wife long dead, of children grown and fled. Of the New World. His world of bloodied chicken feathers. He sits in his wooden hut on a stool and dredges up fragments of prayer and snatches of song. He rocks forward and back, his right foot tapping an unsteady* obbligato.

*The weekly family shopping safari. Crowds of pedestrians from Bathurst, from College, from Dundas, from Spadina converge at Kensington. Walking, jostling, wheeling prams and strollers, spilling onto the roads, dodging dray horses and rattling wagons. A Chevy coupé honks by.*

*The vendors at their stalls. Assaulting the ears:*

—Cherries. Ripe Cherries. Cherry ripe.

—Bananas. Bananas. Bananas.

—Apples. Apples. Apples.

—Apples. Pears. Bananas.

—Fresh fish. Whitefish. Cod. Haddock. Mackerel.

—Herring. Schmaltz herring. *A mechayeh.*

—Oranges.

—Quarter a dozen. Quarter a dozen. Juicy oranges.

—Tomatoes. Cucumbers.

—Potatoes.

—Fresh dills. Sauerkraut. Olives.

The shouts ricochet into the mild evening air. Cheering sounds. Entreating sounds. Buy now sounds. The heaps of produce beckoning with color and profusion. White-aproned merchants and their fat wives scoop up and weigh and stuff into bags and collect money. All is bustle. Saturday night at Kensington Market.

—Don't squeeze the grapefruit, Missus. You want to buy, so buy. Don't squeeze.

Past Prussky's Butcher Shop, sides of beef hanging in the window. Past Greenberg's dry goods, a jumble of fabrics, piled in disarray. Past Issie Reisman's Fruits and Vegetables. Past Weinroth's Shoe Repair Shop. The freshly painted synagogue, two houses joined in prayer. Past Joe Wolfe's herring stand.

Around the corner into Baldwin Street. Past the pots and pans. A greater miscellany of necessities and beguilements. Hoarse shouts. Responses. Crowd thickens. Perlmutar's Bakery exuding warm smells of freshly baked bagels, buns, rolls, breads. Rye. Pūmpernickel. Black. Gabriel begs for a bagel to nibble on. Noah, me too.

—Later, Sara says, and deftly steers the kids past Perlmutar's, crowded with customers. Past Kaplan's Dairy with the hillocks of cheeses, pints of rich sour cream, slabs of unsalted butter. Ripe lactic odors. Past Dora Goodman's Grocery. Into Steiner's Poultry Store. Sawdust sprinkled floor. Fly specked bulbs hanging from frayed electric cords. Mottled sheet metal ceiling painted grey. Executed birds drooping from metal gallows. Massive wooden counter with a pile of newspapers. RED RALLY ROUTED AT CITY HALL.

Impassive Steiner, man of stone, balding, weighs the chickens and wraps them. Makes only necessary conversation with the customers. Yetta Steiner in the back room visible through the rectangular opening amidst a cloud of feathers.

Pluck. Pluck. Plucking chickens is an art. Got no time to even fart.

Thumb and index fingers swoop down on feathered body. Pluck. Again. Pluck. And pluck. And pluck. And pluck. Swiftly denuded chicken becomes dressed fowl. Time: 105 seconds. Yetta sneezes, wipes spittle and feathers from face, tosses the still warm corpse onto the table with dozens of others. She yawns and scratches under armpits. She pokes up her nose, in her mouth, exploration for feather wisps. Snuffling and snorting cleanses the nose. An explosive series of coughs clears the throat. Ears cleansed with rotary fingertip movements. After all, the feathers still cling with magnetic attraction.

In another part of the Steiner aviary the live ones are sequestered in cages. Slatted wooden crates contain jostling, strutting, pecking, clucking, cock-a-doodling denizens, sharp-beaked heads thrust forward outside the confined space.

Sara reached into the crate and selected a fat hen. She felt all over for imperfections. She found none. No scars. No malignancies. An eminently edible hen. It would serve as the *Kaporeh*, bearing the sins of the household. Sara carried the sacrificial offering home in a paper bag, legs trussed, only the head protruding. Noah, unseen by Sara, poked at it and sent the fowl into a screaming paroxysm.

—I have the *Kaporeh*, Sara announced as they entered the house.

Aaron examined it and agreed it was just fine. He gathered the family about him, opened the *Siddur* and read:

—B'nai Adom... Children of men, such as sit in darkness and in the shadow of death... They cry unto the Lord in their trouble and He delivereth them from their destruction. For He saith, I have found a ransom.

Aaron held aloft the frightened, fluttering creature by both its legs and whirled it around and around as he intoned:

This is thy redemption. *Zeh hatarnegol.* This bird shall be sacrificed while thou shalt be allowed a long, happy and peaceful life.

The hen protested, spread its wings for flight, but, finding itself moored in Aaron's grip, released drops of hot lime, chicken shit, onto the celebrants.

—Be all our transgressions upon thee, Aaron concluded and stuffed the frantic bird into the bag. For us all, a long, happy and peaceful life.

—Amen. Amen. Amen. From Sara and the kids.

* * *

The *Shochet* greeted them with pleasure.

—Good evening Mrs. Gottesman. And good evening to you, he said to Gabriel. Are you going to become a great scholar like your grandfather?

—No. An actor, he said.

Sara slapped him.

—Sure, she sneered, and live like a gypsy. Not while I'm alive.

—Maybe you would like to learn the trade of a *Shochet*. Mr. Rabinowitz said. You have to be learned in the Talmud. You must say all the prayers and go to *shul* every day and have pure thoughts about the Everlasting One, praised be His Name. The old man looked skyward.

Somewhere up there on a Golden Throne dwelt the Almighty, surrounded by Angels and Seraphim and Cherubim shouting, Holy, Holy, Holy. The whole world is full of thy glory. Somewhere up there was the god of Abe Silberfogel. Jesus, the Christ. The only begotten son Who came to earth to take upon Himself the sins of the world. Standing at the right hand of his father. Heaven. So many different roads to salvation. The Jews had the one God, the living God. The Christian sects squabbled over the superiority of their divinities. The Catholic god was the most successful. He had many Churches, all over the world. They were full of riches: statues and paintings and ikons and gold inlaid altars. And he had millions of worshipers. He was more powerful than the Protestant god. Probably had a bigger celestial chariot. And more angels singing Sanctus. Sanctus. Sanctus. You could speak to the god of the Catholics through his priests and ask the saints to intercede on your behalf. The man-god, bearded, white-robed, the kind father. Jehovah on the other hand held Himself aloof. You had to pray hard and even then you never really got to know Him. As it is written: Who can comprehend Thee, O Lord. The eye cannot behold Thee. The ear cannot hear Thee. Thou art ineffable, without a form, mighty and powerful, quick to avenge.

Gabriel looked up into the indigo night sky. Vast reaches of interstellar space. The stars winked at him: Don't forget to say your prayers tonight.

—Well, come in and we'll prepare the customer, Mr. Rabinowitz led the way into the small sheet-metal lined room. Feathers everywhere. They carpeted the wooden floor. They hung from the ceiling and wall. Clung to the sides of the metal troughs.

—*Oyfn pripetchok brent a feierl.* Humming softly he bent the bird's head back and removed the feathers from a small portion of its pulsing neck. He said a prayer then picked up a sharp edged knife. With one quick downward stroke like a violinist bowing a chord he slashed the throat. Before the veins began to spurt he plunged the bird head-first into the trough. Gabriel shrank from the shrieking, convulsing creature. As the blood drained out of the body the noise and the activity diminished. Silence. Quite dead.

Mr. Rabinowitz retrieved the doomed chicken. It was beginning to stiffen. The head hung to one side, splattered with clotted blood, the beak clamped shut, sightless eyes bulging open.

—All finished. A nice chicken for a fine *Yom Tov* meal, Mrs. Gottesman. He wrapped the dead bird in several sheets of newspaper.

Gabriel made out the headline: NAZI BRUTALITY CONTINUES. Underneath was a photograph. It showed a uniformed trooper with a raised club in one hand. An old man cowered at his feet. The old man looked a lot like Mr. Rabinowitz.

## 8

—Git along, yippee, I'm a-leaving Cheyenne, Roy Acuff's scratchy voice on the phonograph disrupting the morning calm. Western melodies from Staszek Slomczynski's collection of cowboy records.

—There's a goldmine in the sky...

—He's at it again, Bill! Mrs. Reingold's treble jolted her husband awake. Those goddam cowboy songs.

—Come and sit by my side if you love me... warbled Gene Autry.

—Turn on the radio, Bill said. We'll blast him with The Jewish Hour.

—Romania. Romania. Romania. Romania, chanted Mickey Katz.

—A crazy, worried mind, Roy Acuff cried.

A rope lasso snaked out of Staszek's open window and missed the Reingold dog nosing about a pile of recently-deposited turds. The lariat ascended to the second floor. Toby sniffed at a shrivelled shrub. Lingering odor of a previous contributor. As the mongrel raised its right leg, the rope descended and encircled it. Staszek yanked the lasso tight and pulled Toby yowling across the dusty ground.

—Yippee, exulted Staszek and pulled again, lifting the canine three feet above the porch. Toby pendulum-swung as Staszek shouted and Roy Rogers intoned Tales of the Texas Rangers.

Mrs. Reingold heard the howls and rushed out.

—Bill! Bill! Toby is hanging from a rope! Bill! Come out and see what the *meshugganah shaygetz* is doing to poor little Toby.

She shouted up at the westerner who grinned down at her. Staszek, you idiot! Let go of Toby. Then, Bill! Get out here quick. The dog is strung up.

Bill emerged, hammer in hand. What's happening? he growled. Toby greeted him with a whine.

The hammer hurler let go at the cowboy. OOOPH—in the stomach. Staszek groaned, relaxed his hold on the rope and fell back. Toby dropped thirty-two feet per second per second head first.

Mrs. Reingold rushed to free the battered dog.

—Give me back my hammer, Reingold shouted.

Staszek reappeared at the window, sober, scowling. He threw the hammer at Reingold's head. Missed. Smashed against the fence. The carpenter retrieved it. Brandished it in gesture of defiance at Staszek and followed his wife indoors. Toby was licking his chafed parts.

—Fuck you, Staszek muttered. Fuck'n Jews. Staszek lonely cowboy, bruised cowboy, put on a new record and sang along with it: Tears on My Pillow. He and Gene Autry consoled each other.

—Phone the police, Bill, and report what that big galoot did to poor Toby. I insist you phone the station.

—Doesn't pay, Bill said. They'll only come and ask questions and scribble something in their notebook. Then they'll leave and we won't hear from them till next time.

—We could lay charges. Cruelty. That's it. Cruelty to an animal.

—So, call the Humane Society, Bill said.

—They're no good, she said. They only bother with stray animals. Put them in a box in the van and smother them with gas from the exhaust. I know. I was there when they came for that terrier that used to play outside the Goldman house. No. The best thing is the police.

—O.K. So call them. And make trouble for yourself.

Mrs. Reingold was determined. She shooed Toby into the bathroom and shut the door. She ran with little short steps through the lane into Zimmerman's Grocery.

—Mr. Zimmerman, I've come to use your phone. I must call the police.

—What's the matter? He wiped his sweating face with a soiled handkerchief.

—It's that crazy Staszek again, she said. He almost strangled Toby with his lasso.

—Staszek caught the dog by the neck?

—No, by the leg. Toby was hanging upside down. He was foaming from his mouth. We rescued him just in time. He could have choked. And Bill gave that Staszek something to remember. A real *shoss* with his hammer. Learned him a lesson.

—Bill hit the *shaygetz* with a hammer? Mr. Zimmerman's eyes opened wide behind the spotted spectacles. Did he hurt him?

—He didn't hit him close up like somebody attacking somebody.

—How then, Mr. Zimmerman pursued.

—Well, Bill threw the hammer at Staszek and it caught him in the belly.

—Maybe you better *not* call the police, Mrs. Reingold. Suppose the Polack made a complaint — assault with a dangerous weapon — that would be very bad for your husband. No telling how much trouble you'd get into.

—But what about poor Toby?

—He's only a dog, Mr. Zimmerman counselled. A dog is a dog. An animal. A person is something more. A human being.

—That Staszek is a human being? I wouldn't trade one hair on Toby's body... but, maybe you're right.

—Have a bottle of creme soda and cool off a little. She sat down on a pop box and sipped.

—There are more important things happening in the world than the problems on Leonard Avenue, he continued. Terrible things going on in Germany. That fellow Hitler and his Nazis. And who will be the first to suffer? The Jews. Just wait and see if I'm not right.

—Yes, Mrs. Reingold agreed. Always the Jews first. They should leave Europe and come to Canada. Or the States. Lots of room in Canada. She sucked up the last drops of her soda pop. Things aren't so good here either with the Depression. Bill doesn't work much these days. That's why I haven't paid anything on the bill lately. She hastened to assert the righteousness of her cause. But we will, soon, Mr. Zimmerman, you won't lose a cent. Well, I guess I'll go home now. Thank you for the creme soda.

—Don't mention it, Mrs. Reingold. And listen, stay far away from the Polacks. The whole family is a little...you know... He tapped a finger lightly, knowingly against his temple. Have you seen the midget sister recently? Now there's a sad case. Very sad. A midget with a hump on her back. And a head with no sense. The whole person is no bigger than a kitchen stool. He measured with his hand. This high.

—I saw her last week, Mrs. Reingold said. With her boy-friend. Can you imagine a thing like that having a man? A good-looking *goy* too. Tall and straight. At least six feet tall.

—They're going to get married, Zimmerman said.

—Married? You are a big joker, Mr. Zimmerman. That...?

—Oh yes, the grocer's head bobbed up and down assertively. The mother was in here yesterday with an order. On credit yet.

—Did he do something to her that he should marry her, Mrs. Reingold asked eagerly. Then on taking her leave, she added: Although I can't see any man wanting to sleep with such an ugly person.

Mr. Zimmerman pondered the proposition: How does a giant do it with a midget? Six foot John with a tool on him like a horse shoving it in. All the Polacks have big organs. Just like the niggers. Polacks and Niggers. Zimmerman didn't consider his own anything to boast about. Just a so-so *putz* even at full erection. Jews don't have big ones. And of course the Jews don't go around fornicating all day long. The Bible lays down strict laws. And the *Shulchan Aruch*. No trenning during menstruation and for so many days after. Unclean. Taboo. Don't let the moon shine in. Don't do it in front of the baby. Or in front of a dog or cat. Even have to cover up the little canary bird. Don't want it whistling at you. I see what you're doing. Tweet. Tweet. Meat. Meat. Zimmerman on top of his Gertrude going through the motions. Reverse position? Prohibited. Doggie way? Strictly forbidden. Kiss. On the mouth. On the pussy would be a sin. Don't even finger the pussy. The finger that turns the prayer book pages, that touches the Torah, that winds the phylactery leather around the arm.

Zimmerman, still pondering, sighed. So many restrictions. Still the *rebetzin* had a dozen children. The *rebbe* must know things he himself didn't. Zimmerman had very little pleasure. In his late forties he was over the hill. You're not a *boychik*, his wife Gertrude was fond of reminding him. She was a pinch-faced, thin woman with wisps of greying hair peeping from under her wig. She was two years younger. She was always menstruating or bleeding for other reasons. She was tired at night. Have it if you need it, she told him. It's a *mitzvah*, he replied. Friday night. The sabbath queen. My queen. Gertrude spread her limbs and they coupled briefly, then sundered.

Zimmerman sought other satisfactions. He found them in the *Daily Forward*. International events. Statesmen and politicians posturing and threatening. The sexploits of the Hollywood movie stars. Clark Gable and Carole Lombard. Jean Harlow. All that nooky passing him by. He would settle for the odd piece. A nice, juicy *pyerg*. The other Slomczynski girl, Wanda, would restore his soul. Nineteen and enormous, with a big ass, bulging thighs, sagging breasts. She wore tight sweaters and straight-cut skirts. She had a round Slavic face with straight, black hair worn in a buster brown. She worked in a paper box factory on Carlaw Street. Zimmerman felt her up once in a while behind the counter. He trembled at the heat of her unstockinged thighs against his perspiring palm. The lion reek lingered on his finger. Strong cheese for adventurous appetites.

Wanda instructed Zimmerman in the ways of the world. About the efficacy of Coca Cola.

—I just drink it, he told her. You mean there are other ways to use the pause that refreshes?

—Sure. Look at the bottle. Concentrate. You'll see what I mean.

—It's a bottle, Zimmerman said. Just a Coca Cola bottle.

—Nice shape? Wanda asked. Look at the way the neck tapers. Such a beautiful fit. Zimmerman understood.

—Ah, it would never take the place of a man's thing, he said.

—What man's? Yours? Wanda teased.

—I'll draw you a picture of mine, he offered.

—Don't bother, Wanda said. You've seen one, you've seen 'em all. Look, I'll show you what you can do with

Coke. She put her thumb on the opening, shook the bottle vigorously and released a foaming white-brown jet over Zimmerman's shirt.

—Bet that would put out any fire, she said.

—You mean, he said, measuring his words, ...you mean...up the...?

—Sure, Wanda confided. Coke douche.

—Does it work? For cleaning out... ?

—Nope, she laughed. But my boyfriends like the taste.

—Hmmm. A Coca Cola cock-tail. He would like to try it with Gertrude. He wouldn't dare. She would call him a dirty pig. What a world there was out there... just outside his store. A world with black women and white men. Chinese girls with mysterious slits. Was it true...? Where dogs mounted crouching females. Shepherds shoving it into lambs. Midgets and regulars.

—Tell me, Wanda, Zimmerman said. You get a lot of nooky?

—Enough, she snickered, reaching far up for a can of Heinz beans.

—Tell me, have you ever done it with a midget? I mean a man midget. Like...a...dwarf.

—A midget? Wanda exploded into staccato laughter. Her stomach ripples of jello. A midget? Jesus. That's a funny one. What do you wanna know for?

Perhaps he shouldn't have asked. Can't back off now.

—Well, you know, I've been reading about the sex habits in different parts of the world and it occurred to me that a small man here in this city would have a lot of trouble with normal size girls. I mean...his organ would be so tiny...a little hot dog...or would he have a big one?

—How would I know, Wanda pouted in mock annoyance. Do you think I fuck around with midgets? Jesus Christ. What would I want with a midget?

—Well, you know, for a change. Everybody is looking for a change. I bet you get around a lot. See interesting things. Do interesting things. Me, I'm just a grocery man. I stand here all day. I only know what I read. Mostly here, (pointing to the *Forward*). And what my customers tell me. He patted her ass in a gesture of friendly confidence.

—O.K. Wanda said. I'll tell you. I've never been out with a midget. But my girlfriend Joyce goes out with one. Peter. He's a bellboy at the St. Regis. You know. *Call for Philip Mor-ris!* Looks like a kid. Squeaky voice. Tiny face, tiny hands, tiny feet. Except, where it really counts, he's a regular Tarzan. That's what Joyce tells me.

—Really? Zimmerman marvelled. How big? Measuring a space of almost a foot. Like this?

—Even bigger, Wanda said.

—Does your friend have...relations with this bellboy?

—Oh sure. All the time. At first though, Joyce wouldn't have anything to do with him. Anyway she just split up with her husband, Steve, in Winnipeg and she wasn't in the mood.

—This bellboy must have been a good salesman, huh?

—I guess so. He came up to her room with a telegram from Steve. When she finished reading it he was still there looking up at her. Joyce is taller than me. Must have been funny, the two looking at each other like that.

—Do you want to send a return wire, Peter asked her. Just write the message on this form and I'll have it tele-graphed for you.

—Not right now, Joyce said. Maybe later.

—O.K. Just pick up the phone and ask for the Bell Captain. Tell him you want Peter. That's me. He saluted her and turned to leave.

—Wait a minute, Joyce said. She took a quarter out of her change purse. He accepted it, flipped it into the air, caught it with dexterity and winked as he shut the door behind him. She called Peter to her room later in the day to pick up the message. It read: NO DICE.

—I'll get this out for you right away. He winked again as he scurried away. After awhile her phone rang. It was Peter confirming the telegram, and asking could he do anything more for her.

When she checked out of the St. Regis the next day, Peter arranged for her to stay at his mother's rooming house on Berkeley Street. He gave her the money for the first month's rent. Gradually Joyce began to fancy him. He was her little boy playing at soldiers in his blue uniform with peak cap and bright, pointed oxfords.

She let him into her room the first night about eleven. She told him about her marriage. Three months of bickering. How Steve came home early one day and found Joyce in bed with his buddy, Frank. He gave the stevedore enough time to put on his dungarees, then kicked his ass all the way into the street. He then proceeded to beat her up. A black eye. Two broken teeth. Belt lashes across the back and thighs. He told her to pack and beat it.

—Here, I'll show you the red marks still on my back, she said to Peter. She pulled her terry bathrobe down from her shoulders. Peter climbed onto the bed for a better view. The flesh was criss-crossed with red ridges. The bellboy bent to kiss the welts.

—You're cute, Joyce said. I like you.

—I like you too, Peter said. He kissed her on the cheek. She pulled him down between her breasts. She fell back on the bed and enclosed him with her robe. She laughed as his fumbling became more frantic. What do you thing you're doing down there? Show me what you've got.

She sat up and placed Peter on her lap. He directed her hand to his crotch.

—I don't believe it! she says. Show me. So, he unbuttons and takes out this great big prick.

—Did he really put it into her? Zimmerman asked.

—Sure did, Wanda chuckled. Still does.

—And does your friend enjoy this.

—Well, I'll tell you, Wanda paused and leaned across to Zimmerman, her breasts resting on his counter. Joyce says that Peter has a cock on him the size of a horse. Joyce says he fucks better than any guy she's ever had.

—Maybe your sister will have the same kind of luck, Zimmerman said. I hear she's gonna be married next week to Big John.

—Hell, they've been screwing for months. My old man figures it's about time John started to support her.

—I didn't think John was the type to be tied down, said Zimmerman.

—He isn't, but the old man threatened to cut him off. Look, John, the old man said: No marry Mary, no more whiskey and no more fucking Mary. Get marry and lots of whiskey and lots of fucking. They were getting sloshed. By the time the Seagram twenty-sixer was empty, the old man had a son-in-law and Mary had a husband.

* * *

They were married in St. Stanislaus Church on Denison Avenue. The priest looked down at Mary and up at John and about at the four Slomczynskis. His not to reason why. *In nomine Patris, et Filii, et Spiritus Sancti.* Amen.

After the ceremony the group had lunch at a Polish restaurant on Queen Street. Roman poured whiskey for everybody from his flask. When they returned home the couple retired to Mary's bedroom. Roman and Staszek sat on the porch drinking. Wanda in the bathroom was trimming her overgown bush of coarse, black hair. Too hot in the summer. The shears snipped closer to the pink lips. There. Now to shave the fuzz off the legs. Wanda stroked the shins. Soft. Hairless. Close shave. She put away Staszek's razor.

Mrs. Slomczynski was busy cooking. She had changed into her usual housecoat — gravy-stained, unseamed at the right armpit, unhemmed, missing two buttons at the bosom. There would be a Polish wedding feast that night with lots of *kulbassa* and *bigos.* And lots to drink. Everything on credit where possible. Money borrowed from Wanda and Big John.

The table was set. The room was bright with pictures. St. Mary of Czestochowa, face scarred where the Swedish soldier had pierced her cheek with his sword. St. Teresa and the miracle of the roses. Looking out from an ornate bronze frame was a suffering Jesus, the bleeding heart dripping big drops. Portraits of Roman Slomczynski and his wife set in oval frames. He looked stern in military haircut, white shirt topped with celluloid collar, wide black tie, dark jacket. She, a country girl, her brown hair tied in a bun. Her high-necked blouse with puffed sleeves and four-button cuffs. Virtue about to be assaulted.

Roman wandered in, looked about him, nodded with satisfaction.

—Good job, old lady. Everything look good.

He saw her gazing up at their wedding pictures.

—Goddam! Roman was fine young man. Strong as ox. Work hard like ten men. Hey, *stara*, look at you. Once was pretty woman, hey?

She resisted his overture of reconciliation. It was too soon to forgive last night's drunken attack. Her left eye was swollen purple. She ached everwhere. But she had given him a few whacks in return. Screams and curses. *Psiakrew cholera.* Staszek trying to pull the old man off his mother. Wanda striking at Staszek.

*Carnaval des animaux.* Gabriel perched on the fence in the back yard, listening. Aaron and Sara in bed heard the sounds. None of their business. The *goyim* could slaughter each other.

A light bulb exploded among the combatants. Groping in the blackness. A scream as Roman knocked his wife to the floor. Staszek swung a chair at his father. Wanda pulled a hatpin out of her dress and jabbed it into Staszek.

—Jesus, fuckin christ, I'll cut your fuckin tits off for that.

—Leave the old man alone, you bastard. She jabbed him again. He screamed.

—Wanda, don't hurt Staszek, her mother shouted.

—Kill the son of a bitch, Roman hollered.

Upstairs, John and Mary were fucking. Downstairs, in the bulb-less moon illumination, the shouts and curses fused into grunts and heavy breathing broken by a groan, a cry, a crack of breaking furniture.

—Maybe somebody should do something, Mrs. Reingold from the ringside position outside her door addressed the gathering crowd. She had been witness to these domestic disasters every Friday night.

—Bill, you think maybe somebody should do something?

—Like what, Bill asked.

—Like go in and separate them?

—Are you crazy?

—But Bill, it's worse than ever. They'll kill each other.

Another thud. Another groan. Staszek caught Wanda by the hair and slammed her head against the table.

The Reingold dog began to bark. The Reingold kids, awakened, ran out in their underwear.

—Oh boy, another fight, Felix said. What's happening, Ma?

—The Polacks are celebrating.

The noise aroused Zimmerman. Into the courtyard draped in a brown cotton robe he wandered sleepy-eyed, and greeted:

—Ah, Mr. Reingold, your neighbors are at it again.

The door opened and Mrs. Slomczynski appeared. Her hair hung in a spider web about her face. Her nightdress was ripped, the breasts exposed. She gasped a forced breath halted by the pain in her side. She tried again and coughed up blood.

—Police, she shouted. Police. Somebody get police. *Boze Moj.* Murder. Help. Police.

—Bill, do something.

—Get police, Mrs. Slomczynski fell to the ground and lay there moaning: police, police.

From inside: You rotten, fuckin sonofabitch, Wanda shrieked. Up your ass! Staszek retorted. Oooh, oooh, hurts, from Roman.

Persuaded, the grocer ran to the store and got the night sergeant at the station.

—What's that you're tellin me, he said in his Belfast brogue. A murder? Where? Ah, yes, the Slomczynskis. Sure, it's not as bad as all that. Who's fightin? Ah the father...yea...and the mother...uh-huh...and the boy and the girl....Uhhh. Well now, tis nothin but a family spat.

—But...but...Zimmerman stammered, it looks real bad. You better send somebody.

—O.K., we'll investigate it.

O'Donohue sent a patrol car. When the constable arrived, things were quiet. Only nocturnal gossiping from the crickets and the neighbors.

—Now then, where are the bodies? he inquired.

—They dragged her back in the house. They're all inside, Mr. Reingold, spokesman, confided.

Roman Slomczynski opened the door to the knocking of the law.

—Now then, what's all this about a murder? Anybody been killed here?

—No, Mr. Policeman. No murder. Only family party. Tomorrow daughter get marry. Tonight have few drinks. Celebrate.

P.C. Pritchard directed his flashlight around the room. The old woman against the wall, a bottle of beer in her hand. Wanda cross-legged on the floor, head lolling in fatigue. Staszek straddling a chair, head slumped on the table. Broken bottles, shards of crockery, beer spills, blood stains.

—Pretty messy here. What happened to the old woman?

—Fell. Accident. Be all right tomorrow.

—Well, better knock it off for tonight. Nearly two o'clock. Get to bed now, all of you. And don't be disturbin the peace anymore.

He took another look at the debris spotlighted by his flashlight and asked: Anybody want to make a complaint? Answered in the negative, he bade them good night and heavy-booted his way out. With an air of finality he advised the spectators: All right now. Everything's in order. Nothing more to see. Get on home. The assembly dispersed.

—Tonight, Bill, you better double-lock the front door, said Mrs. Reingold.

Peace re-established, the battle-weary, booze-sodden quartet stretched out, each in the required space on the floor.

—Goddam good party last night, huh? Roman put his arm around her. Making amends. She allowed that it was a goddam fine party.

—We make good couple, is right? No more fight. He felt her torn cheek, the swollen eye. Have drink now. Feel better. Here.

He uncapped the whiskey. She drank a generous portion.

—Good, she said. You too have drink, then put away for after. Alcohol, warm inside her, she smiled at her husband: Was *real* good party last night.

Roman put the bottle to his lips, swallowed, then laughed: Be better tonight. Everybody be here: Gwozdz. Razanovitch. Grabowski. Domaradzski. Mroz. Preniazek. And Father Zyczynski.

Mrs. Slomczynski finished the remaining chores. Two more bridge chairs (Zimmerman's best) placed in the corner. She lifted the lids from the sputtering cauldrons, inhaled, tasted, nodded: *Dobre!* Roman, time for bring in beer. Staszek, help father bring in barrel beer. Come down.

—Bring in myself, Roman said. Still strong. Don' need Staszek.

Staszek muttered, Shit! turned off the phonograph...on the lone prairie... clunked down the stairs in his boxer shorts. He advanced, neo-neanderthal man, arms and genitals swinging, to the shed. He pushed Roman aside and seized the barrel and trudged into the house with it. Roman inserted the spigot, pulled out the bung.

—We have drink now, Staszek. *Zdrowie!*

They gulped non-stop. They tapped another tumbler, then a third.

The musicians arrived at eight. The Polski Trio. A fat violinist with a horseshoe mustache. A lanky bass-fiddle player. A blond, happy accordionist.

—Wanda! Mrs. Slomczynski hollered. Wanda! Orchestra come already. John! Mary!

—Have drink, Roman offered. The Polski Trio tipped shot glasses of whiskey and drained them in unison.

Wanda lay in bed, looking through her collection of reading material. *Spicy Mystery. Satan's Masterpiece. Weird Tales. Love Story* offered: *A Mother At Twelve.* She turned to *Passionate Romances.*

—*Naughty Nola, more sinning than sinned against, led men on to destruction. They were powerless in her torrid embrace.* Should be a good one, Wanda thought and began to read, absently fingering her cropped fleece, as Naughty Nola teased her gentleman callers into a variety of compromising situations.

—*Click went the camera. Trapped you, she whispered in his ear. Now you'll have to pay. God, he cried. I'll pay anything. Only don't let Diane see these pictures. My family. My career....*

—Wanda! the mother called again. She turned to Staszek. Stop it with drinking. Go tell Wanda get ready.

Staszek lurched up the stairs. At Wanda's door he stopped, called. Unanswered, he pushed against it and crashed into the room.

—Time to get dressed, he mumbled, and pulled his sister out of bed.

She sprawled on the floor, a display of flabby flesh.

—Hey, Wanda, how about a quickie? She was on all fours. He approached her from the rear. She collapsed as he mounted her.

—Fuck off, Staszek! Why don't you go jerk off.

She rolled away from him. He pursued playfully and pinned her back against the floor. He was aroused now. He wedged one leg between hers.

—How about it, Wanda? Let me in. He thumped against her.

—Hey! Not so rough, she cried. Her legs widened to his insistence. She clawed at him. She was open to him.

They moved to the one inexorable rhythm. In ecstasy, incestuously, they writhed.

—Staszek, you great big sonofabitch. Ooooooh, Staszek. Ooooooh, Santa Maria.

—Oooooh, finished, Staszek grunted.

—Play now, Roman shouted downstairs. A polka!

The violin took up the theme, lost between the fullness of the thumping bass and the gurgling chords of the accordion.


\* \* \*


At the Kiever Synagogue Gabriel and Aaron helped usher out the Sabbath. First with prayers and spicy fragrance. Then downstairs in the basement with shmaltz herring and black bread and whiskey. All the men of the congregation in an hour of good natured bonhomie.

—*Sholem Aleichem.* They took their leave of each other. Until tomorrow morning. Father and son walked with other fathers and sons in the tepid summer evening, chatting quietly, enjoying the alcohol induced euphoria. Arrived at No. 47 Aaron greeted Sara, who was scrubbing the weekly washing. He bent over to kiss her.

—Lay down Aaron. Get a sleep. The whiskey is making you do funny things. Who provided the bottle this week?

—Greenbaum the tailor. He became a grandfather yesterday.... I'm laying down now. Feel dizzy.

Aaron stretched onto the couch in the dining room. Gabriel cut a thick slice of Chalah and buttered it. He looked out the kitchen window at the rotting fence, the cindery ground with wisps of green hopeful of survival. He could see Mr. Wolinsky next door hunched over the table reading his newspaper, scratching himself.

Sounds of night drifted in through the open window. Snatches of spirited conversation. A shout of derision. A curse relieved by a raucous laugh.

Music. Slow patterns in three-quarter time sustained by the accordion. The Anniversary Waltz. Sara heard and ceased her scrubbing. Recalled her own wedding in the old country. Parents and brothers and sisters. Aaron, her groom, young and straight with sporty moustache. The seven blessings. Seven days of celebrating. A plethora of food. Meat and potatoes and dumplings and borscht. And drink. In moderation. Blessed be thou, Oh Lord our God who hast created the fruit of the vine.

—Oh, how we danced on the night we were wed. Sara wiped a tear, blew her nose into the paper napkin. The waltz ended. The music makers being treated by the merry makers to food and drink. More people arriving. Shouts answering shouts.

—*Dobry wieczor!* Come in! Slomczynski welcome you. Have drink. Be happy.

The music again. An *oberek*. Fast with lots of foot stomping. Hand clapping. Shouts of hoo-rah. A roar as somebody fell to the floor and the piece ended. Roman was orating in Polish. The end punctuated by applause. A violin solo soaring slow and diving.

—I'm going to Marvin's place Ma, Gabriel announced.

—Don't be late, Sara advised him. Don't be late.

—I won't, ma. He headed instead for the Slomczynskis. The long way around via Nassau, Bellevue, hop over the fence and into the courtyard.

The guests were gathered in a wide circle, clapping and shouting: *STO LAT, STO LAT. NIECH ZYJER, ZYJER NAM.* May you live a hundred years.

In the center stood the groom and bride. John offered Mary a glass of wine. She stretched on tiptoes to present him her glass. He, giddy with beer, wine, whiskey, over-reached and knocked her down. She fell on flat, misshapen legs to the floor, John on top of her. He sat up, grabbed for her, and put her right-side-up, her back against his stomach. Cradled between his wide-spread legs, he rocked her from side to side, crooning in her ear.

Staszek handed him another full glass. John took a sip, then presented the goblet to Mary's lips. She gulped. A trickle of red ran down her chin, down her white organdy wedding dress and onto the floor. John, laughing, raised her, squirming, above his head. She freed herself and straddled him, her hands beating against his chest. Staszek presented her with another glass of wine. She splashed it over John's face.

—Hoo-rah! everybody shouted. Hoo-rah!

John grasped Mary to him and hugged the chunky body. He reached for her ankles, tightened his fists around them and without releasing her managed to get to his feet. He was holding her upside-down. She squealed, Let me go, let me go! John swung her in polka rhythm about the room. Faster. Faster. Until he smashed into the table. Mary crawled from under him and smacked baby hands across his face and ran crying out of the house.

—Hoo-rah! Hoo-rah! Roman shouted. He tried to raise John. 'S all right, John. Everything hokay.

John rose unsteadily, swayed and collapsed. The vomit poured from his slack mouth. Staszek hoisted his brother-in-law and carried him into Roman's bedroom.

—Dance everybody! Dance! Roman exhorted. A *krakowiak.* He pulled Mrs. Gwozdz into his arms and pranced with peasant strides across the floor, measuring the beats: Tum-tum. Tum-tum. Tum-tum. Dipping his right arm in a graceless sweep.

After a few erratic movements Mrs. Gwozdz stopped.

—Listen, she said. You want dance? Okay, we dance. Me show you. Roman permitted her to lead him.

—Hey, you be good dancer, Mrs. Gwozdz. *Bardzo dobrze tanczy.* Goddam how you learn to dance so good?

—Huh, dat be nuff for you, she said and flung him from her.

—Hey, Mrs. Gwozdz! Come we have drink now. Roman, gracious host, poured for her, then for him, whiskey, straight, full tumblers.

Gabriel from the doorway enjoyed the revelry. The dancing, drinking, brawling. The grimacing faces, legs flashing by. Stale smells of garlic, farts, alcohol, *eau de cologne.*

Wanda, in a fresh-from-the-cleaners black silk dress, shiny from use, tight about the bulges of bosom, stomach and rump, was coming in his direction. Ambulating as best she could in a line more or less direct. She managed the question through the exhalation of boozy breath:

—Hey kid, wanna dance? An obscene, rolling motion of her body.

—Don't know how, Gabriel said.

—Come on. I'll show you. Easy. She pulled him toward her sweating cleavage, held him vise tight. He felt the heat of her woman's body. She rolled her hips and thrust her pelvis against him. Roll and lunge. Oblivious to the music. Eyes shut. In heat.

The dancers whirled about them to the music of The Polski Trio. Wanda, still rubbing against Gabriel, directed him with counterfeit dance steps into the bedroom where Big John lay snoring on the floor.

She pulled Gabriel beside her onto the bed. She raised her dress. Fat thighs wet with perspiration. Sopping triangle of hair. Rancid roquefort smell.

—Your prick. Pull out your prick. Goddam it, don't you know what it's for? She reached for his fly. Gabriel was trembling, beset by fear and desire.

—Put it in, she urged. Now, now. And Gabriel's flesh found the place.

—Oh, God.

—*Riboyne shel O'lem*, what are you doing to my son? Sara pulled her firstborn from the lusting Wanda. *Cholerna kurveh!* Do up your pants, she commanded Gabriel. Oh, the shame, she cried. The shame. And just before your *Bar Mitzvah*. I'll never be able to keep my head up again.

She pushed Gabriel ahead of her, through the noisy revelers, away from Wanda and her Polish delights.

## 9

—Cherry Nose!

The shouts rang out from the more daring students at Ryerson Public School. The Vice-Principal turned in the direction of the jeers, one finger on the clapper of the brass bell, ready to ring the recess to an end and the shouting, brawling children to attention.

Cherry Nose Campbell, who received his nickname from the fruity hue of his bulbous proboscis, was a martinet. His predisposition came from his Presbyterian background and his authority from his position. By contrast, his superior, David A. Davidson, Principal, was a temperate, dignified person. He showered his beneficence on faculty and pupils alike. His signature on report cards and memos was a model for penmanship classes.

Gabriel had practiced the slanting sentinels and ovals, the pen held at the precise angle, nib barely touching the sheet. At their desks the girls — Dorothy McKeever, Clara Hislop, Beatrice Nesgor — had produced beautiful samples of calligraphy. Gabriel's own efforts had been abysmal.

Miss Ross stopped at individual desks, patted heads, nodded approvingly, said, Good, very good.

—We'll just have to put these on the walls for others to see. I bet they're the best examples of penmanship in the whole school.

Miss Ross paused to observe the work of Rita Leznovitch in the desk ahead of Gabriel.

—Practice your capitals, Rita. Careful of the curves. Not too much flourish.

Stooping to show Rita how to make a perfect L, Miss Ross revealed more than she knew. Bare skin above the silk hose. Gabriel saw more than anyone had ever seen of the admirable Susan Ross. Everyone admired her trim figure, her auburn hair combed off the face, her perfect nose and candid grey eyes. The men teachers vied to date her. She was beautiful, and kind, and easily embarrassed.

When Tommy let a fart and the kids commented on the smell, Miss Ross felt her composure disintegrating.

—Hey fart face, did you shit yourself, Salvatore Puzzo bellowed. Miss Ross, may I open the window? The air ain't so good no more.

She nodded, yes. Salvatore covered his nose as he passed by Tommy. He raised the window and thrust out his head.

—Now don't be foolish, Miss Ross yanked Sal back into the room. Let us continue. Tommy, did you have your hand up?

—Yes, Miss Ross, Tommy feigned bowel trouble. May I be excused? He hurried out to the applause of the boys.

—Now class, get on with the exercises. She bent down to work with Rita. Gabriel, attention drawn again to the white thighs, wished for a wider revelation, employed a ruse. He allowed his pen to roll off the desk between the feet of Miss Ross. He pretended an expression of annoyance. As he leaned forward to retrieve the object he raised his eyes to the sight of white. Within their soft folds lay the private parts of Miss Ross. He felt a kick in the rear. He stumbled under the full skirt. There was a guffaw.

—What in the world... ? Miss Ross surprised.

Gabriel crawled out from under her, pen in hand. He waved it at her. It fell off my desk. I was reaching for it. Slipped.

—Hah, hah. Salvatore roared. *Cazzo duro.*

A flush appeared on the teacher's cheeks and spread across her face. She extended an arm, pulled Gabriel from the floor, pushed him with deliberation, back into his seat. She straightened her skirt.

—I, uh, I want you to know, what a despicable, uh, how childish, how ungentlemanly.... She faltered. The tears began to flow. Susan Ross ran sobbing out of the classroom. Gabriel turned around to Salvatore.

—You shouldn't have done that, he said.

—Who? Me? Wha'd I do?

—Pushed me.

—What the hell ya doin under her legs? Peeking up at her cunt?

Gabriel struck a weak punch at Salvatore. The big fellow jabbed at him and pushed him up the aisle, crash against the blackboard.

104

Norman jumped between them: Anybody fights Gabriel has to fight me.

Three of Sal's friends accepted the challenge. Horny Fox siezed the pointer and held it aloft. The girls stayed in their seats, interested spectators.

—Cherry Nose!

The warning came too late. The Scotsman was in the room, flaying the antagonists with the strap.

—That'll be enough. Stop the fighting. Whack, whack, across the buttocks. Whack. Whack.

Order restored, he glared at the students: We shall now write one hundred times, O Lord, forgive we beseech thee, our transgressions. He stayed with them until the bell rang for dismissal.

Miss Ross, pale and reticent, was at her desk the following day. She kept apart. She no longer ventured close to instruct. She did not incline from the vertical.

Gabriel attempted a rapprochement. After class he approached the front desk and waited for Miss Ross to acknowledge his presence.

—Yes, Gabriel?

—Miss Ross, I want to apologize.

She didn't reply. He stood fidgeting, waiting. He tried again.

—I want you to know how much I love you, Miss Ross.

She looked up from her papers. That's sweet of you, Gabriel. But I think you should lavish your affections on somebody your own age.

\* \* \*

Gabriel fell in love with Deborah Dale. She had a horse's face, short-cropped black hair and a gap between her two front teeth. Her dress hung awkwardly on her bony frame.

He began calling on her brother, Norman, just to get a glimpse of her. One afternoon he found her in the bathtub covered to her pointed chin in soap bubbles.

—Hey, Gabriel, whyncha knock first? Then, nonchalantly, indifferently, she asked, Wanna scrub my back?

—Sure, Gabriel said. Sure.

She handed him a brush and directed the motions across her scabby back.

—O.K. That's enough. Now you'll have to leave. Gotta get dressed.

Unwillingly, Gabriel departed. Lovelost over Deborah. He told not of his love. He patrolled Debbie's demesne, yearning for the sight of her. Down Leonard to St. Christopher, about-face and back, past Mr. Schwartz's gas-lit cottage, then across to No. 47 to wait.

As the twilight turned to black and the yellow street lights came on, Deborah appeared, clad in a blue, cotton night dress. She sat down on the top step of the verandah. She sang: When my dreamboat comes home....

I will arise now and go to Debbie D. Hi, Debbie! He sat down beside her. He smelled the fragrance of lilacs. She gave him a smile. He gave her his hand. She put it in her lap. She closed her legs.

—Gotcha, she laughed. Then she frowned. She pushed his hand away. Don't, she said. Whadda you think you're doing? He reached to kiss her. She slapped him. You're fresh, she said.

He took her hand and put it between his legs. Want to feel it?

—That's not nice, she said, removing her hand. Not now.

—Go on, nobody's around.

—Some other time.

—When?

—When the moon comes over the mountain.

The summer passed. Gabriel, love unrequited, still sought Deborah. She remained aloof, aloft, unloved. He kissed her once, sucking the spittle from between her gaping teeth. He masturbated to a vision of Deborah recumbent in bubbles of bath water.

Deborah was unattainable, but her brother Norman became Gabriel's close buddy. Damon and Pythias.

—Hey Gabriel, there's the milkman's bike in front of your place. Let's go for a ride.

—Can't, Norm. Mr. Balaban warned me not to touch it

again. My mother yelled bloody murder last time I borrowed it.

—Hell, just a little ride, Norman coaxed. Around the block. We'll put it back in the exact same place. He won't even know we touched it.

Norman straddled the seat. Gabriel reluctantly hoisted himself onto the crossbar and Norman began to pedal. The creaky two-wheeler moved arthritically then with increasing speed. At St. Christopher House, Gabriel shouted. Turn here. We're going to crash. Turn.

—Sure, Norman yelled. Sure, right up on the sidewalk here and then we'll circle around.

The front wheel struck the curb, the riders were thrown off.

—Better get her back, Gabriel said. That was a helluva bump.

—You bet, Norman agreed, one helluva bump. O.K. Hop on. Here we go.

Norman pushed down on the pedal but the bike didn't move. He tried again. They got off to inspect it. The front wheel was twisted. Spokes protruded from it; the tire had blown.

They hauled the broken machine up the street to No. 47 and propped it gently against the curb. They hid behind Norman's place and waited.

Mr. Balaban appeared. He put on a pant clip, adjusted his collection purse and eased himself onto his conveyance. He angled his body in anticipation of an easy takeoff, waved goodbye to Sara and toppled from his seat as the bicycle crumpled beneath him.

—What's the matter, Mr. Balaban? Are you hurt?

—The bicycle, he said. The wheel is all twisted. Somebody must have crashed it.

Sara saw and understood. She glanced about the street.

—Gabriel. Gabriel, she hollered.

Norman stifling his laughter, turned to his frightened friend: Let's go to my aunt. We'll stay there for awhile.

—What'll I tell my mother? I'm sure she'll blame me for it.

—Don't tell her nothing. Tell her you were with me at

my aunt's. All afternoon.

They climbed over the fence into the premises of the Western Hospital and out to Bathurst Street. In seventeen minutes they were on Montrose Avenue.

—Hya Auntie, Norman said blithely when she answered the bell. Well, here I am. Told ya I'd be visiting. This is my friend Gabriel.

—Go in the parlor Norman. I'll bring you a treat.

Mrs. Silver returned with glasses of ice cold milk and a chocolate cake on a silver tray. Mrs. Silver cut two giant slabs. Norman reached for his with avidity, crushing the chocolate icing, a cool compress against his dry lips.

—This is for you, she offered it to Gabriel.

—No, thank you, he said. He wanted it. But he said, No thank you.

—What's the matter, it's no good? Norman, tell me, the cake is no good?

—Delicious, Norman confirmed as he gulped his share. Great.

—Take it, she urged Gabriel.

—Yeah, take it Gabe, Norman commanded. Aunt Miriam makes the best chocolate cake in the world.

Gabriel refused. Stubbornly. Desire imprisoned within a catechism of responses taught him by his mother.

QUESTION: What do you say when somebody offers you something to eat?

ANSWER: No, thank you.

QUESTION: Why do you say, No thank you?

ANSWER: Because it isn't polite to accept right away. People will think you were not well brought up.

QUESTION: And suppose the person insists and says, go on, have some?

ANSWER: You still say, No thank you, I'm not hungry.

—No thank you. I'm not hungry, Gabriel told Norman's aunt. His mouth felt sunburnt. He would have liked to be able to say Thank you. Yes. I will.

—No, thank you. I really am not hungry.

—Such a foolish boy, Mrs. Silver said. Here Norman, you

take his piece.

As each forkful of moist chocolate disappeared into Norman's maw, Gabriel felt the anger surging within him.

—My fucking, goddam mother. Goddam my fucking, respectable, Jewish mother.

\* \* \*

The Waldheim's dog, a male German Shepherd, could do all kinds of tricks: Beg. Play dead. Walk on hind legs.

—Eat, Rex. Rex ate everything: bread, cheese, lettuce, apple peelings, left-overs of all sorts.

—Make a jobby, Danny. Perched precariously on his potty in the kitchen, little Danny grinned at his mother. Make a jobby now. Rex is waiting. Rex padded over to Danny and licked his toes. The youngster grabbed at the dog's ears and fell off the potty. The mother rescued potty and child.

—Now Danny, be a good boy and make a jobby. No? How about a wee-wee then? She reached for his baby's penis and pulled it. A cow's teat ready for milking. Make wee-wee, Danny. She shouted to her husband: Jack, turn the water on so Danny will make his wee-wee. As the water sluiced out of the tap, Danny responded with a squirt at kneeling Mrs. Waldheim. She directed the stream into the porcelain chamber pot.

—Turn it off, Jack. He's doing his duty.

Joy in the household. Grandpa Waldheim stroked his beard and grunted approval. Danny's mother clapped her hands, inviting the baby to do likewise. Tinkle, tinkle. Into the pot. Guess what little Danny's got?

—All right, now. Show Mommy how you make your jobby. Show Daddy. And Grandpa. And Rex.

—Woof. Show me, Rex sniffed at the bowl. Danny burped and brought up a trickle of spit. He pulled at his genitals.

—No, Danny, you've already wee-weed. Now it's time for your jobby. She started to grunt. Like this, Danny. She sat down beside him on the brocaded footstool.

109

—Look, Mommy's going to make jobby too. She grunted again, put her hands on her tummy and pressed. Danny, simian responsive, imitated her. His mother grunted again. Then Danny. Then the mother. Then Jack. Then Grandpa. Solidarity forever. The dog yawned.

Danny squeezed out a thin baby fart.

—Oh, goody, goody. That was a goody. Try again. Another one.

Danny complied. From his loosened bowels poured forth a yellow mess of pottage, splash, splash into the receptacle, up against his bare bottom.

General delight.

—Well done. Jack, look. Danny made his jobby. Look. Grandpa. Look Rex.

She kissed Danny, removed him from the bowl, assessed with approval the results of his labor and carried him into the bedroom. Father and Grandfather followed.

Rex trotted over to the chamber and sniffed. A fly buzzed in circles around it. Rex snapped at it, missed, and upset the contents over his snout. He ran in circles, around and around, then into the bedroom.

Danny's mother called: Here, Rex! The dog jumped up and licked Danny's face.

—Stinks! Rex stinks! Danny pushed him away.

* * *

The Leroys of Leonard had seven daughters and one son Gabriel's age. Mrs. Leroy was a wizened old woman at thirty-six. She was married to a religious zealot with side-curls that wound around his ears. He was called Rabbi Jonathan. Or Reb Jonathan. Or simply the Rav. Whenever he came into sight, he was greeted by the kids with: *Shah Shah der Rebbe gayt.*

He had never been ordained. He had no pulpit. He never led the Kiever Congregation in prayer but stayed apart from the other worshippers.

—Hey Albert, how come a nice orthodox kid like you with a praying mantis of a father has a name like Leroy?

Albert grimaced. That's my name, Leroy.

—What was it in the old country?

—Lazarowitz. The old man changed it when he came over. Anyway, what the hell was your name before you changed it?

—Fuchs, Horny Fox said. Same as Fox, only in German.

—That figures, Albert said. Fuchs fucks fox. Horny all the way.

—Better than Alcock or Faircock or Cockburn.

—You're still all-cock as far as I'm concerned, Albert smirked.

—Hey Albert, what does your father do for a living?

—He prays hard and God looks after him.

—He prays for a hard-on, Fox said. Where'd you think all the kids come from?

—Jealous. That's what you are. You probably couldn't even get a hard-on. Probably don't even have balls. I bet you pee sitting down.

—I'll show you, smart-ass, Fox said. Here, what do you say to that? He pulled Albert down to the foxy erection. There, if you ever make fun of me again, I'll let you have it. Only next time it'll be a blow job.

Albert ran into the house. He tried hard not to swallow.

Reb Jonathan Leroy, long, black hair and wispy beard framing a splotchy face, rounded the corner from Nassau Street. His worn mantle was spotted with grease stains. The frayed shirt was big around the neck. A thin, black tie danced against his chest as he marched homeward, his black satchel thumping against his side. His boots needed heels and soles.

Reb Jonathan stopped at the curb to blow his nose. He applied a thumb to one wing and honked out of the open nostril a stream of snot. In similar manner he effected the discharge from the other nostril. He sneezed whole-heartedly, spraying Mrs. Gwozdz who was passing. She cursed him. He shuffled by her, pronouncing a benediction.

Time for *minchah* prayers. He greeted his wife curtly and retired to the bedroom where, facing east toward Jerusalem, he prayed. He prayed with fervor. He added prayers, first for his own safety and delivery from evil, then for his wife and family, then for afflicted Jews everywhere. Finally for the souls of all the dead from time immemorial. Amen.

The Reverend Leroy's livelihood lay in his battered satchel. Metal boxes painted the blue and white colors of Zion, bearing the names of various charitable enterprises. The Home for the Aged in Jerusalem. The Home for Orphan Boys. The Home for Scholars of the Talmud.

Reb Jonathan called at the Gottesman home to install one of his tin cans. Gabriel reluctantly let him in.

—*Eliahu hanavi* has arrived, Gabriel announced.

—*Tzedaka* for the love of the Almighty, the Rav pleaded in Yiddish. A *mitzvah.* A blessing on this household.

He affixed a box to the door frame at the bottom of a line of prior contenders. He stepped back, appraised his work, nodded in silent satisfaction. He shook Aaron's hand.

—An extension to the Home for Orphan Girls in the Holy City. Pious girls. They pray every day for us to help them. He returned the hammer to his satchel, gathered about him the folds of his long mantle, adjusted his faded black felt hat, and swished out, uttering: Bless you. Bless you. Lord bless this house and all therein. He paused at the door.

—Don't forget your contributions. Put in nickels and dimes. Pennies. Whatever you can spare. Your prayers will be answered. I'll be back in a month to empty the *pushke.* A blessing on you all.

He was gone. Gabriel approached the boxes. Each had a slot to receive the contributions. For prayers answered. Ping. In expectation of prayers answered. Ping. During an illness or other family crisis. Ping. Aaron distributed his money equally among the seven pushkes. Gabriel flicked a thumb under each container. A dismal rattle.

—That old fraud. That old fraud. And all those others with their *pushkes.*

He turned to his father. You should get yourself a job like the Rebbe's. Join the Holy Caravan. Then we wouldn't have to be on relief. He smashed his fist into the box of the Orphan Girls of Jerusalem.

—Fucking frauds. All of them.

* * *

Gabriel preferred the simple, unaffected style of the Leshyks in No. 51. Mrs. Leshyk was a charwoman at the Roxy Burlesque on Queen Street. On Saturday nights after the last show she swept, dusted, washed, scrubbed and polished. The stage, the dressing rooms, the theater, the lobby. The manager's office. The box office. She finished her chores at three in the morning. An amiable, moon-faced Ukrainian, small and heavy, she had a smile and a greeting for everyone.

Her husband was a mournful man who chain-smoked Zig-Zags, holding the cigaret between thumb and index finger. He didn't speak much. He worked in a paint factory on Niagara street. He coughed all the time. Their only son, Steve, received the material rewards of their joint labors.

Steve played the violin. Badly. No amount of practice could bring him beyond the beginner's level of musician-ship. His bow produced scratchy scales, and simple off-key melodies. He stood by the window of the upstairs flat, scraping bruised quavers from the ill-tuned strings. Im-mersed in a dream of himself as Heifetz. Moist eyes veiled, head hanging limply on the chin rest, slender, young boy's body tensing and relaxing as he sent the resinated bow across the bridge. Gabriel envied him.

—I'd love to play the way you do. Would you show me how?

—Sure, Steve promised. Sure. We'll form a duo and give concerts all over the world. Paganini. Beethoven. Mozart. Here. I'll give you your first lesson. Easy.

Gabriel mastered the technique of holding the violin, learned the names of all the parts. How to apply the resin; how to replace the strings, and play three notes of the C scale.

—You can get yourself a violin from the pawnshop across from City Hall. Cheap. We'll meet next Sunday.

The internationally renowned violin virtuosi — Leshyk and Gottesman — cancelled the projected tour of the world due to the inability of the latter to obtain the required instrument.

Approached for funds, Sara dismissed him with a bitter laugh. Go sell papers. Gabriel gave up the quest. Steve shrugged and continued to fiddle solo flights of mediocrity.

One Saturday afternoon Mrs. Leshyk took the two boys to the Roxy.

—See funny men, beautiful ladies, dancing. Real. Live. After is a movie.

She brought them in via the stage entrance, up a long, dark, side passage and into the back of the theater. Two seats in the last row.

—Be quiet. I go now to Eaton's. I be back in two hours. Meet outside.

The theater was hazy with cigaret smoke. Far away, on the stage brilliant with colored lights, Gabriel made out two men knocking each other about. One was tall, well-dressed in a white suit, a flower in his lapel. The other was short, fat with a dented bowler perched on his head, baggy trousers held up by wide suspenders, a checkered shirt open at the neck and oversized boots.

—Where I come from the oranges are so big people use them for bowling balls, baggy pants was shouting to the tall man.

—How do you account for that my good fellow? The other seemed genuinely interested.

—It's the climate, my boy, the climate. And do you know the chickens in my state lay eggs so big they're mistaken for footballs?

—And what's the reason for that may I ask? the tall man was saying.

—It's the climate, my boy. The climate. Yuk-yuk-yuk, he slapped his thigh and moved in closer, more confidential, to his partner. And did you hear about the little midget who married the six foot seven chorus girl and had three

114

children with her?

—How did he ever manage that?

—Climb it, my boy. Climb it. The funny man laughed and ran around the stage shrieking, Climb it, climb it, to the audience. The tall man ran after him beating him over the head with a truncheon as the stage lights blacked out.

Cigarets lighting up. Flickering fireflies in the dark.

—And now, ladeez and gennemun we take pleasure in presenting the one and only, the lovely, lushus Lorraine.

A spotlight filtered through the haze and fell an amber pool against the right proscenium curtain. The orchestra led by Curly Kramer was playing, Birds do it, Bees do it. Piano. Trumpet. Saxophone. Drums. Sweet and schmaltzy. Lovely Lorraine sauntered into the light. To Gabriel's astonishment she began to undress. First, she took off her black gloves. Then her wide-brimmed, black straw hat. Then a zip and her sheer crimson robe was in her hand. She was moving in dancing steps. The saxophone was whining, Let's fall in Love. The spotlight changed to flesh color. Now Lovely Lorraine, clad only in brassiere and panties, was drifting across the stage. Deft fingers unhooked the brassiere and let it sway before she tossed it into the wings. Now she was sliding the net panties down the long, smooth legs.

—Even educated fleas do it....

—She's wearing a jock strap, Gabriel whispered to Steve. Hey, look at that. It's even got sparklers on it.

—Beautiful. Beautiful, Steve asserted. The music is beautiful.

Now Lovely Lorraine was turning slowly around, her arms crossed, each hand covering a breast. The spotlight changed to indigo and she let her arms fall to her sides.

—Look at those tits, Gabriel nudged Steve. Wow. Pasties covered the nipples. The law of the land.

The ecdysiast gyrated her pelvis while Kramer's musicmen produced from their instruments growls and purrs and grinding sounds. She reached for the pubic covering, patted it, fingered its perimeter.

—She's taking it off. Now we'll see her pussy. Watch. All will be revealed. A quick tug. Now you see it. The lights

115

went out. Now you don't.

Applause. Whistles. Cheers. Lorraine lovely in her nakedness does not return. The stage lights reveal a doctor's office.

A noisy introduction from the band brings on a comic doctor and a woman patient. He is examing her.

—Breathe deep, he commands as he moves the listening device between her big breasts. He makes a comment. The audience laughs. Gabriel doesn't understand. The girl turns away and bends over. The doctor pretends to stick the stethoscope up her ass.

—Say ah-h-h. She slaps his face. Hilarious. She grabs a seltzer bottle and squirts it all over him. She stalks out waving her buttocks. The travelling curtains close and the stage is dark again.

—And now the management of the Roxy Theater presents for your enjoyment the Roxyettes in a ballet specially produced by our Director Vladimir Sokoloff.

On stage now a forest setting. Tinselled trees and shrubbery. A cardboard fountain. At the rear, a stairway covered in glitterdust. Languorous woodwinds bring in the Roxyettes in short tutus and satin slippers. The prima ballerina leaps on stage, *à grande jetée.* The others circle about her. The tempo quickens. The brasses sound. The drums, savage tom-toms. All is frenzy. The girls rush about in hand-holding sweeps of movement. The follow spot from the projection booth washes the stage in arcs of changing hues, blue, yellow, amber, green, violet. The principal dancer is elevated above the swaying bodies. She is appealing for help. She dies. Blackout.

When the music starts again the lights go on. The stage is empty. The members of the cast come down the stairway to take their bows. The funny men. The bicycle act. The acrobats. The dancers. The master of ceremonies bounds down the stairs; takes a bow.

—And now once again, to close our show, we present our Star, the Lovely Lorraine.

All the artists turn in the direction of the stairs. She floats, down, down, Sophisticated Lady, one step at a time, a black transparent wrapper showing everything, as

116

the lights dim down and out save for one flesh spot on Lovely Lorraine. She steps forward and the red plush proscenium curtain closes behind her. At the edge of the stage, rhythmically in time to the music, playing to the front row, she begins to bump.

—Take it off.

Lorraine pulls back an edge of her robe partially revealing one breast. Baldy Kramer brings the boys to a crashing finale. Blackout. Lorraine vanishes behind the drapes.

As the movie flickered on, Gabriel sought the men's toilet. Safe behind the locked door of the cubicle, with the recurring theme of Sophisticated Lady in his head Gabriel jerked off in tribute to the Lovely Lorraine.

## 10

The *melamed*, a bent man with a trim grizzled beard, came to the house three times a week at four o'clock in the afternoon to prepare Gabriel for his *Bar Mitzvah*. Each Friday he collected from Sara his fee of one dollar.

He was a disappointed man, left behind by life, destined to spend his remaining years in the company of pre-*Bar Mitzvah* adolescents. He trudged into one home, escaped an hour later, and trudged into another. So it went until eight. Five days a week. Extra sessions on Sundays for the slow learners.

Gabriel loathed the periods at the kitchen table, breathing in the old man's stale exhalations. The odor of decaying viscera and dissolved dreams.

At the appointed hour each day, Reb Joseph appeared.

—Where's the boy?

—Gabriel! Sara shouted. Reb Joseph is here.

Up on the third floor, Gabriel was hiding in the old wicker hamper. From amidst the smell of moth balls, he heard the footsteps. Reb Joseph peered into cupboards and under beds. Gabriel sneaked downstairs by degrees and took his place at the table.

—Where have you been hiding? Reb Joseph appeared, out of breath.

—I've been here all the time. How come you're so late today?

Twelve minutes of the hour had passed. For the balance of the time Gabriel showed Reb Joseph how much he had learned since his last visit. He put on the phylacteries, the small leather boxes with portions of the *Torah* enclosed. One cube perched on the forehead. One secured on the inner-left arm with leather strap bound round and round in descending spirals ending about the palm and fingers. *Thou shalt wear them as frontlets before thine eyes. A token upon thine hand.* Every morning at prayer. Except the Sabbath and religious festivals.

Then chanting in Hebrew from the fourth book of the Pentateuch:

*—And Aaron lighted the lamps so as to give light in front of the candlestick, as the Lord commanded Moses.*

They chanted together, master and pupil following the ancient notation beneath the words.

*—And the Lord spoke unto Moses saying: Take the Levites from among the children of Israel and cleanse them. Sprinkle the water of purification upon them and let them cause a razor to pass over all their flesh and let them wash their clothes and cleanse themselves.*

The wisdom of the Torah in the *loshen kodesh*, a tongue holy, reserved for prayer, professing Gabriel's continuity with the prophets.

*—And thou shalt present the Levites before the tent of the meeting; and thou shalt assemble the whole congregation. Thus shalt thou separate the Levites from among the children of Israel; and the Levites shall be mine.*

Reb Joseph prodded. Gabriel enunciated, stumbled, continued. While Sara prepared the evening meal.

On the Saturday morning of Gabriel's *Bar Mitzvah*, the Gottesman family arrived especially early at the Kiever Shul. A quorum of older men had already assembled. Chatting quietly. Donning their prayer shawls. Rocking in prayer.

Sara made her way up the stairs to the balcony reserved for women and took a seat in the front pew. She noted with approval that the Gabbai was ushering Aaron and Gabriel and Noah to the seats facing the Holy Ark. Today Aaron would receive an *Aliyah*. He would say a prayer and pledge some money to the synagogue. The grandfather and the uncles would be honored in similar fashion. Then it would be Gabriel's turn.

Noah spotted and reported the arrivals to his brother.

—Uncle Samson has just come in. And Joshua and Eli. There's *Zayde*.

Aaron greeted them, seated them beside him. The balcony was filling up. Young women in long-sleeved blouses, old crones in ankle-length dresses, children, some in starched, white frocks. The aunts and cousins.

The service began, the voices of the worshipers rising and falling, an anarchy of sound.

119

When the time came for the removal of the *Torah* from the Ark, the congregation arose and sang: Lift up your heads, O ye gates.... As the *Torah* was carried to the *bimah*, many of the congregants dispersed. Into the hall. Downstairs to the toilet. Outside to the small patch of green that was Denison Square. Those who stayed exchanged information with their neighbors about the events of the week—local and international. Somewhere in the hubbub the law brought down from Sinai by Moshe Rabbenu was being read.

Gabriel, growing more nervous, sat waiting, his shiny, silk prayer shawl hot on his shoulders. The *Ba'al Tefillah* sang out Hebraically,

—Let us now call up Yechiel Yosef, the son of Aaron. Noah prodded him, Now. Go up.

Gabriel approached the *bimah*. Throat constricted. Parched. He was shown to the center of the high table where the scroll was unrolled, to the position designated for him. With the *tsitsit* of the prayer shawl he kissed the spot indicated by the reader and recited the prayer.

—Praise ye the Lord to whom all praise is due.

The response arose: Praised be the Lord to whom all is due forever and ever.

Gabriel again:

—Praised be Thou, O Lord our God, ruler of the world who hast called us from among all people and hast given us Thy Law. Praised be Thou. O Lord, giver of the Law.

The *Ba'al Tefillah* read from right to left the words inscribed by some devout *sofer*.

—*And Miriam and Aaron spoke against Moses because of the Cushite woman whom who he had married. Now the man Moses was very meek above all the men that were upon the face of the earth. And the Lord spoke suddenly unto Moses and unto Aaron and unto Miriam. Come out ye three unto the Tent of Meeting. And they three came out. And the Lord came down in a pillar of cloud and stood at the door of the Tent and called Aaron and Miriam; and they both came forth. And He said: Hear now My words: if there be a prophet among you, I the Lord do make Myself known unto him in a vision, I do speak with*

120

*him in a dream. My servant Moses is trusted in all My house; with him do I speak mouth to mouth, even manifestly, and not in dark speeches; wherefor then were ye not afraid to speak against My servant, against Moses, And the anger of the Lord was kindled against them; and He departed. And when the cloud was removed from over the Tent, behold, Miriam was leprous, as white as snow: and Aaron looked upon Miriam and Aaron said unto Moses: Oh my Lord, lay not, I pray Thee, sin upon us, for that we have done foolishly, and for that we have sinned. Let her not, I pray, be as one dead, of whom the flesh is half consumed when he cometh out of his mother's womb. And Moses cried unto the Lord saying: Heal her now, O god I beseech Thee. And the Lord said unto Moses: Let her be shut up without the camp seven days and after that she shall be brought in again. And Miriam was shut up without the camp seven days; and the people journeyed not till Miriam was brought in again.*

Gabriel recited the prayer, *After the Reading of the Torah.* Then the scroll was elevated. The congregation rose up and sat down. The scroll was carried to a bench on the Bimah and was dressed in its mantle of royal blue velvet with a silver crown atop the two ivory handles and a silver breast plate and silver pointing hand.

Gabriel opened the book to the Haftorah for that Sabbath day. His Sabbath day. He read:

—*Praised be the Lord our God for the law of truth and righteousness which He has revealed unto Israel, for the words of the prophets filled with His spirit and for the teachings of the sages whom He raised up aforetime and in these days.*

His moment had truly come. The fulfillment of all the weeks of learning by rote the prophetic portion, *Behaalosecha.* Zechariah 11-14, Chapter 11. He squeaked the first words: —*Sing and rejoice...* He started again.

—*Sing and rejoice, O daughter of Zion: for lo, I come and I will dwell in the midst of thee, saith the Lord. And many nations shall join themselves to the Lord in that day and shall be My people, and I will dwell in the midst of thee. And the Lord shall inherit Judah as His portion in*

121

*the Holy Land and shall choose Jerusalem again. Be silent, all flesh before the Lord; for He is aroused out of his holy habitation.*

It was easier now. His father at his right hand, the *Zayde* at his left. He no longer heard the buzz of conversation from the non-worshipers about him. The moneychangers in the Temple.

The Hebrew phrases, learned with so much effort in the past year, cascaded from his lips like the waters from Mount Hermon. He was a high priest among his ancient people, serving *Yahveh* within the tabernacle.

—*Hear O Israel...* he was nearing the end.

—*Who art thou O great mountain before Zerubbabel? Thou shalt become a plain; and He shall bring forth the top stone with shoutings of Grace, Grace unto it.*

Finished.

A shower from the balcony: Filberts, peanuts, hazel nuts, almonds. Raisins too. Upon his head and shoulders. The young boys scrambled for them where they fell upon the floor and in the neighboring aisles.

Gabriel Gottesman, now truly one of God's anointed, ushered into the ranks of the House of Israel. Aaron was the first to shake his hand: *Soll sein mit Mazel.* Congratulations exploded about him.

Today I am a fountain pen. Gabriel received a Parker, dark blue with a silver nib. And a bottle of Quink. There were also shirts and underwear and stockings. A two dollar bill. A fedora. A pocket watch by Ingraham. A new *Siddur.* A pair of brown Oxfords.

The Bar Mitzvah party was held that night. The old lace tablecloth on the round table. From the kitchen Sara brought plates of corned beef, tongue, salami, pastrami; dill pickles and mustard; potato salad; schmaltz herring; loaves of black bread, rye bread, bagels, buns. On the buffet sat a keg, its spiggot dripping white foam into a pan.

Aaron's family — Sara's tenants — were the first to appear. Samson and Joshua, Sadie and her husband. Freda and her husband and four year old Susie. Eli, recently widowed, with his three children. And the grandparents.

In due time the other relatives arrived. Mr. and Mrs.

Rajansky — who had just recently changed their name to Rain — knocked politely at the door and waited to be admitted. Their good manners accompanied them everywhere, even on their infrequent visits to their proletarian relatives.

Uncle Shlomo Nathanson and his wife barged in with two of their children. Reb Joseph was welcomed effusively by Sara. Diffidently, he extended his right hand to all within reach.

Uncle Eli took charge of the beer. He instructed Sara in her duties: Bring more glasses. Here, wash these out. Mop up these spills. The first of the brood in the promised land, the biggest wage earner, Uncle Eli had an exalted position within the family. No one acted without his advice. God's in his heaven, and on earth, Uncle Eli.

The grandmother sat in the corner munching a herring tail. Her false teeth clicked as she chewed. Judah The Lion, beside her, was drinking rye.

Noah, beside the Stomberg-Carlson highboy, was sipping Punch Dry Ginger Ale out of a bottle and chomping on a corned beef sandwich.

The Rajanskys on the couch nibbling at Sara's sponge cake, hoping Princess would be all right after her latest misadventure.

Uncle Nathanson, worn out at fifty-two, sat on the edge of a straight-backed kitchen chair, complaining in his grating voice about life's difficulties. The Depression. Taxes. He did not mention his daughter's elopement with a *shaygetz* from Rochester. He sighed mournfully, That's the way it is, and pulled out his watch, read the time, looked towards the hallway, listening, waiting for a *tocsin.*

—Worthy parents, honored Rabbi, dear friends and relatives. Today, my *Bar Mitzvah* day....

Gabriel's *Today-I-Am-A-Man* speech. Painfully memorized.

—I want to thank all those who have helped me to reach this wonderful day....

Promising to honor his parents, to attend synagogue regularly, to practice in his daily life those precepts incumbent on a member of the Congregation of Israel.

Young David running about the room bumped into Uncle Eli who overturned a pitcher of beer he had just filled. Eli walloped him on the back and the child fell shrieking against the buffet.

—I owe everything I am to my mother and father who have brought me up with care and kindness. Especially my mother....

Sara rushed in from the kitchen.

—You should teach your brat to have better manners, Uncle Eli shouted at Sara.

—How dare you touch my child! she retorted, trying to hold back the tears. Don't you ever do that again!

—Don't you talk that way to me, Uncle Eli spluttered, you *peasant*, you *lowlife*. You belong in Kensington Market, you...you *fishwife*.

Aaron said nothing. His debt to Eli crushing his manhood. Eli had redeemed them from the Polish *shtetl*, but Sara would not show the reverence demanded by her brother-in-law.

—I'm not your slave. I won't stand for your insults. In my own home. In front of my guests. Taking in your children and their *dreck*. You can move out. All of you.

Reb Joseph began to sing: *Hinay mah tov umanayim.* How good it is for brethren to dwell together in harmony. *Shevet achim gam yachad.*

Eli stalked out. Samson and Joshua decamped with him. Silence except for the chewing. Subdued sobs came from Sara as she cleaned away the beer-soaked tablecloth.

The telephone rang and Noah answered. For Uncle Shlomo. The Bell awaits thee. Nathanson raised his superfluity of flesh.

—Hello? Who? Yes. Yes. No! My God! Right away!

Agitated, perspiring, he returned to report: The house is burning. The fire engines are there. I have to leave. Oh my God! My house! On fire!

His son had done everything just right. With the insurance money he could pay off the mortgage, fix up the house, have something left over for other needs. He mumbled good bye and left.

The Rebbe finished the last phrases of *Havenu Sholom*

*Aleichem* and bowed his way out. The Rajanskys brushed cake crumbs from their clothes. Mrs. Rajansky handed Gabriel an envelope.

—Buy yourself something. She clasped Sara to her and wished her strength to bear the burden of the times. Her husband shook Aaron's hand. Together they intoned *Mazel Tov.* The others, neighbors and friends, took their leave.

All quiet now. Save for the hum of voices from upstairs. The meeting convened by Uncle Eli to plan the next move. It was decided. Ostracism against Sara and her family. The decision, inflexibly adhered to by Uncle Eli, broken by others for necessary favors, including postponement of payment of rent.

\* \* \*

Joshua, assailed by Eros, required specialized assistance.

—Oh, Gabriel, if you still want to come to the Standard Theather next Friday, I-uh-can get you in uh-free. O.K.? Good. Now, you-uh won't forget about my letter, now, will you?

Gabriel wouldn't forget. Supplying words of love, playing Cyrano to a Roxanne from Hamilton. Phrases of delicacy and wit, paeans of grandeur addressed to a young stenographer whose age was twenty-one. A steelcitysylph. Joshua, a machine operator, stitching together ladies garments.

—Write to Polly that I am happy for the letter she sent to me. Say I want very much to see her again.

Gabriel wrote.

—My dearest sweetheart Polly. I have read your beautiful, tender letter over and over. I am very lonely for you. I count the hours until we meet again.

—Fine. Fine, Joshua agreed. Write more. Say how much I love her.

Gabriel seeking bardic strains found courtly iambs:

—If music be the food of love. Your letters are music to me and I sound the words over and over. That surfeiting, the appetite may sicken and so die.

Inspired Gabriel. The selfsame words spoken on St. Christopher's stage. Felix Reingold as the Duke, sighing: *O spirit of love! how quick and fresh art thou.* Horny Fox ad-libbing from the wings: That strain again — and collapsing in mock pain.

—It's from Shakespeare, Gabriel explained. Polly will like it.

Finished, Gabriel read it aloud, the letter to Polly, phrases orotund, laced with metaphor and simile. He added, Yours forever, Joshua Gottesman. Grinning approbation. Hastening to the red metal box. Royal Mail.

Received by return the reply from Polly. Gabriel reading it to his uncle.

—My dearest Joshua. Your letter thrilled me. Such lovely thoughts. You must be very educated to know such big words and to phrase them so well. At the Commercial School where I learned typing and shorthand we also studied English Literature. I didnt like it very much. You say things much better. I show your letters to my closest girl friend. She is so jealous.

Joy suffused Joshua.

—A reply, Gabriel. Write another letter to Polly. This time better than before. More big words, love words.

—Sure, Gabriel said. Sweet, sentimental, schmaltzy.

—*Schmaltz?* No *schmaltz.* Shakespeare.

—O.K. No *schmaltz,* Gabriel agreed then proceeded to pen a salvo of sodden stereotypes exalting the flesh and the soul. Pollyannas in polysyllables to Polly Sachs.

—Fine. Very good, Joshua anticipating his love's delight.

Polly replied on scented stationery with the embossed initials P.S. enclosed in a shield.

—I keep your letter in my bosom and take it out many times during the day just to read and read and read. I can't wait to see you again to hear the words from your own mouth.

Gabriel had to explain to Polly in the next *billet doux* about the superiority of the written word over the spoken language. He included a poem:

When I am with my loving Polly
Everything seems oh so jolly.

When I am far away from her
All the world's bereft of cheer.
Joshua learned the poem by heart. He would recite it to Polly when he made his next visit to her.

When I am far away from Polly
Nothing, nothing seems so jolly...

Theme and variations. There's a small hotel, by a wishing well. Joshua, passionate; Polly, frigid for lack of matrimonial guarantees. The affair fractured, Joshua sulking away the days, searching for the next romance. Gabriel remained the anonymous creative muse. The selfsame series of letters to another girl with another name.

—Write the number one letter this week, Gabriel, the one that starts with, No blemish did e'er on cheek appear.

—My dearest Florence, Gabriel wrote. The note mailed, the certain response received, replied to by Gabriel. Answered in turn. Gabriel, bar-mitzvah-fountain-penned ambrosial words for Joshua who fell in love and out of love and in again and out.

His brother Samson mocked his travails, lectured Joshua and Gabriel on the realities.

—Stay away from women. They'll ruin you. Remember what happened to Samson in the Bible. Sex will make you weak. Take care of your body. Build it up. Exercise. Cold baths. Let in the fresh air. Especially in winter when you go to bed.

—You can't be too careful, he told Gabriel. And keep your hands off your *putz.*

The evils of masturbation. Gabriel read about them in a pamphlet.

—Don't pull off, Samson waved a crooked forefinger at Gabriel. A man should exercise self-restraint. It's written right here in the *Shulchan Aruch.*

He translated from the Yiddish, from the Code of Jewish Law:

Semen is the vitality of man's body and the light of his eyes and when it issues in abundance the body weakens and life is shortened. He who indulges in having intercourse (or jerks off, Samson added) ages quickly, his strength ebbs, his eyes grow dim, his breath becomes foul, the hair of his head, eyelashes and brows fall out, the hair of his beard, armpits and feet increase, his teeth fall out and many other aches besides these befall him. Great physicians said that one out of a thousand dies from other diseases, while nine hundred and ninety-nine die from sexual indulgence.

—Is there more stuff like that in there, Gabriel inquired, I mean about what isn't good for you?

Samson merely said, The wise man grows wiser.

—I'd like to read it all the way through, Gabriel said. Several weeks later, returning the book, he asked his uncle: Tell me, do you think I'm getting stronger?

—Sure, Samson said, you're getting bigger and stronger.

—That's funny, Gabriel mused, you see, before my *Bar Mitzvah* I could bend my penis easily. Since I started reading the *Shulchan Aruch* I must have grown weaker because I can't bend my organ at all.

Samson looked at him, frowned, then understood.

—Idiot. The hard-on kid. Go ahead. Jerk off. You'll be sorry later. Samson wheeled the old bicycle out of the shed, tied his dog to the frame and pedalled off to Cherry Beach.

* * *

—*Bei mir bist du shayn....*

Jackie Borsuk, boy soprano, stood on a stool in the royal box of the Standard Theater and sang to Molly Picon far below him on the stage. The new musical was called *The Widow From Boston*. The golden spotlight enveloped one singer, then the other as each in turn sang:

—*Bei mir bist du shayn,*
*Bei mir hast du chayn.*

The audience applauded, demanded more.

*Bei mir hast du chayn....*

Encore after encore. Again. Again. Gabriel too, adoring, clapping, shouting. *Gloria in excelsis.*

Another Friday evening, Jackie Borsuk, tattered orphan,

standing in the theatrical rain amidst theatrical thunder and lightening, singing, sobbing, appealing:

—*Kupice,*
*Koiftshe papierosen....*

Have pity on a poor orphan. The night is cold and dark. Buy. Buy my cigarets

Gabriel was proud to call six-year-old Jackie his friend. Tying his shoe in the schoolyard. Seeing him home to the flat above the grocery store on Nassau Street. Enjoying the recognition of the neighbors: Look, there's Jackie Borsuk with the Gottesman boy.

Friday nights, after synagogue and supper, Gabriel slipped away to the enchantment of the Yiddish Theater. He presented himself to the spectacled man in the box office just as the show was beginning. The man winked at Joshua. Joshua winked at the doorman. The doorman winked Gabriel into his seat.

—In the shadows when I come and sing to you....

Paul Josephson, the Dick Powell of the Yiddish Theater, sang and danced a full season at the Standard. He affected a mellifluous sing-sprach, a mannered posing, a boyish air. Boy meets girl (an attractive soubrette). Boy loses girl (amidst tears and lamentations). Boy gets girl (reunion in the park).

—In the shadows when I come and....

Tragedy was the forte of Berta Gersten. Gabriel suffered with her even though there was much he did not understand. He could not see why she was so upset about Oswald. And why was the play called *Ghosts?* Oswald crying to her: *Mother, give me the sun.* She screamed: *I cannot bear it. I cannot bear it.* She threw herself on the floor beside Oswald: *No. No. No.*

Maurice Schwartz and his Yiddish Art Theater in Sholem Aleichem's *Hard To Be A Jew.* The blessing of the Sabbath candles and the rendering of the *Kiddush* over the wine. The two students, one Jewish, one Gentile who exchanged identities and how the Gentile discovers how hard it is to be a Jew.

Maurice Schwartz in *Yoshe Kalb*, with an English summary for the non-Jewish theatre-goers who filled the Standard. Joseph Buloff. Miriam Kressyn. Zvee Scooler. Seymour Rechtzeit. Capering, gesturing, shouting lines of bawdy comedy and of anguished heartache. Singing, waltzing, spinning about the stage. A festival of emotions. Engulfing the spectators in a communion of ritual.

Herman Yablakoff arrived one spring and stayed for six months in *Der Payatz*, a Yiddish version of *I Pagliacci*. Giant advertising sheets in the restaurants and gift shops on Spadina Avenue, on College Street revealed *Der Payatz* in clown costume. Clown face a painted, tragic mask.

On the Jewish Radio Hour the announcer urged everyone not to miss *Der Payatz*. MIME. MUSIC. PASSION. POIGNANCE. PATHOS.

Herman-the-clown-Yablakoff played with passion and pathos. Poignantly. When, sobbing, at the end, he collapsed the house applauded and cheered. The orchestra played the clown's theme and the audience shouted. More. Advancing, now hand in hand with the cast, now alone to bow and receive the accolades. Retreating, humbly behind the sweep of curtain. Reappearing. Spotlighted downstage center. One hand raised for silence, the clown spoke in the voice of Herman Yablakoff:

—My dear friends (a gasp for breath), I am honored ...and overwhelmed by the magnificent reception you have accorded me here tonight. (Another deep-drawn breath). On behalf of my fellow actors in the troupe I wish to thank you from the bottom of my heart. (Applause). It is only because of your marvellous reception that Der Payatz has been able to play for so long in the United States and here. If you truly liked the show, please tell your friends and relations about it. Tell them that Herman Yablakoff is grateful to Toronto for helping to keep alive the flame of Yiddish Theater. (Applause). Tell them we'll be here only another few weeks and then we must return to New York. Tell them, dear friends that we perform every night except Sunday. Matinees Wednesday and Saturday. And now dear friends, you can see how much effort we have put into the show. (Deep breath). We're all very, very, fatigued and with your permission we'd like to retire. Thank you and

*Shalom.* (Waves of applause. Fire curtain descends upon *Der Payatz* and troupe, all bowing, bowing, bowing.)

\* \* \*

Bowing to his applauding peers at the Jewish Boys Club Gabriel enjoyed the role of actor in an improvised sketch of comic confusion.

The Jewish Boys Club on Simcoe Street in a three-storey red brick building that thrust out its social consciousness between two whore houses. A polished brass plaque proclaimed its purpose: J.B.I.T. Jewish Boys In Training. In the rear was the baseball diamond. Gabriel played little. Played badly. Got struck above the left eye with a baseball bat. The impact puffed the eye, travelled diagonally down his face and shattered half a tooth in the upper incisor area.

One Sunday afternoon the ball was knocked into the garden of the north-neighboring establishment.

It fell to Gabriel's lot to retrieve it. Up and over the fence into the tall grass. Searching, apprehended by a vicious German Shepherd dog who grabbed Gabriel by the sleeve of his jacket and jerked its head back and forth. Trained to capture Jewish Boys In Trespassing.

—Shake him off, Gabriel, the kids hollered encouragement from the safety of the other side of the fence.

—Don't be afraid. Pat him. Give him a biscuit.

Gabriel, biscuitless, stood motionless. The dog rose on hind legs, pawed at Gabriel in a doggy embrace. The dog penis emerging red from its belly.

From behind the curtained window on the second floor of the house, a female face appeared. Another joined it. Blonde by blonde. Amused gestures from above as the dog continued its thrusts.

A whistle, sharp, two-fingered. A shout.

—Down Hindenburg. Here Hindenburg. Here boy. A burly man in a coarse, brown pullover and corduroy trousers appeared. He carried a leather riding crop.

Swish. He struck the randy dog across the hind quarters.

131

Hindenburg, the pride of the palace guard, gave a yelp and released Gabriel. The dog slouched away into the bushes.

—Now then, the man asked Gabriel, what the hell are you doing here?

—The ball. Looking for the baseball.

—Get your goddam ball and don't come back. And if it ever falls in here again, just leave it lay. Don't send anybody for it... We don't bother you. So don't you bother us.

—There it is Gabriel, the kids pointed. There it is. The man waited while Gabriel scooped up the ball and hurried to the safety of the Jewish Boys Club.

—Fuck off, now, all of you. He shouted to those still clinging on their side of the barricade. Go on. Beat it. Or I'll get my dogs to tear you apart.

—Hey, Horny taunted, how about sending one of your girls out here to play with us.

The man advanced, threatening, and the faces disappeared. Scurrying indoors for safety. For other diversions. Billiards. Ping Pong. Sculpting. Club meetings. Dramatics. Jewish Boys In Training. Jerking off in the lavatory. Printing in large letters: A man's ambition must be small, to write his name on the shithouse wall.

The Jewish girls, in their clubrooms on St. George Street near the Central Library, were in training too. How to say no. How to keep marauding hands away. Jewish girls don't come home to mother with gashed membranes. Pregnant. Hot necking leads to petting leads to disaster. Jewish girls can't be too careful.

The lady social worker sitting primly with cemented legs, hands clasped in her lap, surveys the circle of adolescents, daughters of Zion. The facts of life. A girl has a vagina. A boy has a penis. Daddy and Mummy do it when they go to bed. But they are married, so it's all right. A girl should never let a boy touch her with his penis. One drop. That's all it takes. Damaged goods. Shame upon the entire family.

At the Jewish Boys Club the physical health instructor delivered the straight goods.

—Look here now fellas, we all like the opposite sex, don't we? But we must respect them. You wouldn't want your sister to be hurt by a thoughtless act, now would you? Well then, remember that when you are out with a girl. Don't take advange of her. A girl can't defend herself.

—When is the party, somebody wanted to know.

—Next week. There'll be sandwiches and cokes and fruit. And dancing.

—Shit, muttered Horny Fox. Who wants to go there? A bunch of goon girls. Why don't we have more movies?

An early autumn Sunday afternoon. Gabriel marches with a hundred other Jewish urchins up Simcoe Street along Dundas to the Imperial Theatre. Injunctions from attendant counsellors. Keep in line. Behave. Walk quietly.

Gabriel is goosed by Horny Fox. Horny attacked from the rear by Itchie Meyer. Keep in step. Keep it orderly. Keep it Jewish. Into the vast entertainment emporium, via the Victoria Street entrance. Climbing up to the second balcony, high, high. Finding a seat way at the top next to the projection booth.

The stage show begins. Dancers, jugglers, magicians, acrobats. The spotlights bathe the performers in rainbow hues. Down there, on Canada's biggest stage, little dwarfs going through their acts. Gabriel sees them grow smaller. Tiny. Tiny. Eclipsed by his outstretched pinky finger.

The orchestra begins the finale. Brassy sounds. Up tempo. The wall of velvet comes down then rises again. Curtain calls. The trained dogs bark across the stage, the trainer in pursuit, shouting doggie words of command. The comic comes forward, bows, falls down. Another drags him off. To each his own special technique for eliciting the manna of applause.

Now all the lights are out. Struck blind, the Jewish Boys In Training shout, jeer, whistle. The front curtains part, the movie screen, a big white square stares out at them. The film begins to unreel.

Harold Lloyd wears a straw hat, black-rimmed glasses that never fall off. Running to catch a train. Arrival in the big city. Trouble on a runaway tram. Footing it up the side of the big department store building.

He climbs. He slips. He catches onto a ledge. Higher now. Hands and feet in the spaces between the bricks. At last, near the very top he falls. He grabs for the hand of the big clock and hangs on. The clock face yawns open and he dangles high above Fifth Avenue. The cars down below are toys, the people ants.

At last he clambers to safety to the roof of the building where his girl is waiting to embrace him. At the edge they kiss. He slips — a little slip — just as the movie ends.

—That's what we should have, more movies, Horny complains again.

—Very well, Melville Fox, the counsellor counsels, if you don't want to go to the party you don't have to. I am sure there are others who *do* want to go. All in favor raise their right hands. That's good. Everybody in favor. Everybody. Except Melville.

—Shit. I'm not going. Too late to reverse himself, Horny maintains the negative.

—Awright then fellas, see you next week at 44 St. George. Oh, by the way, there's a special treat downstairs.

Their queued-up patience rewarded by the receipt of one hot dog. One Coke. And a shiny, red Macintosh apple.

Out on the street, munching silently, leaning against the J.B.I.T. plaque, the two, Horny and Gabriel watched the club house emptying of boys. As the lights blinked out, wrapping a mantle of blackness about the Jewish Boys Club, the two Jewish boys observed the house next door all lighted up, the pleasure dome of Kubla Khan. Shining, black sedans arrived and discharged well-dressed young men. In the interval between the opening and closing of the front door Gabriel heard the music.

—Yes sir, that's my baby.

—Boy would I like to be in there right now, Horny whispered. A dog's bark. Silence. Another bark.

—Circus tonight, I bet, Horny averred.

—You mean clowns and horses and bareback riders? Gabriel marvelled.

—Oh yeah, bareback riders, all right, Fox said. Bareass riders.

—How do you know?

—Oh, I know. Fox had a collection of pictures left by a travelling salesman who once lived in his mother's boarding

134

house. He knew. Although a virgin Fox he knew.

—Don't you know what a circus is? An orgy. With naked girls and fucking dogs and things like that, Horny explained. Bet you don't even know what a hoo-er house is. On and off for two dollars.

—Ever been in one? Gabriel asked his all-wise friend.

—Sure, Fox lied. Else how would I know all about it?

—Was it good...the fucking I mean?

—It was O.K. I guess. Only you have to leave as soon as you've come. I had a fat broad with a big ass. She wouldn't let me kiss her. But I sure would like to be in that there house right now, with the circus going on.

—Tell me about the circus, Gabriel insisted.

—Animals fucking girls. And people watching. Men fucking girls and people watching. And girls fucking girls.

—Dogs?

—Yup. Trained to fuck girls. One of the whores kneels on a cushion on the floor. The dog is brought over to her. She has some juice smeared over her twat. The dog licks it. He gets horny and he fucks her.

—Does the girl like it?

—Sometimes. All the guys watching sure do. They throw money at the girl. They make bets about how long it'll take the dog to fuck her.

—Suppose she got knocked up. Would she have a puppy? Other times. Other climes, Pasiphae and the Minotaur.

—Christ no. Doesn't work that way. Good thing, too. Hate to have to wheel a dog-face around in a carriage.

—Good morning Mrs. Klein. This is my sister.

—My, isn't she beautiful?

—Oh, I wouldn't say that, Mrs. Klein. She's a bit of a dog. But maybe she'll grow out of it.

Gabriel enthralled. Apalled. What a piece of work is man! In dog's image. Sodom. It's circus time everybody. Gomorrah. In time past. Time to come. Forevermore.

—Sure would like to be in there tonight, Fox mused. Sure would.

They passed by slowly. Gloomy street, lamplit at intervals. Towards McCaul Street and the spot where the murder was discovered. Quickly pass by. Old man

Steinberg was hanged for it. A Jewish scandal. Another five minutes would bring them to the Art Gallery. Then Spadina Avenue and home.

—Aren't you going to the party next week? Gabriel asked.

—Nah. I got another date. A house party. Real hot broads. Wanna come along?

—Sure. But I wouldn't know what to do, how to act. Gabriel hedged.

—Do like I do. Boy, when I show them this....

Gabriel felt the swelling part of him too. With satisfaction. Some of the other guys, bigger guys, older guys had way smaller tools and not even any hair.

—Meet me at the fire hall, Horny said.

Gabriel thanked him at the door of No. 47. Everyone was asleep. He too, soon, after....

Gabriel, the dog, mounted on a frisky whore. *Cave canem*. All around him his dog friends sat, tongues drooling spittle. Gabriel climaxed. Into the whore-bathtub he shot his jissom. Gabriel wagged his tail down the fifteen steps.

—Woof. Woof. He barked with satisfaction as he curled up for the night.

## 11

Gabriel went to work for Lou Fink. Every day after school he checked in at No. 47 for a glass of milk and a thick slice of heavily-buttered black bread. Then he borrowed Samson's bike and pedalled downtown to Richmond and Yonge where Lou presided over his stacks of newspapers and magazines.

Along Richmond the trams clanged, turned at the Victoria loop and returning clanged. Up Yonge for miles to the city limits and back again to the edge of the lake, they clattered.

Black sedans, jaunty in their new-styled streamlining. Hulking delivery trucks. Bicycles. Pedestrians. Cluttering and congesting.

Lou hustled newspapers, coughing out their names over the din of traffic.

*Star. Telegram.* Get your *Daily Star. Racing Form. Evening Telegram.* Leaning against the plate glass window of L.J. Applegath & Son, Hats, chewing the taste out of a mouthful of peppermint Chiclets. He knew his customers by name.

—Afternoon, Mr. Bradbury, here y'are, *Tely.* Lou thrust the folded paper smartly under the banker's arm, accepted the nickel, proferred three cents change, was advised to keep them, smiled and said: Thank you sir.

Gabriel learned by observation, imitated his boss.

—Hustle up kid. You got a mouth, sing it out. Hustle up and sing out. Don't dream boy. Sell those sheets.

Outside the Tivoli Theatre (Now Playing — The House of Rothschild with George Arliss) Gabriel hustled. Lou bicycled up to the curb, newspapers wedged high between the handlebars.

—Final Edition. Fifty *Stars.* Thirty *Telys.* Hustle up. He threw the bundle at Gabriel and was off again around the corner to Adelaide Street, growling, Hustle Up, to Izzy Ginsberg.

—*Star. Telegram.*

At half-past five out of the office buildings stenographers

and secretaries appeared, rainbowhued in their sleeveless summer dresses. She came up to him, delicate curves in motion hand extended.

—*Star*, please.

Gabriel pulled a copy from under his left arm, smacked it against the right thigh, doubled then quadrupled it and wedged it expertly under her arm.

—Thank you, Gabriel, my you're fast. A tinkle of laughter. See you to-morrow. Goodbye now.

The men, dark-clad, serious, no-nonsense customers.

—Here you are sir, the *Star?*

—No, dammit. Not that communist rag. *The Telegram.*

*The Star*, champion of unpopular causes, building circulation in the process. Anathema to stock brokers, petty clerks on the way up, officer managers, presidents and a sizeable section of the Anglo-Saxon, blue collar community, staunch subjects of King George V and Queen Mary and their surrogates in Canada. They all read, prideful of heritage, the *Telegram*. The Jews rallied round the *Star*.

At six o'clock Lou cycled by, waved.

—O.K. Kid. Pick up your sheets. Time to check in.

Ouside the Royal Bank of Canada Gabriel waited, counted coins, separating the tips from the rest of the change. Seventeen sheets left. Sixty-five sold. Should have $1.30. Right.

When Lou arrived Gabriel scooped the money out of his *Read The Star* apron pockets and deposited it on the Bank's high window ledge for Lou's scrutiny. Lou's index and middle fingers slid coins of one denomination, pennies, then nickels, then dimes, then quarters from the ledge into his cupped, left hand.

The newsboy was stooped and rheumatic. Face leather-tanned, etched deeply during thirty-four years of rain and snow and sun and wind. His one glass eye fixed, unmoving, upon Gabriel. The other darting about.

—You're short. Fifty-two cents. His good orb appraised Gabriel with distrust.

—You took back twenty-six sheets around ten to six, he reminded Lou. The lid winked over the living eyed. Lou smiled broadly.

138

—Yeah, that's right. O.K. It checks out. Here.

He handed Gabriel two quarters and a dime. Then a nickel. Gabriel added sixteen cents in tips.

—Listen kid, tomorrow try to get here before four o'clock.

—Sure Lou, I'll try. Sometimes I have stay in after school.

—If you can't come at four, don't come at all, Lou said. Matter of fact I can't use you anymore. One of my regular boys is coming back.

On Monday Gabriel appeared as usual. Lou didn't say anything. On Friday he fired Gabriel again.

—And don't come back next week. Why don't you see Karl up the street at Shuter? He may need a boy.

Karl Roff, squatting on an orange crate at his news stand outside Adams Furniture said:

—Sure I'll take you on kid. Work from noon to eight. One dollar. You keep any tips. If Lou says you're O.K., you're O.K. by me. Karl checked him in then left for Woodbine promising to return after the last race.

Gabriel exchanged the Sabbath of the synagogue and the Sabbath of movies for the Sabbath of sales.

\* \* \*

June 1934.

Number 2894, cream and red Peter Witt electric trolley stopped steely screeching at the news stand. The front and center doors slid open and disgorged Saturday's children and their parents.

—There it is, Mommy. Shirley Temple at the Imperial. America's sweetheart in *Little Miss Marker*. The blurb on the sandwich board near the cashier's cage screamed: *Her daddy hocked her for 20 bucks!*

Old Pat, the amputee, seated on his roller board, propelled himself along the sidewalk with leather-gloved hands.

Outside Loew's Theatre a queue had formed for *Manhattan Melodrama*. Starring Clark Gable, Wm. Powell, Myrna Loy.

August.

The Yonge Street Mission, swing-doors swung inviting open, was empty. Later the wooden pews would fill up for evening prayers. After the gospel message — Heaven and earth shall pass away but my words shall not pass away — and the hymn singing — What a friend we have in Jesus — led by a mission volunteer — Nothing but the blood — there would be a supper of bean soup and macaroni and bread in the community dining room downstairs. Then handouts of clothing.

—There are no bums at the Yonge Street Mission. Glory Ha-le-lu-jah. The empty wine bottles from under the pews would be collected and dumped into the garbage can in the lane.

October.

The blind poet, whey-faced, grey-tweed-coated, stood erect against the T.T.C. car stop. His white cane curved from one pocket. A silver cup hung from a cord around his neck.

—*There are strange things done in the midnite sun*
*By the men who moil for gold.*

He recited in an even rhythm pausing at the end of each alternating tetrameter and trimeter:

—*The Arctic trails have their secret tales*
*That would make your blood run cold.*

November.

—*The Northern lights have seen queer sights.*

The poet shook his cup, rattling the two coins for attention.

—*That night on the marge of Lake Lebarge*
*I cremated Sam Magee.*

The mother lifted her boy child. Into the cup. Drop it in. Go on. He won't bite you. That's it.

—Thank you, Ma'am. Thank you, sonny.

December.

An offering from the well-dressed lady with the brown fox coat. A priest uttered a blessing in passing. *In nomine.*

The poet removed seventy-three cents and transferred it to his left coat pocket. The chestnut vendor left his brazier of burning coals. He asked solicitously:

—How you feel today, O.K.?

—Yes, the blind one replied. Yes, I'm alright.

—You want roasted chestnuts? Warma you up.

—Yes. I'll have five cents worth. He nibbled quietly.

Tinkle of coin in cup.

—Thank you kindly, he bowed to the unseen benefactor. He ate crumbs of sweet chestnut from California, warming his hands against the crisp, hot shells as he removed them, careful not to lose the contents.

June. 1935.

The sightless musician, heavily sweatered, hobbled on misshapen feet. He carried a folding canvas chair. He carried a tin whistle purchased from Whaley Royce. He held an enameled cup from Woolworth's. He carried his burdensome old age with regret. Outside the Bank of Toronto between Scholes Hotel and the United Cigar Store he sat slowly down. Whistle to lips he essayed a few shrill notes. He spat a brown gob of tobacco juice behind him. Began again.

—*Land of Hope and Glory. Mother of the Free.*

He played forlornly a piping appeal. Unrewarded. He took breath and switched to *Rock of Ages*. After that, a faltering *Chase Me Charlie*. Into his cup fell three pennies and a nickel. He removed the contributions. His repertoire almost exhausted, the best saved for last, he tootled an old man's sorrow:

—*When there are grey skies, I don't mind the grey skies. You make them blue, Sonny Boy.*

An audience gathered around him, singing to his flag-eoleted melody. At the end he heard the shower of metal into the cup.

—Thank you. Thank you.

Up the street the recitation wooed the throng: *And there sat Sam looking cool and calm,*

*In the heart of the furnace roar.*

—Get your *Star* and *Telegram. Racing Form. Star Weekly.*

July.

—Hey kid, where's Karl? The slim young man smiled at Gabriel. A confidential smile. He wore a white suit, black shirt, white tie. On his feet were black and white Oxfords. In his lapel a red rose.

—Don't know, Gabriel said. Should be back soon.

—Tell him Morry was here. Tell him Frederick the Great was just great in the fifth at Woodbine. He sauntered away chewing on a tooth pick. Ping. He tossed a fifty cent piece into Sam Magee's cup. Pang. Two quarters for Sonny Boy. He saluted Nick Maggi, shoeshine man who saluted back from inside the Cigar store.

From the Heintzman building the arpeggios floated pianissimo out to him. Emily Taylor's coloratura high above on the seventh floor. Pedigreed. Trinity College of Music, London, England. At Lowes, Wm. Powell and Myrna Loy were cavorting in *The Thin Man*. Imperturbable super sleuth Nicky, his glad-eyed pouting lady, Nora, and their wire-haired terrier Asta.

Morry turned left at Queen Street and entered Mike's greasy spoon. At the counter he unfolded the *Racing Form*, pretended to read. Liz at the window, staring vacantly out at the crowds. He should find himself a younger whore. Liz was getting too old and sloppy. Wasn't earning much lately. Her tricks were old rummies. The odd horny kid. She gave him all the money she earned.

—I'd do anything for you Morry. Just don't leave me.

Liz suck up the last drops of Coke through the straw and put the empty bottle in the wooden case. She sat on the stool next to Morry. Isn't it time for you to be working, he asked her.

—Can't. Got my monthlies. She itched. She scratched with dirty finger nails around the edge of the Kotex pad. Must visit Doc Murphy. Some sonofabitch must have given me a dose. The next john is gonna get happy returns of the day.

She opened another bottle of Coke, inserted a straw. Sat there, sipping, scratching, looking out where the rain was chasing people into doorways. Summer shower. Soon over. Rainbow. No pot of gold for her at the end of.

142

At five o'clock Karl returned.

—O.K. kid, I'll take over. Get some supper.

—Morry was here, Karl, asking for you. He said something about Frederick the Great.

—O.K. O.K. I'll talk to him. Now go get something to eat. And don't forget to be back in an hour. I have to get away.

Karl put on Gabriel's STAR apron, jiggled the coins in the pockets. Chicken feed. Even with making book you couldn't make enough. And the cops to pay off. And a house to keep up. And a nagging wife. And a no good, lazy son.

September.

—The picture you've been waiting for. Mae West in *Belle of the Nineties*. The Imperial's big Labor Day Attraction. Admission sixty cents.

Red Gallagher, gravel-voiced street evangelist, stood on a box and waved a copy of *True Romances* newly purchased from Karl. He shouted imprecations at a non-existent congregation. His raspy voice would draw them and they would stay to badger and taunt. He would respond with scriptural evidence.

—Repent ye for the Kingdom of Heaven is at hand. Prepare ye the way of the Lord, O generation of vipers, who hath warned ye to flee from the wrath to come.

Gallagher turned the romantic pages of the magazine. Fornicators. Adulterers. Whoremongers. Wallowing in the sins of the flesh. The Queen City has become the city of Sodom. Think not that you will be spared the fire and brimstone that is to come. It has been foretold in Mark...

Gallagher pushed the rolled up copy of *True Romances* into his back pocket, flipped the pages of his Gideon Bible and found the place.

—*The sun shall be darkened and the moon shall not give her light. And the stars of heaven shall fall and the powers that are in heaven shall be shaken. And then shall they see the son of man coming into the clouds with great power and glory.*

He paused, glowered at a handful of silent witnesses,

banged shut his book and thrust it towards the boozer dozing at the curb:

—*But of that day and that hour knoweth no man, no, not the angels which are in heaven. Take ye heed. Watch and pray for ye know not when the time is. Watch ye therefore lest coming suddenly, He find ye sleeping. Watch.*

A shout of approval went up. The sleeping sinner awoke and joined in the general applause.

—That's right, Jerry. Give 'em hell.

The preacher glared at the mockers. He thumped the Gideon and declared, *He that cometh after me is mightier than I, whose shoes I am not worthy to bear.*

—Hear. Hear.

—*He shall baptize you with the Holy Ghost...*

—Hear. Hear.

—*...and with fire.*

Jerry left for a hamburger at the One Minute Lunch.

—Results in yet? Let's have a look. Bill Margolies slapped Karl's shoulder.

—Hello Bill, how's your whorehouse? Beds still creaking at the City Hotel?

—The whores are doing all right but everything else is lousy. The *shmucks* come in for a beer at noon and stay all day. Doping out the races. I shoulda been a bookie.

He scanned the winners and the odds. Groaned — shouda listened to Morry. Threw the paper back at Karl.

—Gotta go. Little cutie waiting for me at the Roxy. Bill pushed his boxer's body towards Queen Street.

Lucky stiff. Nothing to worry about except broads. Gets laid all the time. Maybe a young broad would be good for me. Change of oil.

Married to Sophie twenty-eight years. Karl screwed her uxoriously every three weeks. It took him a long time to get an erection. He fingered her. Dry. Sophie toddled out of bed in her chintz wrapper, reached into the bathroom medicine cabinet for a daub of vaseline. When she heaved into bed again Karl's cock was soft. She played with it.

—Now. Before it gets soft again.

She spread her fatty thighs and he steered it into her.

144

Wallowed about. In and out.

—Are ya coming yet, she heaved to help, and let out a dry fart.

—No. I'm not coming, he breathed heavily as he performed the act, as she grunted and farted. Goddam hard labor. No sky rockets. Another fart, a long, slow, high-pitched sneaker with a foul smell.

—Jesus Christ, Sophie, do you have to do that when we're fucking? Do you have to fart?

—Couldn't help it. Sneaked out. Hurry up. I'm getting tired.

—What...about...me? Karl was slowing. I'm dead beat. I'm only doing this because....

He couldn't think of a good reason. He gave it another try. Could she make it tight for him? Karl felt a slight nudge against his penis. Maybe he would come. He went faster. Sophie bucking up against him, sweat oozing down from her hairy armpits. Globules of liquid on her neck and between her breasts.

—No use, Karl slowed down, stopped.

—Hold it Karl, she shrieked, I'm coming. I'm coming. She held fast against him. Her face distorted into a caricature of ecstasy. A writhing mound of drenched fat. O-h-h-h-h-h-h.

Karl tried to achieve his own orgasm and failed. Sophie jerked him off while he lay back and imagined what it would be like with one of the strippers at the burlesque house.

He came at last. A slight pain with each contraction. Have to see Doc Berger.

—*Star Weekly*, please Karl, the salesgirl from Belgium Glove and Hosiery offered a worn George V nickel.

—Sure, Lois. Trim girl. Legs somewhat thin.

Karl felt the pressure against his bladder. The need again. Pissing frequently with difficulty. Delay and pain. Underwear urine-stained.

—Just getting older, Karl. Doc Berger assured him. But we'll check out everything just to be sure.

—Now then, Karl, off with the trousers. Let's see the crown jewels. Now cough. Good. Fine pair you've got.

Now bend over. Doc Berger inserted his lubricated, rubber gloved finger.

—Hmm. Hmm. He hummed as he massaged the gland. Enjoying it? Karl felt a minor orgasm coming. A drop of fluid at the tip of his penis.

—Prostate is a bit swollen. Normal for a man your age. Back ache?

—Yeah, doc. By the end of the day it really catches me.

—Had any trouble achieving an orgasm?

—So who fucks? I only use it for passing water.

—Any pain?

—Yeah. Burning feeling.

—All right Karl, you can get dressed now. It may be an infection of the prostate. I'll give you a prescription. If it's anything different I'll let you know.

—You don't think it's...Karl asked with apprehension.

—Don't worry. It isn't cancer. A baby can't hold his water and neither can a lot of older men. You should see some of them. You'd feel much better about yourself. He pointed out the window. There. Getting off the street car. Yaponchik.

The old geezer was quite drunk. He was gesturing to the motorman, babbling in Yiddish. He wouldn't move. A trickle of urine was seeping out of him making a puddle on the floor. The uniformed employee of the T.T.C. grabbed a withered arm and helped Yaponchik down the two steel steps of the tram. Moved him like a wind-up toy past the stationary traffic and deposited him on the sidewalk outside Shapiro's Drug Store.

Yaponchik, legs apart, finished peeing. A tremor agitated his bones. He leaned into the gutter. A sour gruel burst from his mouth and splashed down his bristly chin, onto his checked flannel shirt, over his brown twill pants, into and over his stained, black leather boots.

Relieved, the neighborhood's Jewish alcoholic tottered unsteadily to Shapiro's window, leaned his rough cheek against the cool glass, dribbling a design of mucous abstraction. He turned to greet Doc Berger coming from his second-floor office on his way to the Mount Sinai. The physician-surgeon, side-stepped, passed by. Gabriel parked his bike outside the Standard Theater and offered assistance.

—You, boy. You a Jewish boy? Help me. The stinking fingers of the old man tightened against Gabriel's arm.

—Where would you like to go?

—Uh-uh-uh-uh-uh to the beer parlor. Go, he commanded. Gabriel took a tentative step forward, then another. Yaponchik lost his hold and fell heavily on his face. A crowd of schoolboys gathered.

—Ya-pon-chik. Ya-pon-chik, they shouted in glee.

—Uh-uh-uh-uh, he grabbed at Gabriel's outstretched hand and pulled himself up painfully. He turned to the juvenile tormentors and screamed, Ge-raddeh-here. Go way.

Blue bottles were buzzing around his face. The rheumy eyes, partially-closed against the bright summerlight. The white hair, matted and limp around his craggy head.

—We go.

Past Shopsowitz Delicatessen, past Sam the Hatter, past Ginsberg's Barber Shop, the patriarch and the youth advanced one careful step after another. Arrived at the Paramount Kosher Hotel, Yaponchik released Gabriel at the Men's Entrance on D'Arcy street. Inside into the gloom.

Fast exit. Ejected. Sprawled on the dusty pavement.

—It's Yaponchik.

—Is he dead?

—Just can't leave the stuff alone. Boy he's really in bad shape this time.

One eye opens with effort. Mouth gradually closes. Shut.

—Uh-uh-uh-uh-uh-up. I get up. He attempts the vertebrate position for locomotion. He looks about. Familiar faces everywhere. They all know Yaponchik.

—A nickel. A nickel. For a glass of beer. He implores. Brushing away the flies.

—Go on home and sleep it off.

—Yeah. Down in the cellar with the dog.

Bulldog Drummond arrives on his police motorcycle. Heavy of face, heavy of ass, the scourge of Spadina Avenue.

—O.K. Poppa. Let's go. Paddy wagon be here in a minute. He seizes Yaponchik by the frayed collar and

147

props him against a post.

—*Bei mir bist du shayn*, Yaponchik serenades the on-lookers. He tries a little dance, a couple of steps, a marionette held in the bulldog grip. The Police Van arrives.

—Uh-uh-uh-uh-Yaponchik stammers as he is hoisted in-side. The door clanks shut.

—Hooray for Yaponchik somebody yells.

The face appears behind the barred window.

—I be back. I be back, Yaponchik promises. The Black Maria speeds away.

In the Men's Room of Scholes Hotel, Karl stood at the urinal waiting for the flow. It came reticently, in spurts. The pressure relieved, Karl buttoned up, passed through the men's beverage room greeting Shoesie the waiter, white spats on his well-shined boots. Room filling up. Small squares of tables with glasses of draft ale. Ill-lit by low-watt incandescence. The imbibers joking, drinking, singing. *The Sash Me Father Wore*. All good Orange Men.

Karl was in trouble. The big payoff. Fifty bucks to Morry. Ten to Julie Kovics, the hoofer at Shea's. Twenty-five to Froggy, the pawnbroker across from City Hall. Others. All together, a hundred and sixty five. A lot of moolah to scrape together. Borrow it from Bill Margolies. Repay in one week at thirty per cent interest. Pay up or he'd find himself with real bladder trouble. Rubber truncheons against his kidneys.

—*Star. Telegram*. Night Edition. Karl offered the latest news. Waiting impatiently for Gabriel to return. Waiting to flee. Through the concave transparency of Adams store window he regarded idly the array of Mr. Adams' finest furniture. Ponderous, velvet-covered sofas and easy chairs. Heavy, oak dining room tables. Radio highboys with standard wave, short wave, police calls, ship to shore. Big global faces for easy turning. A few shoppers wandered about, looking, testing, not buying. That youngster is going to spill his ice cream on the couch. Yup, great glob of it, chocolate ripple. The ginger-haired father slaps him, drags him away, his girl-wife following. The trio emerges into the street. The kid is bawling. Slap. Keep quiet. Come on. Past Karl's news stand. Lost in the distance.

Go home and make another in the same image. Fuck. And fuck again. Bring them into the world. Go on relief. Shit-stained diapers. Shit-stained assholes. Feeding. Crying all hours. Colds. Measles. Whooping cough. Diphtheria. Pneumonia. If they survive, accidents to kill them. Grow up and want to fuck too. In God's image did man create them. Pulled from bleeding wombs in operating rooms at the General, Western, the Mount Sinai. Every hour. Like monkeys at the zoo, baboons screwing in the bedrooms of the nation. Everybody fucking everywhere. Then fucked out, into the Old Folks Home. Senile but still shooting sperm. The old ones humping away. Finally shrivel up. Die.

* * *

Gabriel, supper-bound, avoided the Honey Dew Shop. Not for him the synthetic orange drink, the pulpy pale Ritz Carlton hot dog.

He turned right at Woolworth's Five and Ten Cent Store. Eaton's next door. Across the way the Robert Simpson Company. Saturday shoppers everywhere. At Bay Street the clock in the City Hall tower showed ten minutes past five.

The Cenotaph, an empty tomb, before the municipal building. A faded wreath of blossoms propped against it. Chiselled into its concrete sides a solemn memorial:

> ZEEBRUGGE
> Dedicated by the City of Toronto
> to the undying memory of
> those who fell in the
> GREAT WAR 1914-1918
> This stone was laid on July 24, 1925 by
> Field Marshal the Earl Haig
> Commander-in-Chief of British Forces
> in the Great War.
>
> Thomas Foster
> Mayor
>
> Ypres. Somme. Mt. Sorel. Vimy
> Passchendaele. Amiens. Arras. Cambrai.
>
> TO OUR GLORIOUS DEAD.

149

A wilted Union Jack flapped on a flag pole nearby. Gabriel read the exotic names of places again. Ypres. Wipers. Passchendaele. Passiondally. A tour of Belgium and France. Khaki clad boys. Now gloriously dead. Bedded down forever in Flanders Field where poppies blow.

Gabriel crossed Bay street to Shea's Vaudeville. The posters proclaimed: Now Appearing: The International Baritone JULES BLEDSOE, Old Man River Himself. *Show Boat's* Great Star in Person. Coming next week: CAB CALLOWAY, KING OF JAZZ.

From the stage door Henry Armetta, frantic Italian comic shouted instructions to all present. They obeyed, mindful of his success in *One Night of Love* with Grace Moore.

—Alla right. Now, ahm gonna look happy. You taka de pich. Armetta in the center of a group of Shea's chorus girls, leg-kicking with the rest of them. The man with the movie camera cranked the handle.

—Nuff, Armetta signaled. Now, you taka pitch of street, den t'eater, den City 'All, den all people, den back to me wit' dancing girls. He reached behind Julie Kovics and pinched her ass. She slapped him playfully.

—Ees feela nice and hard, no soft. *Come la mia signora*, he chuckled. You and me, we have grande festa tonight, after show, okay? She cuddled beside him for the camera.

Gabriel ran over to get Armetta's signature. He had twenty-three pages of autographs already in his book. Eddie Cantor, Georgie Jessel, Ben Blue. On pink and buff and green pages.

A-R-M-E-T-T-A.....Henry. The comedian spelled out his name on the blank orange page. Then he added: To my good friend....hey, whatsa you name? G-A-B-R-I-E-L. Si. Hey, where'sa you horn? Ha. Ha. Armetta returned to his flock of chattering geese.

Gabriel walked back to Queen Street. Dilapidated shops. Luggage. Junk. Electric goods. Jewellery. He would eat at the Better Ole Fish and Chips. An order of fish, ten cents. Chips, five cents. Two slices of bread (buttered) five cents. Coke, five cents.

Inside. Smells of oil and vinegar. Potatoes sizzling.

Halibut frying in the troughs behind the wooden counter, its yellow paint long peeled away. Tables scattered about the room. Kitchen chairs. Linoleum showing in patches on the wooden floor.

Gabriel lifted himself onto a stool beside the doorman from the Roxy.

—The works, Gabriel ordered.

—To go?

—No. Eat here.

Ritual for enjoying the piscatorial provender at the Better Ole:

Separate fish from chips. Sprinkle salt evenly all over.
Pepper heavily. Perforate fried potatoes and fried fish
with fork. Pour on brown vinegar. Let soak in. Pour
more vinegar. More salt. More pepper. Fork fish. Eat
fish. Butter bread. Eat bread. Equal mouthfuls of
fish and bread. Pick up each chip between thumb and
index finger of left hand. Chew. Savor. Swallow. Sip
coke through straw. Another chip. Another sip. Last
of the fish. Sop up pepper-salt-vinegar-oil with remain-
der of bread. Finish coke.

Another order of Better Ole Fish and Chips?
Heads — Yes. Tails — No. Toss coin. Tails. Toss again. Two
out of three. Heads. Once more. Heads.

—Chips. To go.

Into his paper cone he poured abundant streams of salt, pepper, vinegar. Time: thirteen before six. Better be getting back. He retraced leisurely steps. He chewed with relish, protracting the demise of each morsel before he speared the next wedge with the wooden pick and brought it happily to his mouth.

Sated by his evening meal he could manage two more hours at the newspaper stand.

At eight o'clock, Saturday night would belong to him.

\* \* \*

At seven that Saturday evening, Hosiah H. Hunter un-locked the glass door of the storefront Pentecostal Mission at 123 Dundas Street West. He had much hope, more faith and mostly high expectations of charity in the form of offerings for the miracles of healing, promised though not delivered.

Into the mission seeking remission, shambled the penitents. Ulcerous. Arthritic. Deaf. Depressed. Lame. Blind.

Into the Pentecostal Mission, spiritsanctified, fired with zealousness, tripped the pale maidens, bible clutching, eager for song and prayer. Trooping behind them the black-clad matrons and their spectacled spouses. Temperance people. A shouting-to-Jehovah contingent.

Into the Pentecostal on another mission (in expectation of entertainment) loped Horny Fox, early for his rendezvous with Gabriel who promised stage door access to the Roxy Burlesque in time for the final disrobement.

At the half hour while still the congregation was arriving, Hosiah H. Hunter nodded to Miss Chisholm in the front row. She arose and came to the front, embraced the heavy oak pulpit and reedily announced.

—Let us announce our joy in the Lord. Let us all sing. Washed in the blood.

She began, brave but strained in her delivery. Joined by other voices in high treble. Sparrow sounds, rising to heaven's vault. Washed in the blood of the Lamb. Horny Fox sangalong the words his own, the melody learned in class invoking another hunter in a British glade:

—Do ye ken John Peel
With his cock made of steel
And his balls made of brass
With a poker up his ass.
Do ye ken John P-e-e-e-l?

More of the faithful entered and took the remaining seats. The song ended Miss Chisholm shook the hand of H.H.H. and retired to her seat. At his place behind the lectern the man of God commanded silence with hands upraised. His features beatific, his body rigid, he reached for the Book and elevated it.

—Wilt thou be made whole, he demanded.

—We will, the response from the congregants. We will. Praise the Lord. Bless his holy name. Hallelujah.

152

The minister intoned the words from the authorized King James version, a melange of milk and honey, engulfing his auditors:

—*And Jesus went up to Jerusalem. Now there is at Jerusalem by the sheep market a pool which is called in the Hebrew tongue Bethesda, having five porches. In these lay a great multitude of impotent folk, of blind, halt, withered, waiting for the moving of the water. For an angel went down at a certain season into the pool and troubled the water. Whosoever then first after the troubling of the water stepped in was made whole of whatsoever disease he had...*

—Praise the Lord, the woman beside the palsied man cheered.

—*And a certain man was there*, the gospeler continued, *which had an infirmity thirty and eight years. The palsied man rose aided by his companion and proclaimed, Here I am. Jesus.*

—Save him, Jesus. Make him whole, Jesus. The appeal echoed from voices about the room.

—Yeah man, Jesus, save his hole, Horny Fox demanded.

Hunter signaled for silence.

—*And when Jesus saw him and knew that he had been now a long time in that case, he saith unto him, Wilt thou be made whole? The impotent man answered him, Sir, I have no man, when the water is troubled to put me into the pool, but while I am coming another steppeth down before me.*

Hunter put down the book. He looked up and around, pausing for emphasis. All eyes on him. He stepped forth, arms raised, finger pointing, stopped in the midst of the assemblage:

—*And Jesus saith unto him, Rise, take up thy bed and walk.*

Hunter stopped, transfixed, waiting, all with him waiting, for the ultimate utterance. The preacher man opened his eyes, stretched forth his arms and thundered:

—*And immediately the man was made whole and took up his bed and walked.*

Up from their folding chairs of varnished, white pine

they arose and invoked the Lord's saving grace:

—Bless us. Heal us. Make us whole.

Hunter motioned for them to be seated.

—The Lord is the one who heals, he replied. Thy will be done, O Lord. Verily, verily I say unto you: the Son of Man can do nothing of Himself but what He seeth the Father do. For what things soever He doeth, these also doeth the Son likewise. For the Father loveth the Son, and sheweth him all things that ye may marvel.

H.H.H., thumping the page with the living words. Raising a jowly, closely-shaven face to the believers. Barker for the carnival of the Lord. Showbiz of the spirit.

—Will you accept him? Will you accept Jesus Christ? Now is the time. Come forward. Kneel. Pray with me.

Horny Fox advanced, one of the first of a straggly group. He had seen the light. He chose a place next to a thin girl. Blond wisps of hair hung limp about the pocked face. He smelled her fragrance, lily of the valley. He saw through partly-closed lids the cones of her breasts within the simple dress. He shifted closer to her and rested his hand against her thigh as he prayed with vigor:

—Our Father, which art in heaven, hallowed be Thy name.

Thy kingdom come... she swayed against him as she prayed..., Thy will be done.

Horny stroked her lean rump prayerfully. Amen.

—We come now to the laying on of hands, Hunter announced and Horny removed his.

Hunter touched her and she fell back on the linoleum floor, groaning and clutching her hands in tight embrace.

—Slain in the Lord, Hunter shouted. He touched another. Slain in the Lord. A touch. A touch. They fell about him. Humble servant Hosiah Hunter, working miracles after the manner of Jesus, and Phillip, and Paul.

—Is any among you afflicted? Let him pray. Is any sick among you? The prayer of faith shall heal the sick and the Lord shall raise him up. And if he have committed sins, they shall be forgiven him.

He went among the bobbing, babbling throng, exhorting them: Confess your faults one to another and pray for one another, that ye may be healed.

He looked down at the convulsions of the young man and the pale maiden.

—Slain in the Lord, the Hunter marvelled. Amen. Amen. The young man murmured. The maiden groaned.

Testimonies of healing.

—I was blind, the old woman announced. Stark blind. Then I shouted to the Lord, Restore me, dear Lord. Jesus, save me. And He did. She looked with pouched eyes up and about her, daring rebuttal.

—I was a drunkard. I drank everything — hair tonic, rubbing alcohol, a gallon of rubby a week. While my wife went to work, I drank. I was in Don Jail for ninety days. Then I prayed to the Lord, Save me. Save me. Jesus save a sinner.

—Hallelujah, they shrieked. Save that man!

—Then I came to the Mission and repented. In a flash I was saved. I gave up drinking and smoking.

—Cunting, Horny Fox whispered into the ear of the prostrate lily.

Hosiah Hunter nodded to Miss Chisholm who produced a silver chalice and making her way about the congregation asked, in the name of the Lord, for contributions to continue His work.

And the people gave heed, seeing the miracles He did.

# 12

## BROTHER CAN YOU SPARE A DIME

Antonio DeMarco had a small business. He rebuilt car
generators in the garage behind his house. When he went
bankrupt the dealer repossessed his 1932 Ford pickup
truck. Angela DeMarco implored for Christian charity as
the driver slammed the door shut. Her five daughters
huddled together on the veranda sniffled. Her husband
stood helpless at the curb as the vehicle rolled away. He
felt the apple in his gorge choking him. He applied for
relief. Queued for vouchers. On Christmas Eve Mrs.
DeMarco hanged herself from a pipe in the cellar. The
children were taken away by the Catholic Children's Aid
Society. Antonio moved into an attic room on Bellevue
near the fire hall. He turned to philosophy. He penned a
thin volume of aphorisms interspersed with injunctions
about the end of the world. *Lasciate ogni speranza.* An
apocalyptic vision. He set the type by hand and printed
the work on an old Gordon press. He offered the Jeremiad
door-to-door. He accepted coins, coffee and sandwiches.

## STOUTHEARTED MEN

The single unemployed encamped in the bandshell in
Queen's Park behind the Provincial Legislature where the
band of His Majesty's 48th Highlanders performed. Tunes
of glory. Songs of Empire. Military marches. Gilbert and
Sullivan. On newspapers and rags the dispossessed passed
the summer nights. Jobless young men, youths from
school, graying factory workers, loggers from British
Columbia, farmhands from Manitoba, hoboes from other
jungles. Riding the rails to Ottawa.

Their shacks appeared in the Don Valley. A community
of tin dwellings with tar paper roofs. Members of the Communist Party came to Leonard Avenue, knocking on doors
for a handout. They fought with bailiffs, interfered with

their legal duty of evicting families. The bailiffs summoned the sheriffs who called the mounted police who beat up and arrested the dissenters.

Gabriel listened to their arguments in Alexandra Park. Ukrainians from the Labor Temple on Bathurst Street. Trying to articulate grand passions in a tongue not their own.

—Give it us work, no relief.

They were given shovels to dig ditches. Make-work projects.

On a Sunday in the park, a native-born Canadian, descendant of Egerton Ryerson, perched on a box of Sunlight Soap, brushed his blond hair from his face and advanced his thesis.

—Look to the Soviet Union. What do you find? Full employment. This very minute while you and I are languishing under a corrupt and inefficient capitalistic system the Russian worker is busy, happily building the great Communist State. Some of our best Canadian engineers, unable to find work at home, are helping in that mighty task. They have left this country where one million are unemployed. One in ten. Where four million are on relief. Two out of every five of us begging for the right to exist.


## WE'RE IN THE MONEY

—The only solution is Communism. The Soviet proletariat has shown the way to a glorious new life. Down with the Bay Street robber barons. Down with the Liberals. Down with the Conservative Party.

The young fellows from the Duke Street Hostel shouted approval. They had to leave shortly to make the rounds of the middle-class homes north of Bloor Street. They would avoid Christie Pits where the Fascists met to extol the corporate state and peddle copies of *The Protocols of Zion*.

—Hitler has the answer. Full employment in an Aryan State. Wipe out the Jewish cancer in our midst.

R.B. Bennett, the Prime Minister, had a solution. Conscript all the able-bodied unemployed. Put them into work battalions at twenty cents an hour. Let them build the highway. Mr. C.L. Burton, President of the Robert Simpson Company thought it was a capital idea.

## CLAP HANDS. HERE COMES CHARLIE

The mounted police were busy breaking up meetings and bashing in heads. Their authority, Section 98 of the Criminal Code: Promoting changes by unlawful means.

Samson, caught in an onslaught of horses hooves, suffered a broken arm when a meeting at Spadina crescent was disrupted by the constabulary. His bicycle tires were punctured and the frame bent. His dog broke away from the leash and ran down Spadina. Harry Benjamin, Undertaker, observed from the window of his establishment. Reluctantly he left to prepare a cadaver for the next day's burial. He hoped the Lord would spare him for many years to come.

Charlie Millard, Labor leader, submitted the title of his address to the President of the Canadian Commonwealth Youth Movement at the University of Toronto: *Hepburn Must Go.* His talk was banned.

SECTION 98 NOT BRITISH, PASTOR HOLDS.
REV. ELLIS STANLEY CHAMPIONS RIGHT OF FREE SPEECH

—People are being jailed for no other crime than that of expressing themselves. In all ages men have dared to utter ideas that were unpopular. And they have suffered as a consequence. Socrates the great philosopher was compelled to taste of the hemlock. For Jesus it was crucifixion. In other times, Kings, Queens and Statesmen have had to face the noose or the guillotine in payment for their political crimes. Now our nation jeopardizes the freedom of the individual by the most Un-British clause of the Criminal Code, whereby a man is condemned because it is suspected that he has broken the law.

## SOMEONE TO WATCH OVER ME

REV. A.E. SMITH PROTESTS TRUMPED-UP CHARGES

The general secretary of the Canadian Labor Defence

League attacked the Liberal Government as slaves of the capitalist class at a meeting protesting the arrest of six Long Branch workers facing a charge of conspiracy.

—The government has thought to intimidate us but Mr. Roebuck is terribly mistaken if he thinks he has succeeded. The time has gone by when the capitalist class can afford to ridicule the workers. There is only one way for the workers to gain their ends. Organize. Unless the workers save themselves they will never be saved.


## I'D LOVE TO SPEND ONE HOUR WITH YOU

### SIMPLE JOYS NEEDED SAYS TORONTO PASTOR
### SPIRIT OF HOPEFULNESS BEST CURE FOR PRESENT EVILS

The Rev. Foster Gregory took a small sip from his glass of iced-water, blotted his lips with the starched linen napkin, and paused to let the meaning of his words make their impact. He had carefully prepared his after dinner talk, replete with homilies and messages of inspired devotion. The Women's Association had (praise God) done a superb job of supervising the annual event.

—The world needs many things today. But the most needful thing of all is a new spirit of hopefulness. A faith that, ultimately, good will triumph over evil.

He waited for the applause, a most enthusiastic response.

—Take joy in the simple things of life.


## AIN'T WE GOT FUN?

### RED RALLY CURBED. THREE MEN ARRESTED.

More than two score of Toronto's finest moved into action last evening against a group of girls and men walking down Spadina Avenue singing the Red Internationale.

The contingent of mounted police, motorcycle officers and patrolmen broke up a rally scheduled for Queen and Spadina, intended as a protest against the prosecution of nine Toronto Communists. Arrested and charged with obstructing police were Morris Hermann, a German, age 37; James Grant of Oshawa, age 32; Timothy Johns, age 22 of Winnipeg. Several of the constables lost their hats in the course of a wild scramble in a dark lane. One had his uniform splattered with mud and one epaulet was torn off. The police were jeered by the girls and taunted by the men. Constable Peake suffered a bruised finger, the result of a bite from one of the rioters. Grant hurled a brick at Constable Kennedy. It flew past his head and smashed a plate glass window of E.H. Dworkin, Steamship Agents at 525 Dundas. A mounted officer chased Grant into the Liberty Theater where he was apprehended in the women's washroom.

## BOULEVARD OF BROKEN DREAMS

Up where University Avenue embraced the seat of government, in the littered green of Queen's Park, Gabriel sat in the bandstand and shared Red Rose Tea in a chipped porcelain mug and ate slices of Christie's bread smeared with Skippy Peanut Butter.

When the first drops splattered staccato on the sloping slate roof the group huddled more closely together. The air hung humid and stale about the unwashed bodies. The news of the day was all about Comrades Beatty and Baker:

—The accused were charged with advocating force and violence. When arrested Beatty was lecturing to thirty-four men who were on city relief and instructing them to organize and demand what they wanted and to take what they needed if refused. Sgt. Nursey averred that Beatty was a member and organizer of the National Unemployed Council, a Communist organization that incited people to break the law.

## THE CLOUDS WILL SOON ROLL BY

### GOD IS LOVE, SAYS MINISTER

—With the coming of the Kingdom of God there will be no criminals, no robbery. The urge to steal will have been taken away. There will be no police to effect arrests but to do those other courteous acts that make them beloved now by children and travellers. There will be no armies.

160

The League of Nations will flourish because munitions will be nationalized. Economical, political and moral injustice will vanish. Righteousness and justice will flow down as from the hills and all the children of men will be blessed. Thus spake the Rev. Newton Summerfield.

## ANYTHING GOES

The rain had stopped. The moon was a crescent of June light in the star-fretted sky. The bronzed likeness of Albert's spouse, Victoria, planted heavily atop the stone pedestal, stared imperiously south toward the General Hospital. The Banting Institute was dark.

In the bandshell James Stephen Lever, Ph.D., unemployed, pounded his fist for emphasis. His bony face was animated, mouth shaping the words, eyes glinting. In like fashion he had addressed his peers in the Debating Society at the University of British Columbia. After graduation Lever had come to Toronto for his doctoral studies. His dissertation, well-received — Rhetorical Considerations in the Development of the English Language. His extra curricular interests: The effects of the Depression on Canadian society. He became involved in the economics of poverty, joined the Communist Party and was now one of its most zealous missionaries.

James Lever urged his listeners to take action, to overthrow the government of Mr. Bennett, to seize power in their own hands, to establish a Communist State.

Lever utilized rhetorical considerations to advance his argument. He piled metaphor on simile, added onomatopoeia, dissolved into metonomy, interjected apostrophe, used irony with telling effect and applied great dabs of oxymoron and alliteration. His humor was parody and he used it against the dominant families of Canada, his own included, who exploited the masses. Against the robberbarons of America. Against the imperialists of Great Britain who kept enslaved the sub-continent of India and much of Africa.

But was there reason to despair? No! The new dawn of the brotherhood of man was about to shed its roseate hues over the world. Foretold by Marx and Engels. Nicolai Lenin, the first practitioner. The inspired leadership of Josef Vissarionovich, the man of steel, who was even now directing the growing might of the Soviet Union for the benefit of all mankind.

—Oppressors beware. Long live the Socialist Internationale.

The shout echoed from many mouths. Long live the Socialist Internationale. Lever paused, took breath and began the song, his left arm uplifted, fist clenched.

Arise ye prisoners of starvation.
Arise ye wretched of the earth.
For justice thunders condemnation.
A better world's in birth.

As he sang he looked about at his brothers in thrall, eyes commanding response. A rough voice joined his. Then another. Faltering at first then swelling.

No more tradition's chains shall bind us.

They rose, shouting, fists in the air.

Arise ye slaves.

Gabriel, exhilarated, humming the melody where the words escaped him.

Tis the final conflict.
Let each stand in his place.
The International Party
Shall be the human race.

The ragged company shouted, threw hats in the air, applauded, whistled. Gabriel shook the speaker's hand.

—Down with the Henry Tories. Down with Bennett. A job for everybody. No more relief. Long live the dictatorship of the proletariat.

A flashlight penetrated the dark, behind it the voice of Bulldog Drummond.

—Now then, what's all this about? Stop your noise and go to sleep or I'll run in the whole bleeding lot of you.

—Capitalist minion, Lever shouted. Servant of the ruling class. Enemy of the people.

He began the song anew: —Arise ye prisoners of.

Drummond struck him on the head. Rubber truncheoned, Lever fell. Gabriel bent to help him and was

162

kicked in the rear by the police officer.

—Get on home, young fellow. Does your ma know you're out so late with this bunch of anarchists? Go on now. And remember the rest of you. Any more shouting and you'll cool off in the Don Jail.

Nobody to thunder condemnation. The wretched of the earth protested weakly. Mutterings of good night, as they stretched out on the bandshell floor. Bulldog Drummond strode off, mounted his Harley-Davidson, and farted away into the night.

Somebody began *The Internationale* again, hesitatingly, falteringly. It faded and died. All quiet now.

Gabriel heard the echo of his footsteps, the metal cleats of his heels clacking on the cement as he passed the green-house of the University. The panes reflected the moon-light, myriad-shafted. A streetcar bang-gang-clanged by on metal wheels. Last trolley. It was half-past one, Sunday morning. June 4. 1933. Fourteen years ago at this hour in the town of Opatow in the voivodship of Kielce his mother had exerted the final contractions and expelled him into the world.

The City Hall clock tolled the half-hour. The reverberations cannonballed across the city in hollow diminuendos. They called to Gabriel: Sad and lonely. Sad and lonely.

He stopped to rest on a bench outside the Reference Library. Inside was the accumulated wisdom of the world. Tomes arranged neatly in stacks. Words once issuing from living flesh. Authors, long dead and interred. As you are now, so once was I. As I am now, you soon will be. The Psalmists of old knew the truth:

—As for man his days are as grass. As a flower of the field so he flourisheth. For the wind passeth over it and it is gone. And the place thereof shall know it no more.

He was crying softly as he inserted the iron key into the keyhole at No. 47. His mortality had come upon him.

### LET'S PUT OUT THE LIGHTS AND GO TO SLEEP

THOUSANDS IN NEED AS WINTER APPROACHES.

At the central bureau for civic relief the unemployed

163

waited for the card, good for two meals and a sleep at the House of Industry. Or were directed to other institutions: the British Welcome and Welfare League, The British Dominion Emigration Service, The British Settlement Society, Y.M.C.A., United Church Boys Hostel, Catholic Welfare Bureau, Church of England, The Federation of Jewish Philanthropies. Each according to his racial, religious and ethnic background.

Waiting, the men compared experiences.

—I've been sleeping in the bushes below the Princes' Viaduct. A fine shelter too. Virginia creepers, lots of wild ivy, you know. Well, the cops found my place and bust it up. Brought me to No. 1 Station for the night, they did. The next day I found a spot down in the Don Valley. The brickyard. But they kicked me out of there too, you see. Then I tried the box cars for awhile. Gotta look out for the railway dicks though. I liked the church halls best for sleeping in.

The North of Ireland brogue droned on. The shaggy-haired speaker, with a bright, orange stubble entertained his fellows with tales of nightly escapades. Trapping and roasting bed bugs. Searching through Rosedale garbage cans for leftovers. He was an optimist.

—I've just come in for a bit of luck, I can tell you. Got me a cleanup job in a doctor's house up in Forest Hill. It's ten hours work and the pay is five dollars. That'll see me in grand style for awhile. Tomorrow night I'll be sleeping in a clean bed in the Mission. I'm thinkin it's well worth a quarter.

—The Immigration Hall is a good place, interjected the lame man. He leaned on his cane. Slept there last night. Me and about three hundred other guys.

—You should try the St. Vincent de Paul Hostel.

—That's for Micks. Me, I prefer Church of England.

—Red Cross in the place. Treat us ex-service men great. Coffee and donuts, too.

One suggested the armouries. Two meals a day. Another discovered Miss Maison's noon hour treat. Sandwiches at St. Lawrence Hall.

—Just tell the woman you been waiting for a job at the

employment bureau.

Much banter and camaraderie. Announcements of the benefactions of the great men of the city. Wm. Wrigley Jr. had equipped Wellington House as a hostel. The Barker Bread Company was providing the staff of life at Dundas House.

The finest of discipline prevailed in the central bureau waiting room under the watchful eyes of Sergeant Holmes. On the lookout for queue jumpers. Occasional scuffle. The federal authorities were sending reinforcements. Too much for one man. Hold on now, that chap over there appears to be unwell.

—What's up mate? Not ill are you? Have a sit here on this bench.

—Hungry, I guess. Just got in from Saskatoon. Haven't slept much.

—Try the Scott Institute, Holmes advised confidentially. They'll fix you up all right.


## TEA FOR TWO

IMBIBERS OF BEER TO GET NO RELIEF.
WORKER REPORTED ON THE JOB WHEN DRUNK.
RELIEF RECIPIENTS RELIEVED OF LIQUOR PERMITS.


## YOU TAKE ADVANTAGE OF ME

The Minister of Welfare announced that each man must work for his relief. He threatened jail for those who refused. Men will be paid the prevailing rate and permitted to work sufficient hours each week to cover the cost of food and rent needed by their families. Each single man will be required to put in two days work on the drainage ditch in exchange for maintenance. They will also be required to work in the city woodyard sawing logs for a short time and will receive $1.50 for each cord of wood cut. Other work will be provided, digging for sewers and water mains, grading and levelling city park lands. Milk, bread, fuel and clothing will be provided as at present by the government. Household utensils, bedding, glasses and

165

other extras must be provided by the municipality. Special investigators will visit the homes of those on relief.

## DO, DO, DO

—Buy a poppy. Help a veteran. He fought for you.

## OH, LADY BE GOOD

—Single girls and women are assisted on the same basis as single men. But there is a great disinclination to the taking of housework, particularly among girls of foreign-born parents, most of whom are only prepared to consider employment in stores and factories.

## I WANNA BE LOVED BY YOU

—It is greatly to be feared that in very many cases the initiative and spirit of independence of the invidual is being seriously undermined since many of the recipients of relief are better fed and housed than they were when self-supporting. The seeds of dependency are being sown. People are becoming *relief minded* as evidenced by the fact that so many, when employed, make no provision for the time of idleness. They prefer to spend their earnings in many cases on things which are not absolutely essential.

## BODY AND SOUL

The queue, formed since eight in the morning, begins to move as the doors of the Scott Institute open precisely at ten. Old faces, etched by time and weather. Young, pinched visages. Bums and rubbies. Poets. Philosophers. Scholars. Withdrawn. Waiting. Dreaming. The Reverend Morris Zeidman cares for them all at the Presbyterian Mission House on Elizabeth Street.

Handouts of groceries. Clothing. Delousing. Vouchers for haircuts at the Barbers' Academy. Cash in an emergency.

Mostly they come for the meals.

In the kitchen of the three storey building round-bellied

kettles of potato soup and urns of coffee simmer on the black, six burner stove.

The first group shuffles into the dining hall. They take their places humbly at the long tables, caps removed. They study the piles of sliced bread before them.

—For what we are about to receive, make us truly thankful, in the name of our Lord Jesus Christ. Amen.

The convert to the faith of John Knox pronounces the blessing. The Jew from Czestochowa whose forebears, invited by Casimir the Great, settled the country and made it to prosper. And enjoyed the benevolence of Sigismund and suffered the Tartar and Russian oppressions. And the fiats of the Catholic Church. And grew up in the shadow of *Matka Boska*, the Black Madonna. And endured the blood libels. Morris Zeidman, who escaped from the *pan* and the peasant to Toronto. Who worked ten hours each day in a machine shop. Who attended night classes and studied for the ministry and was ordained and appointed head of the Presbyterian Mission to the Jews. Who thenceforth labored on behalf of those who sought his benison. Those who now grab for bread and tear chunks and stuff the pieces into mouths of rotting teeth. Those who sniff appreciatively the sharp smell of steaming spuds spooned out by the good wife Annie.

Stephen Lever, Ph.D. eats quickly, hunching over the bowl, eats silently, composing a revolutionary tract as he munches. By his side a codger with feathers of fine, white hair chews without benefit of teeth his hunk of bread, dipped for soggy convenience into the broth.

The rhythmic slurps from large metal spoons, then the bowls drained, the adam's apples bobbing with each gulp. Mugs of coffee, white with milk from City Dairy. Broken biscuits, salvaged from the wholesaler, a tasty treat.

Soon finished, up from the tables, make way for the others. At the door, hands reach for rolls donated by Silverstein's Bakery. Stuffed into frayed pockets for the evening's repast.

The Reverend appeals to his neighbors, Aaron Eisen and Jacob Wasserman, for eggs and poultry. For everyone he has a kindly greeting. For Jacob Krasnow the junk dealer.

167

For the book man Harry Greenberg. For Jenny Wong who sells cigars. For Foo Wong the barber and Yen Bok Toah the druggist.

In response to his weekly message, *The Good Samaritan's Corner* in the *Telegram*, the Rev. Zeidman receives donations. From church groups and service clubs. From wealthy widows. From businessmen.

—I'm sorry young man, the Reverend apologizes to James Lever. I have no shoes today. No clothes that will fit you. Except this tuxedo. Do you have a waiter's job maybe? No? Pity. It's such a fine suit.

The wiry gent in boxer's shorts pushes his way to the front of the gathering crowd.

—A pair of trousers, guv. My good pair was taken last night at the flophouse. I'll kill the bastard, sorry guv, who swiped them. If I ever find him.

—Hello Jim, the Reverend greets the boxer shorts. See what I can find for you. Hello Steve. Happy to see you again. When did you get out of St. Michael's?

—This morning sir. Good to be well again. Can you fix me up, sir, you know, some clothes, maybe a job? Not drinking anymore. Really gonna try hard this time. Help me, sir.

—How about something to eat first? Come back later this afternoon. We'll talk.

The second shift, waiting for grace. Annie is tinkling one of her hymns on the black, upright Nordheimer piano.


## 'S WONDERFUL

—Employ a married man for the winter, lady? What can you afford? Fifty cents a week? Seventy five? One dollar? The Rotary Club will send you a willing worker. He'll shovel the snow, polish the floors, clean the windows, carry out the ashes, whitewash the cellar. Thank you for helping us to help those in need.


## YOU'RE THE TOP

—Gentlemen. As I look about, I am pleased by the

response from the leading citizens of this community. Representatives of business, social service organizations, service clubs, civic departments and boards. I welcome you to the Mayor's Luncheon to thank you for your participation in the greatest *Spring Clean Up, Paint Up And Beautify* campaign in our history. _____

## BUT NOT FOR ME
### SANTA CLAUS NEEDS $5,000 A DAY

—You'll find the kiddies we're concerned about down near the gas works in an old pile of coal, looking for bits of fuel on the railway tracks. They're wondering these days. They don't see any confidence in their parents' eyes. They haven't noticed any bulky parcels being stored up in the top floor clothes closet. Do you think Santa Claus will come, they wonder. Do you? Do you? Send a cheque to *The Star Santa Claus Fund*, 80 King Street West and there will be no doubt about it.

## OF THEE I SING

—And when you elect me Mayor, I'll put all able-bodied men back to work.

—What about the relief handouts? Poison, that's what it is!

The tainted meat, rolled up in wrapping paper, was flung from the balcony of the auditorium of Riverdale Collegiate. It landed at the feet of Controller Sam McBride. The ratepayers at the civic candidates' meeting erupted into hoots and cat-calls. They stood on seats. They crowded towards the platform to see the package. The crowd was brought under control with the help of police from the Pape Avenue Station under the supervision of Detective Sergeant Wm. Nursey.

## I FOUND A MILLION DOLLAR BABY
## IN A FIVE AND TEN CENT STORE

Labor man, James Gill, studying figures just released has

revealed the existence of thirty-six new millionaires in the city since 1929. The number of unemployed continues to climb.

## STRIKE UP THE BAND

### WAR SCARES CAUSED BY ARMS MAKERS
### DUPONT AND OTHERS CARRY ON PROPAGANDA
### IN ALL COUNTRIES

Senator Gerald P. Nye, N. Dakota, Chairman of the U.S. Senate Committee which conducted the armaments probe, continued his crusade for peace last night as he addressed the League of Nations Meeting of the Forest Hill Village Home and School Association. Nearly 700 persons attended.

—The money of munitions makers actually goes out to create war scares. It builds up people against people and nation against nation. It drives, coaxes and teases them into that position where they are a ready market. They have no hesitation in selling to both sides. It is a great irony that the DuPonts, so fearful of Germany, are not averse to selling their patents, their plans, their specifications to the Germans as they sold them to the U.S. and to the allies. With war profits they have built themselves an industrial empire. They have America and all the world paying toll to them on pretty nearly everything the public purchases. The same forces which are at work in the U.S. educating it against Japan are at work in Japan telling it to look out for Uncle Sam.

# 13

## THE SASH ME FATHER WORE

BELFAST OF CANADA HONORS MEMORY OF KING WILLIAM
STREETS OF TORONTO FILLED WITH MUSIC

At the County Orange Hall, the city Assessment Commissioner, George Barley, tall in gleaming plug hat greets Controller Robbins in morning coat and silk topper.

—Glorious day for the glorious twelfth.

John Pitts, Worshipful Preceptor of The Red Cross Royal Black Knights of Ireland, arrives similarly caparisoned.

In Queen's Park the veteran County Marshall, W.H. Billy Harper, impressive on his white steed, has been supervising since half past eight a great display of Orange power. Eight thousand men, women and children. Waiting for the signal to march to the cheers of 100,000 spectators who have already filled the streets and are occupying coigns of vantage on roofs and at windows. Harper knows the route. His 32nd year in the saddle. From Queen's Park Crescent to Yonge, past Albert and James Streets, a right turn, along Queen Street to the City Hall, then west to Dufferin Street and into the Exhibition Grounds.

The air about Billy Harper is alive with sounds. Drums, flutes, fifes, horns, pipes. Among the streamered buses, bannered trucks, ribboned participants, Harper urges his stallion.

—Ready now, we're about to go.

Nine-thirty-two. Two minutes late. The march begins.

It is old but it is beautiful and its colors they are fine;
It was worn at Derry, Aughrim, Eniskillen and the Boyne;
My father wore it when a youth in the by-gone days
of yore;
So on the twelfth I always wear the sash me father wore.

Gabriel, orange crêpe cap peaked on curly black hair, ribbons of red, white and blue around his waist, is on the march too, waving *papier mâché* swallows with fluttering tails that produce a screeching whistle. Up the previous night assembling them. Imported from Japan.

171

—Get your birdie. Can't enjoy the parade without a song-
bird. The kiddies love'em. One nickel. Five cents.

> Over the hills there came a great noise;
> Oh, who could it be but the Protestant boys.
> Up a long ladder, down a short rope;
> Hurray for King Billy, to hell with the Pope

Behind Harper's horse, the all-girls band of the Loyal
True Blue and Orange Ladies' Benevolent Association and
Juvenile Lodges. In white shirtwaists and skirts, offset by
colorful regalia. Behind them, waving from decorated
buses and motorcars, the women and children. Then the
county lodge officers.

The Drum of Ballymacash booms the approach of the
W.H.G. Armstrong Lodge. Thomas A. Armstrong, Worshipful Master.

The Orange Young Britons marching up Yonge Street
against the flow confront Harper's detachment proceeding
south and give way. For a time marching feet fill both
sides of the street. Contrary to regulations and to the annoyance of Deputy Chief Pogue.

The Young Britons maneuver into position ahead of the
Loyal Orange Lodges representing the north, center, west
and east districts of the city. The band of the Royal
Canadian Naval Volunteer Reserves strikes up:

> And did you go to see the show,
> Each rose and pink a dilly, O!
> To feast your eyes and view the prize
> Won by the Orange Lily, O!

The distinguished visitor walking with the William III
L.O.L. 140 admires the abundance of orange lilies. Right
Worshipful Brother John L. Fleming, Past State Grand
Master of Illinois. Carrying greetings of the Supreme Grand
Lodge of the United States.

Latecomers squeeze into viewing position at the City
Hall. Discord harmonized by the men in blue under the
supervision of Inspector Austin Mitchell. Horse and wagon
of the Ceylon Tea Company rerouted up Bay Street.

—Get your orange drink, the Roxy candy butcher blinks
in the unaccustomed brightness. Owl eyes barely open.

—Eyes right! The brethren doff hats passing the

Cenotaph. District Mistress Catharine Young is laying a wreath on behalf of York District Loyal True Blues.

—Peanuts. Fresh roasted salted peanuts.

Voices are hushed as Tom Brown, bugler with the Pioneer Drill Corps of Toronto L.O.L. 800 sounds the Last Post.

> July the first in Old Bridgetown
> There was a grievous battle.
> Where many a man lay on the ground
> And the cannons they did rattle.

Fighting it again. For the 243rd time. The Boyne Water. Then the battle of Aughrim on July 12 a year later.

—Hey, look at the chicken, the mother shouts through a mouthful of crunched peanuts. She holds her daughter aloft. Look. There.

The white rooster, mascot of the Cock O' the North L.O.L. 2214 carried by costumed, twelve-year-old Dorothy Tamlin. Orange and blue means I am true.

—Up Magherafelt. Billy Harper's Lodge, waving, exchanging greetings with curbside wellwishers.

Maple Leaf No. 455 with red umbrellas. Passing by. Aughrim Rose of Derry in crimson sashes.

William Douglas, eighty-five, hobbles along with the help of his tricolor cane. The pride of Eldon L.O.L.

—Abide with me, the ladies of the L.O.B.A. 539, halted at the Cenotaph, sing with deep-felt spirit the moving hymn.

*Con spirito*, the Italian brethren of Giuseppe Garibaldi L.O.L. 3115 appear behind their own band.

Belfast Purple Star 875. Ulster Black Watch 675. McKinley 275.

In blue and white the Fairbanks Boys Band rounds the Crescent. Then here's to the boys that fear no noise and never will surrender.

—Hold it. That's right. Don't move. Now smile. Look into the camera. The young ladies of Clarke Wallace L.O.B.A. 183 preen for the *Star* photographer. They smooth and straighten orange and blue dresses. They hold proudly on high their Union Jacks.

The Mayor in silk top hat is seated sedately in his limousine, in the company of Controllers Ramsden, McBride and Robbins. The automobile purrs to a standstill. They wait while Billy Harper equestrian advances to the foot of the Memorial. While County Master Cecil Armstrong deposits a wreath. While the Rev. Morris Zeidman utters a brief prayer. And the Rev. F.C. Ward-Whate, chaplain of the lodge, dedicates the floral tribute to the glory of God and the brave men who have passed on. Then rally round the horseman to be recorded for posterity. The flash from *The Mail and Empire's* photographer Johnny Burns. Thank you, gentlemen.

—Buy a lily! Wave a flag! Wear a button!

—For I am a loyal Orangeman, Gabriel, street vendor, hums as he waves his Nipponese aviary. He thrusts one at the outstretched hand of a whimpering child. The mother reluctantly produces five coppers. Gabriel hears the hooves from afar and dodges into the crowd to avoid the mounted policeman. Looking to peddle his trinkets farther along the route. One hand in his newsie apron, jingling his coins. Whistling — *So on the twelfth I always wear the Sash Me Father Wore.*

The blind poet stands outside Adams Furniture, a sheaf of orange lilies and bluebells in his hand. Not reciting today. Taking a breather from the marge of Lake Lebarge and the cremation of Sam Magee. The orbless musician is in his accustomed position outside the bank. He tootles *The Ould Orange Flute* on his tin whistle.

In the midst of the moving mass of color the white-uniformed Pioneer Drill Corps catches the eye. The marchers wear caps with shiny black visors and gold bands decked with maple leaves. Their chromium-plated axes gleam in the sunlight.

—You should have seen the Pioneers in '83, the old man from the House of Industry muses. In red and blue. With yards and yards of gold braid. Cap topped with a gold cockade. The best fancy drill team anywhere. Yessir. Won every prize.

> Teeter totter, holy water
> Sprinkle the Dogans every one.

174

If that won't do, we'll cut them in two
And lay them under the Orange and Blue
Hilliard Birmingham and Russell Nesbitt, M.P.P.'s, make
bold efforts to keep in step.

—Hands Off The Little Red Schoolhouse, threatens the
banner on the float of the John Knox Lodge. The crowd
cheers. The bulldog tight-leashed to the schoolhouse door
shows his fangs.

—Ah, there used to be a lot more Orange in the good
old days, sighs Joe Hays. The good old days.

The beloved padre, the Rev. Capt. Sidney Lambert is
recognized and applauded. Walking with his fellows.

—No Surrender. The Eastern Lily Flute Band, resplen-
dent in blue and gold capes.

—O Valiant Hearts. Capt. John Slatters' Band. Behind
him Fire Chief Sinclair is marching with Metcalf Lodge.

Miss Mary Cullum, founder of the L.O.B.A., erect of
carriage in her seventy-seventh year leads a contingent of
two thousand women in four hundred motor cars, floats
and buses.

The Orange Insurance display floats by. Designed, decorated and driven by Miss Mae Dillon. Attended by inspired
juveniles in orange and white. Assets proudly proclaimed:
Grown from $144,000 in 1920 to $1,132,608 in 1933.
Total death claims paid: $2,000,000.

—Ice Cream Cones! The confection fast becoming a
soggy, dribbling mess.

—Rule Brittania. The Mother of the Free, sceptre in
hand, rolls by on her wheeled throne. Behind her children
on tricycles. Youngsters twirling batons. Babes in fathers'
arms.

The enthusiasm of the girls and boys of the Toronto
Juvenile Orange Association Lodges, thoroughly educated
in the principles of Protestantism and Orangeism:

### THE KING'S PROTESTANT DECLARATION

I do solemnly and sincerely, in the presence of God,
profess, testify and declare, that I believe that in the
Sacrament of the Lord's Supper there is not any
transubstantiation of the elements of bread and wine

into the body and blood of Christ at or after the consecration thereof by any person whatsoever; and that the invocation of the Virgin Mary or any other Saint, and the Sacrifice of the Mass, as they are now used in the Church of Rome, are superstitious and idolatrous.

* * *

At the Exhibition grounds the grandstand fills quickly. There is a brief prayer service conducted by the past grand chaplain of the Triennial Council of the world. The Rev. F.C. Ward-Whate. The Mayor is introduced. He welcomes the brethren in the name of William, the Prince of Orange, who fought for freedom and religious liberty. When the cheering is spent he announces that a Union Jack has this week been formally handed over to the Lord Mayor of Belfast on behalf of the City of Toronto by Canadian delegates attending the Orange Imperial Council of the World. The crowd shows its approval by a demonstration of cheering and noisemaking. When he can again be heard, the Mayor introduces the honored orators.

SPEECHES

—The Orange Order stands for equal rights for all and special privileges for none. One school. One flag. One language and that the English language. (Applause.)

—We here today, are celebrating the deliverance from the oppressors' chains. Liberty was wrought by our forefathers who were willing to offer their lives and all they had before they would allow that most precious gift of God to be taken away from them. Liberty.

—Our organization stands not opposed to any religion. But we are most certainly opposed to a religious group that attempts to usurp powers that do not belong to it. (Applause.)

—Nor will we forgive THE JESUITS' OATH:

I do renounce and disown my allegiance as due to any heretical King, Prince or State named Protestants, or obedience to any of their inferior magistrates or officers. I do further declare the doctrine of the Church of England, of the Calvinists, Huguenots and of other of the named Protestants to be Damnable. And they themselves are damned and to be damned, that will not foresake the same. I do further declare that I will help, assist and advise all or any of his Holiness' agents in any place wherein I shall be, in England, Scotland or Ireland, or in any other territory or kingdom I shall come to. And to do my utmost to extirpate the heretical Protestant's doctrine and to destroy all their pretended power, legal or otherwise. (Hoots, shouts, gibes.)

## WHERE ORANGES GROW

—I come from a part of the Old Land where Orangemen grow. Its name is ULSTER. U stands for Unity. L for Loyalty. S for Steadfastness. T for Truth. E for Earnestness. R for Right. (Peals of applause.)

## BONDS OF EMPIRE

—We stand for the tying of the bonds of Empire closer together. While we are Canadian we are proud of the British Empire. At Ottawa the politicians want a vote of the people before Canada again goes to war for the Empire. What would those same people in Ottawa have to say if England had to have a vote of the people before they came to the assistance of Canada? I tell you, we would not be celebrating the glorious twelfth if the Empire had not stood together in 1914. (Applause.)

—We hear a great deal of talk about a new flag. The Union Jack was good enough for our boys to go out under, to fight under and to die under. I wish to God that they could live well enough under it.

## THE DANGER FACING CANADA

—We must see that we get our share of the right kind of immigrants. We should not allow any law to be passed that will bring in men and women who are not in sympathy with our rights and our ideas. Ideas that are the best in the building of any country.

—As it is, Canada has become half Roman Catholic. One reason why we don't get Protestant immigrants is because our immigration officials are Catholics. And French. When I was at Wembley recently I saw the Canadian Exhibition spelled out in large French letters. The English description was in very small letters. People there asked me if Canada was a French country. A French country!

—So long as certain parties are in power in Ottawa, so long are they going to try to make Canada a different kind of country than a Protestant country.

—Watch out for French Roman Catholic influence. (Cheers. Stamping. Shouts.)

## NEARER MY GOD TO THEE

Thousands of voices swell in an anthem of praise and prayer augmented by the many bands and assorted choirs. Well done, thou good and faithful servant.

## THE OLD ORANGE TOAST

In the Walker House Hotel (Gentlemen Only) Mr. Fogarty (You bet I'm a vet) in the presence of his many friends, wipes the beery foam from his chin and rises on wobbly legs to recite the oath of allegiance.

—Here's to the pious and immortal memory of King Billy, who saved us from knaves and knavery, slaves and slavery, Popes and Popery, brass money and wooden shoes.

The Orangemen stand.

—And if any man among us refuse to rise to this toast may he be slammed, crammed and jammed into the barrel of the Great Gun of Athlone. And may the gun be fired into the Pope's belly and the Pope into the Devil's belly and the Devil into the roasting pit of Hell.

—And may the doors of Hell be banged shut and the key kept in the pocket of a brave Orange boy.

—And may there never lack a good Protestant to kick hell out of a Papist.

—And here's a fart for the Bishop of Cork.

178

# 14

Short and slender, silver-rimmed spectacles on his delicate nose, the principal addressed the assembly. His eyes flitted about the auditorium. He left the rostrum and glided to the edge of the stage. Searching. He passed his right palm in an exploratory sweep across his hairless dome and brushed away flakes of dry skin.

—You! He pointed at the sweatered schoolboy in the second row. The low murmur ceased altogether as the principal leaned down.

—Are you disturbing the young lady in front of you, he purred. Miss, is he bothering you?

The apple in the boy's throat bobbed nervously as he attempted to reply.

—You! Come up, Terence Hawke commanded. The girl molester shuffled up four steps to the platform.

—Yes, sir? he questioned in a wavering treble.

The Hawke extended gaunt talons and pulled the tow hair towards him. Then to the left. To the right. A dribble of laughter issued from the amused students. Mr. Hawke stared the assembly into silence. He released the prisoner with a whispered admonition. Then he addressed the students. Finely enunciated syllables edged with steel.

—This past summer three of our students lost their lives by drowning. Two more were killed in traffic accidents. I deeply deplore the sudden termination of these young lives.

He paused, bowed his head in silent tribute. He resumed his place behind the podium, explored the state of his pate, brushed and continued in a brighter mood.

—I hope you have all had an enjoyable summer. Welcome to our school.

Seated in the balcony Gabriel felt the welcome personally. They would get along fine. Gabriel had no fear of the former boxing champion—classics scholar who controlled the school with a mixture of gentleness and pugnacity. When the Hawke swooped into the boys' corridors, smashing freshmen heads against metal lockers, it was to underline the necessity of decorum. With the girls his behavior was impeccably gentlemanly. To serious students of either sex, he freely gave time and advice. Excellence in Latin was the open door.

Gabriel was introduced to the rudiments of Caesar by Major Dermat Gall O'Connor. *Omnia Gallia in tres partes divisa est.* Big as a bullock, lacking china shop refinement, O'Connor slouched by the window, playing with the shade, tossing case endings of the second declension at the first formers.

—*Us. I. O. Um. E. O.* Nominative. Genitive. Dative. Accusative. Vocative. Ablative.

—*Murus. Muri. Muro. Murum. Mure. Muro.* The wall. Of the wall. To the wall. The wall. O wall! From the wall. Now find the plural in your text. Write it down in your notebooks.

O'Connor gazed absently at the hunched shoulders before him. Jewish scribes from the ghetto that encircled the school. Poles. Ukes. The two Post brothers were English. He designated then First Post and Last Post. Scrawny kids, all of them. Couple of years in the army would toughen them up. Hup. Two. Three. Four. Hup. Two. Three. The major was proud of his physique.

—Look at these muscles. Military training. Posture of Atlas in classic position. I'm in a helluva lot better shape than any of you guys. I'll show you. Grab me here, around the waist. Anybody want to try?

Janusz Przybyshewski accepted the invitation. He hugged the rotund Irishman about the belly. O'Connor *cachuchad* humming *fandango, bolero,* carrying the swinging Pole with him.

—Fee. Fie. Fo. Fum. O'Connor twisted. Janusz hung on. O'Connor snorted, shook his military might. Couldn't dislodge the boy. Grew red in the jowly cheeks. Panted. Przybyshewski, eyes shut, still attached to the Major.

Smash. Into the wall below the blackboard the hurler hurled the clinging student and dislodge a massive chunk of plaster. Still hanging on.

—O.K. that's enough. O'Connor signalled the end of the contest and the dazed Pole unwrapped himself from

180

around the soldier's rumpled trousers and tottered to his seat. Goliath tucked his grey shirt into the flannel trousers and tightened the army belt. His fly was missing a button, a casualty of the encounter. He would have to wear his coat. Miss Galbraith (Physical Health) would be shocked if she saw.

O'Connor surveyed the hole in the wall and the debris on the floor.

—That's nothing, he said. You should've seen the shell holes in the battlefields of Ypres. As big as this room. Went through the Great War dodging them, lying in them.

O'Connor revelled in tales of military strategy. He fought the major battles of history in Latin 1H with the encouragement of the class. He showed his wound. A transverse scar hidden in the folds of stomach fat. Shrapnel. He taught them army songs in several languages including Latin.

—*Ecce Caesar, nunc triumphans, qui subegit Galliam*, sung to the tune of O My Darling, Clementine. *O Delicia. O Delicia. O Delicia Formosa.*

Miss Felicity Wisdom (Geography) was lonely, middle-aged and frustrated. For release she rubbed against the corner of her desk while teaching. Measured movements of pressure and friction. Subdued. Not quite unperceived.

Mr. Hawke was a frequent visitor. He drifted into Miss Wisdom's classroom by the front door and padded up to her from behind and embraced her. She pretended to ignore the exploration of his scholarly hands and continued to expound the anomalies of weather conditions in the British Isles.

—Will someone volunteer to trace the course of the Gulf Stream?

Someone did. Gabriel. Pointer moving across the map from the Gulf of Mexico up the Atlantic, bathing Ireland and England with its warm waters.

—Class, please pay attention to the map. Miss Wisdom with an adroit side-step, extricated herself from the principal. She thanked Gottesman for his demonstration and accepted the tapered stick from him. Mr. Hawke sat in her chair, observing her professional technique. He was

181

pleased. He arose to leave, patting her derriere in passing. The class laughed. The bell signalled the end of the period. Miss Wisdom retired to her desk. Her corner. She heard the sounds of shuffling feet and the teachers' voices marshalling the students and Miss Lorraine Tallmaid in the adjoining classroom shouting, *Dépêchez-vous. Dépêchez-vous.*

The cadet corps. Marching and drilling in the football field. Soldiers' games under the tutelage of Captain Sylvester Rowntree (Ret.) a shellshocked boozer with a facial twitch. Very English, what? very military, swagger stick tucked tightly under his oxter.

A representative from Defence Headquarters, a smooth-shaven young Lieutenant visited, reviewed the cadets, offered courses in First Aid and Communications, and spoke about a career in the Army. Gabriel signed up for Semaphore. A three month course held weekly at the Armouries. Waving of flags to spell out messages. Last resort in case of failure of more sophisticated signalling devices. At completion, certificate of skill. Fifteen dollars reward. Registered Gottesman, G., Cadet No. 135709.

His mother clutched her abdomen when he explained the implications. First to be called. First to be shipped over. To fall while sending an urgent report to his company. Picked off by a sniper. The flag wrapped around him at his burial on a windy hill, the bugler sounding taps. His name added to the Soldiers' Memorial on the school lawn. Dedicated to the memory of the students who lost their lives in defense of their homeland. LEST WE FORGET: BRIG. GEN. GABRIEL GOTTESMAN, O.B.E., M.M., V.C. The metal figure, helmeted, putteed, heavy-booted stood on a rough-hewn, stone pedestal, bayoneted rifle thrust forward in the *let the bastards have it in the guts* position. Brave mannikin, oxidizing greenly, decorated with lime-grey pigeon droppings.

—Don't worry Ma. They won't call me. There won't be a war. Besides I still have three more years of school.

Languages and Mathematics. Physics and Chemistry. Physical Health.

Learning to dive and swim in the pool. Cavorting naked in the cold, bile-colored, chlorinated water. Comparing the sizes of pricks of his classmates. Morty has no bush. Smooth, white flesh where the skinny shaft joined the pubis. His nuts lodged somewhere up his crotch. Undescended. But Morty is a piano prodigy. Plays Beethoven and Bach. Fingers running nimbly up and down the eighty-eight keys. Picking out the notes on the score from behind fat lenses. No time for frivolity. Unaware of the musk smell of the girls' armpits on a summer afternoon. Eyes averted from the show of girl-thigh occasionally revealed.

Gabriel totally aware. Hurrying behind girl students, eyes focused on curves of nubility. *Bella puella.*

The first night of *The Mikado.* Gabriel dressed in the Samurai costume from Malabar's, kneeling, singing:

> If you want to know who we are,
> We are gentlemen from Japan....

Beside him other robed, Japanese gentlemen are kneeling, facing the dark auditorium. They wear heavy make-up. Eyebrows slanting exaggeratedly, orientally upward. Drooping mustaches. Bushy sideburns. Melville Fox. Gilbert Senderowitz. Moshe Goldberg. Malcolm Steinberg. Calvin Goodfellow. Shep Steen. Watching for cues from Dermat O'Connor on the conductor's plinth. Massive body swaying, arms swinging, bass voice rumbling yumph-a-tumph-a-tumph. Nodding to concert master Boris Brillstein. On the downbeat the sliver of baton shatters against the music stand sending splinters into the open-mouthed French horns. O'Connor, *sotto voce,* damns the pain in his wrist and continues *sans baton.* Cue to the chorus. Eyes left.

> If you think we are worked by strings
> Like a Japanese marionette....

Thirty-nine voices in faltering harmony rise in volume to meet the challenge from the brasses: O.O.O.O.

Enter Nanki Poo disguised as a second trombone.

—Gentlemen, I pray you tell me, where a gentle maiden dwelleth, named Yum Yum.

Malcolm's moment of greatness. He takes one step forward. Bleating out the response: Why, who are you who ask this quest-i-on?

The wandering minstrel prepares to expatiate, bidding the chorus gather round. In the wings a trio of Japanese maidens, waiting to swish onstage. Mara, the Ukrainian Yum Yum. Olga, the Latvian Pitti Sing. Francesca, the Italian Peep Bo. Three little maids from school.

In the reserved seats the school trustees sit duty-bound. Terence Hawke, bald eagle, reflecting the spotlight's glare from his pate, scrunches felicitously next to Miss Wisdom, pats her chiffoned thigh and whispers footnotes to the performance. Behind him, the other teachers. Behind them a full house of students, friends and relatives.

—Where's Gabriel, Aaron cannot make him out in the welter of dizzying costumery.

—There. Sara points — next to the funny little man with the pigtail.

—Why isn't he dressed like a sailor? I like the sailor opera better. Aaron confused, remonstrates with her. Remembering Gabriel at St. Christopher House. Arrayed as Admiral of the Fleet. Aaron liked the little jig Gabriel did. That was real good. When Sir Joseph Gabriel Porter Gottesman collapsed in a faint near the end everybody applauded. The well-dressed lady rushed backstage to congratulate him.

—Wherever did you learn to dance like that? What part of England are you from? You must be a true Britisher. To be able to play the role so well...so...authentically. My. Absolutely first class. Are you from London?

Gabriel the true Britisher mused on his ancestry. You might say that I was born not too far from the Royal Horse Mews. Buckingham Palace Road. Within the sound of Victoria Station. My father was a regular visitor to the Court of St. James. We trace our family tree back to the Iron Duke himself. Part of the glorious cavalcade of British History.

Tonight Gabriel is a Japanese. A Yaponchick. Funny man, Yaponchick. He didn't even look Japanese. Aargh-aargh Yaponchick. He should be up there on the stage. He would make everybody laugh. Sara fans her flushed face with the program. Gabriel is catching the sword from the man called Ko Ko.

Backstage on the bridge the director looks down at the

cavorting Poo Bah and drylaughs in appreciation. Noel Fairweather, teach of Ancient History, sucks on an unlighted briar. Beside him at the dimmer board the lighting man in overalls and black stocking cap clicks switches and maneuvers rheostats in response to the cue sheet. Noel Fairweather commends him. Everything is going well. It is the finest production in his twenty-seven years at the school. As good as anything the D'Oyly Carte people could do. Listen to that duet:

Were you not to Ko Ko plighted....

Nanki Poo and Yum Yum. The most delectable female lead yet discovered at the school. Mara, at sixteen, potential Grand Opera diva, exuding professionalism from every pore, plucking the high notes with ease and delivering them to her stage lover like sugared confections. Yum. Yum. Mara was edible and beddable. Mr. Fairweather would have liked to.

Loved one, let us be united....

Mara, heart and head concentered on the conductor. After school hours in the music room. Teacher and pupil. She had sung to O'Connor: List and learn ye dainty roses. He responded: When the foreman bares his steel. She echoed: Tarantara. In a blue funk, preparing to leave for the week-end military exercise at the Armories, the shiver of pain in his head. She soothed him with cool fingers at his temples. He thought of the jolt the kids in his English class would get when they tried to scan the first piece on the term paper:

When you're lying awake with a dismal headache
And your thoughts are confused by anxiety;
I conceive you may use any language you choose
To indulge in without impropriety....

The meter galloped through his head. Flying hooves of a berserk Pegasus.

O'Connor uttered several damns as Yum Yum gave herself a trifle too avidly to Nanki Poo and accelerated the tempo into the next number. Brillstein looked up, questioning, why the hurry. O'Connor sliced the air with sausage fingers. *Allegro vivace.* Into the finale.

In the classrooms adjacent to the auditorium the make-up people were cleaning the spills of face powder, putting away the tubes of Leichner foundation cream, eye liners, eyebrow pencils, mascara, crepe hair and spirit gum. They opened jars of theatrical cold cream and set out boxes of Kleenex tissues and rolls of paper towels.

Mr. Fairweather descended the metal ladder from the bridge. He was pleased with the work of his stage crew. Members of the school's exclusive fraternity. The Little Lost Lambs. He waited in the wings until the cast rushed onstage for the curtain calls, then left by way of the west dressing room. Get out before the crowds. The street car carried him to his stop near the castle. Five minutes by way of the ravine and he was home. His neutered Grey Siamese greeted him at the door. Meowing. Licking at his galoshes, following him about their shared domain, purring and rubbing against him.

Mr. Fairweather's flat was in an old mansion. Lots of room for his books: *The Sagas of the Phoenicians. The Greek City States. The Rise and Fall of the Roman Empire.* Plutarch. Josephus. His furnishings were spare and utilitarian. An easy chair. A couch that pulled out into a bed. A desk. A two-burner gas stove. A sink. A small kitchen cupboard. A table and two chairs. A clothes closet. He shared the toilet with the other tenants on his floor. The w.c. flushed with a prolonged roar—the best Niagara. The high bathtub crouched on green metal claws.

Mr. Fairweather switched on the Rogers Majestic. Between crackles and cascades of interference he managed to make out the announcer's voice:

—...the end of the news read by Gareth Davies. This is the overseas service of the British Broadcasting Corporation. We now bring you a program of light classical entertainment.

Mr. Fairweather lit the gas and placed the iron kettle on the flange. Orange pekoe for him. A bowl of warm milk for his companion Ayutthaya. He sang along with the music — Pour, oh pour the pirate sherry; fill, oh fill the pirate glass.

—Here Tai. Here puss. Ayutthaya, come. The Tai uncurled and bounded from the chair onto the table where

186

Fairweather sat sipping. He nudged the cat to the edge, pointed to the wooden bowl on the floor. There! Milk for Tai. The animal soared in an arc and stopped at the rim and lapped.

Mr. Fairweather drank and dreamed of other times. Of his wedding morning, the same day that Ferdinand was shot in Austria. Of his honeymoon. The departure on the local train from Kidderminster to Birmingham, then the express to London. Of the crash outside Wolverston. Of the death of his bride. His mild concussion. Then the consciousness of loss. The pain gradually receded as the war continued and he was finally accepted into the Royal Signal Corps. He served nineteen months in Belgium, arrived in Toronto after the Great War, still trying to forget. Immersed himself in antiquity, more real, more desirable, more comfortable. Live in the past. Teach the past. Solace for the days of his years. Years that brought no joy. No end to the turbulence in Europe. Upset by the strident pronouncements of Herr Hitler. No joy.

He reached for the playscript, newly mimeographed by the school secretary. *A Day in Babylon.* High jinks at the Court of Altabarantaphoscaphornio. A parody in one act, wedding his own dry humor with genuine content. The Little Lost Lambs would present it at morning assembly.

—All right now, you collection of stiltons, roqueforts and camemberts (that was in the script), the Chief Lamb is about to make a pronouncement.

It was always fair weather when the lambs got together. Boys only. Election by unanimous approval. Rejection by one black ball. Membership highly desired. An elite corps of entertainers, the delight of the students. The despair of the disciplinarians. A group of zanies:

—We present the constitution of the Little Lost Lambs. First item: There shall be no constitution.

The secret society meeting in Mr. Fairweather's classroom at 3:45 whenever the white pasteboard with L.L.L. typed in the lower left corner appeared in the window of the rear door.

The Little Lost Lambs were an admixture of racial backgrounds and religious inheritance. The secret password:

187

Question: How many? Answer: Two bags full.

Miss Audrey Penstone knew there was a rehearsal for an L.L.L. comedy presentation when she heard the bleats in her English class. Lambs signalling the after hours activity. Reingold to Gottesman to Gaines to Little. They would be unable to join in her *Hamlet* venture. Miss Penstone fingered her passementeried bodice. Very well. She would proceed without them. Lower grades for the absentees. Little Lost Lambs indeed!

—Penelope will announce the rehearsal schedule.

Penelope Edelweiss, secretary of Miss Penstone's Literary Society, rose from her seat. Penny bright, pounds foolish.

—List, O list: The first rehearsal of *Hamlet* is scheduled to be held....

Gabriel stared in admiration at Penelope's breasts. Full fathom five my penis lies. Bouncing on the foamy mattress of Penelope's body.

The bell jarred its hourly alarum. Next class Math. Mr. Joey Hughes, pointer sloping over his right shoulder, old soldier, leaned against the greenglassboard, ready to reveal many cheerful facts about the square of the hypotenuse.

—Closing all texts, Mr. Hughes commanded — attention to the board while we going through it. The teacher's idiosyncratic misuse of the English language had been accepted long ago by students and faculty. His favorite grammatical construction was the gerund.

—Sitting quietly now. Not making any noise. Trying it again. Watching closely.

Senderowitz laughed loudly. Mr. Hughes said:

—Senderowitz. Leaving the room. Standing in the hall until the end of the period.

—Taking my books with me, sir?

—Going quickly or getting a detention. Mr. Hughes turned back to the geometry problem on the board.

—Watching closely. Seeing me go through it.

Mr. Hughes also used dangling participles and misplaced modifiers. But he was a friendly chap. More likeable than ramrod McGee (Physics):

—If all the smart alecks will stop disrupting the class we can proceed. That applies to the barnyard comics too. In seven seconds I shall be forced to assign extra homework.

Of all his teachers Gabriel liked Diana Hastings best. *La déesse virginale de la classe française.* Cold and distant *comme la lune.* Grace and beauty in her face and form. *Habillée en vêtements de la maison Dior.* Summer excursions to Paris *pour l'amour toujours.* French phrases flowed incandescent from Diana Hastings' lips like invitations:

—*Je désire. Tu désires. Il désire.*

Full of desire, Gabriel observed the glistening lips of the French mistress as they curved around the vowels. Conjuring a vision of *une liaison secrète et dangereuse.* Her apartment in Parkdale. Crimson velvet hangings, thick *tapis blancs* for bare feet, a deep plush sofa, canopied bed draped in white with embroidery of *fleurs de lis.* One floor lamp, a cupid figure in gold metal. Edith Piaf on the radio: *Sous les toits de Paris.* To french with Diana. In tongue caress.

She disrobes in languid movements. Her Gioconda smile promising, promising.

| | |
|---|---|
| Gabriel *(souffle de coeur):* | *Je désire, chérie.* |
| Diane *(rusée):* | *Tu désires? Vraiment?* |
| Les Chérubim *(aux voix célestes):* | *Il désire. Hosanna.* |
| Diane *(agréable):* | *Nous désirons, n'est-ce pas?* |
| Gabriel *(au grand cris):* | *Vous désirez! Zut alors!* |
| Les Chérubim *(ensemble):* | *Ils désirent. Nom de Dieu. Regardez-y.* |

—Well done, Gabriel, Miss Hastings approved. Her index finger was massaging the tip of her pointer. Very well conjugated.

The Little Lost Lambs applauded. Miss Hastings admonished them:

—Don't add to his conceit. *Désirer.* Just a simple verb. Not much intelligence required to learn how to conjugate.

—Earthworms conjugate. Penelope remembered well her Biology lesson.

—That will do, Miss Hastings said. A hint of a smile hovered about her mouth. *Taisez-vous. Maintenant faites*

*attention aux symboles phonétiques. Regardez ma bouche.*
—Aaa. Aii. Eee. Auu. Ooo. Euu.
Diana Hastings. Enchantress. Oh, to be with Diana in the groves of Arcadia. Diana, high-booted, in short tunic, with bow and quiver. Diana, naked in her bath. Goddess virginal, remote as the moon.

## 15

If you like us, please don't mind
If we bump and if we grind.
We will shimmy and we will shake,
But please don't think we're on the make!
High steppers pony trot. Music brassy and thump, thump thump. Netstockinged chorus girls kick and tap and twirl. Break and reform. Opening number ends in crash bang finale.

—Ladies and gentlemen, a big hand for the Roxyettes. Thank you. Thank you very much. The management is pleased to present for your entertainment the best in Burlesque. And now, Mr. Leader, on with the show.

Thursday in July. The glitter dusted posters outside the theater announce the week's program. Photographs: RAGS RAGLAND, funny man in baggy pants. SCURVY MILLER. MAXINE DE SHON, in the almost-nude, glittering pasties, glittering G-string. NEXT WEEK: BOZO SNYDER, The Tramp Pantomimist. LOIS DEFEE, The Eiffel Eyeful, six-feet-four-inches of pulchritude.

Lunchtime queue forming at the box office. Sons of Adam dispersed from Babel.

—Hello, Mr. Chang. The doorman takes his ticket. Mr. Chang hurries to the front row.

Gabriel walks into the alley and to the stage entrance. Metal door creaks open. Shafts of colored light stab into the darkness. Curley's boys are playing *The Sweetheart of Sigma Chi.* Stagehands in undershirts. Stage manager. Where?

—Wait till the show is finished, kid, one of the crew advises. Stick around. Few minutes. Stand over there.

—*The girl of my dreams is the sweetest girl....* Tony Sands, house singer is crooning. The sweetheart onstage unzips her transparent dress, tosses it into the wings where a chorus girl catches it. Maxine De Shon bathed in a pink follow spot. Rotating her pelvis to the treacly voice of the saxophone. At the end of the phrase the light winks out. Visible now the radium-treated jewelled panties a mass of

191

kinetic brilliants in the blackness. From the drums in the pit issue an insistent rhythm. Tum-ta-ta-tum ta-ta-tum ta-ta-tum. She hums, a little out of breath. Tum ta ta tum. Advancing towards him, she seizes a portion of the proscenium curtain, flagellating against the winey velvet. She ceases suddenly. Drums out. The silence attacks Gabriel's ears. Then full orchestra with the reprise—*She's the sweetheart of Sigma Chi*. Ecdysiastically she releases the pudendal trophy and elevates it gleaming in the restored circle of light for all to see.

Blackout. Reward of applause. Shouts for more. And more, more. Illumined again. Orchestral voices again. As it was in the beginning. Alpha and Omega and Sigma Chi. She smiles wistfully, striking a pose. The spotlight irising down to the patch of flesh-tinted satin, hovering friefly, clicking out.

—That's the show folks. Before we leave we'd like to introduce our star-studded cast. Full lights full on. Curtain calls for everybody. The Roxy chorus, the comics, the acrobats, the exotics, and finally the headliner, the lovely, luscious Miss Maxine De Shon. The orchestra underlines the applause.

—And a great big hand for our maestro, Curley Kramer. Take a bow Mr. Leader man. Curley about-faces, bowing benignly as the music rises to a coda and out.

—Kill the lights, a voice beside Gabriel shouts. In the dark, feet gallop past him to the dressing rooms. The rear traveler parts. On the screen the images appear. Akim Tamiroff in *Michael Strogoff*.

—Kid here wants to see you, Bill.

The stage manager in shortsleeved pullover approaches Gabriel on sneakered feet.

—Yeah. What wouldja like.

—I have an act. Can I audition for you?

—What kind of act?

Gabriel unpocketed the shining Hohner Key of C. Its chromeplated surface bore the name of American Boy Scout. Winner of many international awards including the Grand Prix de Génève. Gabriel cupped his hands about the harmonica and began his audition piece. *Where the deer*

*and the antelope play.* Instructed by Jimmy Lawless at the
Jewish Boys' Club. *And the skies are not cloudy all day.*
—Very good, the stage manager admitted. But we don't
hire anybody here. All the acts are booked from New
York.
Disappointment. Promising career ended.
—Tell ya what though, Bill added encouragingly, I hear
Mushie out front needs somebody. Bet you'd be good, too.
He directed Gabriel to the candy concession in the
lobby.
—Just ask for Mushie. He'll look after ya.
—Wanna be a candy butcher, kid, Mushie sized him up.
He squeezed a glob of pus from a blemished cheek. Sure I
could use ya. Here, try on this tray.
Gabriel slid his arms through the shoulder straps. Mushie
observed and pondered and attacked a fat pimple in the
cleft of his chin.
—O.K. I'll give ya a chance. Work fast in the intermis-
sions and ya can make three dollars a week easily. O.K.?
Gabriel nodded assent. Mushie called to his brother. Hey
Hushie, I want you should meet the new candy butcher.
—Where didja work before, kid? Hushie, acne soiled like
his brother, inquired.
—Oh, all over. Been working for a long time.
—Didn'tja hustle sheets?
Gabriel admitted to having been temporarily employed
at Karl Roff's newsstand.
—That's O.K., kid, Hushie said, I hustle sheets myself
sometimes. This job is better. Pays more. And ya see all
the shows, meet the broads. He winked. Know what I
mean?
—Sure, I know what you mean. Meet the broads.
—Say, I bet you're still cherry, Hushie laughed.
—No, I'm not, I've had my share. Boy, you shoulda seen
the Polish broad I screwed. Ever been to a Polish wedding?
—Nope. What's it like, Hushie asked.
—Well, there's lot of booze. (Go on, build it up, show
this guy how you've been around.) And after awhile everybody is really stinko.
—Pissed, huh?

193

—Yeah, that's right. Really pissed. And the dames get so hot they practically beg you to...you know.

—Did you...? Hushie wanted to know.

—Oh yeah, I scored with a hot hunk of stuff. Boy, could she screw. I came four times with her. Hell, I been around. (All around. With your mother baying about you.)

—Could ya fix me up? Hushie wanted to know.

—Sure thing, sure thing, Hushie. Next Polish wedding comes along, boy you're gonna be in like Flynnski.

—You do that for me, Hushie said fervently, and I'll fix ya up with some of the dames here. Just leave it to me. Only don't let anybody find out or you'll be out on your ass.

—O.K., Gabriel said.

—And stay away from Sammy the Chink. And Chris Augenblick. Yeah, especially Christine. Hushie danced a couple of steps away from Gabriel, then came upon him from the rear and goosed him. Know what I mean, he asked. Just like that. Only Christine won't use his fingers if he gets a chance. Too bad about him. Can't help it I guess. Oh, another thing. Don't get chummy with the customers. Ya never know what can happen. Like that dame we had here last week. The one you're replacing.

—I'm replacing a dame?

—Yup. We had a little broad. Mushie thought it would give the joint a bit of class. So he hires this twat. Good looking she was too. And he gets her this costume. Like in the night clubs. Skirt above the knees. Blouse cut low so she can show her tits. Net stockings.

—What happened to the twat? Gabriel wanted to know.

—Well, I'll tell ya. It was the Sunday midnite show. Couple hours of movies first. Edgar Kennedy short, news of the day, a travelogue about Tahiti, Bugs Bunny cartoon and the feature, a Charlie Chan movie. Ya know, the usual crap. Well, around 2:30 in the morning they're ready to start the stage show. All the lights are on out front and the guys are setting up backstage. At this time the broad struts down the aisle with her tray.

Hushie chuckled, squashed a pustule.

—Yeah, Gabriel said, then what?

—Then the whistling starts. That makes her a little nervous but she begins to sing out — chocolates, ice cream bars, chewing gum — like a little canary — cigars, cigarets. Hushie breaking up. Really funny.

—First thing ya know a lush sitting by the aisle stops her. She smiles at him and asks, what will you have sir? And this guy says two of these and reaches for her boobs. Another *shmuck* behind her grabs for her and before she knows it, she's got one hand on her bazooms and two on her ass.

—No kidding.

—Yeah. Well, she lets out a scream and drops the tray. Her tits are now hanging out and her panties are torn. She gets away and runs up the aisle and locks herself in the ladies' john. The Polish cleaning woman calms her down and helps her back into her own clothes. Mushie pays her five bucks and gets a cab to take her home.

—Boy, that must have been some night, Gabriel said.

—Yeah. Too bad about that broad though. Looked like a good piece. Well, good luck, kid. Keep your ass away from the queers.

Timidly Gabriel announced his presence: Chocolate bars. Ice cream bars. Candy. Orange Crush.

—Hey bud, c'mere, the stale mouth whispered. Got any safes?

Gabriel hurried by. Hushie had warned him about the guys that pulled off during the striptease. Sons of the sheik pumping jissom into condoms, then depositing them under the seats, to be swept up nightly by Mrs. Leshyk. Their spent seed decaying in the garbage can in the alley.

\* \* \*

Gabriel hustled. Cold confections. Sweets. Tobacco. Then the lights dimmed. Up to Mushie's hole-in-the-wall concession. Off with the tray.

—Be back in an hour, kid.

Gabriel sat down to watch the show. Eager to observe, to inform in the fall the members of the Little Lost Lambs

195

how he spent the summer.

The straight man, pinstripesuited, hair sleek with ointment announced from the stage:

—The Roxy Theater presents the *Man In The Street* program. Can I have a young man?

The comic, battered fedora on bald head, glasses on Cyranose, tattered shirt and patched pants, oversized shoes, soles flapping, penguins into view. He nudges the straight man.

#### STRAIGHT

My friend, I asked for a young man. You'll never be as old as you look.

#### COMIC

*(To audience)* You've heard of the March of Time? This must be his son — waste of time.

#### STRAIGHT

Just look at that face. Does anyone out there have a hunting license?*(To comic)* My good friend, you are about to become famous. See this microphone? You're on the air.

#### COMIC

*Grabs mike and begins to croon into it. Straight pulls mike away from comic)*

#### STRAIGHT

Behave yourself. I'd like to ask you a few questions.

#### COMIC

Go ahead. Ask me anything.

#### STRAIGHT

Do you mind telling me your name sir?

#### COMIC

Phillips. Patrick Jehosephat Phillips.

## STRAIGHT

Not the Phillips that makes the Milk of Magnesia?

## COMIC

No sir! I'm the Phillips that takes it. *(Breaks up. Slaps his thigh.)*

## STRAIGHT

Well, Mr. Phillips, may I ask what you do for a living?

## COMIC

I work in a panty factory.

## STRAIGHT

Do you make much?

## COMIC

Oh, I pull down about forty-five a week.

## STRAIGHT

You think you're pretty smart, don't you?

## COMIC

I should be. I was born twins.

## STRAIGHT

Born twins? Does that make you smart?

## COMIC

Two heads are better than one. *(Doubles up with laughter, slides away from straight man who grabs him by the seat of his pants.)* Watch out. You're choking me.

## STRAIGHT

Could you make me smart?

## COMIC

Sure. Here. Rub this liniment on your head. Boy, will it make you smart!

STRAIGHT

Did you ever have any problems with your brother?

COMIC

Hell, yes. Everything he did, I got the blame for it.

STRAIGHT

How's that?

COMIC

When we were kids, playing baseball, if he broke a window I got blamed.

STRAIGHT

That's too bad!

COMIC

If he went into Woolworth's and stole something, I got blamed.

STRAIGHT

That's terrible. Do you remember any other incidents?

COMIC

Hell, yes. When we grew up I fell in love with a beautiful girl. But he married her.

STRAIGHT

That's just awful.

COMIC

But I sure got even with him.

STRAIGHT

You mean to tell me you got even with your twin brother who looks exactly like you?

COMIC

Hell, yes.

STRAIGHT

Do you mind telling me how?

COMIC

Last week I died...and they buried him! *(He stomps, does a little jig, appeals to the audience for applause and receives it.)*

STRAIGHT

My friend, thank you for appearing on the *Man In The Street* program. However, in parting may I tell you that you are—without a doubt—the most ignorant person I have ever met...

COMIC

Go ahead. Build me up.

STRAIGHT

Why, I bet you haven't the intelligence of my youngest son.

COMIC

You have a child? How long ya been married?

STRAIGHT

Three years.

COMIC

That's nice. How many children do you have?

STRAIGHT

Six.

COMIC

Married three years? *(Counts on his fingers)* And you have *(counts again)* six children?

STRAIGHT

Yes. That's right. I have six children.

## COMIC

What the hay! Tell me, how come you have six children and you're married only three years?

## STRAIGHT

*(Haughtily)* It's on account of the reading my wife did.

## COMIC

Reading? What does that have to do with it?

## STRAIGHT

Well it's this way. The first year we were married my wife read a book called *One Night of Love* and at the end of that year she presented me with a bouncing baby boy.

## COMIC

I see. *One Night of Love.* One boy.

## STRAIGHT

That's right. And the second year my wife read *A Tale of Two Cities.*

## COMIC

I know that one. Story about the traveling salesman with one broad in Toronto and one in Montreal. Tail of two cities. Get it? *(Appeals to audience. Laughter.)*

## STRAIGHT

That's right. She read *A Tale of Two Cities* and at the end of that year she presented me with a beautiful pair of twins.

## COMIC

Second year twins, eh? Go ahead, tell me about the third year.

## STRAIGHT

I'm sure glad you asked me. Are you ready? Here goes. The third year she read a book titled *Three Men on a*

*Horse* and at the end of that year she presented me with triplets.

COMIC

*(Doubling up with mock pain)* What the hay!

STRAIGHT

That makes six altogether. See?

COMIC

Let's see now. This requires a lot of co-gi-ta-tion. The first year you were married your wife read a book called *One Night of Love* and at the end of the year — bingo — she had a baby boy. The second year she read *A Tale of Two Cities* and gave birth to twins. Wham. The third year she read *Three Men on a Horse* and hot damn—triplets. Is that right?

STRAIGHT

Yes, my good man. That's absolutely correct.

COMIC

*(Very upset)* Hell. I better get home right away.

STRAIGHT

What on earth for?

COMIC

My wife is reading *The Birth of a Nation.*

Blackout

\* \* \*

Beasley insisted that Isabel Evans had the best legs in the business. Beasley was a flesh expert, knowledgeable about horses and women. Vocation: Gambler. Fantan in Chinatown. Daily double at Woodbine. Avocation: Resident stud in the service of the Roxy hoofers. He was ingratiating and likeable.

Isabel demurred when he first propositioned her. Can't win them all. He tried another time. She laughed away his advances. She had to get home to her widower father. No time.

One snowy Sunday after the midnite show about half-past-three in the morning, he invited her to Bowles Restaurant for chili con carne and a cuppa. He shared half a mickey of rye with her. She consented to stay the rest of the night in his room on Sumach Street. Beasley gave her affection and tenderness. All day Monday she lay beneath Beasley's busy loins.

When Isabel was three months pregnant and no longer able to high step, Beasley proposed marriage. She promised for better or worse in a civil ceremony at City Hall. Isabel's father grumbled that he had lost a breadwinner and gained a freeloader.

After the baby was born Beasley persuaded his wife to go back to work. He would look after their infant son. He did. For a week. Then he slipped the old man five dollars in return for domestic services. Diaper changes, bathing, feeding. There would be regular payments he promised. He had several job offers. Somehow they didn't pan out.

Beasley returned to his seat in the theater. Watched Isabel strut through four a day. Still pretty. Still a high kicker. No wonder she was so goddam tired in bed. More than anything Beasley needed a good lay. Isabel used to be, no longer was, never again would be, a great piece of ass. Besides, the baby would wake and Isabel's maternal reflexes were stronger than her desire. Screwed again, he muttered as his wife rolled away from him to investigate the shrieks from the crib.

Returning, she protested, I need my sleep, Beasley. I'm dead tired after the last show. I wish you'd be more considerate.

Beasley granted her request. For awhile he exercised his manhood with Dolores, number seven, part Chinese, part Greek. Then a young stripper from Buffalo came through on the circuit and Beasley lightened her loneliness. She gave him an allowance and presents.

When she left for Chicago, Beasley wooed Gwen, number eleven, a heavy blond with a real tight box. She had a nicely-furnished apartment. She gave him her spare key.

202

He purloined her squirrel coat, radio, some jewelery and a floor lamp. He pawned everything and put the money on a sure thing. The horse didn't have the same urgency as Beasley. Gwen complained to the police. She wept as she gave her story to the desk sergeant. Beasley was picked up at No. 12 Elizabeth Street. They wouldn't even let him finish his chicken chow mein. He was sentenced to seven months in Don Jail.

Isabel no longer cared. No Beasley. No trouble. No other men in her life. Just the baby and the job.

\* \* \*

Curley Kramer in the pit palms his glistening cranium, wipes five fingers down the side of his trousers and raises the baton. On the downbeat a powerful drumroll.

—And now, Ladeez 'n Gennemun, the Roxy management is proud to present the one, the only, Peaches LaTour. Direct from the New York World's Fair, the undisputed mistress of pectoral persuasion. Let's have a big hand for Peaches LaTour.

Curley's boys begin *Won't You Be My Melancholy Baby.* Into the circle of illumination a massive woman appears. Blond shoulder-length hair. Embroidered brassiere imprisons bulging bosoms. Panels of black muslin float from her hips. She teeters on spiked heels.

From melancholy baby the first gentle undulations. Slight motion of head, in-out belly movements, easy rotation of the hips. One breast twitches. The first tremulous stirring of the silken tassel, a quick flick. Again the rotation to the beat. The LaTour tassel twirls in widening arcs. Circling around the left breast. In the opposite direction. Dextrous. Won't you be my tasselated baby.

Now the other breast twitches. Revving up. Twin propellers, plumes of threads, circling to the rhythm of the pom-pom-pom of the drums. Spinning in one direction. Spinning otherwise. Towards each other. Sustained until the crash of the cymbals. The tassels droop from tired tits. Her outstretched arms invite approval. More.

In the blackout Peaches slips behind the curtain. Re-emerges into the spotlight. Accolades of MORE. But she exits.

The clarinet now into *Blue Moon*. Then the saxophone's husky voice. Curley brings in the traps. The others follow. Muted trombone and trumpet. Piano. Violins. Bass fiddle.

—Once again, Miss Peaches LaTour, Arthur Vale loud-speaks.

The azure spot hisses on and encircles Peaches' derriere where — *mirabile dictu* — a tassel hangs from each dimpled cheek.

*Blue Moon, I saw you standing alone...* for further tassel treats.

—Shake that ass, baby!

In quickening rotation, the LaTour peaches whirl the silks. *Le tour du monde.* The applause starts. Builds. The light changes to amber. *Then I saw the moon had turned to...* Peaches slows down her frantic haunches as the music stops.

Another blackout. Another show. Peaches heaves her bulk into the ladies' dressing room and sits heavily on the tatty couch.

—Bunch of *shmucks*, she exhales Sweet Caporal smoke in a cooling breeze against her fatigued breasts. Rivulets of perspiration ooze down into her steaming crevices.

\* \* \*

—Order in the court!

H.M. Case, King's Counsel, chuckled. A good way to spend an hour before returning to Osgoode Hall.

—The courtroom sketch is my favorite, he put it to his companion. Her fingernails traced patterns about his trousered thigh.

—The true embodiment of everything that's excellent, she whispered, revelling in remembrances of their pleasure together. A *prima facie* case for a bill of divorcement should they be discovered *in flagrante delicto*.

### CLERK

All rise for His Honor, the Judge! *(Enter JOE DE RITA, the Comic Judge in black robe. He trips, bangs pig's bladder over the head of the clerk, climbs onto the chair behind the high desk, falls off, tries again and succeeds in maintaining his perch. He reaches for bottle, takes a swig, stares out at the audience and falls asleep in an upright position. About to fall off chair again but awakes in time, looks about, shouts down to the clerk.)*

### JUDGE

Call the first case. *(Studies docket before him.)*

### CLERK

Katarina Zwiazczych. Miss Katarina Zwiazczych. *(A voluptuous redhead enters. Her breasts are popping out of a white peasant blouse. A short skirt is wrapped tightly about her. She is ushered to the witness box and sits exposing to view a great expanse of crossed legs. Everybody on stage crowds about her. His Honor cranes forward and falls off the chair. A trap door near the bottom of his desk opens and the judge peers out. The door slams shut. Judge re-appears to disperse KATARINA'S admirers, bladder flailing at the cop, the clerk, the attorney, the jury.)*

### CLERK

Order in the court. Order in the court.

### JUDGE

*(Bangs clerk over head with bladder. He sidles over to KATARINA, takes out a small notebook, whispers in her ear, smiling lewdly. KATARINA raises her skirt higher, whispers to the judge. He jots down her response. He produces an oversize carpenter's tape and measures her bust, waist, hips and jots down the vital statistics. At last he gets back to his desk, winks down at her.)*

### JUDGE

Who is representing this lady?

## ATTORNEY

I am, your honor. This attractive, desirable lady is my client. *(He squeezes her hand. She wiggles with delight. Judge leans over and bladderbangs the attorney over the head.)*

## JUDGE

That's enough. There will be no monkey business in my court. Unhand that woman, Mr. Attorney. Get to the seat of the trouble.

## ATTORNEY

She is already sitting on it your honor.

## JUDGE

*(Loudbladderbanging)* I'm the funnyman here. Now my dear, what seems to be the trouble?

## KATARINA

Well, you see, your honor, I have suffered a fate worse than death. I have been... *(She rises, performs suggestive movements which are picked up by the drummer.)* ...confronted, affronted, molested, arrested, seduced and traduced. I seek support for my child.

## JUDGE

Is that so?

## ATTORNEY

Yes, your honor. My client has been confronted, affronted, molested, arrested, seduced and traduced. And we shall prove beyond a shadow of a *podeshva* who the guilty party is.

## JUDGE

*(To KATARINA)* You say, my dear, that you have been... *(imitating her convulsions)* ...confronted, affronted, molested, arrested, seduced and traduced?

## ALL

*(Chanting)* Yes, your honor, she says she has been

confronted... *(As they are about to continue, the judge reaches over and hits them individually with the bladder.)*

### JUDGE

That's enough. *(Paternally to KATARINA).* Now, my dear, will you point out the guilty man? *(She approaches each man in turn, the orchestra bumps and grinds, accentuating her walk. She finally stops before the cop and points an elegant finger at him. She bursts into mock weeping. The attorney helps her to her chair where she recovers immediately and adjusts her skirt upward.)*

### COP

Your honor, this lady asked for a lift in my cruiser and I felt sorry for her. I was only doing my duty. *(KATARINA crosses her legs provocatively.)* I...was...only ...doing...my...duty... *(He wiggles obscenely.)*

### JUDGE

*(Repeating cop's motions)* ...and where did your duty take you?

### COP

I admit we did go for a drive in the country.

### JUDGE

Then what happened?

### COP

We embraced on the back seat.

### JUDGE

You say you embraced on the back seat? *(KATARINA nods, big smile of recollection.)*

### COP

That's right. We made love on the back seat. And when we finished the car was gone. We had to leave the seat in the woods.

## JUDGE

A likely story if ever there was one. Well, it's a wise child that knows its own father. Bring in the little girl. We'll ask her. *(The little girl is a nubile member of the chorus in tight sweater.)*

## JUDGE

Wow. Look at those balloons! *(Leans towards her, salaciously.)* Little girl. *(She throws a hip in his direction.)* Little girl. *(She hip sways to him. He takes out his notebook, whispers in her ear. She responds with rear-end movements that leave no doubt about the conversation. In a final furious rotation of her pelvis she bumps the judge off his chair. He rises from the floor and hobbles stiffly to his desk.)*

## JUDGE

Little girl...will you kindly look at the people in this courtroom and tell me if you can recognize your daddy. Be careful now. We don't want a miscarriage *(he winks at woman in the jury)* of justice in this court. *(As the girl looks around, the judge indulges in a ditty.)* The postman came the first of May. The policeman came the very next day. Who fired the first shot, the blue or the gray? *(He addresses the little girl again.)* Now then, my dear...was it *(pointing to attorney)* him?

## GIRL

Uh...uh. No.

## JUDGE

*(Pointing to clerk)* Was it him?

## GIRL

Uh...uh. No!

## JUDGE

*(Pointing to cop)* Well, then it must have been him.

## GIRL

Oh, no!

JUDGE

Well, if it wasn't him...or him...or him...then who in hell is your father?

GIRL

*(Points accusing finger at the JUDGE.)* YOU! DADDY! *(Judge falls off the chair. Blackout.)*

\* \* \*

Georgia Southern exploded onstage —*Hold that tiger* — zip-wheel-zip-dip — undressing, racing against Curley's boys to a sixty-second photo finish — gesturing to him — up yours — before the final blackout.
Gabriel Gottesman offered Candies. Chocolate Bars. Chewing Gum. Cigarets. Eskimo Pies. Cigars. With zesty theatricality.

\* \* \*

The counterfeit presentment of a flaxen-haired coquette petulant in provocative inquiry:
—What's it gonna be? Wearing a clinging silk print. Whatcha gonna do? in silk stockings and spikes. What seems to be the di-few-calty? a pause for applause.
Then the music, *Sophisticated Lady*, and Bobbette begins the perambulations. Stride. Pirouette. Swinging hips. The face a mask of rouge, liners, mascara, lipstick, blending powder. Mouthing loving words. Throwing a kiss—Say you love me. Tottering at the apron's edge, grinning. Two mincing paces to the curtains and the parody of flagellation. The rape of the drape. Bobbette tantalizes with dress upraised. Peekaboo. Look at those, Gypsy Rose. One stocking ungartered, unrolled to the ankle. Now the other, unrolling down a hairy shinbone. Lightning quick, unzipped. Bobbette disrobed. Black lace panties. Black lace Daintiform brassiere — molds as it firms as it lifts as it separates. Movements now flirtatious. Bobbette dips into the cleavage and discovers expendable foam breasts. Hah! Whatcha gonna do? Here's one for you. And the other. Wide trajectory. Patrons' hands upraised to catch. The

performer unhooks the brassiere and exposes a flat hirsute chest. One hand caresses the entanglement of hair, the other dangles the Daintiform in languorous pendular rhythm. Tick. Tock. Flick. Into the wings. Bobbette, downstage center, caresses *Sophisticated Lady* undies. Music softer, lights dimming, Bobbette wriggling out of the step-ins. Fanfare. *Ecce homo.* Jock-strapped. The cupped manhood of Bobbie Morris, female impersonator and burlesque clown.

* * *

Sunday afternoon. Lapping butterbrickle ice cream cones with Horny Fox and Einstein outside Hershberg's grocery store.

—What's new at the Roxy? Fox asked with horny anticipation.

Gabriel tongued a hefty gob of ice cream and snaked it between widely-parted lips.

—Wait till I tell you about the new comedy sketch. Get ready for some big laughs. Fox and Einstein nodded their readiness.

—You see, Webber and Pincus are riding on the crowded Seventh Avenue subway. All kinds of people get on and off at the stations. Women with big tits. Tramps. Drunks. Webber spits on the floor and right away there's this big cop wanting to arrest him: That'll cost you two dollars for expectorating, he says. Webber is ready to pay, but Pincus, his lawyer, says no. He'll take the case to court. Webber is found guilty. He tells his lawyer, Pincus, pay the man the two dollars and let's get the hell out of here. No, says Pincus, we'll appeal.

—That's right, Webber, appeal it, Horny hollered.

Gabriel continued: They go to a higher court. They lose. The fine is raised to fifty dollars or six months in jail. Pincus, we should have paid the man the two dollars. Now it's fifty. Pay the fifty and let's get the hell out of here. No, says Pincus, we'll go to the highest court in the land. The United States Supreme Court.

—Three cheers for the red, white and blue, Horny sang. Einstein unsmiling listened.

—Well, all kinds of witnesses testify and accuse Webber of all kinds of crimes. Murder. Rape. Robbery. And spitting in the subway. Pincus tries to break down their testimony but fails. A fight breaks out in the courtroom. Order in the court. The judge runs around hitting everybody over the head with the bladder. He falls into the orchestra pit hollering: Order. Order. Pincus shouts back: One beer, Judge.

—Hey *Rov!* pay the man the two dollars, Horny Fox called out to Reb Jonathan Leroy who was rounding the corner. The reverend cursed — *Goyishe kop* — and spat in the gutter.

—It's too late for payment, said Gabriel. Webber is found guilty of murder and is sentenced to hang by electrocution.

—By electrocution? Einstein begged to differ.

—Sure, Gabriel assured him, in Burlesque you can even be electrocuted in the gas chamber.

—So what happens next? Fox asked.

—There's this big scene where Webber is led in, blindfolded, and placed in the electric chair. You should see it. Wires and sockets and a whole dimmer board. Pincus tries to console Webber. A priest all in black enters. The priest reads: *It is a far, far better thing you do than you have ever done. It is a far, far, better place you go to than you have ever been. The bourne from which no traveller returneth.* Webber screams at him, Pincus you should have paid the man the two dollars. The warden says: My good man, you are entitled to one last wish before you leave this vale of tears. Is there anything we can do for you? You say I can have one last wish? Webber asks. That's right my good man. Webber motions the warden to come closer. Warden, he says, when they pull that switch and send a million volts of electricity through this frail body of mine, will you do me one final favor? The warden says, Anything at all, my good man. In that case, begs Webber, sit in my lap!

Einstein ruminated: There's real social significance in

that piece. The common man, subjected to the stresses of our times, held up to ridicule, arrested, incarcerated, the victim of a sham justice. It's all there. The whole corrupt capitalistic society that bears within it the seeds of its own destruction. A good lesson in Marxist dialectic.

—Ah, it's only a bit of burlesque, Gabriel remonstrated.

—Sure, Horny Fox said. Einstein, pay the man the two dollars.

* * *

Jack and Jill went up the hill
To fetch a pail of water.
Jill came down with a two dollar bill.
Do you think she went up for water?

All about him the audience laughed, but the minister from the United Church noted: Jack and Jill...two dollar bill.

There was an old lady
Who lived in a shoe.
She had so many children she didn't know what to do.
There was another old lady who lived in a shoe.
She didn't have any children.
She knew what to do.

Complain about that too. Old lady...knew what to do, he wrote on his pad.

—Your honor, this man molested me in the theatre.
First he put his hand on my ankle, then he put
his hand on my calf, then he stroked my thigh.

—Why didn't you yell out or try to stop him?

—How did I know he was after my money.

Doubtful. Didn't get past her thigh. The minister shifted in his seat to get a better view.

—Doctor, I'm pregnant. I did everything you told me but it
didn't work. Did you say I was to take the orange juice
before or after relations with my husband?

—Instead of. Instead of.

Relations. *That's* obscene. We'll see the manager gets a call from Chief Inspector Draper.

* * *

212

Linda Cunningham in high dudgeon banged on the door marked PRIVATE.

—Mr. Little. Open up, Mr. Little.

The manager admitted her.

—I can't do a goddam thing with that fucking orchestra, she shouted. They're fucking up my whole strip. Lousy, fucking bastards.

—What's wrong darling, he sought to soothe her.

—They're playing my number in the wrong fucking key.

\* \* \*

The groundlings are responsive. On the Roxy stage Scurvy Miller is sitting with a beautiful girl in an open sports car. He starts the engine. There is a sound like a pistol shot. Scurvy jumps out of the car. Who fired it? He looks about. Must have been a backfire.

In the car again beside the pretty girl he sniffs, sniffs, screws up his face and asks her: Who fired it? He jumps out of the car, finger to his putty clown's nose. He asks her again: Who fired it? He addresses the audience: Who farted? Who fired it? Who farted?

\* \* \*

Sunday midnight. The members of the chorus, daubed in bronze paint and glycerine were naked save for three maple leaves. Around and between the tinsel forest they stomped to the tom-tom of the drums. Vladimir Sokoloff cried with happiness.

—Beautiful, beautiful. Gorgeous. Ees best production I haff created. Pair-haps now Meestair Leetle be happy.

The manager had been most unhappy when the melancholy Slav first proposed the idea. The girls would suffocate in all that paint.

—Nyevair mind. Ees all right. Paint make warm, and glycerine good for skin. Hot shower after show take off everything.

—Well, maybe you're right, the manager reluctantly agreed. I hope it's good for business. Christmas week is a stinker.

After three curtain calls the Roxyettes trouped off to the portable showers. Shivering, they turned the knobs.

—Jesus. No water!

—Somebody turn on the fucking water!

—*It's turned on!*

Chill December had frozen the pipes conducting the water to the showers to wash the girls all covered with paint who danced on the stage in the brilliant production conceived to the tune of Ravel's *Bolero.*

The gelid showgirls stumbled back to the dressing rooms and huddled mournfully in a group while water was heated and poured into basins, pails, tubs. Gabriel volunteered to join in the scrubbing of the coated chorines. The splashing dampened his trousers but not his ardor.

\* \* \*

LITTLE LOST LAMB AMONG THE STRIPPERS

SCHOLAR SCORES WITH SHOW PEOPLE

\* \* \*

Michelle Morgan was twenty-seven. To Gabriel, sixteen, she was Venus incarnate of the Queen Street playhouse. Michelle was affectionate. She greeted Gabriel daily with a kiss on the cheek. Her voice was honey-soft. Her inflection was Southern, redolent of magnolia and dogwood. She told him about her childhood in Jonesboro, Georgia. About a black mammy who clouded the water of her bath for modesty: Don't want nobody seeing what's down there, honey, not even you.

Gabriel told her about St. Christopher House and the Little Lost Lambs. He wanted to be an actor. They sat in her dressing room and chatted about Broadway, life on the

214

road, the people in the profession.

As she spoke she tossed her head for emphasis. Gabriel admired her long, red hair, her generous mouth, the wide-open slate-colored eyes, her slender figure. She gave him a photograph and inscribed it, *To my dear friend Gabriel, from Michelle, with love.* He taped it to the wall of his third-floor bedroom. He invoked images of other women when he masturbated but his love for Michelle was not of the loins. He would not besmirch their relationship with gross thoughts.

During the second summer of Gabriel's apprenticeship, on an afternoon in July when the temperature and humidity were wedded at the zenith of discomfort, Michelle sent word that she was dying of heat, could she have some cold drinks delivered to her dressing room.

Gabriel arrived to find her alone at the makeup mirror. She was nude. No pasties. No panties.

She smiled into the glass and welcomed him with a grand sweep of arm.

—Come in. Put the bottles on the table. You're a dear. Let's have a drink together.

She turned in her chair and he saw first the golden ferns of her bush. His breath imprisoned in his throat caused him to gasp. He averted his eyes but they kept returning to the sight. The taut abdomen, the breasts with nipples the hue of orange-pink. The long hair in careless disarray about her face.

She sipped at her glass of Seagram's and Canada Dry. Tapering fingers motioned to him.

—Gabriel, honey, would you please brush my hair? Don't be shy. Nobody's around. They all went down to the lake. Hot as a bitch around here. She gulped the rye and ginger. As she handed him the brush, he was aware of the mixture of perfume and pungent woman smell. It eddied a wave of provocation about him. He brushed awkwardly the tangled strands.

—Not like that, I'll show you. She maneuvered him in front of her. His trousers coarsed against the soft thighs spread slightly for ventilation. She reached for his hand and exposed her hairless underarm moist with bubbles of

215

perspiration. Start at the crown and brush in sweeping strokes all the way down. Like this. Again. Again. She paused to see his furtive glances encompassing her form. She looked up at him, a roguish smile forming about the crimsoned lips.

—Do you like me? she asked simply.

Gabriel kissed her glancingly on the powdered cheek. — Yes.

She widened the span between her legs. Gabriel slipped down between them. He turned adoring eyes up to her. She smiled down at him.

—You're so serious, she said. Gabriel, the romantic. You'll suffer terribly you know. Here, let me see your palm. Just as I expected. The love-line is very pronounced. She placed his moist hand on her thigh. She raised his head.

—Look at me. What are you thinking?

—You're so beautiful, he stuttered.

—Come on, you can do better than that. Tell it to me romantically. One of your poems. The one to Deanna Durbin.

—I couldn't do that, he blushed. You're special.

—What do you see when you look at me, she teased. The kettledrum in his chest echoed in his ears. Above the surge he heard himself saying:

—Behold thou art fair, my love. Thine eyes are as doves. She was pleased.

—Continue Gabriel. Recite for me.

—Thy lips are like a thread of scarlet. And thy mouth is comely. She bent to him, her full, liquor-dampened lips on his dry ones.

—Thou hast ravished my heart.

She pulled him closer, his head in her bosom. She sang, *Sometimes I Feel Like a Motherless Child.* She kissed him tearfully.

—Thy neck is like a tower of ivory. Thy head upon thee is like Carmel. And the hair of thy head like purple.

His fingers glided about her hips.

—The roundings of thy thighs are like the links of a chain. He firmed his arms about her posterior. From his

216

kneeling position he implored: Set me as a seal upon thy heart. For love is strong as death. Many waters cannot quench love. Make haste, my beloved....

She opened for him and the scent of warm musk enfolded him. He kissed the inside of her thigh and she caressed his head and brought it toward the cleft barely visible. He kissed her bush and she eased upward and drew his head closer still and she opened wider and he kissed her vulva and she encouraged him to continue and his tongue began to explore as deep as he could get inside and he felt the contractions and then he tongued her where she directed him, around and around the bit of swollen tissue and her hips were rhythmic in response and her buttocks convulsed and she held him between her tightly closed legs. And then the electric current began to spark inside her and she began to heave, up from the chair and his muffled ears heard the moans and the gasps and then the final exquisite diminuendo.

She leaned back in the chair. She stroked his hair for awhile. Then she pulled him to her and kissed him.

—That was beautiful. Beautiful. You were very gentle. She kissed him again. Now I want to do something for you.

She unbuttoned his trousers and released that part of him straining in his loins.

—Magnificent, she whispered.

She leaned down to receive his manhood within the velvet softness of her mouth. His ejaculation was immediate.

—O my god, he apologized. I'm sorry. Sorry. Sorry.

—Some other time, she assured him. We'll try it again some other time. It will be better another time. Go now before they return.

\* \* \*

Whitey wiped his greasy hands on his splotched apron and threw a patty of meat on the spluttering stove. A puff of smoke ascended from the hamburger and the underside began to sizzle. He pressed down with the spatula, then turned back to the perusal of the *Racing Form*. He puffed quick snorts at a Sweet Caporal.

Gabriel on the revolving stool turned from the counter and watched the street faces pass by. The regulars of the White Spot Hamburger lounged at circular plastic-topped tables, waiting for pickups. Rendez-vous at the Union House (Ladies and Escorts Only) for a Saturday night of beer drinking. Then upstairs into a two dollar room for a two dollar score. Bam. Bam. Thank you, Sam.

The slanting rays of twilight lit up Simonsky's Pawn-brokers. Three balls above the entrance. Shop crowded with binoculars, watches, tools, musical instruments, jewelery. Cyril Loeb, thin, dark hair oiled flat against his skull, pencil mustache, picked his teeth as he leaned against the plate glass window of Cyril's Men's Haberdashers. Enjoying the air. He jabbed between two molars, dislodged a particle, scrutinized it, removed the fermenting flesh from the wooden sliver with careful fingers and inhaled the garlic. Reluctantly he flicked the morsel onto the sidewalk.

Along Queen Street from Bay to York others waited for customers. The petty bourgeoisie in dusty untidy shops supplying food, services and entertainment. Suey's Cafe. A & A Radio Service Supply. Tighe Lee Billiards and Barber. Chinese National League. Army Store. Dart Coon Club. Moler System of Barber Schools Ltd. Quick Service Coney Island Lunch. Harry Toben Pawnbroker. United Cigar Store.

In the gypsy joint next to M. Davis & Son, Men's & Boys Furnishings *(Davis will never willingly be undersold)*, the pock-roughened face of the Romany Sibyl looked out from the curtained store window. Madame Nadejzda. Fortune Teller. Cross her qualms with silver. Reads tea leaves. Phrenologist. Your mental powers analyzed. The diagram of the bald head indicating the thirty-five phrenological organs.

INCLINATIONS (Amativeness) SENTIMENTS (Self-Esteem) PERCEPTIVE FACULTIES (Individuality) REFLECTIVE FACULTIES (Causality). Reads Palms. The drawing of the human hand. Line of life. Line of the head.

218

Line of the heart. She chewed vacantly, a crust of bread. Gypsy, gypsy live in a tent. Have no money to pay the rent.

Gabriel, passing by her draped domicile was stopped by the tapping on the window. Tap. Tap. She opened the door, beckoning with a crooked, black finger.

—Want to see pussy? Look at gypsy pussy?

Gabriel politely enquired as to her fee for viewing. Fifty cents. He declined with thanks in basic English:

—No look at pussy today.

—Maybe you want to feel cunt, she stretched out a silk swathed arm to detain him. How much, he asked. To feel. She hoisted her several petticoats, multi-colored.

—To feel is one dollar. Gabriel demurred again. To do more—how much for—you know, he hinted at the act.

—With telling of fortune or without, she queried.

—Without, he said.

—Three dollars.

—Too much, Gabriel retorted. Not worth it.

—Too much! Go fuck pig! She spat at him and disappeared into the rear of the premises.

—Here y'are son. Hamburger on a bun. Greasestains slapped it on the counter. Gabriel spun round on his seat. Inhaled the steaming aroma of burnt meat. Reached for the Heinz and upended the bottle. The ketchup seeped sluggishly into the neck and plopped in pulpy gouts onto the meat. Next Gabriel wooden-spooned mustard from the container. He added pickle relish and sweet relish and mixed relish and raw rings of onion.

—Cup of tea, please, Gabriel ordered. Tea bag out.

He bit into the hamburger squirting juices from between the bun halves. He bent over the plate as he chewed, saving the droppings for the end. Wolfed down. He licked stained fingers and wiped them on the paper napkin.

—Here y'are. Tea. Bag out. Gabriel poured the water from the chipped china pot into the cracked cup. Held Heinz above the cup, thumping the bottle to force the ketchup. Incarnadine the liquid. He added pepper, a bit of salt, a drop of vinegar. He stirred and tasted. Tomato Soup. M-m-m-m- Good.

—More hot water please, Gabriel begged. Thank you. He reached for an empty cup beside him. Poured out the dregs on the floor. Inserted the tea bag. Made his brew and sipped. Nearby, half a donut, chocolate dipped, lay lonely on a monogrammed White Spot plate. Abandoned by previous diner. Take me. I'm yours. Gabriel sneaked it closer and ate. Drank tea. Fulfilled.

—That'll be ten cents for the hamburger. Five for the tea. Gabriel produced three nickels. They bore the bearded likeness of the late monarch. Georgius V. D.Gra. Fid. Def. Rex et Ind. Imp. His reign had closed in peaceful sleep at Sandringham House on January 20, 1936 at 6:55 P.M. E.S.T. Toronto's Big Ben (elevation 295 feet) tolled as the news was flashed from London. His Worship Mayor Sam McBride presided at the Memorial service at City Hall.

—The reign of a great King has ended. His Majesty served through an eventful period of world history during which he won the love and respect of subjects in the far flung British Empire. The Empire-wide celebrations last year of the 25th Anniversary of His Majesty's accession was striking evidence of the strong ties binding the Throne and the British Commonwealth of Nations. Toronto mourns the loss of a noble and beloved sovereign who labored unselfishly for the good of his people and for the welfare of the human race. His memory will ever be held in universal love and veneration by his people.

Condolences having been dispatched to the Queen Mother, the Royal Family, the Prime Minister, the formal statement of the sad event was interred in a time lock along with other pertinent information about the Queen City: Toronto, Indian name for meeting place is situate on the north shore of Lake Ontario almost due north of the Niagara River. It has a latitude of 43 deg. 39', 10" north and a longitude of 79 deg. 23' west. The City Hall opened September 18, 1899 at a cost of $2,500,000 has five acres of floor space. The city has an area of 34 square miles with 575.07 miles of streets and 157.83 miles of lanes. Population: 638,271. Births: 11,112. Marriages: 6,445. Deaths: 7,150. A list of hospitals, parks, playgrounds and abbatoirs included. Recorded also, the number of apprehended males: 88,908. Apprehended females: 10,422. Lost children: 921. License fees: One dollar for slot machines, freaks, circus performers, rag collectors. Sleight of hand operators: $5.00. Added to the thesaurus of civic miscellany, a comment penned by Charles Dickens a hundred years ealier:

*The town is full of life, motion, bustle, business and improvement. The streets are well paved. Shops are excellent. Many of them have a display of goods in their windows such as may be seen in thriving towns of England. There is a good stone prison here. There are besides, a handsome church, a court house, public offices, many commodious private residences and a government observatory for noting and recording the magnetic variations.*

Whitey accepted the Georgian coins: The King is dead. Long live Edward Albert, he said.

—I understand he has some property out west, Gabriel said. A ranch in Alberta I think.

—I remember when he visited Toronto after the war. Whitey flipped over a hamburger on the greasy hot plate. He sure was popular.

—You know, his motto really suited him: *Ich Dien.*

—Me too, Whitey tossed the meat on the bun, I also serve. But I don't get the same pay.

Edward Albert, Prince of Wales. Welcomed by the city fathers. Prayers for his health by the invested heads of the sixty-four Anglican Churches, fifty-nine Methodist, fifty Presbyterian, forty Baptist, thirty Roman Catholic, five Congregational and the other fifty miscellaneous denominations. And a special prayer by the Rabbi of the Toronto Hebrew Congregation.

—Then he came back in '27 with his brother George — Quiet George — for the dedication of the Princes' Gate. He sure lived it up. The women were crazy about him. Guess he'll have to settle down now.

Summoned to Buckingham Palace for the weighty responsibility of succession. Mayor McBride voiced the approval of the populace:

—Our new King Edward VIII has been the idol of millions throughout the world. The love and admiration of all races and creeds accompanies him as he assumes his grave duties. He ascends the throne with a wider knowledge of human nature than any of his predecessors.

His Majesty in his first broadcast message to his people throughout the Empire declared:

—I am better known to most of you as the Prince of Wales, as a man who during the war and since has had the opportunity of getting to know the people of every country of the world under all conditions and circumstances. Although I speak to you as the King, I am still the same man whose constant effort it will be to continue to promote the well-being of his fellow man.

Edward, the bachelor King. First since William IV. The royal matchmakers were having a difficult time pairing him with one of the bloodless females from the royal houses of Europe.

Chris Augenblick cautiously pushed open the door of the White Spot.

—Come on in, Beasley shouted. The young man eased a dainty shoulder inside, then the rest of the slim body. Hey fellas, look who's here. Christine. Queen of the Fairies.

—What an unspeakably tiring day, he sighed.

—You mean your pretty boy's disappointed you again? Beasley winked at the others.

—Oh no, Chris corrected him, it wasn't that at all. I was at the Library reading Schopenhauer. I'm deep into philosophy, you know.

—Sure, we know, said Jake Grizzle, superannuated newsboy from Queen and Bay. You're deep into everything. Mostly assholes.

—Oh, watch your language, Chris admonished and waltzed over to the counter. Beasley grabbed at him but Chris sidestepped, avoiding the confrontation.

—Hey Beasley, Sammy the chink called out, Christine's particular about who plays with him. He won't let anybody with the smell of cunt on his fingers within a mile of him.

—What'll ya have, your highness, Whitey asked.

222

—I'd like something to eat. I'm famished. But I don't have any money. Chris tucked his open collared, white on white, silk shirt neatly into the skin tight, duck trousers.

—How about doing a dance for us Christine? You perform and we'll buy your supper.

—Yeah, do a strip tease. Like Gypsy Rose Lee.

—Nah. Ann Corio is better. Do it like Corio.

—Margie Hart. Without the G-string.

—Slow. Easy. Like Michelle Morgan.

—What's it gonna be? Bobby Morris?

They crowded about him, urging.

—Aw, come on fellas, Chris pleaded. I just want a quarter for something to eat.

—Dance for your supper, Jake said. Come on, let's see you wiggle your ass. Beasley goosed him. Chris high stepped away. Whitey flicked a towel snap against his ass.

Chris scolded him, Oh stop that! —You're the only one here who understands me, he sat down beside Gabriel. Let's go to Sunnyside tonight, huh?

—Can't. Gotta work the last show. Cigarets. Candy. Ice cream pies.

—Heavens, I'm hungry, Chris surveyed the menu chalk scrawled on the board. I'll do one dance. For twenty-five cents. Right?

Chris started slowly, pirouetting between the tables.

We are dainty little fairies

ever singing, ever dancing.

The dusk of evening turned on the street lights and across the way the electrified legs above the marquee of the Roxy Burlesque kicked high, kicked high, inviting, exciting.

—*Je suis Titania*, the queen announced and the courtiers applauded, as Chris glided about them, caressing his face and neck and nipples. He tossed his head of bleached blond hair.

—Attagirl, Beasley shouted. They were all clapping, urging him on.

Chris swivel-hipped over to Jake and began the bumps. Jake backed off. Chris pursued. Jake fell and Chris straddled him. *And I am once again with you.* He stroked Jake's weathered, stubbled face. Jake swore at him. Fuck off, you queer. Chris abandoned him. He waltzed over to Beasley and executed three deliberate bumps. Beasley fell back. Chris pursued, embraced Beasley and kissed him on the mouth. Beasley pushed him away.

—Let's have a big hand for Christine, said Whitey. Queen Christine the First!

Beasley wiped his lips: Fucking queer!

* * *

Big, burly Rags Ragland in the Crazy House sketch. Face of a boxer. Beautiful timing. Delivers a line just perfectly. Double take. Freeze. Milk the last chuckle.

MICHELLE

*(In white nurse's uniform, sits at reception desk. A good deal of bosom is revealed. She uncrosses her legs frequently showing a lot of thigh. She is reading a book. Jack the Ripper. Enter one of the inmates in a state of agitation.)*

INMATE

*(Rushes to center of stage. Looks up at spotlight.)* They're coming for me.

MICHELLE

Who's coming for you?

INMATE

*(Points)* A flock of wild flying sewing machines. I can hear them.

MICHELLE

What do you mean you can hear them?

INMATE

They're Singers. *(He rushes off).*

RAGS

*(Enters cautiously. Looks around)* I was told you wanted a night watchman. What kind of place is this? A crazy house?

MICHELLE

No. An insane asylum.

RAGS

Oh, that's different. I'll take the job. What do I have to do?

MICHELLE

First, you'll have to be examined by Dr. Kronkheit. *(She does a sexy walk to the accompaniment of grinds towards stage left and rings a hand bell. She returns with the same sinuous movements and sits on corner of desk swinging her legs. Doctor enters carrying satchel, stethoscope around his neck, reflecting light on head. He makes for the nurse, stretches her out on top of desk and begins to examine her.)*

MICHELLE

No. No. Doctor. Not me. Him. The night watchman. *(He releases her and does zany dance step in the direction of Rags.)*

KRONKHEIT

*(Stage German accent).* Vell, my goot man, so you want to be the night watchman here, is it?

RAGS

That's right Doc. Sure.

KRONKHEIT

How old are you?

RAGS

Fifty-three years.

KRONKHEIT

How long you been out of work?

RAGS

Fifty-three years. *(Dr. figures mental arithmetic, comes up with satisfactory answer.)*

KRONKHEIT

What's your father's name?

RAGS

Ben.

KRONKHEIT

What's your mother's name?

RAGS

Anna.

KRONKHEIT

What is your name?

RAGS

Ben-Anna.

KRONKHEIT

*(Nods wisely)* I see. *(Regards him carefully, walks full circle around him. Reverses and walks full circle the opposite way.)* Tell me, do you have a Fairy Godmother?

RAGS

No. But we've got an uncle we're not so sure about.

KRONKHEIT

Prepare for medical examination. On guard. *(Dr. places stethoscope on RAGS' chest, listens, places stethoscope on his own chest, gives the other end to RAGS to listen, motions MICHELLE to come over, places stethoscope on her chest. He and RAGS take turns listening. Reaction: from interest to joy to amazement as she breathes hard,*

*breasts heaving. She pushes them away and KRONKHEIT*
*resumes examination of RAGS. He places the scope at top*
*of RAGS' chest, then middle then the bottom.)* Eeny-
meeny-mighty-moe.

### RAGS

*(Stops scope at waist level)* Stay away from Little Joe.

### KRONKHEIT

All right, nurse. This man is *non compos mentis*. But he
is medically sound. You vill proceed now to make him
comfortable. You want him to be a happy member of our
little family.

### MICHELLE

Oh sure, Doctor Kronkheit. *(She goes into slow*
*bumps)* You can rely on me. *(Doctor and nurse do adagio*
*together towards exit. NURSE executes fantastic last*
*bump and practically hurls him into the wings. She returns*
*to RAGS.)* All right, Mr. Ben-Anna. You can get undressed
now while I make up the bed. *(She turns from him to-*
*wards the small cot. As he starts to undress she turns*
*around to look at him.)*

### RAGS

*(His trousers half-way down his legs.)* Oh nurse...*(he*
*motions her to look away.)*

### MICHELLE

Oh, that's all right. I'm used to those little things.
*(RAGS does double take, then begins pulling up his pants.*
*MICHELLE turns away. RAGS completes undressing, is*
*wearing long, white nightgown.)* Now. Your job is to guard
the door. Don't let any of the patients escape. If you want
anything *(she does bumps and grinds)* just send for me.

### RAGS

If I want anything *(he imitates her)* just send for you?

### MICHELLE

If...you...want...anything....*(bump-bump-bump)*

just...send...for...me. *(She exits. RAGS lies down on cot.)*

### CORPSE

*(Dressed in black, face yellow, staggers in, makes for RAGS.)* Hey mister, did you see a funeral go by?

### RAGS

No. Why?

### CORPSE

I just fell out of the hearse. *(Exits running. RAGS lies down again. MAN runs back and forth across stage, unrolling toilet paper.)*

### RAGS

Hey, where do you think you're going?

### MAN

*(Holds up toilet paper.)* Crap game. *(Exits.)*

### RAGS

*(Prepares to lie down. Each time he is interrupted. Little man chases big girl in short negligee. Drunk enters, whiskey bottle in hand. He sets it on table and staggers about. RAGS reaches for bottle, puts it to his lips and takes a swig. DRUNK notices.)*

### DRUNK

Hey, don't touch that. I'm taking it to the doctor. *(RAGS spits out a torrent of water. DRUNK retrieves bottle and exits. OPHELIA-LIKE CHARACTER appears, sleep walking, carrying a watering can. RAGS freezes, watches.)*

### GIRL

*(Sings)* There are flowers at the bottom of my garden... *(She approaches RAGS, upends the can and drenches him — right down the front of his nightgown. She exits humming. RAGS does a lot of business, wringing out his nightgown, etc. He has twisted the wet fabric into a phallic*

*form at the level of his genitals. MICHELLE comes on. RAGS sees her, stops stage business, holding the material, penis-like in his hand.)*

### MICHELLE

Oh John, lay it on the floor. *(Bumps)* Oh John, lay it on the floor *(More bumps as she moves downstage right.)* Oh John...*(bump)*...lay it *(bump)* on the *(bump)* floor. *(Exits.)*

### RAGS

*(To audience)* Just my luck. My name is Wilbur.

### (BLACKOUT)

## 16

The Saturday night poker game started at nine. Eli presided over the weekly sessions.

Sara, from the kitchen, scrubbing the long johns in the galvanized tub, heard the knock at the door, then the clamorous descent of Joshua, two steps at a time. Old Rachel set out the peanuts and the ginger ale, then joined her husband in their bedroom.

Knock. Knock. Joshua scrambled downstairs again. Three more customers. The others are here? Good. We brought the whiskey.

—*Patchy, patchy.* The grandmother played clap hands with the baby. The grandfather stopped in his prayers, closed the *siddur.* Everything was changing. He wasn't happy about his wife's new chores, feeding Sadie's little one, changing his diapers, taking him for a buggy ride — all interfered with his own comforts. He no longer enjoyed the position Biblically vouchsafed as head of the family. He had to wait until the baby was attended to. What about my supper? He had to remind Rachel.

—Oh, you didn't have it yet? I must have forgotten. I'll make it right away. Scrambled eggs with onions, all right?

—All right. But make already.

Sara hung the washing to dry on lines strung across the kitchen. The underwear and shirts pinned in serried ranks like ghosts.

—Time to go to the market. Hurry up Aaron.

Aaron put down the prayer book. She was waiting in the hall. At the door she stopped, grimaced in the direction of the laughter upstairs. It won't finish till early in the morning. They have no respect for anybody. Come, let's go.

As the evening lengthened the residents returned to No. 47. Sadie and her husband, the cap maker, from a visit to his family on Phoebe Street. Samson and his mutt from a bicycle jaunt up Bathurst to Bloor and back. Freda from an evening at the Orange Hall. Hadn't won a game all week. Didn't Bingo tonight either. She would not tell

Solly. Lucky he wasn't home yet. Out with the shop steward at an executive meeting of the Union. That's what he told her. She knew what kind of a meeting it was. *Klubyash.* Solly the Blackjack giant. Fat Solly, darkly mustachioed. Hey Solly, imitate Pancho Villa. First a drink. Solly emptied the shot glass of rye, wiped his two chins with a flabby palm. He sat back and hollered: Hola Señora, breeng nodder bottle Tequila for Pancho Villa. He dug thick pistol fingers into Moishe's wife's ass.

Eli slid the small pile of poker chips towards him. The house was doing well tonight. Your deal Max, he pushed the pack to the foreman of the Delight Dress Company. Have a salami sandwich Victor. You too, Lazar. Eat. Play. Be happy. Joshua, tell Ma to make some coffee.

Returned from Kensington Market, Sara stowed the apples and oranges, the meat and eggs into the ice box. She wrapped a cloth around the frozen cube. Had to last till Monday. Put the sign in the window for the iceman. She checked the pan and emptied the water. Time for bed. She walked in stockinged feet into the hallway listening. Still pokering, she muttered as the snatches of levity from above drifted down. Tomorrow she would deliver one of her cease-and-desist orders. In the bedroom she removed her housedress then the corselette allowing the tires of flesh to hang loosely, glad to be free of the encumbrance.

—Blessed be the Lord by day. Blessed be the Lord by night. Our God who art in heaven, reign over us for ever and ever, Aaron, in his white combinations, finished the prayer.

—Check the front door, make sure it's locked, Sara said. He did so. Pull down the window blinds. Make sure the window screen is in the window. He did so. When he was in bed she clicked the light switch on the wall and groped to her bed. She lay for awhile looking up at the heavy brass chandelier, three bell shapes with bulbs screwed into them. She turned over on her side. Aaron was breathing heavily. Perhaps tonight he would not dream-scream. The recurring nightmare. Chased by a pack of mongrels through the streets of Opatow into the Market Square. Seeking sanctuary in the Cathedral. Refuge refused by the black-bearded, black-gowned priest who shouted: Dirty Jew, get out. Stumbling down the hill through the medieval town gate, the barking curs nipping at him. Sara slapping him awake.

—God in heaven. What's happening? Open your eyes. His thrashing body relaxed. Oh, oh, uh-uh-uh, his cries subsided. You scared me to death with your screaming. How many times have I told you not to sleep on your heart. Turn over on your right side. Maybe you won't dream.

Aaron apologized, obliged and fell asleep again. Sara couldn't sleep. The mechanism of memory replayed the events of the day. Of the week. Of all her years. Replayed the injustices perpetrated against her by her husband's family. Despite her own tireless efforts on their behalf. Did she get any thanks for her unselfishness? No sir! She was rebuffed by the whole kit and kaboodle. After all she had done. Taking them in for practically nothing. She could have rented the rooms to strangers and received more appreciation and more money. Nobody in the Coxie Army upstairs even spoke to her. They came and went with averted faces. The old woman proferred the nine dollars once a month. She didn't speak. Just handed Sara the bills and stood there in Parsifal innocence until Sara told her it was all right, she could go back upstairs.

—Two weeks late, Sara complained to Aaron.

—You should have asked for it at the beginning of the month, he advised.

—I wouldn't lower myself, she snorted.

She informed him (again) that she came from a much better family. Wasn't her father Shmuel Grynszpan, a land-lord with a house, a farm and many head of cattle? Wasn't he respected by the whole community, even by the *goyim?* Aaron was lucky to have gotten her for a wife. She could have done better. Many young men were after her hand. Educated, well-to-do young men, even *yeshiva bochurs.* Oh yes, the best in Opatow. But her father had chosen the sensitive Aaron, with his trim beard and piercing eyes, for his eighteen year old daughter. He will honor you all the days of your life. You'll learn to love him. The engagement was announced at the synagogue and the contract deliver-

232

ed to the prospective bride. The dowry, generous as befitted a man of Shmuel Grynszpan's position, was paid to Aaron's father. Aaron gave his bride-to-be a prayer book, a fine silk veil and a gold ring. She presented him with a prayer shawl and silver pocket watch with a silver chain. The full moon the night of the wedding vied in illumination with the flickering light from the many lanterns held by the guests. Bright shining faces. Freshly-laundered blouses and dresses and trousers and coats. Polished boots. There was Hershel Weisskopf, the hunch-back, with his wife, Shayndl, who spoke through her nose. Zalman Guttkind, the bootmaker, who employed five assistants including Aaron. Itzik Goldwasser, the silversmith. Yechiel Polakievitch, the young dandy who rolled cigarets for a living. All the relatives and many children. And the musicians.

Aaron, dressed in a new *chalat* over a white *kittel* (Remember the day of thy death and repent), was led to the *chuppah* canopy and stood with his face to the East (If I forget thee, O Jerusalem...). Then came Sara, purified that afternoon in the *mikvah*, white-gowned and veiled, led by her bridesmaids. The groomsmen and the Rabbi and her father's close friends, all prominent members of the Jewish community, dressed in their black coats and fur hats, walked towards her. A chanting arose: Our sister, be thou a mother of ten thousand. They turned away from her and proceeded to the *chuppah*. The singing began: a hymn of praise to the Lord for His goodness. The bridesmaids brought Sara under the *chuppah* and her parents walked with her seven times around the groom. Standing at Aaron's right hand she heard the *Chazzan's* deep baritone: Blessed be ye who come in the name of the Lord. Tova, her closest friend, raised Sara's veil. The Rabbi, long-white-bearded with many valleys etched in his old face, took a step towards them. Is this young man pleasing in thy sight? he asked. Sara answered softly, Yes. The singing began again. *Hinay mah tov umanayim.* Sara was led to a stool and her rich auburn hair was sheared close to her head. Henceforth she would always wear a wig for it is written that a married woman has no longer any business to please a man. Her mission in life has been fulfilled.

Sara absently braided strands of greying hair. The tears washed her eyes and trickled down her cheeks as she remembered the ceremony. Aaron's avowal as he placed the golden encirclement upon the forefinger of her right hand, Behold Thou art consecrated unto me by this ring according to the law of Moses and Israel. The seven benedictions enunciated by the rabbi ending with, Blessed art thou O Lord, who makest the bridegroom to rejoice with the bride. Sara and her groom sipping from the wine glass. Aaron's heel coming down-smash-on the glass — remembrance of the ancient grief tempering the joy of the moment. Shouts of *Mazel Tov*. A beautiful and gracious bride. Handfuls of hops thrown over them, for prosperity and fertility. After the rite of consecration they were led to her chamber by the rejoicing parents.

Their wedding dinner. She and Aaron partook in private of the food and wine. From the courtyard the shouts of merriment, the singing and the dancing.

The *klezmorim* were tuning up. Five itinerant musicians who had come from Sandomierz. A fife player, a violinist, a drummer, a flutist, a trumpet player. They played firt the *Mazel Tov* dance. Then the dance for the parents of the bride and groom. Then folk dances. Hebrew and Polish themes. Zalman, the *badchen*, sang mock laments and joked and cavorted with the guests. Sara and Aaron joined the others and danced and accepted the good wishes heaped upon them from all sides. Later they returned to her room and prepared for bed. In the dark, fumbling under the goose-feather comforter she fulfilled the obligation encumbent upon a Jewish bride. As it is stated in Genesis: Be fruitful and multiply.

A woman's scream from the Western Hospital. May she have a safe delivery. Sara had suffered three miscarriages and a stillbirth. When the bleeding wouldn't stop she saw Dr. Rothbart at the Mount Sinai. Her final cleaning. You'll be all right now, Sara, he assured her. We had to remove the ovaries. A cancer? No. No malignancies. You should have a full life. A long life.

How long is a lifetime? Long enough to see her family

234

again? If only her father hadn't been so obstinate. After the business trip to New York (she was seven) he vowed never to return to the New World. Too frantic. Everybody rushing, working, no time for prayer. Better to live here in the little shtetl where a Jew can still be a Jew and follow the precepts of his forefathers. Every Passover Shmuel Grynszpan prayed, Next year in Jerusalem. But he remained in Opatow. With the lice and the bedbugs, with the herring and the garlic, bowing *Dzien Dobry* to the Lord of the Manor, jostled by the beggars as he passed by them, unheeding of their cries, *Piece groszy, proszy pan, piece groszy.* Shmuel Grynszpan was comfortable in his village, the streets with their wooden pavements crowded with Jewishness. Jews with peaked caps and rough peasant attire, the *tzitzits* proclaiming their identities. Jews in *chalats*. Talmudists. Tradesmen.

At the market the bartering. Buy fish. Nice, fat fish. Do you think I'm so stupid to pay thirty-four *groshen* for such a small carp? Who says it's small? The *goya* spat. *Parszywy zhyd.* The Jewish merchant placed the undernourished fish back in the tank and muttered: *A kaporeh oif dir.* Shmuel, sitting with friends at the inn where Josef sold vodka and sausages, listened to the gossip. From all over the Kielce *voivodship* the latest information was delivered and interpreted. Who died. Who was married. There was a fire at the synagogue in Sandomierz. The *sefer Torah* was saved. The Jewish corn factor from Staszow was beaten by a *goy*, a *shikker*. The Jews in Ostrowiec had to stay indoors on Easter Sunday. Nobody was hurt, praise God. Not like 1906. Corpus Christi Day. The terror on horseback. White smocked Cossacks in loose trousers and high boots sweeping through Bialystok firing into the Jewish houses. The hooligans looting, breaking furniture, cutting off noses and ears. It was much worse in those days. Even during the Great War they had managed.

They had barely survived, Sara thought bitterly. Digging in the wintry fields for roots. Happy to find a shriveled carrot or a turnip. Terrified at the approach of the Kaiser's soldiers. Relieved to find them well-mannered and courteous. Their quarrel with the Tsar. After the peace treaty, new borders, the same old problems for the Jews.

—Father, we're finally leaving. She showed him the remittance from Aaron. Shmuel wasn't listening.

—The anti-semite, Pilsudski, is the new head of the government. I heard the news this morning. More trouble.

—Leave Opatow, she pleaded. Come with us.

—My home is here, he insisted. We'll survive. We're Jews. We managed in Sinai. In the desert. We'll manage here.

Having transacted his business, a good price received for the new calf, Shmuel pushed past the haggling vendors. Buy. Buy. Buy a chicken. Pretty lady, buy some ribbon for the hair. Cucumbers. Strawberries. Cherries. Shmuel was eager to get to the *Bes Midrash* where the Rabbi and others learned in the law were pondering over a passage from Deuteronomy: If it is eleven days' journey from Horeb unto Kadeshbarnea by the way of Mount Seir, why then did it take Moses forty years to lead the Children of Israel to the promised land?

So Shmuel and his wife and four sons and two daughters stayed in Opatow. He and Sara exchanged infrequent letters. Full of the small talk of the daily round: First I wish to tell you about the health of all of us here, hoping to hear the same from you. A healthy child, a girl was born to your sister Rosa. Your brother Yankel moved into his own house on the hill. The *aktsiyah* lent some of the money. The cow gave birth to another calf. Marshall Pilsudski died recently. (Blessed be the everlasting.) Now things will get better. Everybody here is well. We send our love to you and to your husband and your children.

Sara wrote that she was well. The Depression had to end soon. She didn't say anything about her loneliness, her apprehension that she would never see them again. She didn't write about the bunch upstairs.

The expletives exploded beyond the closed door as one of the players won a hand. The smell of tobacco was filtering down into her bedroom, a harbinger of the suffocating smoke from the coal stove in the coming months. She would have to visit the Jewish Federation soon for second-hand clothing for her sons. She was a bit ashamed

236

that they should be working where the naked ladies dance. Not home yet.

* * *

Maxwell Plum light-fingered the closing arpeggio. The Roxy orchestra crashed out the coda. 11:37 P.M.

—Kill the lights. Strike the set, the stage manager shouted. Work lights. The proscenium curtain swung open. Bring up the houselights The crew dismantled the scenery. The casual help stood by to assist. Sammy the Chink. Chris. Noah. Clambering with props and sets up three flights to the storage area. Michelle Morgan carrying a suitcase came by Gabriel at Hushie's concession. She kissed him.

—Goodnight, sweetheart. See you next time around. In six weeks.

—Goodbye, he smiled in sorrow. She moved on colt's legs, her hips a rhapsody, under the flowered jersey dress. Cyril was waiting for her in the lobby.

—Where to, lady? My Chevy's outside.

Michelle far away in time and space. The red clay fields of Jonesboro. The old railway station. The old jail at King and McDonough streets. The old plantations, clapboard houses with sagging porches, the Fitzgerald place, the Talmadge estate. The visits to Atlanta with her mother. Dancing lessons. Shopping on Peach Tree Street. Growing up all too soon. Meeting Dexter Cartwell at the vaudeville theater. Running away to marry him. Going on the road with him. Joining the chorus. Graduating to the feature attraction: Michelle Morgan: Exotic. The marriage breaking up. Matinée idol Dexter Cartwell and his lady friends. Separation. Then the loneliness. Then the men clamoring for her favors with gifts and propositions.

Michelle Morgan fighting nihilism with lavish sexual grappling. Drowning in Lethe waters. *Ménages à deux, à trois, à quatre*. The daisy chain established. The daisy chain broken. The circuit via Detroit, Chicago and Buffalo ultimately bringing her back to Toronto. To Cyril. To Whitey. To Shoesie. To Sammy the Chink. To Beasley. To eager Gabriel and his uncontrolled orgasm.

—My place. The V.I.P. suite at the Ford. Ha. Ha.

—O.K. First we'll get the corned beef and stuff from Shopsowitz. I've got a bottle of rye in the glove compartment.

He made a U turn and headed for Spadina. He placed a warm hand on her lap. Warmer still his desire.

At 1:55 A.M. the incandescence blinked off at the Roxy. Homeward bound the brothers, accompanied by Frenchie, sounded echoes along lonely Queen Street. Stringy-haired, cadaverous Frenchie had no abode. *Un petit chien perdu.* He washed dishes at Bowles, sold scratch sheets at Woodbine, peddled papers for Sam Meister, worked as hopper for City News.

—Good show next week, Frenchie said. George Ferguson. Peanuts Bohn. And Ann Corio. *La poitrine magnifique. Les fesses extraordinaires.* In all my years I have not seen such sculpture of flesh. *Sacre tabernacle!*

—*Ferme ta gueule*, Gabriel responded.

—*Foures-toi*, from Frenchie.

—*Cochon*, Gabriel countered. Noah listened with admiration. Foreign words. Frenchie's Québecois. Gabriel's assiduously acquired school French.

—*Auprès de ma blonde.* Frenchie turning nostalgic for the girl he left behind. For the Côte Joyeuse that sloped from the highway down to his village.

—*J'attendrai...le jour et la nuit...j'attendrai toujours...ton retour.* She is not waiting for me, he said. *Seulement une nuit d'amour.* Den she tell me she is *enceinte* (he showed the big belly). Her fadder come after me with shotgun. *Mon dieu*, I run away fast. Out of St. Raymond. Get ride to Montreal. Nobody find me in the rooming house of Rue St. Denis.

—Would you like to go back? Gabriel asked.

—Never. Always wanting to get away. Away from goddam parish priest with beads and Hail Mary. Get away from brothers and sisters. Eleven.

—Where you headed next, Frenchie, Noah asked, excited to know.

—Out west maybe. Winnipeg. St. Boniface. Vancouver.

238

Travel boxcar style. First class.

—Well, tonight you're coming home with us. Huh, Noah? The younger brother agreed. Right!

—*Très gentil de toi. Très gentil.* I accept.

The trio moved by Osgoode Hall, Noah trailing a splinter of wood along the iron railings. The funny gates once kept cows from trespassing upon the grounds of the Law Society of Upper Canada.

—*Vive la Canadienne. Vole, mon coeur, vole.*

At Spadina the Orpheum Theatre, a tomb of ghosts. Memories of Frankenstein's monster trailing Gabriel through the dismal basement corridors. The shade of Fu Manchu hovering over him at the urinal. Velly sharp razor cut off balls and cock. Roasted and ground into powder for the Chinese aphrodisiac. Served to tired Jewish business-men in the garment center down the street. The lights in the lofts of the old buildings showed yellow against the black of brick and sky. Always somebody designing a dress, cutting a pattern, stitching, pressing. The Jewish en-trepeneurial system. Instant capitalism.

At Dundas the church bell announced the quarter hour. Almost three. Westward Ho, past small shops, silent and dark except for the reflection of the crescent moon pacing their stride. Clop. Clop on the pavement. Past Augusta. Up Denison to the parkette where the worshippers from the Kiever Shul promenaded on Yom Kippur, avoiding the water fountain on the day of fasting. Along Bellevue Place, renamed Wales Avenue in honor of Edward Albert.

—That's St. Christopher House. Gabriel bowed before the neighborhood shrine.

—And there's old man Wineapple's grocery store, Noah whispered. One small bulb flickering in the ceiling. Ward off thieves. The gray tabby curled around the display of oranges s-t-r-e-t-c-h-e-d a furry leg. Frenchie tapped the flattened catnose behind the pane of glass. The lids opened lazily, green eyes questioning, then lowered again.

—My street. Leonard. Home soon. Sleep soon.

—*Auprès de ma blonde*, Frenchie sang out.

—Sh-h-h. Wake up everybody. Get hell from my mother. If she sees you it'll be S.O.L.

Sara heard the tinny insertion into the keyhole, the turning of metal and the creak of the unoiled hinges. Her two boys were home. Perhaps she would sleep now.

—You got party going on? Frenchie whispered.

—Upstairs. Poker game. Should be breaking up anytime now. Gabriel preceded Frenchie down the dark hallway, past the parents' bedroom, beyond the dining room, stepping cautiously between the heavy circular table and the squat buffet, into the kitchen.

—Watch out for the clothes lines. Sit here at the table. Gabriel switched on the light.

—Christ, Frenchie gasped, you take in washing? Look at the goddam stuff hanging here.

—Quiet. Keep it down, Gabriel admonished.

—Yeah, Noah said, I think I heard Ma. Noah at the sink, stopped peeing, listened, heard nothing, resumed, aiming for the drain, the warm yellow of his stream diluted by the gush from the faucet. Finished, he dipped fingers in the water, wiped them on his pants and said a prayer.

From the ice box, Gabriel eased a plate of apple strudel and a bottle of milk. The three ate and drank. Frenchie asked for more. Gabriel found a chicken leg, plump, roasted, savory with garlic.

—*Mon dieu, j'ai faim.* Frenchie tore off strips of flesh, stuffed into mouth and chewed and swallowed and finished with half a bottle of milk.

The three undressed. Gabriel and Noah in their combinations on the couch. Frenchy in jockey shorts on the frayed Oriental rug beside them, a cushion under his head, the linen slipcover over him.

—Goodnight. *Bonne nuit. Merci pour le repas.*

—That's  O.K.

—*A demain.*

In the silence Gabriel thought of Michelle. Frenchy remembered the Saturday night dances in St. Raymond; the thin girls with their small breasts and bony asses. Noah wondered if he had washed away all traces of his urine.

—Let's call it a night, boys, Eli yawned. He stood up and the chair crashed to the floor. Joshua accompanied the poker players dowsntairs.

—Goddam those fuckers, Gabriel growled.

—*Maudits bâtards*, Frenchy echoed.

—Lowlifes, Sara muttered.

Aaron on his right side lay in dreamless sleep.

—Night. Goodnight. See ya next week. Same time. Joshua locked the door and left the key in the aperture. Everybody home.

From her attic bedroom Freda heard the clang of the clock in the Fire Hall Tower. Half past three. Solly not in yet. Solly had an accident? Tonight would be her night of misery. She knew it. Destiny. She squirted drops into her nose and sniffled and blew into one of her supply of orange wrappers.

Gabriel poked Noah in the side. Noah stopped snoring and turned over.

A knocking brought Sara frightened from her bed. Who's there? She pulled on a robe and hurried in bare feet to the door. Somebody was sing-shouting on the verandah. She knew who it was before she unlocked.

Pancho the bandit, sick in the head.

Pancho the bandit, long due for his bed.

Freda from the head of the stairs shouted, Is it Solly? The others behind her, pushing to confirm. Is it Solly?

—He's drunk, Sara said. Look at him lying there. He's all covered in vomit.

—My darling wife, he moaned. I love my darling wife. I love my darling children. Who says Solly doesn't look after his family? Who says so?

—So you're home at last, Freda shouted. Did they let you stagger through the streets?

—No-oh-oh. In the car. Brought me home in the car, he sighed.

—Sure, Freda sniffled, they get you drunk, cheat you at cards, take your money and throw you back to me. Fine friends you've got.

—Good friends, Solly agreed. The best. The shop chairman. All the boys. For the Union makes us strong. Glory, hallelujah, he tried to rise, fell back. Freda grabbed him. Joshua on the other side of Solly. They pulled him inside and propelled him up the stairs.

On the landing Solly lurched. The fermentation swirling in his gut erupted through the grinning mouth and splashed, a bile green shower, onto his wife.

—Freda, the toilet, the toilet. I have to shit. She pushed him inside the chamber. Pulled down his puke-stained trousers and sat him down. The loose stool poured from his bowels, coated the long-johns, dripped through the fabric and splashed plop, plop, in the bowl.

Solly groaned, Oh my head. My stomache.

Freda alternately soothed and lectured him. There. There. You'll feel better. Keep this cold compress on your head.

The others withdrew. Solly fell off his perch. Freda helped him on again.

—One more affair like this and I'm finished with you, she cried. You should be ashamed of yourself. A fine example for your children.

Sara locked the front door and retired to tell Aaron the complete story in detail.

—Promise me you'll never get drunk again, promise me, Freda sniffled.

—Never. Never again. I promise, my darling wife. From his seat on the pot he embraced his spouse. She waited until he was finished, washed him, changed his underwear and led him to their bed.

Solly, King of the Revellers, outstretched, sceptre in hand, slept, dreamed of a Royal Flush.


* * *


On the tenth day of the ultimate month, *Anno Domini* 1936 HRH the Duke of York, Albert, Fred, Arthur, George — Quiet George — succeeded his brother. By the instrument of abdication: *I cannot carry on as King of England without the help and support of the woman I love.*

—Too bad about Edward, Whitey attacked a grease spot on the counter, looks like that Simpson woman has him by the knackers. Throwing away throne and all.

—I'd like a lover like that, Julie Kovics, munching on a hamburger, sighed. Somebody who would give up the whole world. Just for me. That's what I call a real grandstand performance.

—Yeah. Top banana, Whitey said. Crown Jewels and all.

—Ah, it must be a wonderful thing to lie under a King, Chris the queer tremoloed.

GOD SAVE KING GEORGE VI, the banner headline in purple on the front page of the *Star*.

At a special meeting of the City Council, W. D. Robbins, mayor, in the chair, the following resolution was unanimously passed on a motion of Controllers Wadsworth and Conboy:

—We, Your Majesty's most loyal and devoted subjects, the Council of the Corporation of the City of Toronto, assembled in special session this twelfth day of May, 1937, to do homage and service to Your Majesty's Throne and Person, desire to express our feelings of willingness and joy at Your Majesty's Coronation and greet Your Majesty with clamorous acclaim as our only lawful and rightful liege lord, to whom we do acknowledge all faith and constant obedience. Today, from every hill and valley within the far-flung Empire, echo answers echo as Your Majesty's loyal subjects with one heart and voice cry out: God Save King George. We humbly pray that God's richest blessings may be outpoured upon Your Majesty, Your Most Gracious Consort, Queen Elizabeth, the Queen Mother, the Princess Elizabeth and all the Royal Family, that by His assistance Your Majesty may be granted the spirit of wisdom to preserve the people committed to your charge in wealth, peace and Godliness.

—So don't forget, Zayde, the new King is George. Remember that when they ask you at City Hall. George the Sixth, Gabriel coached his grandfather. That was the only alteration in the weeks of preparation.

—Now, let's have another rehearsal. Judah Lion Gottesman, approach the stand. Before we grant you citizenship the law requires that you answer a number of fundamental questions about the country of your adoption.

Gabriel translated the preamble into Yiddish. The Lion nodded. He understood. He looked at Gabriel through clouding vision, the shaggy grey eyebrows uplifted to catch the first question.

—Name the capital of Canada. The grandfather stroked the greygroomed beard, adjusted the skull cap on the gray thatch and answered.

—Ottawa. A proud, learned response. Ottawa it is capital of Canada.

—Very good. Now, who is the Prime Minister?

—King.

—No, not the King, the Prime Minister.

—Is King. William Lyon King.

—That's right. His full name is William Lyon Mackenzie King.

—Many names for one man.

—Who is our King and what is the name of Her Gracious Lady the Queen?

—George Six and Elizabeth.

—No, admonished Gabriel. You say it like this: His Majesty King George the Sixth and Her Royal Highness Queen Elizabeth.

—George and Elizabeth, the old man repeated.

—Can you name two of the provinces?

—Ontario.....

—Another?

—...Ontario...and Quebec... and King Edward Island.

—*Prince* Edward Island. Ontario and Quebec. Remember these two. There are nine provinces altogether. From the Atlantic to the Pacific. What is the date of Confederation?

—Con... ?

—When did Canada become one country?

—Eighteen hundred, sixty-seven.

—Name two of the Fathers of Confederation.

—Johnny Walker and...

—No. No. Sir John A. Macdonald. And who else?

—And...and...Brown. John Brown?

—No. George Brown.

—That's right. John and George. I pass?

—You pass.

The day of the interrogation Gabriel delivered the Lion to the flag-draped Citizenship Court in City Hall.

—All rise, the clerk nasalized. All stood for the entry of the black-robed figure. Be seated. All sat.

The judge gazed sternly about him. He nodded, a perfunctory acknowledgement of their collective presence. He perused the sheaf of documents before him. Names, dates, statistics.

When finally Judah's name was called, Gabriel motioned to him to advance and face the Judge. Timorously the old man shuffled before the bench of the court. Stripped of anonymity, exposed in all his Jewish frailness looking apprehensively at the Christian Lawgiver. Instinct stronger than reason expected opprobrium. A hurled epithet — Christ Killer. In Opatow at Easter the blood libel. Mixing Christian blood with Jewish Matza. Pass-over, O God. Stay the violence during this the season of our deliverance from bondage.

—Gottesman, the voice omnipotent sounded the Teutonic syllables. Are you familiar with the history of this country, its chiefs of state, the political system, the names and location of our provinces, the extent of our vast country, *a mari usque ad mare?*

The cobbler from Opatow was familiar with the view from the basement window that looked out on the hilly street of the ghetto. Names bounded across his vision. Staszow. Kielce. Radom. Sandomierz. Ozorow. A wider awareness was expected of him. Gabriel nodding vigorously a sign for him to answer, Yes, Sir, Your Honor.

—What is the capital of Canada?

—Ottawa. Your Honor.

—Who is the King of Canada?

—His Majesty King George Six and Royal Highness Queen Elizabeth.

No need to badger the old man with other questions, considering the time it would take to process the entire group. He dismissed Gottesman and queried in similar fashion the other citizen-aspirants. Satisfied as to the suitability of the candidates the Judge bade them rise.

245

—I swear by the Almighty God that I will be faithful and bear true allegiance to His Majesty George the Sixth, His heirs and successors according to law. So help me God.

In fealty the chorus repeated the oath phrase by unfamiliar phrase.

The judge addressed the incumbents:

—From this moment you are entitled to all political rights, powers and privileges and subject to all obligations, duties and liabilities to which a natural-born British subject is entitled or subject, and that you have to all intents and purposes the status of a natural-born British subject. The flag of Great Britain is now your flag. The Magna Carta belongs to you. Take pride in your new country. Cast off all foreign allegiances. Welcome my fellow citizens.

The judge shook hands with each, presenting each with the certificate tightly rolled and secured by ribbons of red, white and blue.

—Now I am Citizen? Judah asked Gabriel on leaving the magisterial chambers. Gabriel affirmed that without doubt the honor had been conferred.

The new citizen framed his Certificate of Naturalization (No.22665 — Series B) and hung it above his bed. The Secretary of State himself had certified and declared in favor of Judah the Lion Gottesman and had affixed his official Seal. Each night before retiring the old man drank his ounce of whiskey to the health of his monarch:

—*L'chayim*, King George Six.

Seven months later his cardiovascular system broke down. He was invalided to the Jewish Home for the Aged, two converted residences on Cecil Street reeking of stale piss. The Home was a repository of used-up humanity afflicted with chronic and degenerative ailments. Superannuated crones, grinning toothlessly in wheelchairs or hobbling about the halls. Arguments. Curses. Childlike jealousies. The cackling of senility. The sexual drive, unabated, spurring on the wizened oldsters to hopelessly unfulfilled couplings. Whitesmocked attendants intervening. Come clean. Separated. In this corner, aged eighty-three, weighing 107 pounds, Samuel Manischewitz, the Kensington Mauler. In the opposite corner at eighty-three pounds (a lady doesn't tell her age) Sadie Landsberg, great-grandmother from Crawford Street. The verdict of the referee: *Coitus interruptus.*

Citizen Judah Lion Gottesman, loyal subject of His Majesty, attached to a greater fealty by a spiritual umbilicus extending through five thousand years prayed three times a day in the residents' Synagogue but could not prevent the current of his life from draining into the abyss.

He was transferred to Mount Sinai, newly rebuilt, with one hundred beds. The family gathered to pray for him. Eli, in command, sent instructions to doctors and nurses alike to spare no effort, but the periods of unconsciousness grew longer.

Judah the Lion was a youngster. The Polish children had encircled him. Taunting. Accusing. It's your fault. Look. These blots on my copybook. Jew blots. They threw burrs at his clothing. He couldn't tear them off. Jew-burrs. He thrust pleading arms towards them. Don't let him touch you, they shouted. You'll get the mange. The Jew-mange. They threw stones at him and he awoke. My Citizen Paper, he whispered hoarsely. Show. Citizen Gottesman.

The old woman, Rachel, who had cooked his meals, washed his clothes, and had borne him nine children, she who all these years had walked silently three paces behind him, sat outside his hospital room. Her eyes were closed. Images of the past assailed her. She conversed with them in plaintive tones.

Aaron stood in a corner vocalizing the Psalms of David. He swayed as he prayed. Eli sat grimly silent with Joshua and Samson in the waiting room. Sadie, stockings loosely hanging about her blotchy legs, wandered in a daze wailing sporadically. Freda circling in the opposite direction, stopped at the wall, banging her head against the white plaster in an outpouring of grief. Sara waited at Aaron's side.

The final report was delivered by Dr. Rapaport to Eli: I am sorry to inform you that your father has passed away. Aaron, the firstborn heard, wept tearlessly among the clamorous keeners. Aaron and Sara walked home alone.

\* \* \*

The funeral was arranged by Eli. An unfinished pine casket, expressly so willed by the deceased,contemptuously referred to as the Rowboat Model by the undertaker, enclosed the remains of Judah the Lion. The family sat in the front rows of the chapel. Aaron, Eli, Joshua, Samson. Behind them the womenfolk, Rachel, Freda, Sadie. In black. A portion of the apparel knife-slashed in token of bereavement. Gabriel and Noah sat with Sara. Beside them and around them the relatives and friends, landsmen from Opatow, the regulars of the Apter Shul who had broken bread with Judah the Lion and dipped it into the herring juice and shared the whiskey at the end of each Sabbath.

Isaiah Steiner, poultry merchant, sat with his wife Yetta freed from the poultry plucking for the afternoon. He didn't like these modern funerals. Not at all like the old country. Judah the Lion, God rest his soul, would have been given a better send-off in Opatow. Taken to the cemetery building by his closest friends and laid out on the plain table in the center of the bare room. He would be sprinkled with water and the *minyan* would pray over him. Then the preparation for burial. The fresh water pumped through the rubber tube placed in his mouth. The stomach pressed with the rolling pins and the syringe inserted to cleanse his bowels. The process repeated until the evacuated water was clean.

What kind of a shroud is he wearing, Rachel wondered. In Opatow it would have been of fine linen, sewn from one whole piece of fabric. Eli had assured her. Everything is being done according to his wishes. Was he wearing the Yom Kippur shirt? Did they remember to put on his gloves?

In the old country, Steiner mused, the nails of the fingers and toes would be scrupulously cleaned. The hair and beard combed. The sticks between the fingers. Rise up when the trumpet calls on the last day.

The moaning subsided. The Rabbi in black coat and broad-brimmed black fedora approached the pulpit. He spoke in Yiddish about his old friend, at peace at last. He spoke quietly, unemotionally, stroking his full, white

248

beard as he paused to emphasize a thought. Was it fifty-three years ago that he danced at the wedding of Judah and his bride Rachel? Man is like grass. We are all doomed to die. But weep not for this pious person who left behind him years of devotion to God and a respected family and many grandchildren. The Rabbi rendered up to God the soul of Judah the Lion, son of Rachmiel. He bade the congregation rise. He intoned in a voice quavering with the fatigue of years the *El Mole Rachamim:* O Lord full of mercy, have compassion upon Thy servant. Sour breaths of the living mingled with the overheated air in the chapel assaulted Gabriel's nostrils. The unctuous Director motioned to the pall bearers. Out into the sharp February air they carried the casket of Judah the Lion. Out to the black, shining hearse while the Rabbi intoned in the Ashkenazi Hebrew of the Polish *shtetl.*

—He restoreth my soul. Yea though I walk through the valley of the shadow of death...

The mourners follow the coffin. A shriek of anguish erupts from Sadie. She hurls herself against the pallbearers. She is restrained by the Director. Decorum. Must have decorum. No unseemly conduct. There. That's better. He breathes solace into her ear and guides her into Freda's embrace. Citizen Judah Lion Gottesman, safe in the row-boat is slid inside the hearse.

—Surely goodness and mercy shall follow me... The rear door closes securely. The hearse moves forward noiselessly. Behind it, the limousine, black beauty, with the members of the family, seated close on luxurious, cushioned seats. Down Spadina to the Synagogue, the other mourners follow on foot.

A short stop. A brief prayer outside the Beverley Street Shul. Then the pedestrians disperse and the vehicles continue to the field.

Everybody out at Dawes Road Cemetery. At the section marked *Anshe Apt*, everything is in readiness. Mounds of turf heaped brown against the snow. The coffin is placed on slats that span the grave. The Rabbi bids the family gather about. He summons Aaron to perform the last rites. Aaron places a handful of earth beside the unseeing Judah and the coffin is closed. Aaron says a prayer. More meaningful the way it's done in the old country. A shard from a new earthenware basin placed over each eye. In lieu of a coffin, planks of wood at the sides and above him. Nothing under the body. Earth to earth. Adam. From the earth wert thou created.

The straps are pulled away and the pine box lowers out of view. The wailing begins anew. Sadie and Freda thrashing about. The sons sob, lavish tears. All except Aaron who is impassive, beyond weeping. Old Rachel too. Her own demise foreshadowed.

The gravediggers sink flashing spades into the stiff earth. The clods drop — thud, thud — into the grave. Then muted clomps. Earth upon earth. Soon filled.

The Kaddish. The sons of the late, lamented father enunciating in the Aramaic, the avowal of faith: *Yis-ga-dal v'yis-ka-dash sh'meh rabbo.* Praised and glorified be the name of the Holy One.

The seven days of mourning during which peace reigned among the brethren. Plans for an everlasting memorial in honor of the patriarch, Judah the Lion. The redemption of an acre of land in *Eretz Israel.* They would never quarrel again.

Eli embraced his elder brother and his sister-in-law. They wept, clutching each other, promising love and affection. Mother, you'll see. We shall be one happy, devoted family.

At the end of the *Shiva* period the reality of life intruded. It was Aaron and Sara against the others. All over again.

**17**

The Flyer hurtled towards the crowd below then climbed, I-think-I-can-I-think-I-can. At the top the roller coaster paused. In the first car the two clutched each other for fear, for joy.

—There's the Fun House where we met, she pointed and Gabriel squeezed against her to see. She was thin, skin covering bones. A wisp, frail and-forlorn.

—Yes, he said.

He had found her wandering through the labyrinth inspecting her distorted figure in the curved glass sheets. Coming up behind her he maneuvered his belly bulging in the reflection to touch her. She screamed and ran into the next chamber of drolleries. The inane electric laughter of the bobbing womanniquin with the red wig and the watermelon breasts echoed through the Fun House and out into the summery Saturday night.

Trapped in the *cul de sac* she waited. Gabriel ran towards her until bang he smacked into the plate glass. Hand signals. You go that way for the exit. Follow me. I'll show you. With parallel steps on his/her side of the partition each moved cautiously in search of an opening. Finally emerging she thanked him for showing her the way.

—The way is narrow and strait the gate, he said.

—Lead me not into temptation. I am just a girl not yet sixteen.

—Fear not, O maiden, I am just a boy turned seventeen this very evening. The occasion of my birth has not been celebrated by me or by those to whom I am near and dear. I seek some gratification for having lived so long, some *raison d'être*, some small departure from the daily round, some solace in the company of an unknown beloved.

—Will you take me away and show me the heavens full of stars?

—I shall transport you to the heights of desire, to the constellation of Orion, past where the twins Castor and Pollux frolic. Perchance we can explore the Milky Way together. My head in your bosom.

—My breasts have not yet matured.

—My face in your hair, then.

—Alas, the bob is boyish, too short for nestling.

—My arms around your waist.

—You'll crush my bow.

—My hand in your lap.

—Please hold me, she urged, as the roller coaster swerved around a curve, high above the earth.

—Look at the stars, he whispered into her ear, his breath issuing Wrigley's spearmint. She turned her face, a tattoo of freckles, in his direction and he pecked a kiss on her lips just as WHOOSH the Flyer dropped.

—Hold me, she shouted, eyes averted from the screeching descent. Along the straightaway she removed his hand from her breast. Don't, she admonished. Up again WHOOSH and a sharp turn sent her against him, blowing wide her blue and white gingham dress.

—Oh-h-h-h, she exclaimed and smoothed her dress in place, Oh-h-h-h, another sharp turn, Oh-h-h-h and down again and the Flyer slowed and she eased away from Gabriel as the cars halted at the end of the ride.

—I enjoyed that. Thank you. Now I have to meet a girl friend. So goodbye, she said.

—Stay, he entreated. *I* have no one waiting. We'll have potato chips in a paper cone. Hot dogs and Honey Dew.

—No, I have to go, she insisted.

—We can see the Great Wallendas and Zacchini, The Human Cannonball.

—Well, I don't know...

—Come on. The merry-go-round.

—I get dizzy, she grimaced.

—The ferris wheel then.

—I'll stay for awhile, she said. Let's walk.

Test Your Skill. He threw three wooden balls for a dime and failed to knock down the grinning wooden cats. He received a balloon for consolation.

—Test Your Strength. Ring the bell and win a prize. He walloped with a will but sent the disc only half way up the column. He apologized for his inadequacy.

—Let's go dancing, she pulled him towards the lake, to

the open air Seabreeze Dance Pavillion. They entered through a gap in the wire fencing. Tendering the ten-cents-a-dance ticket to the attendant. Gabriel foxtrotted around the marble floor with what-did-you-say-your-name-was? Fern. Mine's Gabriel. He held her close and breathed down her skinny neck and insinuated a daring leg between hers.

—Let's go to the Palais Royale, she begged. I love Bert Niosi. Along the boardwalk, from the Seabreeze eastward ambling, hand-holding, hearing the waves on the beach and the calliope music of the carnival, Gabriel led her, sideways-glancing to fix her image. The knife-blade nose, the protruding chin. Bone and gristle. Gabriel offered her a smooth-as-silk Roxy Cigaret. She didn't smoke. Gabriel puffed, like George Raft, blowing the smoke between tightened lips, surveying the scene, ready for action. He dusted a speck from his blue flannel jacket. Searched in his white flannel trousers, found several small coins.

—Can you spare a quarter, he asked Fern. I'm a little short.

From her red leather shoulder strap bag she extracted the price of admission. The Palais Royale and the big band sound of Bert Niosi. Where Yiddish boys pick up *shikses* because Jewish girls don't fuck.

Inside the vast hall, a cacophany of horns and drums. The dancers jitterbugging, lindy hopping. Contorted. Over the shoulders and between widespread legs. The management attempts to cool down the calisthenics in deference to the older couples and the romantics who prefer dancing cheek to cheek.

Around the periphery, stand the ladies. Unescorted I-don't-care-if-you-never-ask-me-ladies. When solicited, icily refusing, No thanks. Gay ladies. Sad ladies. Teenage and overage. Waiting.

—Case that broad over there, the mechanic from Lou's Garage, out for a night of happiness, pleads with his buddy. Let's ask her.

—Sure, the shipper from the paper box factory is game. Maybe she's got a friend.

—Maybe. The blond with the big tits. Next to her.

—They both got big tits. Come on. Jesus, what a score.

—Sorry, I'm not dancing just now, the first refuses. Me neither, the blond echoes, haughtily. Rebuffed, the mechanic protests, Who're ya kidding?

—Fuck off, the blond retorts.

—Geez, the mechanic makes the appropriate sign with his forefinger. Queen shit. The ladies saunter off to the soft drink bar. They buy two cokes and retire to a table. From her carry-all the blond removes the flask and adds the rum. The two drink and observe, waiting to be approached so they can turn down the proposition.

—Don't you just love the music? Fern seeks confirmation from Gabriel. Shouting to be heard in the noisy Bert Niosi dance hall. Gabriel agrees. When the number has ended he excuses himself leaving Fern among the hopefuls.

In the Men's Washroom, littered with butts, the talk is boastful.

—Jesus, you shoulda seen the one I picked up last week. Hot little bitch. At first she wouldn't come across. What do you think I am, she asks. So I tell her, Bet you've had it in your mouth hundreds of times. That's the only way to treat them, ya know. So I take it out and stick it in her hand. Boy, she goes down on me just like that.

—No kidding, his friend says shaking the last drops into the choked urinal.

—Best blow job I ever had. That mouth was made for sucking.

—Did you fuck her too?

—Are you kidding? I wouldn't put my cock into her stinking cunt. Never know who got into her last. Could get the clap. I'm particular. Look here, isn't this a beauty, showing off his penis, pulling back the foreskin. His friend agrees. Super! You should see it when it's hard. As big as Seabiscuit's. He returns it proudly to its concealment.

Alone Gabriel takes his out and pees. Observes the length (not bad) the circumsized head (smooth velvet). More than enough for frail Fern.

She is gone when he returns to the dance floor. Just my luck. Shit and goddam. He walks about, scanning faces, inhaling the melange of scents. He stops at the bar and buys an O'Keefe Ginger Beer.

254

—Hey, how about a sip? Fern's voice behind him. Had to go to the Powder Room. Was it ever crowded. She takes a ladylike sip from his bottle.

They had one more dance, then the band played God Save The King. Midnight. All over the city, pubs and dance halls closing down for the Christian Sabbath. Regulations strictly enforced under the powers of the Lord's Day Act. Don't want you up so late that you won't come to Church on Sunday.

Sunnyside was shuttering up. Rectangles of painted plywood enclosed the open spaces of the concession stands. The horses in the Merry-go-Round stabled. Fun House locked up. The Flyer motionless. The Seabreeze dark. Lights out everywhere.

They walked slowly among the dwindling pleasure seekers behind the Ferris Wheel up the section of stone steps to Queen Street. The night club was shadowed. Only the Top Hat, neon outlined, was visible. The last patrons were leaving. One threw a whiskey bottle smash at the curbside. His female companion berated him, warned against a possible confrontation with the constabulary.

At the tram stop Fern reiterated her conditions: Yes, Gabriel could take her home.

—But don't try anything funny.

—Funny? What do you mean? Gabriel asked.

—You know what I mean. No monkey business. And you can't stay long. I have to get up for Mass. Promise? Gabriel raised one hand.

—I hereby renounce all my knavish tricks. I promise to respect your person and your honor and to keep inviolate those parts of your anatomy sacred to yourself, your mother and to the god Hymen. So help me Eros and Aphrodite.

—You say things so poetically, she murmured as he helped her aboard the street car. Accelerating, clattering, braking, the tram proceeded to Bathurst then Bloor, where they transferred for the long ride past Yonge where the street became Danforth and the viaduct spanned the Don River. In the almost empty car Gabriel sat close to Fern. He kissed her cheek. She squeezed his hand.

*—We stroll along through the heather.... The Isle of May.*
The song wouldn't leave him. Everybody was singing the plaintive melody. Tchaikovsky's *Andante Cantabile.* Gabriel sang softly and Fern closed her blue eyes to better enjoy.

At Carlaw they descended and walked down the street of shabby row houses, the flickering street lamps showing peeling paint, green, red and white. Fern unlocked the door of 328 and preceded him down the dark hall into the tiny parlor.

—Sh-h-h. Mom's a light sleeper. Sit down. Be back in a minute. She indicated the scraggly sofa, a four-seater.

Gabriel sank through the yielding springs. There was a matching chair, an oak-stained end table with cigaret burns, a wrought-iron bridge lamp with a faded shade. A patch of thin, dun-colored carpet. No father to provide. Ran away years ago. Mother sprays rosebud lips on kewpie dolls at the toy factory down the street.

He heard the gurgle of the toilet and after awhile the soft slap, slap of slippered feet. At the door she paused, looked toward the bedroom and listened. She placed a finger to her lips and closed the door.

She selected *Music for a Mellow Mood* coming to you from CKCL, Toronto's all night radio station. She turned the volume low.

*—Only a poor fool... never caught in a whirlpool...*
Ravel, popularized, eighteen weeks on the Hit Parade. *My Reverie.* Fern was waltzing languorously about the room. Gabriel caught her hand and pulled her down beside him. She lay on the sofa, her head in his lap. He bent down to her. She presented her tightly-closed lips to his ardent open mouth.

—Not that, she slithered away. No frenching. He coaxed her back. He stroked her hair. You promised to behave, she whispered.

—I will, I promise. He pecked at her ear.

She kicked the furry slipper into a corner, stretching out full length beside him. He sat still until he heard her measured breathing. With casual fingers he reached into the V opening of her dress and under the flimsy brassiere. Her little teat cold as a witches. He caressed the nipple.

256

Cracked. Inverted. Inert.

—No. Don't. She removed his hand. He let it stray down her dress, lightly drumming in rhythm to the music. Drumming along the bare legs, slowly upward. His fingers roamed over her panties. By degrees, aided by her slight movements he removed them. Her eyes were closed. He attempted to unbutton her dress.

—No. You musn't. Not that. Kiss me.

He thrust his tongue between her teeth and she bit it.

—Goddam, that hurts.

—Serves you right. I told you no frenching. She soothed him with a kiss and played a game of touch-and-run all over his body. He reciprocated and she succumbed.

—Come on top of me, she invited.

He lay over her. She heaved against his hardness. Her lips, unfurling petals into which he carefully sent his wounded tongue. This time she did not protest. He unbuttoned his fly. He tried to lift her dress but she resisted, all the while continuing her upward thrusts.

—No. Don't. No. No. Ever-thrusting, the gingham scraping against his organ. He kissed her long and open-mouthed and at the same time reached into his pocket for the packet. She was writhing underneath him. He was rolling the condom onto his penis when she broke away from him.

—No. I told you not to try anything. He grabbed for her and they tusselled on the couch. He ripped three buttons from her dress and he attempted to enter her. She kicked him in the groin. He fell away for an instant but was back against her bare pubis. He pried apart her limbs and pushed his face against her bush. Moist and gamey.

—No. Don't. I'll call my mother. Stop that. She pummelled his back and his head and managed to push him from her onto the floor.

—You bastard, she sobbed. You sonofabitch. Trying a thing like that.

—You encouraged me. You're a bloody cock teaser.

—Only animals do what you just did, she glared at him. It's ugly. Humans don't do such things. It's filthy.

Gabriel going down on Michelle's sweet softness. *Honi*

*soit qui mal y pense.*

—Nobody has ever tried that with me. Wait till I tell my boyfriend. He'll kill you.

(That jewboy did *what* to you? Why, that muff diver! I'll tear his cock off. Where is he, the cunt lapper?)

Gabriel buttoned up hastening to go. He put on his tan shoes and retrieved his jacket from the chair.

—I'm sorry I upset you. He left her. She threw his tie after him.

In the silent early morn he hurried with some difficulty to the tram stop. The ache in his scrotum presaged an agonizing case of blueballs.

\* \* \*

Sunday. Breakfast at noon. Smoked fish and bagels and scrambled eggs. Glass of Postum. Sara housecleaning. Aaron hammering a leather sole on Noah's boot.

Sunday. See what's playing at your neighborhood tabernacle. Turn to the Church page of yesterday's edition: United Church. Anglican. Baptist. Evangelical. Pentecostal. Christadelphian. Salvation Army. Lutheran. Presbyterian. Spiritualist. All beating the drums for Christ Jesus.

*Sex Without Marriage* at St. George's. *The Man Who Wrestled With God* at Blythwood Church. *The Loneliness Of Sin* at the Kingsway.

At The People's Church Dr. Gerard S. Manleigh of the Southern Presbyterian Congregation and one of the most prolific evangelical preachers of our times tells the fascinating story of his conversion: *Out of Darkness.* To be followed the following Tuesday by the conclusion: Into His Marvellous Light. Operatic Tenor Robin Christopher and Soprano Phyllis Cooper will be featured at 11 and 7.

Nothing in my hand I bring.
Simply to Thy cross I cling.

The Rev. Dr. Thomas Todhunter Shields sermonizing at the Jarvis Street Baptist Church: I have not a farthing to pay. I am a poor, empty-handed, bankrupt sinner, looking to the sacrifices of Christ, and thanking God I am saved.

258

Are there Roman Catholics here tonight? You do not need a priest. The one High Priest Jesus Christ has offered that one sacrifice. All you need is to receive that, believe it and rejoice that the debt is paid and then all will be well.

*The Good Samaritan Corner.* The homily of the week in prose and verse. A touching case history of a deserving man helped by the Scott Mission. An appeal for funds. An invitation to worship. The Rev. Morris Zeidman, B.A. M.Th. Director.

The Evangel Temple. Sunday at 7. Monday through Friday at 8. Burton Stanfield Smith — A Great Minister For Today. Join us in the auditorium as faith and expectancy rise. See and hear testimonies of healing including an up-to-date, medically-verified cure of cancer. See the operations of the Holy Spirit exactly as in I Cor. 12:8-10. Come early for best seats.

The Salvation Army Temple Downtown. Old Fashioned Gospel Meetings with the Modern Message of God's word. Bible School 9:30 A.M. Family Worship 11 A.M. Gospel Rally 7 P.M. Youth Group 9 P.M.

Knox Church. *Destination Heaven.*

In the Catholic Cathedrals masses to suit your convenience. No need to proselytize. The one true apostolic. *Ad Majorem Dei Gloriam.*

—Aaron, don't forget the meeting of the Society, Sara shouted to him. The payment on the cemetery plots. From the basement Aaron mumbled back, — I remember, through a mouthful of shoe tacks, hunched over the cast iron last. Painting the edges of trimmed leather with black dye. Applying polish to the entire boot and brushing to mirror lustre.

Sunday. A day for replenishment of spirit. A sunny, warm day for strolling, for swimming, a day for watching girls at the lake. Avoid the eastern beaches. Kew Beach guarded by Joe Farr's Nazi paramilitary Swastika Club. *Judenrein.* Toronto Islands O.K. Except for the Manitou Hotel. No Jews or Dogs Allowed. By Order. Sunnyside was best. Stick to public beach. Brooker's Boathouse: Gentiles Only.

(If you haven't seen Sunnyside you haven't seen

Toronto. Thrills and amusements for young and old. Games. Rides. Boating. Canoeing. Bathing. Swimming. Races. Diving Contests. Refreshments. The Sunnyside Bathing Pavilion has accommodation for 7,700 bathers at one time. Diving Platforms and Towers. The Swimming Pool is one of the largest in America. It is 75 feet wide and 300 feet long with a depth grading from 2½ feet to 9 feet and has a capacity of 750,000 gallons. The water is filtered continuously, making a complete change every 10 hours. It is also chlorinated. A heating plant maintains a temperature of 68° Fahrenheit. Life Guards patrol the beach and swimming pool.)

Alone on the Queen street car Gabriel recalled last night's fiasco with Fern. The lingering pain in his testicles. *Keep your Sunnyside up.* The shops flashed by in the afternoon sunshine. Good thing her mother didn't wake up. Could have been arrested. Jewish Youth Incarcerated in Don Jail. Department of Correctional Services investigates young man's predilection for cunnilingus. He dreamt last night of (muff) diving into (cunt) lapping waters. Lac Sainte Michelle. Cheered by Mademoiselle Morgan as he swam amidst her gently waving golden fronds.

Euclid Street. Chris Augenblick danced aboard. Searched in his wallet for the fare, withdrew the ticket.

—Well, hello, Chris breathed a fragrant exhalation of Sen Sen and eased his newly-washed, perfumed elegance next to Gabriel.

—Isn't it a divine day? Chris patted Gabriel's knee. Just divine.

Gabriel pushed away the manicured fingers. I'm not your man, Chris, he protested, mildly.

—Would you like me to get it up for you, Gabriel?

—Listen Chris, stop trying to make me. Go bugger somebody else.

Rebuffed, Chris turned away, scanned the pages of his book.

—Look Chris, I don't want to hurt your feelings but I'm not like you. I enjoy being with girls. That's why I'm going to Sunnyside. I have a great desire to get laid.

260

—Women aren't necessary, you know, Chris said. Some of the greatest men ever lived preferred their own sex. Oscar Wilde. Pope Claudius the First. Napoleon. King James the First. Ever heard of the King James Version? Chris laughed. There was an American President too. I forget his name.

—Ah, you're making them up, Gabriel said. Just fairy tales.

—No, I'm not. You can read about them at the library.

—Sunnyside, the conductor called.

They strolled about the closed-for-Sunday amusements, Gabriel searching for a friendly female face, Chris expounding on the love that dare not speak its name.

—Did you know Tchaikowsky was one? The great Piotr Ilyich had two women — his wife and Madame von Meck. He didn't touch either of them. Michelangelo. Da Vinci.

—Well, sensitive artistic types I suppose get that way, Gabriel conceded.

—Yes? What would you say about strong-minded, strong-limbed military men? Heroic types who changed the world?

—Like who?

—Like Julius Ceasar. Like Alexander The Great. Nero fiddled a lot too.

—The debauchery of the Greeks and Romans doesn't make the whole world queer, said Gabriel.

—You can go back to Sodom and Gomorrah and come forward all the way to Kitchener, Ontario, Chris said. Nice little town. Used to be called Berlin, you know. Then they changed it in honor of Field Marshal Kitchener of Khartoum. Horatio Herbert Kitchener. One of us.

They patrolled the boardwalk, Chris instructing. Gabriel interjecting with a question or an expletive of disbelief. At the Weston's Band Shell they stopped. Gabriel sat on a bench, Chris beside him.

—In ancient Greece, Chris averred, homosexuality was normal. It was even encouraged. Where do you think the young boys learned about sex? From the older men. Have you heard about Plato's ideal army? A military force made up of lovers, fighting side by side. It's all here in his

*Symposium.* Listen, I'll read you a portion. Chris had marked the page: *For what lover would not choose rather to be seen by all mankind than by his beloved, either when abandoning his post or throwing away his arms?*

—Wow. An army of queers, Gabriel laughed. It would never work.

—Inded it did, Chris corrected. Epaminondas, the Theban general commanded such an ideal army. Greater love hath no man than that he lay down his life for a friend. Damon and Pythias. David and Jonathan. Such relations were considered natural and desirable. Until *they* came along.

—Who? Gabriel asked.

—The early Christians. The psychopaths. Then the converts. Then those born into the faith. Out there. Chris pointed to the good burghers of the city enjoying the sunshine in their Sunday best. Their prejudices inherited from St. Paul.

—What did Paul teach? Gabriel asked.

Chris put on a gloomy face, shook a finger at the cumulus fleece in the sky.

—The Kingdom of Heaven shall be open to neither fornicators, nor idolators, nor adulterers, nor effeminates, nor abusers of themselves with mankind.

—Does that include masturbators, Gabriel wondered. Cock suckers, yes. Gabriel in the lane, seven years old, forced to suck off Big Irish. Fear. Revulsion. Swallow it, Irish comanded. Irish held him and made him lick the stickiness off his pecker. Released, running home, crying, puking on the porch.

Chris leaned over to kiss him. Gabriel pushed him away.

—Go see a doctor, he urged Chris. I've told you before. Or get one of those pamphlets from the Public Health Service at City Hall. Promise me you'll try to do something about it, Chris. There must be a cure.

—Sure, Chris said. Maybe religion will help. I'll see my Rabbi. Take it out and show it to him. Have him bless it. And now ere we depart let us pray for Chris the queer. May the Lord who made Chris a fairy reverse His mistake and cause His countenance to shine upon him and send

262

Chris forth a man among men that he may choose to shoot his seed into a daughter of Israel and cause her to grow big with wombfruit so that the children of Israel may proliferate and become as multitudinous as the grains of sand at Sunnyside beach. That Chris may be a blessing upon his aged mother and neurotic sister and embarrassed Jews everywhere. Amen.

Chris rose to leave.

—I'm a changed creature, thanks to your advice, Gabe, old man. The queer in me has vanished. From now on I shall amuse myself only with wide-open beavers.

—That's great, Gabriel said. We can go cunt-hunting together.

—Sure thing, Gabe. I want to thank you for your advice. He kissed Gabriel ardently on the lips and reached for Gabriel's penis.

—You fucking queer, Gabriel shouted. You've been putting me on. I don't want you near me again. You better watch out. The cops will lock you up.

Chris wandered away. Gabriel was disappointed. All that talk, trying to help Chris without success. Shameful perversion. Everybody agreed. Doctors. Social workers. Teachers. Minister. Everybody. Everybody except Chris, the resident queer of the Roxy Burlesque.

Along the boardwalk mothers push strollers, their infants licking on ice cream that dribbles down the sides of fat little mouths and onto seersucker suits. Along the boardwalk, girls in their flimsy dresses swing hips and handbags, past whistling, chain-dangling youths. Gabriel makes for the hot dog stand. He orders a thin, pink Ritz Carlton and a diluted Honey Dew. When he finishes he walks along the shore. The clear lake water rolling up in sheets of wet, devours sand castles and rushes back slurpily under the onslaught of new waves.

Gabriel stops at the Sunnyside Pool, dense with splashing, diving, cavorting humanity. His happy hunting ground.

It was here he had collided with Monique under water in the deep end. They surfaced together and after a long breath he dived between her legs and rose up and threw her from his shoulders. She flailed after him with awkward strokes and he allowed her to push him under. When he came up for air she was clambering out of the pool. He ran after her onto the beach. She stubbed her toe against a rock and fell to the sand. He dropped beside her and kissed her. He fondled her breasts. She pulled his hand away and with it part of the halter. One tiny titty appeared, the red eye of the nipple asking what's up? She jackrabbited from him zigzagging between sunning couples and dashed to the lake and swam far out. He followed. They grappled gleefully in and out of the water. Enough. She splashed back to the beach leaving the top of her swim suit adrift on the waves. He darted after her, cupped his hands about her and whispered in urgency. She cried Oh No! and hastened to the Women's Lockers. He called Monique. Meet you later. He dressed and waited. And waited. She didn't appear.

Other recollections. Remembrances of things past. Opportunities missed. Encounters gone awry.

Gabriel selling funnyface balloons at the Canadian National Exhibition. Biggest annual exposition in the world. A horde of joy seekers jamming the Midway. Step right up. Dancing girls. Paris cuties from Omaha. Step right up. See the bearded lady. The Indiarubberman. Assorted freaks. Step right up. See the miracle of birth. Never before shown in its entirety. No entrance to anybody under the age of twenty-one.

Lots of possibilities for pickups. The girls in their infinite variety in gossamer dresses brushing against him. Have a Mickey Mouse balloon. Go on. Take it. No charge. 'Cause I like you. Meet me later. At the Grand Stand. Super spectacle. Fireworks at the end. Yes, I'll meet you, she nodded vigorously and dissolved in the crowd, the inflated rodent wafting above her. She was waiting for him that evening. Ginger-haired, acne-faced, nearly six feet tall in sandals. Climb it my boy. Climb it. They queued for admission. As the gate opened there was a surge from the ticket holders. Gabriel was pushed against her. He felt it hardening. She eased away from him.

Another surge brought his hand against her bottom. He patted it. Good stock. She laughed. Masked by the crush and encouraged by her good nature he fingered her. She remained unperturbed. He stole under her dress and into her panties and still she was complaisant. Now he was in her summer-drenched cunny. In and out. In an excess of zeal he pulled back the finger and shoved it unexpectedly against her anus. She screamed in disbelief. She swung her parasol thud against his shoulder. Thud. Over his head. Shame suffused him. He escaped into the crowd, into the dusk and distance.

The chairs are beginning to fill up for the Sing Along With Weston's. The Master of Ceremonies bounces on stage. The orchestra greets him with a brassy chord. He exhorts the audience to sing their best because, We'll be on the air soon. Warm-up time. Before the announcer says into the microphone: And now, from Sunnyside Beach in Toronto, the Canadian Broadcasting Corporation presents.... The M.C. draws attention to the projected words on the screen. He jokes and clowns and leads the singing in a whiskey voice.

The sun is low behind the Bandshell, going down in the direction of Hamilton. When it sinks will it boil the water? Crimson twilight now. The Lord's Day almost ended. Have you ever been to Toronto? Yes, I spent a whole month there one Sunday. Yuk. Yuk. Get away from the Queen City. From the blue laws and the dour faces. Shuffle off to Buffalo for a Sunday movie and a Sunday drink.

—Pony boy, pony boy, won't you be my Tony boy. Everybody sings. *My Pony Boy.* And now a sentimental tune, one of the old favorites for all the lovers. If you were the only girl in the world. Lots of only, lonely girls here tonight. And I was the only boy. Take me. My body. Where are you my only girl in the world?

* * *

—Wait till you see her, you'll have no trouble getting into this one, Benny Kirsch had assured him. The Langer's new Mother's Help. Comes from Come By Chance. Comes every time she screws.

—Did you lay her? Gabriel asked.

—Not yet. Waiting for you to join me, Benny said. Told her how long your wang is. She's dying to meet you.

Gabriel wanted to know how much of a dog she was.

—She's not Jean Harlow, Benny admitted, but I've seen worse. Besides, you don't have to marry her. Come on over this evening after six. The Langers are going to a *Bar Mitzvah.* She'll be alone with the kids.

The slabs of beef had been removed from the display counter and from the metal hooks and put into chilly hibernation in the floor-to-ceiling ice box. *Boser Kosher.* Licensed by the Vad Hakahillah. The Rabbinical Council. Strictly Kosher. Kalmen Langer had a reputation for honesty and piety. He served as the *Ba'al Tefillah* at the Hebrew Men of England Congregation. A fine tenor. Almost as professional as the Cantor.

—There she is. My new neighbor. Watching the College Street cowboys. Benny taps on the butcher shop window.

—Let us in, Benny mouths the words. Let—us—in. She thinks about it. Benny points to the door and turns an imaginary knob. She saunters towards them. Unlocks.

—Kids aren't asleep yet.

—Sure they are. The Langers left about an hour ago.

—All right, make it twenty minutes. Around the back.

—This is my friend, Gabriel. The one I told you about.

—Oh yeah, she smirks. See you later.

Benny steers Gabriel into College Ladies Wear. Piles of bloomers, skirts, brassieres, silk stockings, hair nets, piece goods, handbags, hair curlers, lipsticks, nail polish.

—Hello, Mrs. Kirsch. She does not hear Gabriel's greeting.

—This dress was just made for you Mrs. Bluestein. See how nicely it fits around the bust line. Go look in the mirror. If it needs any alterations my husband will do them while you wait. Go look. Beautiful. It really is. While Mrs. Bluestein is preening in the glass, Mrs. Kirsch proceeds to finalize the other sale. The blouse is the latest fashion. An American original. Copied from a high-priced French model. Very attractive on you, Mrs. Prokosh. By the way your daughter Jane was in here yesterday. Beautiful girl. She's not married yet? She looks so mature. A nice figure she's got.

Benny directs Gabriel through the living quarters. We have to go through my sister's room. I'll see if she's in. Benny looks No. All clear. Let's go. Out the window.

They tread carefully the loose shingles of the roof. A three foot space separates them from Langer's house.

—Come on. Jump across. Don't be all night, Philomena taunts from the window.

—Go on, Benny pushes Gabriel to the edge. Don't catch your balls on anything.

—*Après vous*, Alphonse, Gabriel bows.

—Don't be a *shmuck*, Benny says. Hurry. If Selma finds us here I'll get shit. Go ahead.

Gabriel first, then Benny leaps onto the Langer roof and runs to the open window. A sprinkle of gravel rattles down the drainpipe.

—Christ! Benny remembers. Forgot to close Selma's door. Hope she's not home.

In her chamber Philomena lounges on the bed. Benny beside her begins fondling her breasts. Gabriel on the floor is looking up through her parted hairy legs, wondering if he dares finger her up there inside the dark patch. Philomena chews gum with bovine contentment.

—Benny! Are you in there? Selma screeches from her room. I'll tell Ma, Benny.

Philomena stops masticating. You guys better leave. If the Langers find out I'll be canned. Get out of here.

Downstairs there is a pounding at the door. Selma in hair curlers is screaming: Open up! I know you're in there with the *shikse*. Benny, Open up.

—Go on. Out you go. Philomena pushes Benny to the window. You too, buster.

—Wait. Have to buttom my goddam fly. Give me a lift, Gabriel.

—Sure. He gooses Benny upward out onto the roof.

Back in Selma's room they wait and listen, then run across the hall.

—Open up. Selma still pounding away, her quilted bathrobe unbelted from the exertions.

Philomena straightens her plaid skirt and buttons her

mannish blouse. The Langer children are wailing. She clomps downstairs into the butcher shop. Selma is grimacing at the door. Behind her the passers-by stop to observe. Philomena unlocks the door.

—What's the matter? Is there anything wrong, she asks?

—Don't play the queen with me, Selma shouts. She strides in. Where's my brother?

—Your brother? I haven't seen him all day.

—BENNY!

From the nursery a bawling in tandem. Philomena runs to investigate. The infant is whimpering in the crib, fat lips puckering for the lost pacifier. The older child is wobbling mournfully in his cot, pudgy hands clutching the bars, his diaper a damp mass at his feet. Selma comes over to comfort him. He begins to wail as she picks him up.

—See, you've upset him. Philomena snatches the tot from her.

—*Shtick dreck*, Selma hurls the epithet at the mother's help and scurries out of Langer's Kosher Butcher Shop, past the crowd of onlookers. Mind your own business, she bellows. I'll break every bone in his body when I find him. I know he was in there.

—Ma, did you see Benny?

—Did he go out? Mrs. Kirsch turns for an instant from a customer.

—Aw, shit, Selma stamps upstairs. On her way to the toilet she hears muted voices and throws open her brother's door. She looks down at Benny and his friend amidst a collection of test tubes.

—You been here all the time? she asks.

—Sure.

—Didn't you hear me hollering for you?

—No. Guess we were concentrating on this project for Science. That right, Gabriel? That's right, Gabriel corroborates. Been here for the past half hour.

—Say, we better get this sal ammoniac outside. The white puffs billowing from the vial are beginning to fill the room with an acrid odor.

—Okay if we go out on the roof through your window, he asks. She nods. On the roof Benny places the test tube of ammonium chloride on the chimney. The fumes dissipate in the night air.

—Close call, eh? Benny grins. Too bad we had to leave so quickly. Bet she'd make a good piece.

—That's what your sister needs, Gabriel says. A good piece of ass.

—Yeah, she thinks her pussy is only for peeing.

—That's what I have to do right now. Take a leak.

—Me too.

They direct their streams into the Langer's back yard.

—Flow gently sweet Afton, Gabriel sings, among thy green braes.

—Say that's an idea. Let's invite Philomena to a picnic. Out Port Credit way. Ass on the grass.

—By the forks of the Credit, she opened up to me.

—Shine on, shine on harvest moon... Come on folks, let's hear it good and loud for the radio audience. Let's show the folks out west how much lung power we got down here, the man from Weston's exhorted.

Sing. Forget the depression. The hunger marches. The strikes. Mounted constabulary on whinnying, charging horses. Foot patrols at Balmy Beach. The Red menace. Sing tonight. Tomorrow be sure to buy Weston's Bread who bring you this hour of diversion.

—I ain't had no loving....

On that other occasion when Benny had phoned from High Park. A sure score. Picked her up at Grenadier Pond. Meet me at the docks after supper. Don't worry, she'll be there. I told her about you coming. Benny looked out of the phone booth to see her sitting on the picnic table, pick-nicking her fat nose.

—I'd like you to meet my friend Simon Browning, the fella I told you about this afternoon, Benny introduced his old buddy to his new-found friend. He winked at Gabriel. Never give the correct name in case of trouble. For this adventure Benny was Trevor Goldsmith. Simon, this is May Smith. Gabriel shook her hand.

—It's a pleasure to meet such an attractive girl, Gabriel lied.

—Beauty lieth in the eye of the beholder, Benny pronounced gallantly.

In the thigh of the behoover. Close your eyes, undo your fly. Enter the grotto of Helen, the joy of Paris. Or Lesbia, the inamorata of Catullus. Choose any beauty of any time. Diana. Athene. The Queen of Sheba. The Queen of England. Or Madame Lupescu. Is there anyone better I ask you. Michelle Morgan.

The pain of remembrance. Oh, to be in England now that April's there. To lock limbs with high-assed April Morgenstern who graduated to the D'Oyly Carte Opera Company. Or Jane Prokosh, Queen of the Fairies on a midsummer night. Or descend into this May blob of jelly and lie quivering on her belly.

She trotted up the gangplank behind Benny. Silently obedient. They stood at the rail of the Sam McBride and watched the city recede.

—Look at that smoke stack, Gabriel pointed. How would you like to have one that size, Mr. Trevor Goldsmith?

—It's almost as big as yours, Mr. Browning.

Mr. Browning protested. Mr. Goldsmith turned to May. You should see the stack on him.

May said,

—I'm hungry.

Gabriel pushed through the passengers to the boat's snack bar. He bought three hamburgers and three root beers. Benny wiped the ketchup from her face with her paper napkin and threw the stained, crumpled ball into the frothy wake. He folded his own napkin carefully and inserted it into his back pocket.

Half way to Centre Island, May excused herself.

—We'll do it on the beach. You know, near the clump of trees. Me first, Benny advised.

—She doesn't look like much of a lay to me.

—What do you know about it? Benny asked. By the time I'm finished with her she'll be dying for more *putz*. Anyway, you can't tell by appearance. Remember the *Rov's* daughter? The one who was shagged in Alexandra Park? Boy was she a hot *shtup*.

—I wasn't there, Gabriel said.

—I wasn't either, but your heard what Horny Fox said about her. Anyway, I know for a fact that May is one terrific lay. I was fooling with her all day. Smell. Gabriel pushed away the proferred finger. And I told her what a great fucker you are. So she's really expecting it from you. Bam. Bam. Bam.

—Oh sure, Gabriel laughed. Me, speedy Gonzales.

—Need one of these? Benny presented him with a condom. Know how to use it?

—What kind of a question is that? Remember, me great fucker. For you, yourself have said it.

—Right. You are. And it's greatly to your credit.

—For I am an Englishman, Gabriel assumed the pose of Sir Joseph Porter, K.C.B.

—Okay. Okay.

May returned, face washed, lips newly painted, a smear of rouge on her cheeks.

—Guess we're about ready to land, Benny told her. The passengers were straining against the ropes as the gangplank thudded onto the Island dock.

They were the last to leave. They walked along the gravel path, Benny's arm around May. Gabriel trailed behind. Benny started to sing in Yiddish. It was a message for Gabriel. Say goodbye now. Come back in half an hour.

—I have to meet a friend, Gabriel shouted to the two ahead. One of the guys from school. See you later.

Gabriel turned away. Nothing to do while waiting. Stroll around. Should have gone to Hanlan's Point where there's a roller rink and an amusement park with a Merry-Go-Round. Easier to pick up somebody there. He walked to the dock. The Sam McBride was churning back to the city. Across the harbor the Toronto skyline was dimly visible. The Bank of Commerce. Random pinpricks of light. Tallest building in the British Empire. Thirty-six floors. To the left the Royal York Hotel, the grandest in the British Empire. On which the sun would never set. Gabriel wandered about, drawing out the minutes. He gave Benny a quarter hour beyond the agreed time.

They were sitting on the bench beside the wire trash can. Benny greeted him jovially.

—It's a terrific night, he winked at Gabriel. I'm going to the John, Will you stay with May? I'll be awhile.

—Sure, Gabriel said. Sure, I'll keep May company. He sat beside her.

—Would you like to go for a little walk? he asked her.

—I don't mind, she said. I know a nice place. She found the trysting spot where minutes before, she and Benny. Nearby the chestnut trees waved whispering leaves. Nought but the wind. He lay on the sand and pulled her to him. She did not protest. He rolled over on her. Nor did she deny him. In love's prologue he kissed her on the mouth. She lay there and looked at the three quarter moon. He unrolled her rayon stockings. He felt upward with zealous fingers, along the legs, heavy with baby fat. Her panties were open at the crotch. Benny the wild man must have torn them. He wouldn't have to remove them. She lay wordless, unmoving in the sand. Do what you will. She was wet and loose. She lay flat outstretched and his penis slipped out. Eagerly, he went into her again, the sandy grains adhering to the rubber. She screamed.

—Jesus, you've got sand in me. Jesus. Don't. He withdrew and brushed the particles from the moist latex. Inserted the tip of his organ again, and climaxed.

—Christ, I'm full of sand. She threw him off and sat up to examine the mischief. Don't touch me. I'm sore. She got up and tore off her sandy panties. Gabriel gave her his handkerchief.

She wetted it at the water's edge and applied the cooling compress. O-o-o-h. A-h-h-h. She was squatting, moaning.

At a little distance from her Gabriel unrolled the condom. He knotted the top and hurled into the lake, a capsule of squirming sperm sailing into oblivion.

# 18

> Violate me in the violet time
> In the vilest way that you know.
> Ruin me, ravage me, utterly savage me,
> On me no mercy bestow....

It was Norma's song. She taught it to him one blossom-scented evening as they sat on the stone stoop of the Bank of Nova Scotia across from the United Church on Bathurst Street.

> To the best things in life I am utterly oblivious.
> Give me a man who is lewd and lascivious....

Gabriel would gladly have acquiesced. Norma was as desirable as she was impenetrable. Many were attracted to her but few were chosen.

> Violate me in the violet time
> In the vilest way that you know.

Norma's playful fingers darted about Gabriel's torso as she sang. Her eyes sparkled as she waved honeyed hair in time to the song. She enunciated precisely, the lips separating as the sound issued from her throat, then closing shut, then opening. She winked as she warbled, teasing.

—Hands off, old chum, she cautioned as she wriggled out of his reach. Not here. Cold stone is cold comfort. When I want to be violated I'll let you know, where, when, how.

The door behind them opened and Seymour Davis D.D.S. emerged grey and rumpled.

—Hi Doc, Gabriel greeted him, all finished for the day?

—Yes. Had to stay on a bit to complete a fitting. Old Mr. Waldheim. Difficult case. Gums won't heal properly. Told me all the new tricks his dog can perform. Dr. Davis shook his head in disbelief.

—Oh, yeah, that dog has been performing for years. Waldheim didn't have the beast with him, did he?

—No. No. He came alone. By the way, Gabriel I'd like to see you sometime next week. Want to examine your new crown. How does it feel? Comfortable?

—Oh sure, Gabriel tongued the alien smoothness and contours.

Dr. Davis took care of the casualties from the Jewish Boys Club. Gabriel, clobbered by a baseball bat at close range by Goudie Garfinkel, suffered a swollen mouth and the loss of half of the right front incisor. The Jewish Federation sent him to Davis who extracted the nerve and ground the jagged projection to gum level and cemented the radiant, manufactured tooth into place amidst the grey-tiredness of Gabriel's own mashers.

—Phone Miss Ellenstein for an appointment. We'll X-ray the others for caries. Give you a cleaning too.

—I'd like you to meet my friend, Norma.

She flashed the whitest white in a grand smile.

—A beautiful mouth, Seymour Davis acknowledged and left.

—Ruin me, ravage me...Norma sang after him. Why don't dentists smile at people, she asked Gabriel. Don't know? Because they're always down in the mouth, that's why, Norma poked Gabriel in the rear. He chased her into King Edward School and trapped her near the water fountain.

—I will thrust this maid to the wall.

—On me no mercy bestow.

—I strike quickly being moved. My naked weapon is out.

—Gotta sit down. She dodged away and collapsed in the doorway. He closed in on her.

—Got a cramp, she cried. She got up and stretched her beautifully-formed seventeen year old's limbs.

—Uh, uh, n-n-n-no. Don't touch.

—Come on. Just between friends. Let's have a look then. Nobody's around.

—Okay, look, she pulled up her dress.

The hair was an amber shrub. Oh, she grimaced, I forgot to put them on. Fancy that. Musn't catch cold. Picture show finished. She grabbed his advancing hand and flung it away.

—That's all, folks. Pussy in the pantry, she sang out.

—Aw Norma, you're cock teasing again. I'm stiff with desire.

—Put it under a tap, old chum.

—Bet you've never been laid, he challenged her.

—Look, smartass. She rummaged in her school briefcase

and found a square cardboard container. From it she withdrew the moulded rubber diaphragm.

—Voilà! A simple device to frustrate conception. The latest thing. Inserted up where the best of friends must part. I use it all the time.

—Yeah? With whom? One of the bohemians in the Rainbow Tea Room, I bet. Which one? Nicholas the painter? Balzac the poet? Tarnowsky the Trotskyite? Adler the piano player?

—Nah. No fucky-fucky. My period. When it flows it pours. Fills up the rubber cup. I empty the chalice when it's full. Behold. This is my blood.

—Christ, he whistled, I don't believe it.

—Would I fool you, old chum? Remember, your heard it first from Norma, the only female with two diaphragms. One for respiration. One for menstruation. Remember me, when this you see. Norma stuffed the pessary into its container.

—Hey, I've got a little ditty for you, Gabriel remembered. Horny Fox swears he heard a kid singing it outside St. Christopher.

> Around the corner and under a bush
> He gave his girlfriend a little push.
> He gave a push, she gave a grunt,
> A little wee bugger came out of her cunt.

—Improbable, Norma said. Biologically impossible.

—Fast motion, Gabriel countered. Artistic license such as utilized by serious writers and pornographers alike.

—Enough of this love-making, Norma said. Let's do something. If I go home now I'll have to stand behind the counter slicing cheese, weighing potatoes, reaching for cans of Campbell's tomato soup. Trying to avoid the embraces of my mother's new husband. The gorilla. Jesus, the thought of it makes me want to upchuck. Gonna move out one of these days. Get a room with a Victrola and some records.

—How about the Society of the Friends of Music, he suggested. Beethoven tonight. *The Seventh Symphony.*

—What else?

—*Romeo and Juliet Overture.* Tchaikovsky.

—I know the song, she said: Love...I see you every-
where...
—Also Beethoven's *Consecration of the House.*
—Oh no, you mean Constipation of the House.
—Conception of the Louse.
—Consternation of the souse.
—The more the *mulier.*
—The mare the *melior.* If you're so disposed.
—It doesn't matter. With the waiter. Or the mater.
—*Mater dei?* Blessedly conceived.
—Up the crack without a paddle. Immaculate. No ejacu-
late.

The two paranomaniacs cerebrimming with gusto. Throw
me a phrase. I'll go you one better. Portmanteau words.
Words without fetter. Words that in polite conversation
non-mutterable. Jonsonian words, un-in-one-breath-
utterable.

—Honorificabilitudinitatibus. In one Costardrawer's
breath, alack, love'slabour'slost. Wordcatchers. Loftybrow-
flourishers. Vaingloryosophers.

> What are they who pay three guineas
> To hear a tune of Paganini's?
> Pack o' ninnies.


* * *


The members of the Society of the Friends of Music
were serious listeners. An élite group bonded by intellect,
wombed in the high school, sired by Siggie Stein, the
maths and science wizard. In his Palmerston Boulevard
mansion, untouched by The Depression, the Friends
gathered for this Friday evening's symphonic fare. They
reclined on Indian rugs in the salon, squeezed together on
the carpeted stairs, lounged in wing chairs and overstuffed
sofas. They leaned against walls. Attentive, listening to
Siggie's explication of what they were about to hear.

—In the Dance Symphony, Beethoven employs a com-
plex contrapuntal technique, much more involved than the
pure contrapuntal art of Palestrina and Byrd, for example.

As we all know, counterpoint is the combination of simultaneous voice parts, each independent but all conducing to a uniform, coherent texture.

Gabriel and Norma found places in the hallway, at the foot of the banister.

—The third movement opens with a brilliant display of exuberance. It is the apotheosis of the dance. A separate melody intrudes, solemn, hymn-like then fades away. It returns and is finally drowned by five mighty chords to end the movement.

In the candlelight Gabriel moved closer to Norma. In the lune-light Siggie was sharpening the thorn needle before inserting it into the pickup arm and thence into the groove of the 78 r.p.m. heavy shellac disc. The music poured out of the huge speaker.

Gabriel's eyes gradually adjusted to his surroundings. He could make out the forms, then faces. Vivian Zeidenheimer sat like Rodin's Thinker atop a plush ottoman. Fine-boned, no tits, Viennese Vivian with ink black hair, sculptured in short waves about the pale tight-skinned face. Eyes like Luise Rainer's. Her *Wienerblut* cooled during the flight through the Tyrol.

—I am no good to anybody, she had explained simply in response to the goodnatured banter that erupted among the Rainbow habitues. I couldn't give a man any pleasure even if I wanted to. I am sexless. No figure. No feeling.

—No fooling? Gabriel said. I don't believe it.

—I don't even have tits as big as yours, she said.

—They must be hiding, Gabriel ventured to guess as his hands encountered only bone.

—Are you satisfied, dahling? Vivian shrilled triumphantly. No tits and no womb. Surgically sterile. *Schluss.* Courtesy the *Anschluss.* No good to anybody.

Nobody joked with Vivian anymore. She found comfort in the private embrace of Rivka Blumenthal of the Scheuer House.

When was it the enchantment of music was first revealed to Gabriel? Before his *Bar Mitzvah.* An occasion of serendipity. Lying on the couch after supper, listening to the radio. His favorite fifteen minutes.

—The studio clock goes tick-tick-tock, and such is life's queer workings.... That a fellow named Ray Perkins ambles over to the microphone.

Comic patter and popular ballads. Then network trouble. In the studio of radio station WBEN the technician reached for a recording to fill the time. An interlude of Schubert. *Ave Maria gratia plena...* The soaring cadences, so different from the cantillations of the synagogue, filled Gabriel's spirit. He sought for it again the next Sunday just before the news. Marian Anderson sang the *Ave Maria*, then *Jesu, Joy of Man's Desiring*, then *Bereite dich Zion.* Every Sunday the New York Philharmonic played symphonies and tone poems and overtures, music programmatic and music absolute. On Saturdays the Metropolitan Opera presented for his listening pleasure *Faust* and *Carmen, Rigoletto* and *La Boheme.*

—Shut off that noise! Sara hollered. I can't stand it. Turn it down, you're waking the child upstairs. Church music he's listening to. He's becoming a *goy.* Go listen someplace else. Company's coming.

He searched for a place and found Stella at the Promenade Concerts at Varsity Arena. Stella Fisher obtained musical satisfaction from every possible source. From listening to the Masters at Siggie Stein's as she was now, stretched out beside Vince on the sofa. Stella Fisher, artist, actress, student, writer, loved to live to love.

Stella swooned to the sound of the oboe. She vibrated with the strings. Pulsed with the tympany. She was listening now, eyes heavy-lidded, to the pensive second movement. Only the slightest convulsions betrayed her ecstasy.

—Mendelssohn. Beautiful. Goes very well with Shakespeare's comedy. I played one of the main roles at St. Christopher House.

—Are you an actor? she gushed. I am too. My whole life revolves around the stage. But I adore serious music. Can't hear enough of it.

—Why don't we listen together? Next Saturday at Eaton's.

In the listening booth with the Ninth Symphony of Beethoven. Serge Koussevitsky and the Boston Symphony

Orchestra. After eighty-five minutes with the *Ode To Joy* ricocheting inside their heads, they returned the weighty album to the serious woman at the counter. Sorry. This isn't the interpretation we wanted. Then across to Simpson's. We'd like to test the Schubert Great C-Sharp Major Symphony. The most recent release. Stella coquetted with the young clerk and he hastened to do her bidding. While he searched he whistled a fragment.

—It's the Number 7, Gabriel advised. With Furtwaengler conducting.

—Certainly. Certainly. Number 7. Be very careful not to scratch the discs. Here is a supply of new steel needles.

\* \* \*

Siggie was sharpening another stylus. Easier on the grooves than the metal ones. Only thorn was capable of reproducing all the harmonics in the frenzied Fourth Movement. Truer sounds, he explained.

—Vince and I are going to the Rainbow. Are you coming? Stella invited Gabriel. Bring your friend.

—Sure. Meet you later.

Talk for hours on one cup of coffee about art and theater and music and philosophy and dialectics and politics and religion. Solve every problem. Boasting about sexual escapades. Imitating the preacher in the wooden church next door: *Il salario del peccato e la morte. Ma il dono di Dio... e... una donna molta calda.*

Let's walk for a bit, Norma said. I'm tired of the pretensions of those phonies. Not an original thought among them. God, I wish I could get away from here. So goddam provincial. Everybody here is paralyzed.

—Where would you go, he asked.

—New York. I'm planning my exit. And let there be no wailing at the bar when I put out to see.

—When?

—Soon. Maybe not tomorrow. But soon. *Un bel di* you'll find me gone. Gone with the wind. Gabriel's sad eyes grew more mournful.

—Lackaday, he groaned. My days will be a desolation.

—But I'll come back to you. *Un bel di.* Wherever you are I'll come to you.

—Even if I'm in Hamilton?

—Yes.

—Even in Kingston? Or Montreal?

—Even if you're in Montreal. *Cherchez l'homme.*

—I'll miss you.

—Oh, you'll have moo-eyed Stella for comfort. And the constant expectation of a reunion with me.

—I'll miss your jibes, your sallies, your antic disposition.

—*Iamque vale* I'm off to bed. Norma turned away abruptly. Gabriel saw her coalesce with the patrons coming out of the Bellevue Cinema. He ran to catch up with Stella.

Stella. What is she that all the swains commend her? She enters a room and the air becomes charged. She tosses her coarse jet locks. Her eyes are emphasized with liner and mascaraed lashes and luxurious brows. Her lips are thick and red. Her smile is open-mouthed. When Stella pouts in protest or in sadness, it is a bravura performance. Stella kisses ardently, with abandon.

Hail to the Blithe Stella, star of the Underground Players. Changing costumes for the second act, she and Gabriel behind the cheese cloth scrim, behind them a sheet of glass. An elbow jab would shatter the window, three floors above Spadina Avenue, and pull them down past Arcade Press, past Switzer's Delicatessen, and all the king's horses and all the king's men couldn't... ever again. With minimal movements Stella unsweaters. She wriggles out of her skirt. The slip clings about her legs. Off balance she teeters toward him. *Sauve qui peut.* She kisses him, Thanks. She removes the slip and twists into the powder-blue wool afternoon dress. Hair brush, then hair ribbon. Ready. Enter Stella as Elvira. Who is Duse? Who is Bernhardt? Compared to Stella. Gabriel enters, bearded and mannered as the Doctor.

Offstage they enjoyed the role of sometime lovers. Holding hands at the Symphony Concerts in Massey Hall where Sir Ernest Macmillan presided over the Jewish strings and woodwinds. On Sundays, picnics at the edge of the city.

She assembled a lunch of sandwiches on rye bread, potato salad, Coca-Cola. The Yonge Street car took them to the end of the line. They hiked the rest of the way to Hogg's Hollow. Funny name. They scrambled down the grassy slope, waded across the trickle of the Don and camped on a knoll surrounded by birches. After lunch he lay in her calico-skirted lap. She stroked his hair and sang *Poor Butterfly* in a hoarse contralto. Race you to the river and back. She started off. She slowed down so he could overtake her. She feigned a fall and whomp, he was on top of her. Caught you. His prize, a kiss, passionate, as was her nature. Another. He unbuttoned her blouse and she allowed him to kiss her breasts. That was all. He wouldn't sully her. He placed her high on a column of adoration and composed lines of love to her. Let us adore the ever-loving Stella Fisher and render praise unto Him who created her.

He photographed her in romantic poses with flowers in her hair and a dimple in her cheek but made sure to minimize the sharp angle of her nose. He entered the snapshots in contests and received Honorable Mention once.

On opening day they took the tram to the Exhibition and visited the Industrial Building, the Electrical Building, the Flower Show, the Automotive Building and the Midway. The Tunnel of Love.

—You have educated fingers, she sighed. They know just where to go. They tell *me* it's time to return home. A slight squeeze on his arm sent a message of anticipation to his cortex.

—Oh fiddle, she said, my mother is still up. We'll have to stay on the porch for awhile.

It was dark on the verandah. They kissed and fondled. He recited a poem of love and loneliness, of despair without her. He called her Lesbia and quoted Catullus. She was warming to his touch. He mouthed her, starting at the temple and progressing down cheek and neck.

—I love you, he said.

—Let's go inside. I have something to tell you.

In the dark she led him to the sofa.

—I love you, he repeated. I want it to be just you and me. Nobody else.

—Ah, the greeneyed monster, she sighed. I'm so sorry. That's what I wanted to talk to you about.

—Don't you love me?

—Of course I do. But I've been seeing another man. Gabriel sat up.

—Who?

—A soldier. With the Irish Regiment. He wants to marry me.

—But you're only eighteen.

—Old enough. He's in his thirties. He's being posted soon. I would stay with him for a few weeks until he's sent overseas.

—But I love you.

—I know you do, she said quietly, and I'm sorry. He turned away.

—Don't cry. Please don't cry. I'm so sorry. I don't want to hurt you. I feel just awful. But I love Greg ...and he may never come back...after this is all over. Think of the sacrifice he's making. Please understand. I know you'll understand.

—I *don't* understand, he said. After all we've done together. Haven't I pleased you?

—Oh yes, you have. Very much. In every way. But circumstances have now decreed otherwise. And we have to live with changes. I won't forget the wonderful times we've had.

—I'd better go, he said harshly.

—I'd like you to have a happy remembrance of this night. Make love to me, Gabriel.

She removed first the black mohair sweater. Then the skirt. Then the bra. They dropped in a little pile beside the sofa. Gabriel turned away. He stared out the window, vaguely conscious of the rain splattering the road.

She embraced him from behind. He felt the softness of her breasts against his back.

—Make love to me, Gabriel. Now. She coaxed him back. She owed him something. What is it men in women do require? She would not refuse him anything. Gabriel. Gabriel. I love you.

Gabriel, fully-clothed, responded to her provocations. He

kissed her with dry lips — her eyes, her cheeks, her mouth, her breasts, all her woman's body.

—O-o-o-o-h, that's so good, Stella exulted. Now do it, put it in.

He hesitated. The image of a khaki uniform stood sentry between them. Suddenly he pulled away from her. He put on his shoes.

—Gabriel, not like this. Don't leave like this, she cried.

He muttered goodbye and stumbled out of the house.

For awhile Stella lay on the couch and meditated on Gabriel. Then her thoughts turned to Greg. Soldier, soldier, will you marry me? It's oh for a fife and drum....

Gabriel wrote his estranged beloved: *Ich weiss nicht was soll es bedeuten.* He sent her poetry:

### MEMORY OF STELLA

When I think of you
The breath stops in my throat.
The pain begins anew.

### EROS-BOUND

From your anointed flesh
Rare unguents release a fragrance
Exotic as a dream.

### APOCALYPSE

I feel the knife-sharp wound of my mortality
The inundation of my life by time's inexorability.


\* \* \*


March 15, 1939: The announcer read with professional imperturbability: This morning troops of the Third Reich occupied Bohemia and Moravia.

Noel Fairweather stopped in mid tea-sip and addressed his cat: Bad Show. Mr. Fairweather reluctantly resumed his study of the Punic Wars in preparation for the next day's history lesson.

March 16, 1939: The *Star's* headline: SLOVAKIA

PLACED UNDER GERMAN PROTECTION.

In the Upper School German class Gabriel sang:

*Ich weiss nicht was soll es bedeunten*
*Dass ich so traurig bin.*

Included in his book of German selections. *Die Lorelei.* Traditional German poem. Author unknown.

—But didn't Heinrich Heine write *Die Lorelei?* Gabriel asked Miss Bancroft.

—Of course, she said, everybody knows that.

—Do they know it in Hitlerland?

—Herr Goebbels has forbidden the mention of his name. Miss Bancroft was becoming annoyed. We're wasting valuable time. We must get on to the next assignment. Turn to page thirty-seven and translate into idiomatic English.

One of the less difficult pieces: *Der Staat ist ein Mittel zum Zweck. Sein Zweck liegt in der Erhaltung und Forderung einer Gemeinschaft physisch und seelisch gleichartiger Lebewesen.*

—Miss Bancroft, why do we have to work with Nazi propaganda? Norma protested. How about Goethe or Schiller?

—Or Moses Mendelssohn, said Gabriel.

—*Mein Kampf* is a fascinating personal document. You don't have to agree with everything he says. Anyway the material is prescribed by the Board of Education. Let's get on with it. We haven't all day. *Mach's gut. Heute. Morgen ist zu spät.*

—Tomorrow the world, Gabriel saluted stiff-armed, from his desk. The Triumph of the Will. The glorification of Fascism by Leni Riefenstahl at the Nazi party convention in 1934. Nineteen cameramen. Hitler the star. Supporting roles by Himmler, Goering, Streicher, Goebbels. One million extras brought to Nuremburg. A masterpiece of cinematic technique. The apotheosis of der Führer.

*Ich weiss nicht was soll es...*

At Christie Pits a rally of the Canadian Nationalist Party. Local brown shirts. Jackbooted goose-steppers, pimply-faced, brave-in-uniform. English speaking protestants, members of the Loyal Orange Lodges. Joe Farr on a soap box:

—The Jew has always been a parasite in the body of other peoples. That thereby he sometimes leaves his previous living quarters is not connected with his intention but is the simple logic of his being thrown out from time to time by the host nation he abuses. But his spreading is the typical symptom of all parasites; he always looks for a new feeding soil for his race!

From Spadina, hastily transported in trucks and taxis, the Jewish Cowboys arrived armed with iron bars and rocks and knuckle dusters. Farr was haranguing an audience of a dozen summer loungers. His Storm Troopers formed a circle about him.

—I have here absolute proof of a plot by the International Jew. He waved the pamphlet: *The Protocols of the Wise Men of Zion*. It's all here. The plot to undermine our society and then to overthrow our government and then to destroy the Christian way of life.

—It's a goddam forgery, Moshe Greenberg, the Physical Health instructor at the Y.M.H.A. shouted. He pushed his wrestler's bulk closer to the speaker. Farr's elite guard tightened the circle around the leader.

—Here now, one of the police constables advised the Spadina group. No violence. Mr. Farr has a permit to speak. Stand back now.

—We must root out this cancer, the International Communist Jew, the enemy of civilization. Let us take a lesson from Brother Adrian Arcand in Quebec. Let us also say, Jews are not wanted here! *Sieg Heil*.

Farr clicked his heels and saluted and shouted again, *Sieg Heil*. It was then the battle was joined. Before it ended there were broken bones and bloodied heads. Samson sicked his dog: Go, boy, get'em. Tear the pants off the bastards. Samson was arrested and carted away with nine others and charged with causing a disturbance.

—It pays to be in good condition, he boasted. I knocked out two of them. I exercise everyday. Feel my muscles.

In the school gymnasium, Captain Evelyn Blackthorn was shouting:

—Get that flab off. Thirty push-ups. What you guys need is a summer in the militia. God help us if we have to send guys like you against the *Wehrmacht. Die Schule muss...endlich mehr Zeit frei machen für die Köperliche Ertuchtigung.*

April 27, 1939: Hitler Denounces Anglo-German Naval Agreement.

Britain Invokes Conscription.

—And if in the course of events we are called upon once again to come to the aid of the Mother Country, I know that every man student in this assembly will go willingly, just as former classmates of this great high school marched away to tweak the Kaiser's nose twenty-five years ago. Terence Hawke paused, removed a handkerchief from his pocket and delicately blew his nose before he spoke again. *Dulce et decorum est pro patria moriri.*

May 16, 1939: Stripper Found Dead.

The nude body of exotic dancer Melanie Washington, who performed under the stage name of Michelle Morgan, was found in the bathtub of her suite in the Ford Hotel yesterday afternoon. Death was attributed to drowning. Miss Washington, a native of Atlanta, was a frequent visitor to Toronto where she headlined numerous revues. The body was discovered by the Hotel Manager after Miss Washington failed to appear at the Roxy Theater. The possibility of foul play is being investigated.

May 23, 1939: Westminster Approves Independent Palestine by 1949.

At the meeting of City Council, the chaplain delivers the invocation:

—Let us offer a prayer for the health and comfort of His Royal Highness King George VI and His Sovereign Lady Queen Elizabeth whose impending visit to these shores is eagerly awaited.

\* \* \*

*...die nacht is kühl.....*

—Come on, Benny insisted. It'll do you good. Help keep your mind off Michelle Morgan.

—I don't feel like screwing some old whore, Gabriel said.

286

—She's not so old. And she doesn't charge. Does it for love. Can't get enough of it.
—Oh sure, Gabriel said.
—Yeah. She's a nympho. A Jewish nymphomaniac.
—Fancy that.
—Come on.

*...die schönste Jungfrau sitzet....*

Teeny Kaplan, munching on a chocolate bar, opened the front door. She was tall and skinny. A mole with a wisp of hair blemished her left cheek. Her pale blue bathrobe gaped open above and below the waist.
—Come on-a my room.
—This is my friend Gabriel, Benny said.

Teeny crumpled the chocolate wrapping and aimed for the wicker basket and missed.
—Shit, let it lay there. She plopped onto the bed. The springs sighed.

Gabriel sat on a kitchen chair next to the circular table. Benny pulled off his trousers and boxer shorts. Gabriel watched as Benny, bare-back rider, urged her to heave faster, faster.

Benny came quickly but she held him with locked legs and arms. More, more, she cried.
—Give my friend a chance. Benny dismounted and signalled to Gabriel.

Gabriel unbuttoned his combinations. Where was the safe? He got it on and asked her politely would she lie back. Once in, she responded with shrieks of ecstasy.
—I love it. I love it. More. Fuck me. Jazz me. Deeper. Faster. She was perspiring, untiring, screaming for more. Her fists pounded his back. He was trapped within her unsatisfied loins. He was about to plead for deliverance when he felt a hand on his bare arse, pushing him deeper.
—Christ, Benny hollered, you gonna be all day? Here, I'll help ya. In with the good air, out with the bad air.
—No use, Gabriel gasped.

Teeny Kaplan was begging him to continue. Please don't stop. But Gabriel withdrew, unfulfilled. While he was dressing, Benny mounted her again from the rear. He came a second time.

—Don't pull out yet, she pleaded. I'm coming, any second now.

—Let's get out of here, Benny said. I'm all fucked out. I don't want to die on top of her.

She was staring at the ceiling, whimpering. Gabriel pulled the quilt over her quivering frame.

—Come on, for God's sake, Benny said. She'll be running after us in a minute. Too bad you didn't make it. Better luck next time.

There was no joy in this encounter. A haggard creature afflicted with an obsession for the unattainable.

—I feel ashamed, said Gabriel.

—What did you expect? Cleopatra?

—Age cannot wither her nor custom stale her infinite variety. Over a hundred men in one night. She makes hungry where most she satisfies. The serpent of the Nile.

—A Bacchanale. That's what we want. Drink and dunk.

—Ah, but where can one find in this city and this age the mighty buttocks of a classical courtesan? Messalina. Valeria. Twenty-five Roman lances of flesh at one time. *O tempora. O mores.* An empress who sought out brothels. With a wig for disguise and gold leaf on her nipples.

> There she received all comers,
> getting top price until the doors shut tight.
> The lust though, still raged hotly in her bosom.
> Dirt-stained, she left the house and journeyed
>     home,
> Exhausted, but undaunted by the sweat.
> Thus smeared with lampsoot she returned unfazed
> To settle odors in the royal pillows.

—Wow! Is that what you learn in Latin?

—Juvenal. Satires. Available in all libraries. Vicarious pleasures with Catullus and Aphrodite. In a less lascivious mood:

> Gentle virgin, you besides,
> Whom the like event betides
> With the coming year;
> Call on Hymen! Call him now!
> Call aloud!
> A virgin vow best befits his ear.

A paucity of advanced Latin scholars, seven in all, sit in Miss Hortense Fotheringham's special class. Gray-eyed, behind her precariously adjusted *pince-nez*, Miss Fotheringham commands absolutely perfect renderings of Horace, Ovid, Livy, Pliny, Sallust. She articulates the syllables of Virgil:

—*Arma virumque cano.* Translate please.

Penelope rises. *Arms and the man I sing, the first who came, compelled by fate....*

What man the match for Penelope, essaying the power of the rippling thighs and the circumference of the hyperbolic breasts? Aeneas, the exile out of Troy? Gabriel avid to conquer. Penelope concurring. But Hymen watches over her.

—Shall we move on to Book IV?

—The Queen finds no rest. Deep in her veins the wound is fed. She burns with hidden fire....

What does Penelope discover in the metered verse? New truths? Does a trickle of love's balm seep through her enchanted tendrils as she sounds the dactyls? She pauses in the middle of Dido's bedchamber.

—That will be all, Penelope. Well done.

—Will this be on the examination, Miss Fotheringham?

—You will be required to translate some portion of the *Aeneid*, yes. And perhaps the ode by Horace: *Exegi monumemtum.*

I have built a monument more enduring than... more enduring than... my own lofty erection, a prey to time. If Penelope only knew how I have lusted after her.

> *O tuae mammulae. Mea manus est cupida illam*
> *captare*
> *Petulante manicula!*
> *Tu es Venus,*
> *In tuo ingente amplexu tota est mihi vita.*

Unassailable Penelope. Will you bidmetolove elsewhere? I have lain with poxy wenches. I have probed with finger and tongue. Presented my impetuous youth before altars erogenous. Searched for truffles in abodes of filth.

I have sat in Jarvis Street luncheonettes entertaining the

whores with my poems. Classical allusions far above their comprehension.

I have waited outside the Tusco Hotel when the drunken cow clattered down the stairs, her head banging against the concrete. Come with me, young man. Two dollars. The stale beer dribbling down the hairy chin, down between her flopping udders.

The night I spent with the drab on Larch street. The four infants bedded in one bunk. It's all right ducks, me old man ain't to home. Not to worry. She pulled off her dirty cotton dress and paraded lewdly before me. Afterwards I felt sick.

Later the embarrassment of the drip. Hmmm, where did you get the dose, the myopic Scottish doctor examined the discharge. Who was your last contact? I'll have to report this. Oh no, doc, you don't think it's gonorrhea. I must have picked it up from the toilet seat in the Men's washroom at Alexandra Park. He replied with a half-laugh, Hell of a place to screw a girl. It turned out to be non-specific urethritis. Dr. Macintosh prescribed sulfanilamide and a pouch to catch the pus.

Will this appendage between my legs, ritually mutilated on the eighth day, not rebel at last and cast me off?

\* \* \*

August 5, 1939: British Military Mission Leaves For Moscow.

August 23, 1939: Chamberlain Warns Hitler Britain Will Stand By Poland.

—Sex can be a beautiful experience. Only it has to be initiated by somebody who knows how. All the medical students go to her. Want to try your luck?

—Why not? Gabriel said. Pinky Goldstein put down his Basic Anatomy and consulted his black book.

—Here it is. Mooney. Mrs. Prudence Mooney. She's a friendly woman. Runs a select establishment. Her flat is on Bathurst Street above Moishe's Delicatessen. Phone for an appointment. Tell her you're a friend of mine.

290

August 25, 1939: Anglo-Polish Treaty of Mutual Assistance Signed In London.

Gabriel pressed the button. It uttered a polite buzz. He glanced up to Bloor Street hoping nobody familiar was coming. A child-bride wheeled a baby carriage past him.

He buzzed again. A dog barked inside the house and Gabriel heard footsteps.

—Good afternoon, the heavy gray-haired woman greeted him. The pekinese at her breast snarled.

—How do you do...er...Mrs. Mooney? I'm Gabriel Gottesman.

—Yes. Do come in. Don't mind Winnie. She barks a lot but she's really very gentle. Aren't you, darling? She kissed the dog on the flat, wet nose. Mummy's pet, that's what you are. She locked the door and trudged up the stairs, bidding Gabriel to follow. Isn't it a grand day? I think it's the nicest we've had all week. Just grand. She pointed to a chair. Please sit down. We can have tea while we chat.

—Well now, she spoke between sips. Was it Dr. Goldstein that sent you? Ah, he's a nice young man. I'm sure you are too. Otherwise you wouldn't be here. One has to be so careful. I mean what with the police. And the neighbors. And goodness we don't want anybody bringing in any illness...you know, a disease. All my girls come from good homes. They're so keen on personal hygiene. I can see you come from a better class of people. Have another scone.

Gabriel reached for one. The lap dog erupted into an epileptic yapping. Mrs. Mooney stroked the tiny wrinkled head.

—Now, now, Winnie. Be a good little pup. Gabriel is our guest. She's a thoroughbred you know. A little skittish. She'll get used to you. See? She's stopped growling. There. Winnie likes Gabriel.

Winnie thrust out a wet tongue and licked the hand extended in friendship.

The keeper of the house rocked in her chair. Somebody's mother. The Pekinese drowsed in her lap.

—Are you Jewish? she asked Gabriel.

—Yes, ma'am, I'm Jewish. My father's a Rabbi.

—Oh my, isn't that grand? I'm sure you know the Bible

by heart. I read the good book myself. It is a solace in these times. I attend services every Sunday. I'm United Church. Just the other day our Minister spoke about how Jews and Protestants and even Catholics should be brothers. He said we should draw near to one another. He said that the Jewish people should be of good cheer because the Lord of Hosts is with them.

—What doth the Lord command of thee? Gabriel expounded the homily for the day: To do justly, love mercy and walk humbly with Thy God.

—God bless the Jewish boys, she said. I don't know how I'd survive without their help. They are so generous. So courteous. So well-educated. Lawyers. Druggists. Social Workers. They are very popular with my girls. By the way, young man, what is your profession?

—I just graduated. I'd like to be a writer. Study journalism at Columbia. But I haven't decided. Maybe I'll work for awhile. Maybe join the Royal Canadian Corps of Signals.

—Yes. The times are so uncertain. I'm so afraid there will be war. Mr. Chamberlain is trying so hard to prevent it.

*Peace in our time. Herr Hitler has convinced me that he has no further territorial designs.*

The Prime Minister and his umbrella. Fragile defense against bombs by Krupp.

—I do hope the King and Queen will be safe. Did you see them during the Royal Visit? I waved at Her Majesty — and she smiled and waved back. It was so thrilling. Just thousands of people on University Avenue, shouting and singing.

—It was a thrilling occasion, Gabriel agreed. And profitable. The free-enterprise system making possible the hawking of patriotic symbols along the route of the procession. Union Jacks for waving, for lapel trim. Red, white and blue ribbons. Souvenir medallions with the Royal profiles and the inscription: In Honour of the Visit to Canada of their Majesties King George VI and Queen Elizabeth.

—Will you have more tea? Trudy will be with us shortly. She's very sweet. Yesterday was her twenty-fifth birthday

292

and the other girls had a party for her. They presented her with an overnight case. She was so pleased.

A door opened and Gabriel heard feet (two pairs) descending the stairs then the outside door opening and closing, then the sound of footsteps returning. From the bathroom the splash of water and a pleasant soprano voice singing *Bei Mir Bist Du Shayn*.

—Ah, here she comes now, Mrs. Mooney announced. Gabriel, I'd like you to meet Trudy. The dog awoke, sniffed and dozed off again.

—How do you do, Gabriel rose awkwardly from his chair.

—Hello, a laughing voice responded. Her blond hair was set in tight curls. She had lively blue eyes. Her face had been freshly made up. She wore a teal blue linen suit with a blouse that had cascades of lace ruffles down the front.

—Gabriel is a friend of Dr. Goldstein, advised Mrs. Mooney. Isn't that nice.

—Oh yes, Trudy smiled. Any friend of Pinky's is welcome. Well... would you like to come along now?

—See you later, Mrs. Mooney said.

Behind the secured door, Gabriel stands by the mirrored wardrobe. A double bed with brass headboard. Two plump pillows. White sheets. A plush, turquoise boudoir chair. A three-drawer dresser. The wallpaper shows bluebirds in flight. Overhead the Tiffany shade. Beyond the window, visible through the marquisette curtains, the Stitsky's Textiles sign.

Trudy has removed her shoes and suit. Her half-slip is orange. As she casually unbuttons her blouse, Gabriel uncreases the banknote in his pocket.

—Would you like the two dollars now?

—Just put it on the dresser. She smiles, encouraging, not hurrying. First time? she asks.

—You mean with a .... Yes. First time.

—Don't be nervous. You'll be all right.

—Shall I take my clothes off?

—Of course. It's the only way. See? I'm getting ready for you. She lays the blouse neatly across the chair on top of the other items. She sits on the bed in her brassiere and girdle. Waiting. A big armful of woman. Watching as Gabriel peels downs to the summerweight combinations.

—You'll be more comfortable with them off, she advises.

—Oh, sure, I was just going to. Seven buttons and the moulting is complete.

—Now, let's see what you're like in bed. Come on, Gabriel. I'll show you a good time. Did you bring a safe?

—Oh, yes, it's in my trousers.

—Good. I won't have to douche after. Here, let me help you. Operation safe conduct. There. Now we're ready.

Together in bed, she maneuvers him on top of her. Caressing his lean buttocks. His flesh encounters the coarseness of her girdle. His hand feels for the hair below it, the warmth between her legs.

—Don't try to get it in yet, Trudy says. Let's play around a bit.

—Will you take off the...?

—Girdle?

—Yes. Please.

—You can do it. Reach behind. She arches her back. Undo the hooks. She wiggles. There. Now the bra.

He noses between her breasts and she presses them against his cheeks. Her thighs are tight against his gristle. He wants to kiss her on the lips.

—No, not there.

The rest of her body is his for exploring. But he is impatient to begin the ritual.

—Wrong spot. She steers him into her haven. The vulvar boatman. Gradually he penetrates her. Trudy begins a counter-thrusting, slow, controlled. Not too fast, she cautions. Enjoy it longer.

—Can't wait. Can't hold off. Oh-h-h-h, God. O-h-h-h. The explosion from within his core. The gush of semen.

Drained, he remains clasped to Trudy, conscious finally of the tepid pool between their bellies.

—You'll be a grand lover one day, she sighs. She sends a spate of contractions along his flaccid penis. He feels it growing inside her again. This time she does not advise. She does not urge or caution. He reaches his orgasm in a mighty upheaval. They lie there for awhile. She laughs and

294

pats his arse. He grins and says, Thank you.

—You'll have to leave now. I have another appointment, she says.

—I'll be back, he promises. Next week.

* * *

Friday, September 1, 1939: At 5:00 A.M. today the troops of the Third Reich marched into Poland.